Dov Silverman, a winner of Japan's prestigious Suntory Merit Award for Mystery Fiction (1988), was born in Brooklyn, New York and now lives in Safed, Israel. He served as a US marine in the Korean War and has worked as a railroad conductor, auctioneer, teacher, college lecturer and high school principal. For the present, he writes, teaches and serves as a Safed city councilman.

S0-BFA-440

DOV SILVERMAN

Tairo

The Great Elder

This edition published 1994 by
Diamond Books
77–85 Fulham Palace Road
Hammersmith, London W6 8JB

First published in Great Britain by
Grafton Books 1990

Published in paperback by Grafton Books 1991

Copyright © Dov Silverman 1990

The Author asserts the moral right to
be identified as the author of this work

ISBN 0 261 66503 0

Set in Garamond

Printed in Great Britain

For my granddaughter, Anav Helen
With all my love

ACKNOWLEDGEMENTS

To my wife Janet,
Editor of all my works

For Support and Encouragement Along the Way

Edyth H. Geiger
Dr Morris and Dora Molinoff
Malka Rabinowitz
Sylvia and Mel Springer
Paula and Leslie Tint

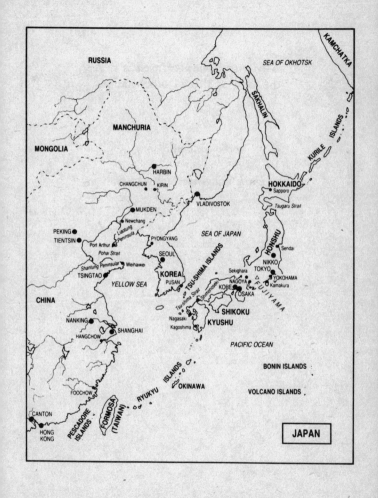

JAPAN

A country's view of itself is never
the same as that of other nations.

Springtime and song
or
Dark wings and bare trees.

Dov Silverman

Part 1

Chapter 1

1 March 1894

From his apartment in the imperial palace, John Mung's eyes followed the rising sun. Diaphanous rays lacquered the tiled rooftops of Tokyo a molten gold. Mung – Moryiama Ishikawa – assumed a yoga stance. He inhaled the fiery light into his belly and up into his lungs. The sight of the distant peak of Mount Fuji sharpened, and Mung spread his arms wide as he exhaled. This was an exhilarating part of his day. Although chief of the Emperor's personal intelligence organization, the Black Dragon was a man who preferred solitude. Now, at the age of sixty-seven, he had been recalled to public life.

The shoji screen behind him slid open and, unconsciously, Mung smiled. Without turning, he said, 'Noriko?'

The beautiful eighteen-year-old daughter of his closest friend, Count Iyeasu Koin, entered the room on her knees. For the seven years since his stroke she had brought his breakfast before her school day, looked in on him when she returned, and again at night before he retired.

Although fifty years her senior, Mung enjoyed exchanging views with the girl. During the period of his illness he had kept in touch with the future generation of Japan's leaders through her. Often he used Noriko to funnel his thoughts into the classrooms of the nation's most prestigious high school. The two spoke freely, in a way few Japanese did. But, like her deceased mother, the girl had a mind of her own. She modified his ideas with her opinions.

'Are you nervous, Uncle?' Noriko asked. She poured his tea and placed pickled vegetables atop the steaming rice in his bowl.

Mung sat opposite her at a low table. 'In the days of the shoguns, few people were consulted about decisions to go to war,' he said. 'The shogun would summon his lords, issue orders, and armies marched.'

'Uncle, we are on the threshold of the twentieth century. Our leaders must now consult Parliament and the Emperor before a major policy change is taken. Japan is a constitutional democracy.'

'Yes. I fought to make it so. But it is a slower and more complicated process than I ever imagined.' Mung pushed at the rice with his eating sticks until he caught Noriko's frown. He took a few bites to please her. Food was fuel to power his tall, wiry body. He consumed enough to keep fit to serve the Emperor. 'My call from retirement places your father in a peculiar position. He has always advised the Emperor to maintain a strong military in order to implement an aggressive economic policy. But too many of our people want war. I shall attempt to dissuade our army from using its power.'

'Father does not want war,' Noriko said. 'The others believe it is necessary if Japan is to be accepted as a modern nation state. They say that just as we copied western industrialism, we must imitate imperialism.' She paused and waited until he began eating again. 'Many believe it is now time to copy the American takeover of Mexican territory, Britain's previous occupation of India, its present activities in Africa, and France's conquest of Indochina. To gain respect in the eyes of the world, Japan must also become imperialist.'

'Is this what they teach in the American college?'

'The Japanese instructors do.' Noriko reached over and pressured the sides of an exquisite lacquerware bowl, breaking the heat seal. She uncovered the miso soup.

Mung lifted the bowl with his right hand, balanced it with the stump of his left arm and drank.

'My father is less concerned with the respect Japan

12

receives from foreigners,' Noriko said. 'He believes a strong military is necessary to maintain overseas markets. He reminded me of Korea's insult to our trade delegation twenty years ago.'

'Your father's brother will never forget or forgive the Koreans. Hideyoshi was with the trade mission ejected from Pusan.' Mung thought of his adopted son Udo, who had been twenty years in the Korean capital of Seoul. Udo led Genoysha, the overseas branch of the Black Dragon Society. His agents had recently reported Russian troop movements into Manchuria and North Korea with the unofficial cooperation of the Chinese and Korean governments. In addition, a full division of Chinese troops had bivouacked on the outskirts of Seoul. Japan's centuries-old fear of an invasion from the South Korean peninsula led many of its leaders to call for an invasion of Korea. Mung had been summoned out of seclusion to prevent that. He was certain that either China and/or Russia would become involved in such a war, and Japan would lose.

'Uncle, please finish your soup,' Noriko said. 'It is almost time to meet my father and appear before the Emperor. Do you wish for me to walk with you?'

'That would be pleasant. Your father will appreciate your presence. I see more of you than he does.'

'When I return from school, will you have time to discuss your son's wedding?'

'I doubt that will be possible. I expect to be very busy. It is the reason I asked you to oversee the festivities for Shimatzu and Kazumi. If there are questions of formalities, appeal to the Emperor's master of protocol. Problems regarding food and other arrangements can be addressed to the imperial household staff. They are at your service. I wish the wedding to be a tasteful blend of tradition and modernity. There will be many foreign guests, as well as the most powerful men in Japan. This marriage is certain to affect the future of our country.'

✳   ✳   ✳

Seoul, Korea, 1 March 1894

'The Black Dragon has ordered us to return for Shimatzu's wedding,' Udo said.

'Am I included?' Gin-ko asked.

'We were Shimatzu's parents until he was fourteen. Certainly, you are included. I cannot help but think of how proud Ukiko would have been to see her son married. And that Mung deserves some happiness. The loss of two wives, then his firstborn son Yoshida, have all taken their toll on him.' Udo looked at his wife, wondering if he could ever bear losing her. Although she wore the traditional kimono, her jet black hair was cut short in the modern style. It curved on either side of her high cheekbones and framed her exotic eyes. At forty-two she was still the most beautiful woman he had ever seen.

He turned back to the letter. 'There is a separate note from Iyeasu Koin's daughter,' he said. 'Mung has put her in charge of the wedding. Our sons will escort Shimatzu at the ceremony.' Udo knew how much Gin-ko longed to see Shimatzu and their two older boys.

Hiroki looked up from the map he was studying. 'Do you think we will be allowed to remain in Japan?'

His mother was also anxious to hear the answer. They had been too many years in exile.

'I do not know,' Udo said. 'We of Genoysha are servants of the Emperor. I am to prepare reports for Mung. Shimatzu's wedding provides the Black Dragon an opportunity to gather key agents without causing a stir. Whether Mung will allow us to remain is unclear.'

'Grandfather must be fully recovered from his stroke,' the nineteen-year-old Hiroki said in Korean.

'Use Japanese,' Udo said. 'Your speech is accented like those seal hunters from Hokkaido.'

'I was born in Korea, Father. Outside of this house I rarely speak Japanese. The last three years in the American college have added to my accent. I am more at home in Korean.'

'Never answer so impolitely in Japan!' Gin-ko said. 'Growing up in an international community has taught you bad manners. You should have been educated in a Japanese school like your brothers.'

Hiroki rolled his eyes at his mother, and smiled. He had learned as a child how to melt her heart. It was at her insistence he was not sent away to school with his older brothers. 'Excuse me, Father.' He bowed.

Gin-ko's eyes met her husband's over their son's broad back. They both smiled. The boy was tall, with natural grace. Young children were drawn to him. Little girls asked to hold his hand. Gin-ko had seen jealousy in men's eyes when their wives cast furtive glances at the handsome young man. Hiroki, like so many gifted people, was oblivious to the attention, taking it as his due. It is his major fault, Gin-ko thought. Everything comes so easy to him. He has little patience with those who are not as physically and mentally gifted.

'Do you think the foreign balloonists will be in Tokyo when we arrive?' Hiroki asked. He pulled out a newspaper article advertising an aerial performance at the Plum Blossom Festival in Ueno park.

'You are not to go up in the air!' Gin-ko said. 'I know that you hung on the back of a giant kite. Queen Min herself saw you from her apartment window. She told me you were higher than the top of her pagoda palace.'

'Mother, balloons are the transportation of the future. They are much safer than kites. You told me Grandfather Mung went up in a balloon to direct artillery during the siege of Sapporo.'

Udo anticipated his wife's appeal for help. 'Heed your mother,' he said. 'Do not repeat such a performance again.'

'Yes, Father.' Hiriko bowed, suppressing a smile. He

15

too was a member of Genoysha. It was his father who ordered him aloft to spy on the Koreans. He had observed Russian soldiers training Royal Korean Army officers on the imperial palace parade ground. He identified the new Gatling guns, modern light artillery and mortars. I will ask Grandfather to arrange a ride for me in one of the foreign balloons, he thought. From stories I have heard about the old man, he might even go up with me.

'You two had better start packing,' Udo said. 'We leave tomorrow.'

Kobe, Japan, 1 March 1894

'If your so-called uncle could memorize the entire plan of a goddamned whaling ship, it doesn't matter how old he is,' James Alburg said. 'He won't ever forget that Americans killed his first wife.'

William Whittefield, Jr levelled his pale blue eyes at the president of the Kobe Club. 'James, you may represent the most powerful organization of western businessmen in the Far East, but I will not tolerate foul language.'

James Alburg excused himself. 'Bill, the question stands. Will he do business with us or not?'

'Mung constructed that ship over forty years ago, shortly after he returned to Japan. His first wife was killed some two years after that.'

Alburg pointed to the closed door of his luxurious office. 'There are fifty Kobe Club members out there waiting to hear what you have to say. Those men control most of the business this side of the Himalayas. If there's to be a war, they want the fat military contracts with Japan. Because you're a relative, you're the only member of this club to receive an invitation to the wedding. You have an obligation to us.'

'I know my obligations,' William said. 'They're first and foremost to a higher power than the Kobe Club. I was raised to believe a man can earn an honest living without

16

transgressing. I also feel this war talk may be premature. I believe Mung's return to public life means he'll try to influence the new constitutional government to peaceful expansion.'

'Bill, only men like yourself who have occupied my chair know of your uncle's role as Black Dragon. Our agents in Tokyo say that Mung remains head of the Emperor's personal intelligence corps. Now, with the excuse of a wedding, he's calling in his key people from Manchuria, Mongolia, Siberia, China, and his son Udo from Korea. We believe the war will begin in Seoul. Have you ever met Udo Ishikawa?'

'Not yet. I've heard he speaks several languages, and can be ruthless. That's why Mung exiled him to Korea. In August 1874 Udo usurped Mung's power as Black Dragon for one night. Japanese refer to it as The Killing Night. Udo ordered the deaths by strangulation of military and political leaders opposed to a constitutional monarchy. Their elimination was a major step towards the restoration of power to the Meiji Emperor.'

James Alburg leaned forward. 'This wedding is more important than anyone thinks.'

'Yes. Mung is selling his natural son Shimatzu in an arranged marriage to benefit Japan. When Udo Ishikawa and the Black Dragon come together, crucial decisions will be taken.'

'Wouldn't the son protest at being sold?'

'Shimatzu is an intelligent young man,' William said. 'I met him in Washington three years ago. But no Japanese would object to serving his country.'

'And the Emperor.'

'The Emperor and Japan are synonymous, like Christ and God. Christianity is nothing without both. Japan is the Emperor and the Emperor is Japan. Shimatzu is marrying for the benefit of the state. It's his payment of Chu.'

'Sometimes you sprinkle your sentences with Japanese words I don't understand.'

'Every man, woman and child in Japan is born with an indebtedness to the Emperor. Chu is the honour gained by dedicating oneself to acts of gratitude to him.'

'When is the debt repaid?'

'Never,' William said. 'The lives of all Japanese are dedicated to obedience. The individual is unimportant. In Japan, one's existence is a perpetual act of gratitude to the Emperor for being who he is.'

'And who is that?'

'The one-hundred-and-twenty-second descendant of the Sun Goddess, Amaterasu-o-mi-Kami.'

Alburg nodded his head. 'You lived here with your late father, the ambassador. You speak the language. I'll take your word for it as the third generation involved with this country. But tell me, please, what the Emperor or Japan gains by this wedding?'

William Whitefield, Jr noted that James Alburg still did not understand the oneness of the Emperor and Japan. There were some things about Japanese society almost impossible to explain. 'The wedding is a straightforward business deal,' William said. 'Mung is marrying his son into the Inei family. The head of the Inei clan will receive the title of marquis and be seated in the House of Peers. He rises in rank from merchant to member of Parliament.'

'What does Mung's family receive in return?'

'Chu. The honour of serving the Emperor. The Inei merchant fleet will be put at the government's disposal, and the Inei steelworks converted to production of weapons.'

'Then there will be war!' The Kobe Club president slapped the table.

'Not if Mung can prevent it. His actions may appear contrary to his policy, but in the eyes of a Japanese it is logical. He's coming out of retirement to prevent Japan from going to war. The merchant fleet and arms factories are concessions to the militarists. Toys for the soldiers to occupy themselves with while Mung seeks a peaceful solution.' William lit his pipe. 'My grandfather saved Mung from a shipwreck and adopted him in 1842. My father and Mung grew up together as brothers. They studied at Harvard High School, whaled together, fought the shogun together. My father held Mung's left arm while they sawed off his infected hand to save his life. Later, when my father returned to Japan as ambassador, they worked together to modernize this country. I know Mung personally, but mostly through my father's stories. He's committed to aborting the unequal treaties with the Europeans by peaceful means. He wants Japan to expand peacefully. His intelligence-gathering organization is used primarily to improve Japan's economy. But there is another side to the coin. Iyeasu Koin – adviser to the Emperor and Mung's friend. Iyeasu believes Japan can maintain a sound economy only if the country is protected by a strong military.'

'That sounds logical to me.'

'Mung thinks maintenance of a major military force is a waste of time, money and manpower. He hopes to satisfy Iyeasu's political faction with the benefits gained by the wedding. Then there are the extremists led by Iyeasu's older brother, Count Hideyoshi Koin. They dream of conquering the Far East. Hideyoshi would probably be elected prime minister if there's a war. He seeks a showdown with the West to abort the unequal treaties.'

'It's only fifty years since Commodore Perry opened Japan to the modern world,' James Alburg said. 'How can a small agricultural country like this conceive of attacking the Russian-backed Korean navy? The Chinese would have Japan for dinner if Japanese troops appeared in Seoul. China has the largest army in the Far East. It would be folly for Japan to seek a war.'

William tapped his pipe into a tray. He pointed at the

closed door, to the sound of impatient voices on the other side.

'I'm going to tell you something I would never say to our members. The Japanese can defeat the Koreans and the Chinese! What's more, if the Russians stick their nose too close to these islands, they'll get it bloodied.'

'Bill, you're right. Don't tell anybody out there what you just said. They would call you crazy.' The president of the Kobe Club steepled his fingers in front of his chin. 'I think otherwise about China and Korea. But they're Orientals, and only God knows what they'll do in a fight. However, when you tell me a yellow army can defeat a white army, I say not on your life! The Russians sent Napoleon packing. They defeated the Chinese in a number of battles. They built the Trans-Siberian railroad, a triumph of intelligence, determination and technological expertise over the cruellest elements of nature. Japan will never defeat a white army!'

William touched his finger to the tobacco ash in the tray. He drew a circle with extending lines on the desk. 'The imperial flag is the rising sun with sixteen rays. It represents Japan. The moment this nation goes to war, the power of the light from that sun will be focused by these rays into one cutting edge to defeat the enemy. This is the land of the gods. The people's concept of Chu – the desire to repay the Emperor – is the major factor. An order from the lowest ranking officer is as if the Emperor has spoken. Bushido, the warrior code, teaches only success in battle. To lose is unforgivable. To be wounded, a shame. Victory is the Way of the Warrior.'

'Sounds like a harangue most generals give their troops before a battle. We'll see when the time comes if the Jap will fight or flee. The original question remains, will Mung do business with the Kobe Club?'

'Yes,' William said. 'Saiyo, his first wife, was killed by American privateers, but he does not hold our country accountable. Mung is an amazing man who has suffered.

20

His first son took ill and died at seventeen. His second wife passed away in premature childbirth brought on by an assassination attempt paid for by Hideyoshi Koin.'

'You mean the present opposition leader? If so, I would have expected Bushido required Mung to kill him.'

'Mung performed Chu by not doing so,' William said. 'He forswore his right to revenge in exchange for Hideyoshi's father's vote on a crucial issue favouring the Emperor. That was twenty years ago. Mung has kept his word.'

'I hope he'll keep the Emperor's word and help us clean up Kobe. That should be his first task. This town has become a hell-hole. You need an armed guard to walk the streets.' Alburg came from behind his desk and led William to the door. He paused with his hand on the polished brass knob. 'You told me the name Mung came about because your father's whaling crew couldn't pronounce Mangiro. That they named him after Mung stew, a South African dish the ship's cook was serving the day he was rescued. After this meeting, let's go out and see what kind of impressive and influential wedding present we can stew up for Mung's son. You may not believe war is coming but the Kobe Club does, and we aim to profit from it!'

Chapter 2

Noriko followed Mung down the palace corridor. 'Father will meet you outside the Emperor's reception room,' she said.

'I find it difficult to converse with you behind me,' Mung said.

'It would be unladylike to be at your side in public.'

'And I thought you to be one of those liberated, athletic women of the Asiatic League.'

'Uncle, you are teasing again. Certain customs have changed forever, others temporarily, but there are those we will never modify. For now, I shall walk behind.'

'I would like you to visit the United States,' Mung said. 'Americans create new traditions.'

'They have little respect for the past, or for family. I asked my teacher where Abraham Lincoln's relatives live. He did not know. Neither did the principal of the American college.'

'I see your father,' Mung said. A sunlit window silhouetted the five-foot block figure of Iyeasu Koin, first adviser to the Meiji Emperor.

The two old friends bowed. 'Welcome back,' Iyeasu said. 'You are needed.'

Mung glanced at the door of the imperial reception room, then to Noriko. 'Your beautiful daughter has been of great help these long years. I am recovered because of her.'

'A worthless, lazy girl of plain looks who takes after her father.' Iyeasu beamed at his daughter.

Noriko blushed as she bowed. 'May I be excused for my studies?'

'Yes. Do not disgrace the family name.' Iyeasu watched her walk away.

'I have not met my youngest grandson, but have heard positive things about him,' Mung said. 'He will be here for Shimatzu's wedding. If he pleases me and finds favour in your eyes, may I introduce him to Noriko?'

'The man she marries will have to possess an especially strong character. My daughter is as physically active as she is mentally alert. In addition to studying in a foreign college, she practises the martial arts.'

Mung shrugged. 'We shall see.'

The two friends entered the imperial reception room. Mung recalled the first time he had appeared before the Emperor and crawled on his belly. Now, he and Iyeasu stood before a vacant, polished teakwood platform, and waited.

'The wedding of Shimatzu into the Inei family will not put off my brother Hideyoshi and his militarists,' Iyeasu said.

'Is your political faction satisfied?' Mung asked.

'I do not want war, but I believe we must prepare for it. The westerners are gobbling up one country after another. The Chinese, Koreans and even the Russians are becoming persistently more active.'

'I have a trick or two up my sleeve that may prevent a war,' Mung said.

Iyeasu tapped Mung's starched shirt-front. 'You forget we wear American-style tuxedos nowadays, not the loose-fitting kimono. There is little room in our sleeves.'

The Meiji Emperor entered the reception room. Mung and Iyeasu remained bowed until his imperial highness was seated on the single rosewood chair on the platform.

'It is good to see the Black Dragon at court again,' the Emperor said. At thirty-seven, the sovereign of the Land of the Gods looked youthful in his custom-made silk tuxedo. He motioned the two men closer. 'Mung,

I have perused your reports and proposals. Specifically your recommendation to circumvent the next session of Parliament. I am not convinced that the benefits derived from your son's marriage will deter Hideyoshi and his band of expansionists. If it comes to a vote, Parliament may declare war against Korea.'

'Your imperial highness,' Mung said. 'The Inei shipping fleet will give our armed forces strategic mobility. That and the retooling of Inei's factories as arms producers will satisfy Iyeasu and his faction.' He glanced at his friend. 'As for Iyeasu's brother, I have the Black Dragon Society working on a complicated strategy to placate Count Hideyoshi and his war party. My plan involves two limited military operations, one of which your imperial highness requested. If I am able to convince Hideyoshi of the second, voting on a decision to invade Korea will be delayed for some time.'

'My brother swore revenge against you because of his twelve-year exile to Hokkaido,' Iyeasu said to Mung.

'He brought that on himself, however much he blames me. He disgraced his family by conspiring with common criminals. But it has been two decades since we met. Perhaps he has mellowed,' Mung said with more conviction than he felt.

'Where specifically do you intend these military operations?' the Emperor asked.

'In Kobe and Formosa,' Mung said. He stepped forward with several maps.

The Imperial Palace, 9 March 1894
'The years have treated you well,' Mung said.

Udo bowed. 'I am thicker in the waist, grey at the temples, and a bit slower rising in the morning.'

'Gin-ko does not appear changed at all. She is more beautiful than ever.'

'She has made our life away from Japan bearable.'

24

'This recall of your family was not for vacation,' Mung said. He turned to look at his grandson.

Hiroki clenched his teeth as the bright, dark eyes raked over him. The old man's stone-face sent a chill through the young man. Hiroki tightened his muscles to hold his heart in place, and bowed. 'I am honoured to serve you and the Emperor.'

'First the Emperor,' Mung said.

'Serving the Black Dragon is serving his imperial majesty,' Hiroki replied. 'I have been taught there is no difference in the order of priorities.'

Mung held the young man's eyes to see if he would waver, and was pleased when he did not. 'I understand you went up on the back of a kite to observe the Russians,' Mung said in English.

'Yes, Grandfather. Royal Korean Army officers were being taught to dry-fire machine guns, artillery and mortars.'

'Explain dry-fire,' Mung said in French.

'Pardon, Grandpapa,' Hiroki answered, changing languages without hesitation. 'Dry-fire means to simulate loading and shooting of weapons without ammunition. They use aiming stakes, horse-drawn targets, and coordinate battery fire by semaphore and heliograph. They have not yet incorporated the telephone into their military.'

Mung turned to Udo. 'Does the Russian presence in Seoul mean the czar will attack Japan?'

'Genoysha agents in Moscow and St Petersburg say no. Russia is seeking to improve its commerce with Manchuria, Korea and China. They want a warm-water port for access to the Pacific trade.'

'Speak in English,' Mung said. 'You and your son will use that language in Kobe.'

Udo nodded. 'I contacted the Chinese tong chief in Canton regarding Kobe and possible negotiations with Peking about Okinawa. Chin Shu succeeded Kang Shu as leader of the largest tong in China. If a bribe can be placed with the Chinese military, Chin's tong-men will do it.'

'The Emperor received a request from the Kobe Club to clean up the port area,' Mung said. 'Is the earring still respected?'

Hiroki saw his father reach into his pocket and produce a gold clip-earring with geometric patterns.

'It was honoured by Chin,' Udo said. 'I don't know if it will be accepted everywhere.'

Mung motioned for Udo to put the earring away. 'There's a large Chinese community in Kobe,' Mung said. 'They're causing as much trouble as the white riffraff in that treaty port. The western nations hold jurisdiction in Kobe but have lost control.'

'The whites forced the treaty ports on Japan,' Hiroki said. 'If they can't govern, they should go.'

Mung ignored his grandson's interruption and spoke to Udo. 'The description of life in the Kobe port area sounds like the gold-mining towns of California when I was young. Several foreign ambassadors, in addition to the Kobe Club, have requested we help clean it up. If all goes as planned, you'll set up the operation for General Nogi and Admiral Takamora.'

'But they're Hideyoshi's men and he's your enemy.'

'Yes. And my return to public life should begin with an agreement between us. Hideyoshi's military supporters must be kept so occupied, they'll not think of invading Korea.'

Hiroki was fascinated by the rapid exchange between his father and grandfather. They spoke of things that would be recorded in history books. He was excited to be part of it all.

'Two Spanish merchantships will carry French, British and American marines to Kobe,' Mung said. 'The marines will remain on the ships. The foreign undesirables in Kobe will be taken aboard, then dumped in Macao.'

'Including the Chinese?' Udo asked.

'No,' Mung said. 'Use the earring to settle it quietly with our Oriental cousins. If that's not possible, give those Chinese who have the means an opportunity to pay their passage out of Kobe. Hand the others over to our army.'

'Hideyoshi's men will kill them.'

'Only the whites must board the two ships,' Mung said. 'The others are unimportant.'

Hiroki was amazed at his sixty-seven-year-old grandfather's memory and decisiveness. The young man had never spoken to anyone older than his father and never met anyone as old as his grandfather. People rarely lived to the age of forty-five in Korea. Even the counting of one's age in Japan began again after sixty, as if the person was reborn.

'What assistance can I expect?' Udo asked Mung.

'Your two oldest sons are already there. Members of the Kobe Club and the municipal police will identify those whites to be deported. You are to advise General Nogi, Admiral Takamora and their officers in the roundup.' Mung pointed at Udo. 'Do not put yourself in danger! Twenty years ago I sent you away to establish a spy network in China, Korea and Russia. By virtue of your experience, you are in a position to help Japan avert a war. If that fails, you'll be needed to help us fight it.'

'But it was because of The Killing Night we were exiled,' Hiroki blurted out.

Mung froze. He did not look at Hiroki, but stunned the young man with his harsh tone in Japanese. 'The first breach of etiquette was your mistake when you interrupted! The second mistake was mine for not reprimanding you!' Mung's nostrils flared; his lips quivered. He turned and directed the full force of his will upon his grandson. 'Do not ever let there be a third mistake! One whose mouth runs ahead of his mind will certainly fall, and hurt others when he does!'

Hiroki bowed until his forehead and both palms lay flat on the floor. 'Forgive me, Grandfather.' He choked. 'Please forgive me.'

'You are of Genoysha! I, the Black Dragon, command both organizations! Not even your mother is aware the exile was a screen for your father to establish what has become the most efficient spy network in the world! Your father travelled to Prussia to learn from the master spy himself, von Stieber. When you marry, your wife must accept that you live in two worlds! Duty to the Emperor takes precedence!'

'So it is ordered,' Hiroki said. 'So it is done.'

'Your father and I have much to discuss,' Mung said in a softer tone. 'The guard will direct you to Shimatzu's room. Take him to see your mother. The three of you will dine with Count Iyeasu and me this evening.'

There was a tap on the screen door. 'Enter,' Gin-ko said.

The young man in his business suit looked like the photographs of western fashion models. A severe, straight line parted the centre of his slicked-down black hair. He wore wire-rimmed spectacles. A gold watch chain hung across the front of his vest.

'By the gods,' Gin-ko cried. Her hands fluttered to her lips. 'Shimatzu. Oh my dear Shimatzu!'

'Mother.' He hurried to Gin-ko and held her by the shoulders, gazing down into her tear-filled eyes.

Gin-ko reached up and touched his cheeks. She squeezed his arms. 'Here in the palace you must call me aunt,' she said in a choked whisper.

'You are the only mother I have ever known.'

'It could embarrass your father.'

'He and I speak of you as my mother. We refer to Ukiko as my dead mother.'

By supreme force of will, Gin-ko stopped her tears. She gazed up at Shimatzu. 'The years have passed slowly without you. Tell me of your travels in America and Europe.'

'There is a great deal to tell. My first university degree was in economics. I studied the influence of corporate structure on international finance and trade.'

Gin-ko patted his shoulders. 'You must sit and explain these things. I would also like to hear about your bride-to-be.'

'I want to listen too, dear Uncle.' Hiroki peeked into the room. 'Remember me. I brought you here.'

Shimatzu smiled. 'It is strange to have a nephew who is taller and broader than oneself.'

'You had better tell your stories quickly,' Hiroki said. 'It is only five hours before we all go to dine with Grandfather.'

The time spent with his mother and Shimatzu helped Hiroki to forget Mung's reprimand. His spirits were high when he seated himself at the lower end of his grandfather's table. They soared again when the young woman took her place across from him. Noriko commanded his full attention. Her movements were naturally graceful, her face exquisite. The sweep of her neck flowed into delicate shoulders that looked soft, yet powerful.

'Are you part of the Ishikawa family?' Hiroki asked her.

'No.'

She did not drop her eyes as young women were expected to, and it excited him. 'I am an Ishikawa by adoption,' Hiroki said.

'I know about you,' Noriko said.

'But we have never met.'

'Uncle Mung reads your mother's letters to me. When he first had the stroke, I read them to him. You do not write often.'

Hiroki leaned forward to breathe in Noriko's perfume. 'Does my grandfather frighten you?' he whispered.

'Of course not.' Noriko wrinkled her forehead. 'Do you have a cold? You keep sniffing.'

Hiroki pulled back and rubbed his nose. 'It is nothing,' he mumbled.

Noriko saw him cast a furtive glance towards Mung at the head of the table. 'He is proud of you,' she said. 'Your mother wrote about the episode on the back of the kite. That was daring.'

'I stepped on the old man's toes this afternoon.'

'Do not call him the old man.'

'He can be very intimidating.'

'His bent nose and the deep lines on either side of his mouth give him the appearance of a graven image,' Noriko said. 'I suspect he uses that to impress people. Moryiama Ishikawa is really a gentle man.'

'Did you know his nose was broken fighting in Hawaii when he was a boy?'

'I never thought of Uncle Mung as a physical person.'

Hiroki looked down the table to be certain they would not be overheard. 'My father says Grandfather has a bullet hole in him from a gun battle in the California gold fields. My blood grandfather died saving Mung's life. That is why my father was adopted.'

From the other end of the table, Mung said, 'Noriko, show Hiroki and Shimatzu the best places in the palace gardens for viewing the plum blossoms. The buds should be open when they return from Kobe.'

Chapter 3

In an isolated part of the palace, unseen hands slid open a shoji screen between two rooms. Mung and Udo Ishikawa and Count Iyeasu Koin sat facing Count Hideyoshi Koin, General Nogi and Admiral Takamora. All bowed.

'You have read the plans for Kobe,' Iyeasu said to his brother. 'Do you approve?'

Hideyoshi's hooded eyelids fluttered. His thin lips parted, but he remained silent. He pointed a finger at General Nogi.

'No honour is to be gained chasing rabble-rousers and drunkards from Kobe port,' the general said. 'I prefer to train my army for the invasion of Korea.'

'It is the imperial army, not yours,' Iyeasu declared. 'The Emperor wishes the Kobe operation completed in ten days!'

'His majesty commands and we obey,' Takamora said. 'However, to mount such a troop movement in so short a time is difficult.'

Following Mung's coaching on how to reveal the Inei agreement, Udo asked the admiral, 'How long would it take the navy to integrate the Inei merchant fleet into its service for training purposes?' Without waiting for a response, he turned to Nogi. 'The army will soon be asked to send advisers to the Inei factories for retooling to produce arms. Would that take more than ten days?'

The two senior officers were unable to conceal their delight. Udo had confirmed rumours circulating since Shimatzu's wedding announcement.

Hideyoshi frowned. 'Once again you give the lion a ball to play with so he will not attack,' he said to Mung. 'The

31

time has come for Japan to assert itself! If not, China or Russia will! Korea is within Japan's sphere of influence and should be under our control!' He flashed an angry look at Nogi.

'Army intelligence reports a division of Chinese troops outside the Korean capital of Seoul,' the general said.

'Furthermore,' Takamora added, 'the two new Chinese battleships purchased from Holland are in Korean waters.'

Mung and Udo glanced at each other. They had known of the warships but not their whereabouts. Such a movement indicated a major policy change for China.

'All the more reason to test our men in limited engagements,' Udo said. 'They have never been tried in combat.'

'Cleaning up that hell-hole of Kobe cannot be considered combat,' Nogi said.

'My son was also referring to the more complicated amphibious operation against Formosa.' Mung saw interest light the faces opposite him. He baited the two military men with the dream of every Japanese warrior for three hundred years – battle against foreigners. 'If the Emperor ordered a battalion-size attack on a bandit stronghold from the sea, could the army and navy be ready? Keep in mind they would have to travel several hundred miles.'

Nogi threw back his shoulders. His chin jutted forward. 'If it is ordered, it will be done!'

'Hai!' the admiral responded.

Mung handed a scroll to the general. 'These are direct orders from the Emperor for a campaign against Formosan pirates. They become effective the moment the Kobe mission is completed.'

'What is all this?' Hideyoshi demanded.

'Two months ago, sixty-three Okinawan fishermen were murdered and their ships seized by Formosan pirates. China claims sovereignty over Formosa, Okinawa and the rest of the Ryukyu islands. We claim the Ryukyu islands as ours, therefore those fishermen were under our protection. The Emperor holds China responsible for the action of the Formosans.' Mung's confidence in his own intelligence network was confirmed by Hideyoshi's surprise. 'The plan is to take the pirates, dead or alive, to China, and claim international jurisdiction over both the Ryukyu islands and Formosa.'

'The Ryukyus perhaps, but China will never concede Formosa,' the admiral said.

Mung bowed. He smiled and said, 'I will relent on Formosa and take the Ryukyus.'

'What makes you believe they will be given so easily?' Hideyoshi demanded.

'If we are successful in Kobe, the Americans will back our claim to the Ryukyus,' Mung said. 'The Russians agreed to this twenty years ago when I negotiated the Sakhalin–Kurile islands agreements with them.'

'Why should the Russians help us?' Nogi asked. 'They are absorbed in the search for a warm-water port in Korea.'

'Prior to this meeting, the Russian ambassador in Tokyo confirmed that his country will honour Peter the Great's signature on the Sakhalin agreement,' Iyeasu said. 'The ambassador from St Petersburg is pleased to keep our army occupied with China and out of Korea.'

Hideyoshi pointed at Mung. 'You want to keep us out of Korea too! I see Kobe and Formosa as your diversions! If Japan is to be accepted as a major power, we must take significant military action! Cleaning up a waterfront is police work!'

'Three hundred years ago our ancestors invaded Korea and were repulsed,' Mung declared. 'It is a disgrace recorded in history for all the world to see!' He played on Hideyoshi with the twin Japanese concepts: Giri, the social obligation of every Japanese to maintain the unspotted reputation of his family and country; Chu, the obligation to the Emperor which takes precedence over parents, children and self. 'His imperial majesty will not tolerate a second failure in Korea,' Mung declared. 'Japan would be dishonoured forever before the entire world! Those are the Emperor's words!'

'Our troops are untried,' Iyeasu said. 'Our officers have no combat experience and the general staff does not have the background for a major sea-to-land assault. Let Kobe and Formosa be your testing grounds.'

'Count Hideyoshi, we agree Japan needs a strong military,' Udo said. 'It must be an army and navy of quality. We can never match the Chinese or Russians in numbers. Let us begin slowly and move from success to success.'

Hideyoshi glanced at Nogi and Takamora. The two military men nodded agreement. 'Kobe within ten days,' Hideyoshi said, and motioned for the screen between the two rooms to be closed.

'Kobe in ten days, Korea in ten months,' Hideyoshi whispered to his military aides behind the closed screen.

'Success in Kobe, victory in Formosa, and international recognition of Japan's rights to the Ryukyu islands,' Mung said. He motioned to the closed screen. 'This will satisfy their appetites and give us time for a peaceful solution.'

Chapter 4

'Did I tell you I am in love?' Hiroki asked.

Shimatzu pulled the quilt over his head and moaned. 'All last night.'

Hiroki sighed. 'I am ready to join you in a double wedding.'

'It will be a single murder if you do not let me sleep.'

'She is beautiful, intelligent, and kind.' Hiroki jerked the quilt off Shimatzu. 'You cannot sleep. You promised to take me to see her this morning.'

'I only promised last night so you would let me sleep.'

'I leave for Kobe this afternoon. If you do not dress immediately, I shall drag you to the centre of the imperial gardens in your hakka shorts.'

Shimatzu rolled off his sleeping pallet. 'Do you know kendo?' he asked.

'What does stick fighting have to do with Noriko?'

'Your little beauty trains with the Modern Women's Asiatic League in the Imperial Hall of Martial Arts. She will be there this morning.'

Hiroki pulled Shimatzu to his feet. 'What are we waiting for!'

They stepped out of their sandals at the entrance and entered the martial arts hall. Hiroki suited up in a kendo training uniform of leather skirt, padded chest protector, mittens, arm guards and black screened helmet that obscured his face.

Shimatzu hailed a friend and presented Hiroki. 'This is my nephew. He is rated on the intermediate level in Korea. I must leave. Could you do me a favour? Find him a partner for an exercise, and arrange to have him meet Noriko.'

'She is practising on the other side of the hall. Why does he have to meet her?'

'My nephew thinks he is in love.' Shimatzu winked at his friend and Hiroki blushed behind the mask. The three laughed, unaware of the young army officers nearby.

'There stands Shimatzu Ishikawa,' Akichi Shibata said. 'Son of the pacifist, Moryiama Ishikawa.'

'Shibata, you have an evil gleam in your eye,' his fellow officer said.

'Listen to the nephew's accent,' Shibata said. 'He sounds like a Hokkaido farmer. He comes to simulate battle while his grandfather crawls out of retirement to keep us from the real thing.'

'He is big, and looks strong to me.'

'I will make him look like a dwarf before he leaves,' Shibata said.

'You are a senior in kendo. They seek an intermediate.'

'He wishes to meet Noriko and I will help him,' Shibata said.

'She is rated intermediate only because she is female. A man with her expertise would be an instructor anywhere in Japan.'

'Then let the farmer be defeated by a woman.' Shibata sauntered over and addressed himself to Hiroki. 'I overheard you are visiting Tokyo and wish to find a partner.'

'You are rated senior,' Shimatzu said.

'That is correct.' Shibata bowed. 'The intermediates practise on the other side of the hall. I shall bring one here for you.' He turned and made his way across the floor, around combatants practising cuts, slashes and stabs with the two-handed bamboo swords.

Hiroki took a stance and began to warm up, keeping an eye out for Noriko.

'Be careful,' Shimatzu warned.

36

'I am here for love, not war. Will we meet before I depart for Kobe this afternoon?'

'If not, then on your return.' Shimatzu bowed and left the hall.

Shibata bowed to the headmistress of the Modern Women's Asiatic League. 'I have found a man who is prepared to combat your star pupil.'

The older woman removed her helmet. 'Are you serious?'

Shibata pointed to Hiroki on the other side of the hall. 'That big one warming up.'

'Noriko,' the headmistress called.

A helmeted figure in a long, black-hooded robe bowed to her opponent and stepped back. She placed the bamboo sword in her sash and presented herself.

'It has come,' the headmistress said. 'Finally, a man has challenged you.' She pointed across the hall. 'That one.'

'The challenger has one condition,' Shibata said. 'If he wins, your league of liberated women will be forbidden to practise in this hall.'

'That is unfair,' Noriko said. She began to remove her helmet.

'Leave it on,' the headmistress ordered. 'This is an opportunity to set a precedent for male and female combat on equal terms.' She turned to Shibata. 'Is the challenger an instructor?'

'No, he is a visitor on the intermediate level. Strong in body and the belief that women should be driven from this hall. He intends to do just that before he leaves here today.'

'We accept the challenge,' the headmistress said. 'Who will judge the match?'

'We must wait until the instructors go to tea.' Shibata grinned. 'It is to be a fight to the finish on the nine metre square, with no judges and no points. The one who is driven from the square loses.'

'Not acceptable,' the older woman said.

Noriko bowed to the headmistress. 'You have told people I am underrated. Now is the time for me to prove you correct. I shall not disappoint you.'

A bell sounded. The kendo instructors in the great hall bowed to their students. They formed a column of twos and marched out.

Shibata bowed. 'Ladies, opportunity awaits.'

He hurried across the floor to Hiroki. 'Your match is set.'

Hiroki felt uneasy, and turned to ask advice of Shimatzu's friend. The young man was being led away by four army officers. 'I am here to exercise, not enter into combat,' Hiroki said.

'You refuse?' Shibata sneered. He pointed at the slim figure across the nine metre square wearing the long, black cloak of the intermediate yudansha class of kendo.

Hiroki looked about. People from all over the hall were gathering around the square. To refuse would brand him a coward for life. He tried to measure his opponent. From the stance, from the position of the raised three-and-a-half-foot bamboo sword, nothing was revealed. They both wore the same armour, although he was without a cloak. Their faces were masked by similar padded helmets. Hiroki was taller than his opponent. He felt stronger, but knew that training and experience are more important than strength in kendo. His Korean instructor rated him high in the yudansha class, but this was the Imperial Hall of Martial Arts. The greatest practitioners of kendo were employed here as teachers. He looked at the crowd gathered around the square. Perhaps Noriko was here. He had no choice but to fight. His honour was at stake. He took a stance, then looked around for the judges. Before he could question their absence, Shibata shouted out, 'Begin!'

The black-cloaked figure sprang towards him. Hiroki tightened his two-handed grip on the leather hilt of the bamboo sword and struck for the wrist, then the side. The black-robed figure danced out of reach, then darted forward and struck for his arm. He parried that blow, another to his head, then stabbed for the chest. The black figure leaned away, and stepped forward with an overhead stroke that became a stab for his throat. Hiroki retreated, and parried a series of lightning blows. His attacker backed off and stood still.

Hiroki, in a cold sweat, could hear his breath whistling through his teeth inside the helmet. He was facing an opponent of the renshi teaching class. Unless he discovered a unique solution, he would be defeated.

Again the black figure darted forward to attack. Hiroki retreated under a barrage of cuts and slashes, forced backward to the very edge of the square. He crossed swords with his opponent and shoved with all his strength, surprised by how easily the black figure was thrown back. He attacked, striking again and again with all his power. But the black phantom blocked, parried and avoided every blow. In a last desperate effort, Hiroki uttered a cry and leapt forward, bringing his bamboo sword down with all his might. The black figure blocked his weapon and also cried out. Hiroki froze. It was a woman's voice.

Before entering the nine metre square, Noriko had used Zen meditation to concentrate her mind, her soul, every muscle in her body, to win. She had seen that her opponent was taller, more muscular, but after a few parries she ranked him low in the yudansha class. His technique was stiff. He avoided being struck only by superior strength and speed. He froze when she cried out and she struck hard at his side. He grunted, but stood like a tree. Noriko brought her sword up, around, and down on top of his helmet. With the classic thrust, she drove the blunt end of the bamboo hard to his throat pad. He fell to his knees, sword upraised. She knocked it from his grip.

Around the square there was stunned silence. A woman had defeated a man.

'You have won,' the headmistress cried. She started forward.

'He is still in the square,' Shibata shouted, and motioned the older woman back.

Noriko advanced on the kneeling man.

Inside his helmet, Hiroki tasted shame in the blood pouring from his nose. He was angry at being deceived, furious at being tricked into fighting a woman. He was enraged at being brought to his knees before everyone. He heard Shibata tell the black phantom to drive him from the square.

She pointed her sword, adding insult to injury, and motioned Hiroki to rise and retreat. His sword lay to his left. He sucked in the blood running down into his mouth. He choked on his fury and stood up, vowing to die rather than surrender. Again the black-robed figure motioned him to leave, but he feinted towards his fallen sword. She moved between him and the weapon, and kicked it from the square.

There was a great sigh from the audience. Many turned to leave rather than witness Hiroki's disgrace.

He took off the padded mittens and deliberately flung them away. From the recesses of his embittered mind, the first lesson of his karate instructor came into his consciousness. 'Undirected anger is mental suicide. Concentrate your fury on a single target and use your skill to destroy it.' Hiroki looked at the black-cloaked figure. The white-hot rage in his heart welled up through his chest and into his throat. He channelled it to his brain.

Noriko, seeing the man in front of her throw away his gloves, assumed he was surrendering. She relaxed her stance. But then he took an unusual pose – his left foot bent forward, the right leg back. He raised his hands high in front of him, and moved them slowly through the air like two serpents in a deadly dance. Without warning he bounded towards her, throwing punches. She thrust her sword at his head, but missed. 'A lightning kick numbed her left arm. If not for the padding she knew the bone would have been smashed. She struck again, expecting him to dodge, but he purposely took the full force of the blow on his shoulder guard without flinching, and swept her legs out from under with a kick.

The crowd was stunned into silence as the man, like a hunting leopard, pounced on the fallen woman. But Noriko wriggled away and leapt up, trying to collect her wits as she avoided a terrible rain of punches and kicks that would not allow her to set her feet.

Hiroki, a fourth-degree black belt in the art of unarmed combat, tore off his helmet. He feinted a front kick and threw a whirling backhand punch with all his might. The black figure was frozen with sword upraised, and his blow caught her in the chest protector. The resounding smash echoed from the high beamed ceiling. She was lifted off her feet and flung backwards out of the square. Her helmet fell off.

'Noriko!' Hiroki gasped. He saw Shibata's leering face. People crowded in. An older woman held Noriko's head in her lap. He saw the beautiful dazed eyes try to focus on him, then roll up into her head. Noriko slumped unconscious. Hiroki's knees buckled.

From the Hall of Martial Arts, Hiroki went directly to the Tokyo dock. He boarded the Kobe mail-boat and locked himself in his cabin.

For hours he lay on the sleeping mat, eyes wide, examining his shame and humiliation. The instructors had returned sooner than expected and were quick to react. Noriko was carried off and treated by the women.

Hiroki's nose was packed with gauze. He had brushed off Shimatzu's friend's apologies for allowing Shibata to trick him. The kendo students were made to stand in ranks. They were sworn to secrecy for the honour of the hall and their teachers.

Shibata and his followers had been permanently banned. They and other young officers made quick bows and left the hall before the senior instructor finished speaking. At the exit, Shibata had whirled and pointed at the instructor. 'When the military holds power, you will be banned from this hall,' he roared.

Hiroki moaned. His lifelong dream of returning to Japan had turned into a nightmare. He closed his eyes and clenched his fists. 'The shame,' he muttered through his teeth. 'To be beaten by a woman in front of everyone!' He knew men like Shibata and his friends. They would brag. Soon all Tokyo would know. Hiroki contemplated seppuku, but his ritual suicide would not release his family from the disgrace. The whole world would know the reason. Noriko had conspired with Shibata to trick him. He had to shame her. 'That is most important,' he said aloud. 'She must suffer!' He ground his teeth. 'Her shame must be private or Grandfather Mung will be hurt. After that I will kill Shibata. Then I can commit seppuku.' He fell asleep with a vision of driving a knife blade into his own abdomen.

Hiroki's thoughts relaxed him and the tension dissipated. Deeper and deeper he went into his subconscious until his mind entered his soul. He rose up, up and out of his body. He wandered over the rolling hills of the Kanto plains. He glided down to a crowd of people gathered in two groups near a stand of scrub oak, with their backs to him. All wore the long black robes of kendo warriors. Suddenly they turned. On the front of the helmets of one group was the face of Shibata, on the other, the face of Noriko. The two came together and held hands.

Hiroki went rigid. He trembled. He did not feel the sweep and sway of the ship, nor did he hear the drum of the steam pistons when the boat pulled away from the dock. His clacking teeth awakened him. He sat up and brought his callused fists before his eyes. 'I swear Giri,' he whispered. 'Revenge! Revenge! If I kill him, then I must kill myself. I would not see her pain. I have to know she suffers and be close enough to witness it.' He slammed his fist into the palm of his hand. 'The longer she suffers, the better! Yes,' he nodded, 'but her shame must be private while Shibata's is public. I will kill him with a blow to the lungs. He will choke on his own blood. Then I will commit seppuku.'

A knock on the door startled Hiroki. 'Sir,' a voice called, 'your father summons you.'

Hiroki became aware of the pitch and yaw of the ship as it left Tokyo harbour and breasted the big ocean rollers of the Pacific. 'I will be there shortly,' he called, and put away his thoughts of revenge, carefully, like rare gems. While he changed clothes he peeked in on his precious treasure, savouring each glimpse, revelling in the anticipation of the solution. He hurried to his father's cabin, convinced of his mission in life – Giri! His love for Noriko had been destroyed by her deceit.

'How was the kendo workout?' Udo asked.

'Good,' Hiroki muttered, relieved his father did not know of the day's events. 'What are our instructions for Kobe?'

'We meet William Whittefield at the dock. He will guide us.'

'Is William the son of Grandfather's adoptive brother?'

'Yes. We are all related to him, but not by blood. Grandfather Mung was adopted by the Whittefield family of Massachusetts and later by the Ishikawa family in Kagoshima. When my father died protecting Mung, Mung adopted me. How would you feel about being adopted if it improved your position?'

'I have never thought about that.'

'You are the youngest son and will inherit nothing from me.'

'Except your family name,' Hiroki said.

'Which is an adoptive name taken from Mung's adoptive name. Shimatzu and your older brothers will continue the Ishikawa line.'

Hiroki caught his father looking at him with love in his eyes.

'Scholars write that a man's oldest son is most important, the middle son more comforting,' Udo said. 'But they also say the youngest is most precious, for all the father has learned from raising the others he puts into the last of his line. I want you to be careful in Kobe.'

Hiroki bowed. He looked up with a question in his eyes.

'Shimatzu told Mung and me why you went to the Imperial Hall of Martial Arts.' Udo saw his son pale and drop his eyes. 'It is not a shame to fall in love. Some day I will tell you of my courtship of your mother. Are you in love with Noriko?'

'What!'

'That was the reason you went to the Hall of Martial Arts?'

'Yes, but . . .'

'Noriko has been extremely kind to Grandfather Mung,' Udo said. 'He and Iyeasu are most enthusiastic about the possibility of a love match. They suggested a mi-ai.'

'A premarital viewing,' Hiroki gasped.

'Do not be alarmed. There is no obligation to marriage. Although your refusal to participate in a mi-ai could hurt your grandfather and insult Iyeasu. If you decide the girl is not for you, I will end the matter in good taste. There is a condition that will make your refusal easier. Iyeasu wishes you to take his family name because he has no son. He would adopt you.'

44

Hiroki hardly heard his father. Details of a plan for revenge on Noriko suddenly blossomed. The sweet smell of it made his head spin. Oh yes, he would go to a mi-ai. He would look across the table at her and smile. 'Why did you deceive me?' he would ask. 'Is Shibata your lover? Did you two plan my disgrace together?' He could not tell his father of his thoughts. 'Yes, Father, a mi-ai would be appropriate.'

'Your mother and I are in favour of the wedding, but you must decide,' Udo said. 'You would inherit title, wealth and land from Iyeasu Koin. Such a wedding could put you in a position of power to serve the Black Dragon and the Emperor.'

'First there must be the mi-ai,' Hiroki said, smiling in eager anticipation.

'First is our mission in Kobe,' his father said. 'The time draws near. Your two brothers were sent ahead to Kobe as scouts for the army and navy. They have familiarized themselves with the treaty port. We will reconnoitre with them and make a plan to round up the undesirables.'

'There will be action?' Hiroki grew excited by the thought of death in battle to atone for his disgrace.

'No swords or guns will be used,' Udo said. 'The Black Dragon gave his word there would be no killing of white people.'

'Then how can it be done?'

'The soldiers will march overland equipped with kendo sticks. The Kobe police will carry clubs. It should prove to be an interesting experiment in discipline. We must finish it in ten days to return in time for Shimatzu's wedding.'

Chapter 5

Kobe

A Chinese footman assisted Udo and Hiroki into the closed carriage, opposite William Whittefield.

The American returned the bow of father and son. 'I believe we are related,' he said in Japanese. 'If not by blood, at least by common cause. Our immediate task is to clean up Kobe.'

'You have warmest regards from Mung,' Udo said. 'My son and I are honoured to meet you.'

Hiroki looked through the shuttered windows. He could see out without being seen.

The American tapped his cane on the carriage ceiling and the driver sent the horses forward at a walk. 'We are passing through the beginning of the waterfront area that must be evacuated,' William said. 'It is a relatively quiet place during the day. But when the sun goes down, the vermin come out of the bars, brothels and gambling dens.'

The carriage stopped and its occupants peered through the shutters.

A white man with rifle in hand and a pistol on his hip called to the driver in pidgin English. 'You group one dollar all visit one hour. Each payee one dollar all day stay. You try go no payee, I breakee you fucking slanty-eyed head!'

A silver coin arched from the driver's seat into the guard's outstretched hand. He waved the carriage on.

'Does he have the right to charge us?' Hiroki asked.

'I'm pleased you understand English,' William said.

'My son and I speak French, Chinese, and Korean as well,' Udo said.

'That will be helpful when we collect the swindlers,

46

thieves and murderers. The scum of all nations have washed up on these shores. The private guard you saw protects this area known as Duke's Ground. For one dollar each, the Iron Duke guarantees twenty-four hours of protection from the law.'

'You mean this Duke has the power to keep out the western authorities and the Kobe police?' Udo said.

'There is no western authority. Look to the tops of the buildings on either side of the street,' William said.

Udo and Hiroki peered up through the window slats. Armed men roamed the flat roofs of the western-style clapboard buildings.

'In good weather as many as fifty guns cover Duke's Ground,' William said. 'See that large sign – THE IRON DUKE. That bar is Duke's headquarters. He never leaves the building. He has men standing by like firemen on duty. Duke is the key to cleaning up Kobe. The warehouse next to The Iron Duke houses three French cannon and a German Gatling gun. Chinatown begins at the end of this street. The tong chief and Duke have an agreement. All opium trade goes to the Chinese. In return, the Chinese come to Duke's assistance, if necessary.'

'How many Chinese are there?' Udo asked.

'Between four and five hundred fighting men. Chinatown exists on its restaurants, brothels and contract labour exchange for foreign countries. They buy and sell their own people, mostly from southern China.'

William tapped the ceiling with his cane and the carriage turned inland, past another guard. They rode out of Duke's Ground onto a wide, clean boulevard. Solid stone buildings lined both sides.

'Who controls this?' Udo asked.

'After dark it becomes no-man's-land,' William said. 'The human rats from the waterfront scurry out of their holes and come up here. No decent person ventures out alone or unarmed.' He read off the names of the more impressive structures as they passed. 'Carroll's House. Bellevue Hotel. Masonic Hall. Dutronquoy's. These are all clubs formed by merchants seeking a safe place to meet, conduct business and sleep. Here they won't be sickened by the water. In the port area, dysentery, cholera and diphtheria run rampant.' He pointed to the red and white flag bearing the letters K.C. 'That's the Kobe Club. Please don't be insulted, but we have to use the rear entrance.'

'Because we're Orientals?' Udo asked.

'Mixed bloods, white sailors and sea captains are also barred from membership. I would have it otherwise, but the situation evolved out of necessity. Kobe was a clean, peaceful Japanese town when it became a treaty port. But the first European administrator was weak and corruptible. The riffraff of the Pacific washed ashore and found a home here. Soon they were running the place.'

'If westerners can't administer a treaty port, it should revert to Japanese control,' Hiroki said.

'I would go further,' William said. 'Even if Europeans could control Kobe, it should revert to Japanese administration. The clean-up campaign is the first step in persuading foreign ambassadors to negate the unequal agreements with Japan. All treaty ports should revert to Japanese control. The use of Japanese troops in Kobe has been carefully planned. Mung and I wish to show the western powers that your country has a disciplined military with a sense of Christian justice.'

The Japanese father and son glanced at each other at the words 'Christian justice', but made no comment.

'Now let's go meet the president of the Kobe Club,' William said.

Udo and Hiroki followed up the back stairs and into the president's office. Greetings were exchanged.

'Gentlemen,' James Alburg said, 'the plan to dump three hundred or so westerners on the beaches of Macao may sound cruel, but you would have to spend just

48

one night on the Kobe waterfront to appreciate our position.'

'I intend doing that this evening,' Udo said. 'What support can we expect from the Kobe Club for our operation?'

'Right to the point,' Alburg said. He blew on the tip of his cigar. 'I've arranged for members of our club to participate in the clean-up. Only they will carry firearms. They'll identify and attempt to convince those whites slated for deportation to leave quietly. If your men can't handle the situation, our people will use their firearms. The Kobe municipal police will guide your soldiers into Chinatown. The club members won't participate in that part of the operation. If Japanese shed Chinese blood, no one will be held accountable.'

'Tonight my sons and I will tour the entire area,' Udo said. 'Afterwards we'll finalize our plans, then coordinate our moves with you and the Kobe police. My two oldest boys, officers in military intelligence, have been gathering information in Kobe. We haven't seen them for years. You will excuse us. They're waiting.'

Outside the port area, in a peaceful part of Kobe, Udo and Hiroki entered a Japanese house. Udo's two sons bowed to their father. 'Even in civilian clothes you both have military bearing,' Udo said. 'Your mother and I are proud of you.'

'I hope Mother did not accompany you to this hell-hole,' Yaka, the eldest, said.

'No, but she yearns to see you. It has been too long.' Udo motioned at Hiroki. 'Do you remember your little brother?'

'He is bigger than the two of us put together.' Yaka laughed. 'What do they feed you in Korea?'

'I chew nails and spit swords,' Hiroki said. 'How are my brothers?'

'Still strong enough to protect you, little one,' Uraga said. 'Do not look so grave. With the army and navy on its way, we will handle this situation.'

'Your little brother has a fourth-degree black belt in karate,' Udo said. 'Have you two kept up your training?'

'Military intelligence officers are given jujitsu courses by police instructors,' Yaka said.

'It appears the army and navy spy networks are more efficient than before,' Udo said. 'The Black Dragon and I were surprised by Hideyoshi's knowledge of Russians in Seoul and the new Chinese battleships in Korean waters.'

'That information came from a merchant captain,' Uraga said. 'We use many civilian spies.'

'Military intelligence is not half as effective as the Black Dragon Society,' Yaka said. 'Untrained people flood us with useless information. Our best men remain behind desks sorting irrelevant reports. The military will soon try to incorporate the Black Dragon Society.'

'Genoysha too?' Udo asked.

'They are not aware Genoysha exists,' Yaka said.

'How do they expect to gain control of the Black Dragon Society?' Hiroki asked.

'If Hideyoshi is successful in promoting a war with Korea, he will demand that the entire nation mobilize behind the effort,' Yaka said. 'He expects a spirit of patriotism to sweep the country. When nationalist fervour reaches its peak, he plans to send Nogi and Takamora to the Emperor. They will claim that incorporation of Black Dragons into the military is necessary for the proper conduct of the war.'

'That would isolate the Emperor,' Udo said. 'Only through the Black Dragons is the Emperor kept informed of what really takes place in the nation.'

'Which branch of the military does Hideyoshi intend will control the Black Dragon Society?' Hiroki asked.

'The army and the navy are always in competition for

power,' Uraga said. 'I have heard young army officers, followers of Hideyoshi, say he personally will take charge of all intelligence services.'

'Then handing control of the Black Dragon Society to Hideyoshi would simply exchange one civilian leader for another,' Hiroki said. 'If Grandfather Mung could expose Hideyoshi's intentions, he and the society would remain independent.'

Udo smiled at his youngest son, and the two older brothers looked at Hiroki with respect.

'The information you have brought is important,' Udo said to Yaka and Uraga. 'I will apprise the Black Dragon of the situation. Now it is time to bathe and talk, to dress and talk. Then you two will give Hiroki and me a night tour of the docks, Duke's Ground and Chinatown.'

Chapter 6

Dutch Henry barrelled through the swinging doors into the Iron Duke Bar. Armed guards, waiters and bartenders made way as he hurried up the aisle between the two long bars that paralleled each other from the front of the building to the rear.

Orientals, blacks and those of mixed race drank at the bar on the left. They gambled at tables behind that bar, and fornicated in the open stalls placed around the walls. The whites drank, fornicated and gambled on the right side of the hall. From a balcony, riflemen watched the bedlam below.

At the back of the large hall, the parallel bars came together. Seated atop the platform on a high-backed chair draped with a large tiger skin was the escaped Australian convict, three-hundred-pound, six-foot-five Tom Tiddler – The Iron Duke. He wore a Samoan sarong and an open black vest that showed his hairy chest and accentuated his muscular arms. His pink, oval face was framed by long, silky blond hair.

Flanking the Duke sat Mervin Kilday, a deserter from the Irish Fusiliers, and Black George, a Fijian renegade. Each held a shotgun in hand and wore a pair of pistols in his belt.

'Let Dutchy through,' the Iron Duke shouted.

'It's what you been waiting for,' the Dutchman called. He held out a telegram. 'The ship with the wenches passed Kasaoko point. They might make it on time if the weather holds.'

'What's it like outside now?' Duke demanded.

'She's going to blow tonight,' Dutch Henry said. He handed the telegram to Black George.

'The weather in this country is dirty like that British gunboat patrolling outside Kobe harbour,' Black George said. He handed the telegram to the Iron Duke. 'The English bastards may not come ashore to get us, but they sure go hell for leather after any slaver at sea.'

'You're right, mate,' the blond giant said. 'So take the Dutchman and get your black arse to the telegraph office! Tell our men on the beach to signal the *Maria-Luz* not to enter Kobe harbour! Have the girls put off on Akahasi beach a half mile up the coast!'

A shot roared from the balcony. Some people ducked. Others dropped to the floor. There was silence. A man staggered towards the front door with a red stain spreading on his back. He fell to his knees.

'What did he do?' Duke called up to the balcony.

'Pickpocket,' came the reply from above.

'Throw the bastard out,' Duke roared. 'And any other son of a bitch what got funny ideas!' He wagged his finger at his customers. 'The show's over! Get up and enjoy yourselves!'

Two guards grabbed the dying man under the armpits and dragged him to the door. They kicked it open and heaved him into the street.

'What the hell you two waiting for?' Duke shouted at Black George and Dutch Henry. 'Contact the *Maria-Luz*!'

The two men hurried away. Duke reached out and grabbed Kilday's shirt-front, pulling the man's face close to his. 'Check your men and the guns next door! Just in case that British gunboat decides to land marines and come after those women when they get here!'

Kilday forced a gap-toothed grin and struggled to free himself. 'Little worry from her majesty's swabbies. They come ashore to gamble, drink and get laid.'

The Iron Duke's eyes narrowed. 'There are more wanted men in Duke's Ground than in half the jails of Queensland. Someday the limeys will come for them.'

53

Kilday pulled backwards, bucking until he broke free. He tumbled from the platform and bolted through a side door that connected the bar to the warehouse. 'I'm on my way.'

Fourteen-year-old Shen Yan, of Hoppo in southern China, stood naked and shivering between the two men. She had been sold by her parents for seventeen dollars to the master of the *Maria-Luz*, a three-hundred-ton, two-masted, square-rigged brigantine slave ship.

'Should I offload her with Duke's merchandise tomorrow?' the ship's mate asked.

'I want no trouble with that blond ape,' Captain Emilio Belviso said. He dipped a cloth in a water basin and washed the semen from his loose-skinned, hairy belly. 'She's a good fuck. You can take her for the night.'

'This cruise will kill me,' the mate said. 'All I do is fuck. These chink girls are so tight my cock is rubbed raw.' He threw the girl an old blanket and shoved her towards the door. Neither man noticed Shen Yan's hand slip out from under the blanket and snatch a knife from the food tray.

'You have two hundred cunts to choose from, but nobody touches the Duke's fifty,' Captain Belviso said. 'There's enough to go round till we reach Lima.'

'If this tub holds together that long,' the mate said. He shoved the girl out of the door and followed her.

The captain dried himself and looked around the cabin. This ship and I started life together in Lima sixty years ago, he thought. Finally, in my last year of sailing, I got to own something. I'll retire, but she'll go on.

He looked in a mirror and pointed a finger at his chest. 'Now you're owner, captain, and you'll make big money,' he said to his reflection. 'I'll make another fortune in Lima from the sandalwood platforms the women are squeezed into.' He pulled on his trousers, stepped into his sea boots and crossed himself. 'With God's help,' he mumbled as he opened a porthole and sniffed the evening air. 'Dirty weather coming, and the British patrolling outside Kobe harbour.' He spat, and slammed the window shut. 'The message from Duke's men said to unload the girls at Akahasi beach. I'll do it tomorrow, and be on my way to sell the rest in the whorehouses of the mining towns along the Peruvian coast before the British hear I was in the Far East.'

At 8 p.m. Yaka and Uraga led their father and younger brother towards the docks. Each carried a Colt .44 tucked in his obi.

'This is no-man's-land,' Yaka said, pointing down the wide, deserted boulevard. 'Right now it is quiet, but there is a shootout almost every night. We believe Duke encourages bands of rowdies to come up from the docks in order to expand his area.'

'How do the municipal police handle the situation?' Udo asked.

'They are not allowed firearms,' Uraga said. 'It is forbidden to maim, kill, or imprison a white man in the treaty port area.' He shrugged. 'The police disappear.'

'How do they deal with non-whites?'

'Lawbreakers are put in jail and fined. For repeat offenders, the police have an understanding with the Iron Duke. They hand them over to Duke's shanghai gangs, and the villains are soon working at sea. It is one way to reduce the outlaw population.'

Yaka and Uraga moved closer to their father as they entered the dock area. The street was lit by cooking fires and light spilling out of grog shops. Large tents lit by electricity projected the shadows of couples drinking and fornicating on the canvas walls. The area smelled of urine and human excrement. Dead bodies and drunks lay in the road. Japanese, whites and mixed breeds chased women across planks laid over the mud-rutted street. Loud Italian opera music from a wind-up gramophone competed with the shouts, curses and off-key singing of drunken men. The mellow sounds of a West Indian iron drum band melded into the clamour.

Hiroki was distracted from his thoughts of revenge by the piercing shriek of a bearded seaman. The man staggered from a tent, screaming and holding his bloody crotch. A screeching white woman charged out after him. She leapt on his back and reached over his shoulder, going for his throat with a straight razor. The seaman flung her into the mud and jumped on her. With both hands on the back of her head, he pushed her face down in the muck. The woman's limbs thrashed. They flopped, they quivered. And she lay still.

Five men staggered out of the tent in various stages of undress. 'She ain't no good to you, Jock, cause you ain't got the balls you was born with,' the first man shouted.

'She ain't no good for nothing no more.' The bearded sailor staggered to his feet. He looked down at his bloody crotch, then at his friends. 'I give a silver dollar to the first bastard what pisses on her dead arse. Do it myself but she almost cut my pisser off.'

The five men circled the woman's body.

'It is more of the same until we get to Duke's Ground,' Yaka said. 'Then the orgies and violence become a bit more organized.'

'Lead us there,' Udo said. 'I wish to see this Iron Duke.'

Hiroki followed his father and brothers onto Duke's Ground, into the Iron Duke Bar itself. His thoughts were far from the plans being discussed to clean up Kobe's waterfront, or the mayhem surrounding them. 'I will attend the mi-ai,' he said aloud, startling himself. He looked around to see if he was overheard. His brothers and father were looking at the blond giant on the platform and the riflemen along the railing of the balcony above.

Hiroki slipped back into the webby cocoon of his imagination, revelling in his dreams of meeting Noriko. People will say, 'What a charming couple. Well-suited, those two.' When others are not looking, I will break her down with terrible stares. I will ask permission of the nakoda – matchmaker – to stroll with and speak to the girl. Then I will clench my teeth and whisper, 'Deceitful woman you are, to act the part of a man. You wore the robe of a kendo apprentice when you are clearly of the teaching class. You tricked me.' He choked on the memory of being brought to his knees. He trembled with anger. Compelling himself to remain composed, he followed his family from the bar. Noriko may cry out in public when I confront her with the truth, but I will be calm. To others I will appear caring and concerned. When they question, I will hint at her masculinity in such a way they will know it is the reason for my refusal. Her reputation will be ruined by those vicious whispers that kill in Japanese society. 'I feel so good,' he said aloud.

'You do seem excited about the forthcoming clash,' Uraga said. 'You have more of the old samurai blood than I do. You say little but dream of battle.'

Hiroki frowned. 'Father,' he said, 'you and William Whittefield spoke of a party.'

'Yes. We plan to host every westerner in the port to all the free whisky they can drink. And tell them it is a holiday sponsored by the government. When they are drunk enough, the army will move in. Lord Takai almost succeeded with such a trick against Commodore Perry in 1854. Grandfather Mung and John Whittefield, William's father, managed to get the Americans back to their ships before they were attacked, and the treaty was saved.'

'How is it that Grandfather and John Whittefield saved the westerners then, and now we work to throw them out?' Uraga asked.

'We had to accept European dominion over our port

57

cities because the whites were militarily stronger,' Udo said. 'But it gave us the opportunity to observe them at close range, and learn from them. It has taken twenty years to incorporate their technology into our society. We now have merchantships, telephones, street lights and the telegraph. The level of Japanese education is higher than England's or America's. The time has come for us to teach the West a thing or two.'

Yaka leaned forward, eyes bright. 'Will we ever fight them?'

'One day we must,' Udo said.

'Grandfather does not think we can defeat them,' Hiroki said.

'Your grandfather is a brilliant man, but he is overly impressed with western nations,' Udo replied. 'He saw them as a young fisherman and learned from them before Japan began to modernize. But he has been a recluse for almost a decade. We now have our own steel mills, coal mines and railroads. Twenty years ago the only wheels in the empire were found on the imperial carriage and funeral cart. Now we have teamsters in every city, and wagon roads crisscrossing our four major islands. One day we shall connect our islands by bridges.'

'I believe we can defeat the Koreans today,' Yaka said.

'And the Chinese tomorrow,' Uraga said.

'If we cannot clean up these docks,' Udo waved at the drunken men and women in the street, 'even the military will not sanction any action against a foreign country.'

The four passed from Duke's Ground into Chinatown. It was quieter, and cleaner.

'Where are you taking us now?' Hiroki asked.

'Wong's Palace,' Yaka said. 'He rules Chinatown. The bordello restaurant is headquarters for the tong-men of Kobe.'

'It has been some time since I had a good Chinese

meal,' Udo said. 'When I married your mother, we had a Chinese cook.'

'I recall one of Mother's stories,' Hiroki said. 'She told me the Chinese cook disappeared one night and was never seen again.'

Udo made no comment as he followed his oldest son into Wong's Palace and to a table. He had killed the chef who helped him poison the then Russian ambassador's wife and her lesbian lover.

The sweet smell of opium mixed with the savoury scents of exotic foods permeated the crowded restaurant. Red, black and gold lacquered carvings decorated wooden pillars. Delicate screen paintings covered the walls.

'I have a special request for this evening's meal,' Udo said to the waiter in Mandarin Chinese. 'I hope your chef will accommodate me.'

'We shall do our best,' the waiter answered in a Cantonese accent. He watched Udo take a gold earring from his obi and fix it to his ear. The waiter stared at the geometric patterns. 'My sons are unfamiliar with Chinese food,' Udo said in the Cantonese dialect. 'I would like to order for the Japanese palate.'

The waiter's eyes never left the earring. 'It will be a pleasure to serve one so articulate as you.'

Udo accepted a menu but did not look at it. 'Bring us stir-fried squid flowers, braised prawns in the shell, and steamed lobster. We shall have dim-sum to begin and shark's fin soup to conclude the meal.'

The waiter bowed. Udo unclipped the earring and placed it on the menu so the gold piece slid into the waiter's hand. The man bowed again, and hurried off.

Hiroki tugged at his ear. 'What does it mean?'

'Twenty-five years ago in Canton, Grandfather Mung made Kang Shu the most powerful tong chief in southern China,' Udo said. 'My brother Uraga died in the battle against Kang's rivals. For years I remained in Canton and

59

worked with the tong chief. We became close friends. He supplied the Black Dragon Society with much information. Twenty-two years ago, before I returned to Japan, Kang gave me the earring as a sign of identification to call upon any member of his tong for help. Kang died some years ago. I recently used the earring in China. Our waiter here is clearly impressed by it.'

The Chinese waiter returned and placed a charcoal fire-pot in the centre of the table, and a bubbling bowl of brown gravy on top. 'This is called Four Seasons Dressing. Around it I place cabbage hearts, cooked chicken breasts, gizzards, tripe, omelette, fish maws and dumplings. Compliments of the proprietor.' He bowed. 'The dim-sum will be served shortly. Mr Wong requests the pleasure of your company, master.'

Udo nodded to his sons, then followed the waiter through a beaded curtain and up a flight of steps. He was ushered into a quiet room with a thickly carpeted floor, and walls hung with rich tapestries. A young man, dressed in a magnificent silk brocade, royal blue robe, and round hat with red tassel, motioned Udo to be seated opposite.

'I am told you speak our language and know our food.' He lit incense in a burner between them.

'I learned both in China.'

'How did you come by this?' The young man held out the gold earring.

'Kang Shu of Canton gave it to me many years ago for favours rendered.'

'You must have been extremely kind to my father,' Wong Shu said. 'He was not prone to generosity.'

'I did not know Kang had a son,' Udo said.

Wong Shu smiled.'He had fifty-four children, although he rarely spoke of us. To him we were like the air one breathes and takes for granted.'

'You must have been very well-behaved too. The many

times I visited your father's barge, I never once heard children's voices.'

'My father lived among the boat-people in Canton harbour. His wives and my siblings lived ashore. We did not see him often.' Wong Shu held the earring up to the light. 'What exactly do you expect from this earring?'

'According to your father, if it is within the power of the Shu tong, its members are obligated to assist me.'

'Can you prove your friendship with him?'

'I was present when my father, Moryiama Ishikawa, or Mung as he is known, made Kang Shu the greatest tong chief in Canton. My brother Uraga died blowing up the junk in Canton harbour that killed most of your father's rivals. Kang Shu armed his barge, several scrambling dragons, and his floating bordellos with weapons supplied by Mung, and finished off his enemies that same night. For years after, I delivered five pouches of gold to your father every three months, in return for his protection and information about China's government and its economy. Your father and I also had many business deals together. I was comprador for the Tillim Trading Company.' Udo saw Wong Shu's eyes light up.

'Then you are the one who took the fifteen hundred contract labourers turned down by the Germans, transported them, and sold them to the same German company for twice the price.'

Udo bowed. 'It was the last piece of business Kang and I contracted before my return to Japan. Your father was a bit tight with his money. He fed his contract labourers so little that 70 per cent died in passage to Hawaii, and the rest soon after they reached the cane fields. That is why the Germans refused to buy from him.'

'My father was not a little bit tight with money,' Wong said. 'He was very very tight. He had fifty-four children and twenty-one wives to house, feed and clothe.' He smiled. 'You are Udo. You, your father and your dead brother are remembered in the Shu clan. Are those your sons at the table?'

'Yes.'

'Kobe is a dangerous place. If I were not obligated by that earring, you and your family could already be dead.'

Udo brought up the Colt pistol from beneath the table and pointed it at the tong chief. 'You and several of your men would not have attended the funeral.'

Wong Shu nodded. 'It is said you are as ruthless as my father.'

'Your father was more than my friend, he was my teacher.'

'What favour do you request?' Wong asked.

'Obey the law. Stop selling opium and women. It is forbidden in Japan.'

'True. But we live and work in the treaty port. Here, westerners govern. The laws are theirs.'

'And only for them, not Orientals,' Udo replied. 'You and your people come under Japanese law. In addition, you will consider any mutual assistance agreement with the Iron Duke as cancelled. We Chinese and Japanese may have our differences, but we are Orientals.'

'Even if you isolate the Duke, he can hold off the police and the whites. He has done it before. And threatened to destroy old Kobe with his cannon. The wood frame buildings stand so close together, the town would be ashes in hours.'

'He will not have time to use those weapons stored in his warehouse. A battalion of the imperial Japanese army is on its way to support the police and the white administration in Kobe.'

'You take a great chance in telling me these things,' Wong said. 'We Chinese in Kobe depend on opium and prostitution for a livelihood.'

'Opium must go. Use Chinese girls for your brothels, not Japanese. Your people will earn added income from gambling, drinking and restaurants after the docks and Duke's Ground are cleaned up.'

'I will show this earring to the elders and let you know tomorrow,' Wong said.

Udo shook his head. He cocked the pistol. 'I cannot leave without your written word, signed and stamped with the chop of your family. You are tong chief. You decide.'

'If I refuse?'

'The military operation will go ahead with one change. I will instruct the Japanese battalion commander to kill every Chinese man, woman and child in Kobe. Your property will be confiscated and enterprises appropriated. But if you agree, I have a business proposal for your tong-men on the mainland. To bribe certain Chinese officials in the forthcoming negotiations regarding Formosa and the Ryukyu islands.'

Wong Shu looked calmly into the muzzle of the Colt revolver. He sniffed the incense. 'What is the amount of the bribe?' he asked.

'Five million yen will be deposited to your account in the Shansi bank of your choice. Use what is necessary. The rest is yours.'

Wong nodded. 'A substantial sum.' He clapped his hands and the waiter entered, pointing a shotgun at Udo.

'Bring my writing kit,' the tong chief ordered.

Several minutes later, Wong signed the document Udo had dictated, and stamped the family chop to it, top and bottom. He handed it across the table. Udo read the document, then put the rice paper onto the incense burner. He watched a brown spot expand on the paper and burst into flame. 'As the smoke rises to Heaven carrying your words, thoughts and promises to your parents and their ancestors,' he intoned, 'so the Shu clan – past, present and future – are responsible for them. The gods obligate you to do as you have written.'

Wong met Udo's eyes and smiled. 'I would not have

betrayed you. At least I think not. You learned well from my father, but he was right in what he said. You are a man without a heart. I believe you would have killed every Chinese in Kobe.'

'Without his word, a man is nothing,' Udo said. He bowed, tucked the pistol away, and backed out of the door.

Approaching the table, Udo saw a stranger sitting with his sons.

The man stood and bowed to Udo. 'Mother of autumn.'

Udo responded with the Black Dragon countersign, 'Father of spring.'

The man held out a rain-cape. 'The weather has turned nasty and the Black Dragon awaits you at the Kobe Club.'

Chapter 7

The storm ripped through the Kii strait and down the inland sea in search of prey. It tore long, ugly scars on the surface of the rising sea, and found the *Maria-Luz* fifty miles off shore. Winds hammered the ship without mercy.

Below-deck 250 Chinese girls, aged twelve to sixteen, huddled in the darkness, clinging to each other. Captain Belviso fingered his rosaries and prayed. With a ship full of slaves and a British gunboat patrolling Kobe harbour, he could not run to port for safety and chance life imprisonment.

'Reef the sails and lay on a sea anchor,' the captain shouted into the wind. 'We can't navigate in this gale!'

'We may not survive it,' the mate called back through cupped hands. 'Taking out those bunker walls to make room below-deck weakened the hull. The timbers are screaming louder than the women.'

'Keep those hatches battened down! Forget the chinks or making land tonight! Heave-to! We'll set the fore and main sails at dawn, and head her into Akahasi beach! According to the last signals from shore, Duke's men will be waiting for us. Now get the crew into the rigging before we capsize!'

'I am glad Father left,' Uraga said. 'I will not have to finish this Chinese food. How anything can look so good and taste this ugly is deceitful.'

'If Grandfather is here in Kobe, the action will begin soon,' Hiroki said. 'This is the first time in twenty years the Black Dragon has been out of Tokyo.'

'You are both right,' Yaka said. 'Since we shall soon see

action, we should take our pleasure now. Women can also remove the bad taste from your mouth.'

'I want to sleep with one, not eat her.' Uraga laughed.

'Waiter,' Yaka called, 'we would like three ladies for the night.' He took out his purse but the waiter refused the money.

'I have orders from Mr Wong to give you every courtesy,' the waiter said. 'Tonight you are special guests of Wong's Palace. Please follow me.'

Upstairs, three young Japanese girls in kimonos were led into the room by an exotic Chinese woman. She bowed. 'Gentlemen, please choose,' she said in stilted Japanese. 'These young ladies are the finest Kobe beauties.'

'I claim privilege of age,' Yaka said, and pointed to his choice.

The girl bowed. 'Thank you, sir. I will try to please you.'

Uraga took a second girl by the arm and the two couples started out the doorway.

'Is there anything wrong?' the madam asked Hiroki.

His brothers turned to see him standing and staring at the floor.

Yaka returned to his side. 'Is this your first time?'

'No. Prostitution is legal in Korea.'

'Then what is the problem?' Yaka nodded at the last girl. 'You will hurt her feelings. The madam will probably cut off her ears and serve them in the restaurant downstairs if you do not take her.' He laughed.

'I cannot,' Hiroki said.

'Why?' Yaka insisted.

'Would you rather leave?' Uraga asked.

'No, my golden rod yearns,' Hiroki said.

'Do you want my girl?' Yaka asked.

'No.' Hiroki shook his head. 'I want a Chinese girl.'

The two brothers moved closer to Hiroki. 'Are they better than Japanese?' Uraga asked.

'That is the problem,' Hiroki said. 'I cannot perform with a Japanese. It would be like sleeping with a sister.'

The older brothers considered Hiroki's idea.

'I never felt that way,' Uraga said. 'Especially since we do not have a sister.'

'It must be that he grew up outside Japan,' Yaka said. He clasped Hiroki around the shoulders. 'If you want a Chinese girl, then we shall all have Chinese girls. And another bottle of sake,' he said to the madam.

The conversation between the brothers had been animated, and heavy with Japanese idioms. The Chinese madam misunderstood, believing the younger brother had demanded they all be serviced by Chinese only. She beamed at Hiroki. 'You may be younger, but it is clear in matters of love you know more,' she said in rapid Cantonese. 'I shall personally see you are well satisfied.'

Although he understood, Hiroki remained silent. The madam repeated her comments in Japanese as she showed the girls out.

She soon returned with three Chinese girls, and brought one directly to Hiroki. 'He does not understand our language,' she told the girl, 'but you have been trained to speak with your body. Give him special attention. He appreciates Chinese ways.'

Yaka and Uraga led their women from the room. The screen door closed. Hiroki and his girl were alone. She moved closer and he looked down at her. She was the same height as Noriko. Her delicate body revealed itself through a neck-to-ankle green silk gown. Seeing his eyes on the nipples of her small breasts, she reached up with long lacquered fingernails behind his stern jaw to draw his head to her breast. His lips closed on her nipple and sucked through the material. He placed his hands on her buttocks and pressed her to him. She was fragile, as he knew Noriko would be. The girl undid the loops down the front of her dress and offered her bare breast. He sucked hard and she

67

cried out, but did not pull away. Her quick, deft hands undressed him, and she attempted several techniques, but his hard, young body demanded satisfaction its own way. Hiroki wanted to make love to Noriko, and to punish her. He was rough, yet he caressed her body. Her pleasure and pain excited him. He grew more and more frenzied.

The prostitute moaned and cried out at the proper times, then unexpectedly her body was lit by Hiroki's fire. She began to lose control. He threw her down on the quilt and stood over her, his golden rod straight out from between his muscular legs. He dropped to his knees and spread her thighs. The expression on his face frightened and excited her.

Hiroki saw Noriko under him. He cradled his penis in his hand. 'This is my weapon! I will humiliate you as you did me!' He flexed his muscles, then lifted Noriko's buttocks and plunged into her, driving full length on the first stroke, not caring if he hurt her. She screamed and tried to push him off, but he drove down again – harder, deeper, wanting her to feel the pain and shame he felt. He moved back and forth inside her, up and down violently. She tried to pull away, then expertly coordinated her movements with his to bring him to a swift climax. He shuddered and gripped her arms. She could not move. Hiroki released her suddenly, and withdrew. Still kneeling between her thighs, he glowered down.

The girl gasped for breath, her eyes languid with passion as she looked up at him. 'You are still hard,' she said. 'Come back inside me. I need you,' she panted, and tried to pull him down, but he resisted. She cupped his golden spheres and gently massaged. She took his wet, throbbing penis in both hands and squeezed, pulling him to her. 'I need this inside me,' she moaned.

Hiroki's eyes closed. He was back on his knees in the nine metre square, with everyone watching. Noriko stood over him, naked, taunting him with her beautiful body.

She pressed her hips forward, urging him to submit to the final degradation and lap her like a dog. Hiroki prised her fingers from his rock-hard penis. He held her hands in his and tightened his grip. He saw her eyes widen with pain. He squeezed and she cried out. He thrust forward between her thighs and filled her, working his hips back and forth, keeping the pressure on her hands. Pleasure filled him. With each stroke his revenge grew larger and larger. Until it exploded. His legs quivered, his body shook, and he slipped off her, away into that blissful darkness where neither time nor space exists.

From far away Hiroki heard the girl say in Chinese, 'He was frantic.'

'Did you satisfy him?' the madam asked.

'There will be no complaints. But he aroused me and . . . and . . .'

'You are not paid to be satisfied,' the madam said.

'He did not care about me,' the girl said.

Hiroki maintained his slow, steady breathing. He opened his eyes just enough to see the madam reach out and caress the girl's breasts. 'I can see you are in need. I will help you.' She embraced her, kissed her neck, massaged between her thighs. 'The Iron Duke is sending men to Akahasi beach tomorrow morning,' the madam murmured. 'Many new girls will be coming ashore. Mr Wong has bought most of them.' She led the prostitute from the room. 'I will see you are not called upon to perform too often.'

Hiroki closed his eyes and fell into a troubled sleep. He and Noriko were sitting at a table side by side, dressed as bride and groom. He felt her desire for him, and he wanted her. They both lay back. Her breathing and his own echoed in his head. With each beat of his heart, his passion for her increased. He reached out and touched her incredibly soft hand. She turned towards him and smiled. He climaxed and she laughed at him.

Hiroki awoke with a start. His legs were wet with

semen. He rolled off the quilt and washed himself from a basin of water. Suddenly the madam's words burst into his consciousness. He knew how to trap the Iron Duke's men! He dressed quickly, and hurried out of Wong's Palace into the storm, towards the Kobe Club.

Chapter 8

'Your presence in Kobe is an unexpected honour,' James Alburg said. 'I'm pleased the storm did not deter you. We'll try to accommodate your every need.'

Mung bowed. He, Udo, and a third Japanese sat across the table from the Kobe Club president and William Whittefield.

'By imperial appointment I was recently given responsibility for the Department of National Decorations,' Mung said. 'My first task is to beautify the Kobe dock area. From the shantytown along the waterfront, through Duke's Ground, up to Chinatown, it will be razed by fire.'

'The rest of Kobe could burn too,' Alburg said.

'We think not,' Udo replied. He placed a map on the table. 'The wide lane on which the foreign clubs stand separates the dock area from the Japanese portion of the city. The brick and stone clubhouses will act as a firebreak. The city's population and fire departments will be put on alert. In addition, the rain will probably continue.'

'You intend moving sooner than expected,' Alburg said. 'It will be difficult for all our members to participate.'

'Recent events make it necessary,' Mung said. 'A battalion of imperial troops under General Nogi arrives tomorrow morning. Yesterday Admiral Takamora decreed the navy must be here first. Our military is in a race for glory.'

'Won't this weather delay them?'

'It may,' Mung said. 'The mail-boat I came over on was almost swamped at the entrance to the harbour. But I must tell you there are other reasons for my presence. Word has reached Tokyo that the Korean revolutionary leader, Kim Ok-kyum, was killed by Chinese soldiers and his body given to Sugyup, a Korean nationalist group. They quartered Kim's remains and sent the parts to the four corners of the Korean kingdom as a warning against political uprisings.'

'Didn't Kim lead the Korean Special Forces?' William asked. 'It was some kind of paramilitary reform group with connections to Japan.'

'Several years ago I recommended he seek asylum in Japan,' Udo said, avoiding a direct answer. 'Kim was a popular speaker in Tokyo. Unfortunately, he returned to Korea too soon. We now fear Hideyoshi Koin will use Kim's death to instigate a Japanese invasion of Korea.'

'There is more,' Mung said. 'Prior to leaving Tokyo I closed down all telegraph lines from outside the city to prevent further inflammatory news from reaching Hideyoshi and his war party.' Mung nodded to the stiff-backed young man in civilian clothes. 'This is Captain Togo of the imperial Japanese navy. He has brought word that could cause an immediate declaration of war on Korea.'

Togo spoke heavily accented English in the loud, cadenced sentences of a career military officer. 'Intelligence agents, from the same Chinese army unit that murdered Kim, combined forces with the Korean Sugyup and incited a mob to burn the Japanese embassy in Korea. Twelve Japanese wounded. One killed.' Captain Togo did not mention that the dead man was a fellow member of Genoysha who had been drilling the Korean Special Forces in the art of unarmed combat.

'Is that why you blocked the telegraph?' Alburg asked Mung.

'I am here to prevent war. The Chinese General Li Hung-Chang issued the orders for Kim's death and the attack on our embassy. Li is in Seoul with a division of his best troops. His agents control the Korean king and queen. On Li's instructions, the Korean king sent home all Russian military advisers.'

72

'That means Korea is a puppet state of China,' William said.

'My son Udo has lived in Korea for twenty years,' Mung said. 'His words will be of interest.'

'Captain Togo's information indicates that General Li now controls the Korean monarchy,' Udo said. He placed another map over the first, and pointed to northern China. 'Li advocates Chinese imperialism, but knows he can't defeat the West.' Udo moved his finger over the map. 'Therefore, Li turns to Korea and Japan to outflank the Europeans. Once his hold is consolidated in Korea, he'll look to conquer Japan. The attack on our legation was a warning. It's little more than a hundred miles from Pusan to Hiroshima. Kublai Khan attempted an invasion from Pusan in the thirteenth century, and we Japanese have an inbred fear of another such move.'

'What do the king and queen of Korea want?' Alburg asked.

'Oriental monarchs rarely seek the time-consuming responsibility of leadership,' Udo said. 'They leave administration to others, while they make an art of enjoying life. My wife and I were frequent guests of the royal couple. They're connoisseurs of good living, and have little interest in affairs of state.'

'You can't keep news of the attack on your legation from Tokyo much longer,' William said.

'If Kobe is cleared by tomorrow night, I can delay any move to invade Korea for at least a month,' Mung said.

'If there's to be a war, a swift strike may be your only prayer of winning,' Alburg said.

'For Japan to embark on a war with both China and Korea would be unwise,' Mung said. 'Japan must isolate her enemies from their allies before going to war. That is my task.'

'An impossible one in the case of China and Korea,' Alburg said. 'Korea has been a vassal state of China's

73

for hundreds of years. Japan fighting China is like a flea attempting sex with an elephant. Great expectations, poor performance.'

Captain Togo leaned forward, hands balled, eyes blazing defiance. Mung realized the shrewd leader of the Kobe Club believed what he was saying, but was also baiting them. Mung had his own doubts about Japan's military capabilities. It was more than three centuries since they had fought abroad. He needed to hear the opinion of one of Japan's finest warriors. He nodded to Togo.

'There will be war!' the captain said. 'Japan will win!' He looked directly at James Alburg. 'You consider China's vast size and multitudes of people. Victory will not be determined on land, but at sea. China has only one rail-line, in the south. Korea has none. Both China and Korea have no major roads to the north. Troop movements will be made at sea. They have to come to us!'

'Even so, the Chinese fleet outweighs, outnumbers, and outguns Japan's, three to one,' Alburg said.

'Spirit, training and superior military equipment will be the determining factors,' Togo said. 'We will win!'

'If a peaceful solution isn't possible, I'm determined to reduce the odds,' Mung said. He opened a folder, turned it around, and placed it in front of the two Americans. 'These are detailed lists of Japan's military needs. They range from sidearms to warships, and include a steady supply of food, clothing, and weapons to be delivered as far on the Asian mainland as Japan might advance.'

James Alburg and William Whittefield leafed through the folder. They clarified certain points with Mung. Not once did he refer to notes. On two occasions, he corrected the figures without looking at them.

'I heard of your infallible memory, and am much impressed to see it in action,' Alburg said. 'But tell me, Mr Mung, why did you come to the Kobe Club for this purchase? William here could be considered your nephew. He has great influence in the US State Department. England, France or Germany could invigorate their economies with an order so large.'

'Dealing with you avoids governmental formalities, votes, treaties, under-the-table concessions. This will be a straightforward business deal. The order is too large for one country to fill in time. It would engender national debates, and perhaps allow our enemies to determine our intentions. Whereas the Kobe Club members can purchase from various countries. They can pressure politicians through their purses to support Japan's policy and undermine our enemies.'

Alburg sat back in his chair. He clasped his hands over his vest. 'I can't guarantee that our members will agree with your provision of persuading politicians.'

'The total amount of our order is one hundred and forty million dollars,' Udo said. 'For that sum we expect certain benefits not related to hardware. Need I remind you there are several other business clubs on this street.'

William forestalled Alburg's sharp reply. 'You came to us because of the special relationship between your family and mine,' he said to Udo. 'And because the Kobe Club is the only business group large enough and powerful enough to fulfil your requests in a minimum amount of time. To the best of our ability, we'll deliver the weapons and goods to the snow-filled wastes of Manchuria or the rice paddies of southern China. You may call upon our members to pressure their governments, as long as it doesn't conflict with their own national interests. You have my word as a gentleman and a samurai, the rank I inherited from my father on whom it was conferred by Lord Shimatzu Nariakira of Satsuma in 1853, that the Kobe Club will make every effort to execute this contract.'

'All inherited rank in Japan was abolished with the constitution and new reforms,' Udo said. 'The rank of samurai no longer exists.'

William smiled. 'I'm aware of that. It's why I mentioned gentleman first.'

The five men turned towards the sound of running feet mounting the outside staircase. Udo drew his pistol. The hurried steps reached the landing and the door opened. Wind and rain rushed into the room.

Mung pushed Udo's gun barrel up. 'You should teach your son to knock!'

'Close the door before we blow away,' Alburg said.

Hiroki shut the door, and bowed. 'Pardon the intrusion,' he said. 'You are here to plan the capture of the Iron Duke and his men after they have drunk up all your free whisky. I have learned of a better way to take them.'

In central Tokyo, not far from the Imperial Hall of Martial Arts, stood an unprepossessing two-storey building. It was surrounded by a stone wall and masked by tall hedges on all sides. This was the headquarters of the White Wolf Society, a membership of military men sworn to the tenets of State Shintoism. Their creed, affixed over the inner door, read:

The mission of the Japanese people
is to bring the nations of the world under one roof.
All humanity must share the benefits of
being governed by the Divine Emperor.

Lieutenant Shibata was in the duty room when the telephone rang. He listened to the caller, then asked him to repeat the message. His hands trembled with excitement as he wrote. He hung up the receiver and deliberated, then rushed to the door and shouted to a man in the exercise area. 'Get in here and take my place! I am duty officer and that is an order!'

The others in the room smiled. They knew Shibata's habit of puffing himself with importance.

Shibata hurried upstairs to the billiard room where his

four friends were involved in a game. 'Come with me,' he ordered. 'I have a message to deliver!'

'We have runners for that,' a fellow officer said.

Shibata pulled on his rain-cape. He was filled with the gravity of the moment. 'This cannot be entrusted to anyone else! I will need protection!'

'Afraid you will blow away or melt in the rain?' another friend said, chalking up his cue.

Shibata grabbed the stick and racked it. 'This is no time for playing,' he whispered. 'Big things are about to happen. We are reporting to Count Hideyoshi Koin. It could mean a step up in our careers.'

The other men put away their cues. They took their capes and followed Shibata out into the storm.

The five officers trotted through narrow streets, onto the wide lane across from the imperial palace, to a sprawling villa. They were challenged at the gate by armed guards, again on the veranda, and led into the foyer by two coarse men carrying sidearms. Only Shibata was ushered into a large study.

Light from a green shaded lamp shone on an empty bottle of Suntory whisky, and cast sinister shadows on Count Hideyoshi's thin, pockmarked face. The count's shifting eyes raised up but never settled on one spot. 'You had better justify dripping on my tatami mats or you will be surveying anthills in Mongolia!'

Shibata bowed. 'Excuse the intrusion,' he said. 'I believe the message I carry warrants your immediate attention.'

'Bring it here and do not wet my desk,' Hideyoshi said. He read, then looked up and demanded, 'Where did this come from?'

'Telephoned from Yokohama. The storm has cut all telegraph communications to and from Tokyo. The man who relayed this is a member of our society.'

Hideyoshi Koin, founder and leader of the White Wolf Society, stood up and walked out from behind his desk. 'If it is true that our legation in Seoul has been attacked and one of our people killed, my dream of leading this country to war will soon be realized.' He paced the floor, and looked at Shibata. 'I see you understand the implications too. Keep a grip on yourself. Whom have you told?'

'No one.'

'Not your companions outside?'

'No, sir.'

'You are a man to be considered, Shibata. Tell your friends they will have to wait. I have plans to make, messages to send, people to meet before morning.' Hideyoshi reached out and placed a long bony hand on the young lieutenant's shoulder. 'Japan's time for glory grows near. The White Wolves will lead our nation to victory! I wish to see General Nogi and Admiral Takamora! Get a message to them in Kobe! They must return immediately! We cannot start a war without the commanders of the army and navy!'

Chapter 9

13 March 1894, 5 a.m.
From three miles off Akahasi beach in gale force winds, a weary lookout aboard the *Maria-Luz* sighted land.

The mate turned his back to the rain. 'Captain, the crew is done in. The bulkheads below-deck have sprung. We're taking water.'

From his position on the poop deck, Emilio Belviso watched the awe-inspiring effects of the heavy waves pounding the Japanese coast. The offshore wind held the waves up to a height he had never seen before. Then the weight of the waves overpowered the wind, and they crashed down on the black volcanic sand. Through his telescope he saw a large crowd standing back from the beach, hunkered against the wind. 'Duke's men are waiting for us to put the women ashore,' the captain said.

'We should beach this wreck and abandon ship,' the mate said. 'Once on Duke's Ground, nobody will dare touch us.'

The deck shuddered under the captain's feet. The moaning women below, the howling wind in the cross-trees above, set a weird tone to the chaotic scene around him. He fingered his rosaries. Tears streaked his weather-beaten face. 'Mr Mate,' he choked, 'make a last effort for deeper water! Pull in the sea anchor! Set the mainsail this time! If it doesn't work, I'll beach her and send the fifty women ashore at slack tide. We can make repairs and float her again at high tide. We'll take her out to sea with the wind at our back.'

'I'll try the men once more, Captain, but I think you're mad!'

The mate picked up his megaphone and a belaying pin. He bullied the men into the rigging. They climbed the lines but could not set the mainsail. The helmsman brought the ship about to face the oncoming waves and the men were whipped around like wind chimes in the storm. They slid back down to huddle behind packing cases on deck. Marching waves broke over the bow, burying the deck in roiling foam. The sea was stronger than the offshore wind. The top and foresails alone could not overcome the sweep and surge of angry water. The *Maria-Luz* was driven backwards.

Below-deck the girls huddled in their cramped bunks, their throats raw from screaming throughout the long, dark night. Their sobbing increased with the attempt to beat seaward. The entire bow came out of the water as the ship breasted the big waves. The forward part of the hull hung in midair, then slammed down in a trough. Sea water spurted through the old planking. In a moment of soul-stirring calm, the three-hundred-ton ship settled in the dark green water. Then a thunderclap sounded above as the following wave broke over the bow. Water poured down through the decking into the hold. It sloshed back and forth with the pitch and yaw of the ship.

Shen Yan lay in one of the lowest bunks in foetal position. A large wave stood the *Maria-Luz* on end. The ship crashed down and water washed into Shen's bunk, soaking her and her blanket. She threw the soggy covering off. Still gripping the table knife, she rolled out of her bunk. Naked, she waded in knee-deep water to the ladder of number three hatch. She was knocked to the floor, and grabbed a bunk to stop herself from being washed away. She rose to her knees, timed a leap for the ladder, and caught it. She scrambled to the top and felt for the hasp holding the bolt that fastened the hatch cover from outside. Grasping the ladder with one hand, the knife in the other, she worked the point around the hasp. Although the bucking ship made the task painfully difficult, the old, soggy wood came away in soft splinters.

Shen Yan felt a hand on her leg. 'You are right to disrobe,' a naked girl below her on the ladder said. 'If we must swim, clothes will weigh us down.'

'I do not know how to swim,' Shen said.

'If we get out of here, I will help you,' the girl said. 'My name is Xu.'

'Can you lock your hands around my waist and the ladder?' Shen asked. 'It will give me support.'

Xu moved up a few steps. She put her head in the small of Shen's back, placed her arms around Shen's waist and grasped the ladder.

Shen chipped and dug at the wood. She pulled splinters away with her fingernails. The knife dropped from her cramped fingers and the two searched side by side under the filthy water that surged back and forth. Xu relieved Shen at work with the knife as the storm battered the old ship.

His voice edged with anger, Mung addressed General Nogi and Admiral Takamora. 'Gentlemen, your valiant efforts to reach Kobe in this storm are commendable, but will be for nothing if you do not act now! The timing is perfect.'

'My soldiers are asleep on their feet,' the general said. 'They have been forty-eight hours without rest.'

'We not only fought the storm to reach Kobe,' the admiral said. 'My men spent six hours in the rescue of two Spanish transport ships foundering at the harbour's entrance.'

'Your actions are to be applauded,' Mung said. 'However you will not be judged by your peers and the government for these heroic deeds. Their interest is in the completion of this minor operation. Failure now could mean a delay of years before Parliament would allocate money to expand our military.'

'When you return to Tokyo, will you tell Count Hideyoshi your men were tired?' Udo challenged.

'Let us hear your plan,' Nogi said. 'Then we shall decide.'

Mung unfolded a map. 'Half the Iron Duke's men went to Akahasi beach to await a shipment of Chinese slaves. My grandson Hiroki, Captain Togo, and armed members of the Kobe Club will lead half our soldiers to the beach. They should outnumber Duke's men four to one.'

'What about the port?' Takamora asked.

'Bring your five ships broadside to the dock area,' Mung said. 'Load your cannon with blanks and aim them at the shantytown and Duke's Ground. When you see the buildings burning, fire three blank rounds from each gun.' Mung turned back to Nogi. 'You will lead the remainder of your men and the Kobe police in a sweep through the dock area up to Chinatown. William Whittefield and fifty members of the Kobe Club will assault the Iron Duke Bar from the front.' He looked at his watch. 'It is 5 a.m. We must move swiftly to catch half of Duke's men away from the bar.' He looked at the two officers. 'Before you decide whether or not to implement this plan, these are for you.' He handed each man an envelope bearing the imperial seal. 'If you are successful today, you may open these. As I promised at the meeting with Count Hideyoshi, here are your orders to proceed to Okinawa and then on to Formosa. You two will lead the first Japanese overseas military expedition in three centuries. If you do not succeed here in Kobe, you are to burn these envelopes. All officers over the rank of first lieutenant, in both services, will commit seppuku.'

Nogi and Takamora touched the imperial seal to their heads and bowed. 'So it is ordered, so it is done.' They left the room.

'I understood the Emperor to be against seppuku,' Udo said.

'He is,' Mung said. 'I added that on my own. They will not know it until they open the envelopes.'

'And if they open the envelopes, they will have already succeeded.' Udo smiled. 'Where is my place in this morning's action?'

'I am too old and you are too valuable to enter the fray,' Mung said. 'We shall watch from the Kobe Club carriage. If our goal is achieved, you will leave immediately for the mail-boat. The moment the weather breaks, you will sail to Formosa. Use your agents there and the earring to locate the bandits who killed the Okinawan fishermen. The Emperor's orders will keep Nogi and Takamora in Okinawa until I arrive after Shimatzu's wedding. This will allow you time in Formosa. But first, let us oversee the beautification of the Kobe docks.'

Yaka and Uraga accompanied William Whittefield and the fifty Kobe Club members. 'Why must there be newspapermen with us?' Yaka asked William.

'One for General Nogi in the sweep through the port. One to observe us attacking the Iron Duke Bar, and one with Hiroki and Captain Togo to Akahasi beach. The journalists will report to the world that Japanese carried no firearms and shed no white blood.' He looked at his watch. 'Time to leave.'

The rain had stopped, but the wind blew stronger. James Alburg led twenty heavily armed Kobe Club men towards Akahasi beach, Captain Togo guided four hundred Japanese soldiers and Hiroki interpreted for the journalist.

Two Kobe Club scouts met the column as it approached the beach. 'Seventy of Duke's men are on the other side of those dunes. They're watching that ship offshore with their backs to us and the wind.'

'Very well,' James Alburg said. 'Each of you will lead half the Japanese in a semicircle right and left to surround them.

I and my group will take the centre.' He addressed Captain Togo. 'Please instruct your men to approach quickly and quietly. They must get as close as possible to negate their lack of firearms. Hiroki, remain close by me with the journalist.' Alburg turned to the grim-faced Kobe Club members. 'Gentlemen, check your weapons. Let's proceed at a trot.'

The wind at their backs pushed the column forward. It kept the men on the beach looking seaward. The four hundred weary soldiers plodded through the soft black sand, and surrounded Duke's men.

Dutch Henry ran towards the contingent of white men. His hand rested on the butt of his pistol under his rain slicker. 'Who the hell are you?' he shouted in James Alburg's face. He motioned around at the Japanese. 'What you got all the slanty-eyes with you for?'

Black George bulled his way through the crowd and positioned himself, hand on pistol, next to Dutch Henry. He sneered at Alburg's double-barrelled shotgun pointing at his stomach. 'Who the fuck are you?'

James Alburg gently squeezed both triggers and Black George was blown back into the crowd. His blood and guts spattered the men behind him. Alburg dropped the shotgun and whipped a pistol into his left hand. The gun pointed at the Dutchman's head. 'Everybody drop your weapons,' he shouted.

Dutch Henry fumbled for his gun and James Alburg shot him between the eyes. 'Drop your weapons in the sand or you're all dead men,' Alburg shouted.

Leaderless on the wind-swept beach, facing twenty shotguns and surrounded by four hundred grim Japanese soldiers brandishing Kendo swords, the Iron Duke's men threw away their guns, knives and picks, and surrendered. They were formed into two lines and marched towards the Spanish transport ships.

'Don't leave yet,' the journalist called to Hiroki. 'I got

to take more pictures.' He scrambled around the departing column of prisoners to the bodies of Black George and Dutch Henry. He built sand pillows under the lifeless heads, placed their guns in their hands, and photographed them from numerous angles.

'Are you finished?' Hiroki demanded. 'The dock area is where the important action will be.'

'Not yet.' The journalist headed towards the water. 'I want a picture of the ship they were waiting for. Look. It turned around and is coming towards the beach. Someone said there are over two hundred young women aboard. I'd like to get a shot of them.'

Fascinated by the size of the ship heading straight for the shore, Hiroki followed the journalist towards the water's edge. A large group of villagers had also moved down the beach.

Hiroki addressed the village elder. 'It seems strange to see that foreign captain sailing his boat into shallow water.'

'Yes. The alien captain thinks he will save his ship from the storm by running it into the soft volcanic sand. It is low tide and he probably thinks to ride out the weather until flood tide floats him and the offshore wind takes him out to sea again. But he is mistaken.' The old man shook a horny finger. 'When the tide turns slack, the wind stops for an hour. If he is a smart captain he will leave his ship then, because it will be smashed apart and everybody who remains aboard will be drowned.' He spat and the wind whipped it away. 'When the tide runs high, the wind will come from the sea with more force.'

'You mean a 180 degree change?' Hiroki said.

'It has always been so on the inland sea. No beached ship built by man can withstand the flood tide and the onshore wind. That is why we have come, and more are approaching.' He pointed to other villagers moving onto the beach from all directions. 'Much wreckage will be washed ashore.'

Hiroki looked from the old man to the doomed ship. 'How long before the wind stops and the tide goes slack?'

'About half an hour. Only if the crew comes ashore will they be saved.'

'Captain!' The mate scrambled onto the poop deck. 'Let me dump the crates of spices and tea overboard. It will lighten the ship so we can get closer to the beach.'

'This ship is mine,' Emilio Belviso shouted. 'She is my life! I'm only beaching her now so we can float her off at high tide! Those crates will fetch a good price in Lima!'

'The damned tub is falling apart,' the mate cried.

'Any man who touches one of those crates is dead,' the captain snarled. He pulled a pistol and shouted to the helmsman behind him. 'Bring her about and head us into the beach!'

The helmsman looked to the mate. The captain fired a shot in the air, and pointed the gun at the helmsman.

'Do as the crazy bastard says,' the mate shouted.

The *Maria-Luz* turned slowly, taking waves broadside over her port rail until her stern pointed to the sea. The big waves picked her up like a cork and carried her towards the beach. Six hundred yards from shore, her keel scraped sand. A wave lifted her stern and catapulted her forward another fifty yards. She grounded solidly on a sand bar some distance from the beach.

'Captain Belviso, I apologize,' the mate said. 'We may make it yet. In the last fifteen minutes the wind has slackened. The men will be fed while we wait.' He pointed. 'Someone is wading out from the beach.'

'Forty-odd years at sea have taught me a thing or two,' the captain said. 'Send the messenger to my cabin! I've got to put on some dry clothes. Prepare to offload the Iron Duke's women!'

'Lower the rope ladder and lift the swimmer aboard,' the mate ordered.

Crewmen pulled a naked man over the rail.

'A Jap,' the mate said in Spanish. 'Are you one of Duke's Men?'

'I don't understand,' Hiroki answered in English.

The mate spoke again, this time in Peruvian Aymaran.

'You're in great danger,' Hiroki said in French.

The mate handed Hiroki his rain-cape and spoke in broken French. 'Come below. The captain wants to see you, and not bald-arsed naked.'

In his cabin, Captain Belviso was elated. 'So the heathen speaks the language of love. Ha! Where's my money?'

'You must evacuate this ship immediately,' Hiroki said. 'The storm will smash it to pieces!'

'What kind of trick is Duke trying to play?' Emilio Belviso demanded. 'Duke pays for his fifty women! The others remain aboard!'

'You don't understand,' Hiroki said. 'Duke's men on the beach have been arrested. Two were killed. The Japanese army and police are cleaning up the Kobe docks. The Iron Duke is finished!'

'What the hell you jabbering about?' the captain demanded. 'I saw Duke's men on the beach an hour ago.'

'Yes, they were there. They've been arrested. The tide's gone slack. You've got to abandon ship now or you're doomed! When the tide runs, the wind will change and come from the sea! It'll pound this ship apart!'

'Abandon hell!' The captain pushed Hiroki aside and rushed out of the cabin. 'Bring the slanty-eyed bastard topside,' he shouted to the mate.

From the deck, Emilio Belviso pointed triumphantly to the beach. 'There they are! Duke's men!'

'Look again,' Hiroki said. 'Those are villagers come to scavenge this ship's wreckage!'

The captain snatched a telescope from its case and

peered at the beach. 'Oh sweet Jesus, Mary and Joseph,' he moaned.

'What do you see?' the mate asked.

'Vultures. They sit there like vultures waiting to pick our bones. Duke's men are gone.'

'We can still make it ashore,' the mate said. 'The wind is down, the tide is slack.'

'No! The police and army are around. Didn't you hear the Jap? We'll be arrested for slaving.'

'But this is a treaty port,' the mate said. 'They'll turn us over to a white man's court. The British navy can't touch us either. We'll be safe.'

The captain shook his head. 'Peru doesn't have diplomatic relations with Japan. We'd rot in a Jap prison or have our heads chopped off kneeling before some Oriental potentate. I'm a God-fearing Christian.'

'I don't understand your language,' Hiroki said, 'but I warn you there is nothing to discuss. The tide will turn, the wind will come from the sea, and your ship will die! If you don't want to leave, at least allow the women off!'

'We have only one chance to save ourselves,' Captain Belviso said to the mate. 'That is to stay aboard, make repairs and wait to float her off at high tide.' He fingered his rosaries and pointed his pistol at the mate. 'Send the Jap back! No one else but him leaves this ship!'

The mate licked salt from his lips and locked eyes with the captain. He looked down at the pistol, and shrugged. Pulling his slicker off Hiroki, he pushed him towards the rail. They both froze at the sound of a cannon from Kobe port.

'The attack has begun on the docks,' Hiroki said. 'You must get ashore now!'

Facing Hiroki, the mate motioned with bloodshot eyes towards the captain. 'Tell someone the master of this ship

88

has gone crazy,' he whispered. 'He won't let anyone leave. There's 20 crewmen and 250 young Chinese girls aboard. Get help.' He picked Hiroki up and threw him into the sea.

Chapter 10

Udo pointed up at the Kobe Club flag. It waved from the roof of the tallest building overlooking the port – Masonic Hall. 'The club's sharpshooters are in place, and William's men should be in position across from the Iron Duke Bar,' he said to Mung. They could see General Nogi's troops and the Kobe police up ahead.

Mung motioned at the deserted, mud-rutted street. 'The storm has driven everyone inside. It will make our work easier. Order the shantytown demolished! Burn every building in Duke's Ground!'

Udo raised his fist and pumped it up and down twice, signalling the general. His troops and the police moved forward at a trot, kicking down and smashing shacks and tents in the shantytown. The few men and women who offered serious resistance were swatted with bamboo swords and driven with clubs to the holding compound set up near the transport ships. The others were massed together in the street.

Thirty policemen, armed with torches and kerosene, raced behind the buildings and set fire to the clapboard structures.

Udo and Mung followed the action from the horse-drawn carriage.

'What the hell is that shooting outside?' Duke shouted from his platform in the bar.

The guards on the balcony shifted in place and looked around, but none responded.

'Kilday,' Duke shouted, 'get your arse on the roof and see what's going on!'

The Irishman hurried upstairs and climbed the ladder to the roof. He nudged the trapdoor open and peered out. Fifteen feet away, a pool of blood spread from a hole in a guard's head.

'Help me.' The voice startled Kilday. A second guard, in bloodstained jacket, had dragged himself to the trapdoor. Kilday pulled him halfway through the opening, but ducked when a bullet splintered the wood over his head. He lost his footing and they both tumbled down the ladder.

Kilday rolled off the wounded man, and shook him. 'What the hell is happening up there?'

'Policemen setting fire to the backs of buildings,' the guard mumbled. 'We couldn't stop them. Sharpshooters with telescopic sights picked us off from the top of Masonic Hall. Help me.'

Kilday raced downstairs to report.

'Get your cannon and the Gatling gun into action,' the Duke ordered, and shoved Kilday from the platform.

Duke pointed to the riflemen on the balcony. 'Down here, all of you! Chase everyone into the street! We've got to know if there's a trap waiting for us out there.'

'Fire! Fire!' The alarm came from the women's quarters at the rear of the building. Smoke drifted into the main hall. Men and women from both sides of the bar bolted for the front door. Chairs were flung through the windows on either side of the entrance. People jumped through, falling over one another, crawling out into the street.

Alongside the dock opposite the Iron Duke Bar, William Whittefield gave his signal. He and fifty Kobe Club members, each armed with a shotgun and two pistols, climbed from their hiding places in the boats. They formed a line and advanced on the warehouse attached to the bar. Yaka and Uraga darted to William's side.

The sudden deafening roar of blank shells fired from Admiral Takamora's big guns cowered the people who had fled the brothels and gambling houses. The warehouse doors flew open. Fifty-one shotguns roared into the building, with devastating effect. Those of Duke's men not killed or wounded crawled out and surrendered.

'We have not seen the Iron Duke,' Yaka said.

William pointed at the burning warehouse. 'The back of the bar must be on fire too. He will have to come to us.' The warehouse survivors seemed desperate to get away from the building and William grabbed a wild-eyed man. 'What is stored in there?'

'Ammunition! Gunpowder! Barrels of alcohol!'

'Get back,' the American shouted in English and Japanese. 'Everyone down to the water! That warehouse is about to explode!'

Kilday stumbled through the warehouse's connecting door to the bar with blood running from pellet wounds in his body.

The Iron Duke leapt from his platform and grabbed the dying man. 'What's going on?'

'They were waiting for us out front,' Kilday whispered. 'We lost the cannon, the men, everything. The ammunition is on fire.'

Duke smashed Kilday in the face and let the unconscious man drop. He gathered the remaining thirty men. 'We got to leave quick! The warehouse will blow!' He shoved several men towards the gambling area. 'Grab a couple of card tables to throw through the back wall. They won't expect us to go out through the fire.' He ran to his office and unlocked the safe. Carrying a strongbox, he hurried to the rear of the building.

A table was heaved at the flaming wall, but only two wallboards cracked. A second table sailed through the air and broke a few more boards. Fire spread to the ceiling. Smoke choked the men. They crouched, shielding their heads from the heat.

Duke handed his gun and strongbox to his henchman. He reached into the fire and dragged out a table, lifting the weight by himself. Swinging it around in a circle, he heaved. The table broke through the burning wall and the men cheered. Duke snatched his strongbox and gun and leapt through the hole. Others followed, but sharpshooters from the Masonic Hall filled the burning opening with dead bodies. Only three made it out alive.

'Take cover! Take cover!' Yaka and Uraga ran towards the platoon of Japanese infantry entering Duke's Ground. They led the soldiers behind a burning building a moment before the ammunition in the warehouse exploded. The entire building disintegrated. The roar and concussion echoed for miles. Thousands of Kobe residents fled into the streets in fear of an earthquake.

'Sir.' A lieutenant reported to Yaka. 'Some people ran from the rear of the bar.' He pointed. 'Into that shallow ravine.'

'Capture them,' Yaka ordered the platoon leader. 'They must remain alive!'

Thirty soldiers followed the lieutenant at a run, and jumped blindly over the edge of the ravine. Yaka heard shots. Bamboo swords whistled through the air. Three prisoners were brought out.

Yaka stood on the lip of the ravine. Below, the Iron Duke flung Japanese soldiers off him like a dog sheds water. He bashed one man's skull with the strongbox. He shot three others. Then the pistol was knocked from his hand and the blond giant was ringed by furious men. Other soldiers dragged their dead and wounded aside. All waited for orders.

James Alburg came rushing up. He glared down into the ravine at the Iron Duke. 'Your men can have a few minutes to punish this animal,' Alburg said to Yaka. 'But they mustn't kill him!'

Yaka translated the order and the grim-faced soldiers closed in.

'Alburg,' Duke shouted, 'you're a Jap-loving son of a bitch!' He charged the nearest soldier, but the small man ducked and stepped forward to trip Duke with his bamboo stick. The big man crashed to his knees. The soldiers rained blow after blow on him. Duke grunted; his body jerked.

James Alburg motioned to Uraga. 'Bring a journalist!'

The Iron Duke fought his way up to his full height. Blood matted his blond hair. It ran down his face. His big, bare arms were covered with angry welts. He threw the strongbox at a soldier's head and rushed him. The man lunged forward, driving the blunted point of his bamboo sword into the giant's stomach. Duke bellowed. He doubled over and plopped down, gasping for breath.

'Enough,' Alburg said, taking a pistol from his belt. 'Now where is that journalist?' He turned to see Uraga approaching with a man holding a camera. James Alburg threw his pistol into the Iron Duke's lap. 'As one white man to another, I will give you this chance.' He pointed his shotgun at the pistol. 'Pick it up, Duke!'

The blood-streaked yellow hair hid the big man's face until he raised his head. 'I done things,' he declared through swollen lips and broken teeth. 'I done things that deserve hanging.' He spat blood. 'But I never sided with no Jap against a white man. Like you done, Alburg!' Duke put the pistol to his own head and pulled the trigger. The cameraman snapped a picture. The Iron Duke's shot was the last heard in Kobe that day.

The tide at Akahasi beach turned and the wind blew from the sea with a vengeance. Waves marched in, pounding the *Maria-Luz* with unremitting fury. Below-deck, some women had drowned in their bunks. Others had slipped under the rising waters.

The living looked to Shen Yan and the girl clutching her legs. They crowded around the ladder of the number three hatch, shivering in sea water breast-high. Shen worked the knife point under the last remaining screw. Rotted wood fell away. She held the knife in her teeth and pulled the screw loose with bloody finger tips, then looked down and nodded.

Xu called to those crowded around the ladder. 'Take off your clothes or they will pull you down in the water. When the hatch opens flee from this dark hole, no matter what! Or you will drown!'

Armed with a rifle, pistol and pockets full of ammunition, Captain Belviso roamed the poop deck firing at his crew on the forecastle to keep them from deserting. Afraid to go below-deck, they took refuge behind crates. The captain shot at two men attempting to lower the longboat. A sailor dived over the rail and was killed in the water. Crewmen pleaded with the wild-eyed shipmaster. His response was a gunshot.

Wind and waves came from the sea as Hiroki had warned. A huge wave hit the stern and lifted the ship, turning her sideways. Her hull stretched over the sand bar; the old timbers groaned and creaked. Like a cannon shot, the sixty-year-old keel snapped in two.

'Captain,' the mate shouted, 'her back is broken! Abandon ship!' He scurried forward behind a crate that had broken loose amidship. 'We're all going to drown if we don't get off now!'

Emilio Belviso pumped the lever action of his rifle, firing until the weapon was empty, all the while shouting, 'No! No! No!' Then he pulled out his pistol.

Shen Yan lifted number three hatch and peeked out. A wave struck the side of the ship and she was almost washed down the ladder.

'Jump over the side with me,' Xu said. 'I will help you ashore.'

Tears rolled down Shen's smooth cheeks. 'I am already dead.' She pushed the hatch aside and slipped out onto the deck, timing the next wave to crawl behind a packing case. Her eyes fixed on the captain reloading his rifle. She ran for the poop deck ladder and began climbing.

The captain saw a stream of naked young women come pouring out of number three hold. He fired, and they died, but others kept coming out over the young, sleek bodies. One slim girl leapt to the starboard rail and prepared to dive. He took aim at her, unaware of the one behind him. Shen Yan stabbed the kitchen knife into the captain's back, but the blade bent. He whirled, and shot her with his last bullet.

Chapter 11

The *Maria-Luz* lay five hundred yards from shore with her back broken. Every man, woman and child from three miles around Akahasi beach had come to watch its death throes. Hiroki struggled out of the water and eager hands wrapped him in blankets. Hot rice, soup and tea were pressed on him.

A cry went up from the crowd on the beach. Naked women swarmed onto the deck of the big ship. The wind carried sounds of gunshots.

A village elder hunkered down next to Hiroki. 'The runners you sent to Kobe for help have been turned back by soldiers rounding up the whites,' the elder said. 'If we could get a line to the ship, some of those young women might be saved.'

'Is there a line that long?' Hiroki asked.

The old man looked into Hiroki's eyes. 'Do you think one Japanese life is worth all those foreigners?'

'Get the line,' Hiroki ordered. 'The tide is coming in fast.'

People on the beach moved back as the onshore wind drove the waves inland. It was now six hundred yards to the ship.

Seven young men returned to the beach carrying the top rope of their community net. Hiroki shed his blankets and the young men stripped. He tied the rope around his waist and led them into the surf. They waded out to the sand bar, within one hundred yards of the ship.

Each time an exceptionally large wave broke over the *Maria-Luz*'s port side, Hiroki saw several girls swept down the deck and over the starboard rail. They were

97

whisked southward, and disappeared in the deep, turbulent water.

Hiroki shouted to the man behind him on the rope. 'I will swim out to the left of the ship and let the current pull me by. Then try to make the rope fast to the ship for the lifeline.'

The man waved and Hiroki struck out, his powerful strokes angling into the current. He was lifted to the crest of a wave, dropped into a trough, and kept swimming.

The shooting had stopped on the battered craft. Hiroki saw men in the bow rush to a longboat, and recognized the mate overseeing the lowering. A swarm of girls jumped over the side into the boat before it touched water, and the longboat capsized. The mate, crewmen and many girls were swept away.

There was a pitiful wail from girls still on deck. They tore at their hair, they screamed. Hiroki saw a few push packing cases into the water, then jump in and try to ride them. But there were no handholds on the sealed cases. One by one, the girls slipped into the water and drowned. He saw crewmen in the rigging push girls off and climb higher above the angry sea.

Hiroki reached a point thirty yards from the rudder. He rose up on the crest of a wave to take his bearings and saw a mountain of water descending on the ship. His shouted warning was whipped away by the wind. The giant wave struck the *Maria-Luz* broadside, crushing the hull. It turned the ship over on its side and tore away the poop deck. Hiroki had a brief glimpse of the gutted ship and girls being thrown into the sea. Then the wall of angry white water crashed down on him, slamming him to the bottom, tumbling and rolling him in the black sand. He fought for the surface but was tangled in the rope. He clenched his teeth and pressed his lips tight, knowing if he opened his mouth his starved lungs would suck in the sea. On the verge of oblivion, his head broke water and he drew great gulps of air into his aching lungs. He flailed the water to stay afloat and kick off the rope wound about his legs.

The men on the line behind Hiroki had been washed away by the giant wave. The current was taking him past the ship, with no one aboard to cast him a line. Dead bodies floated all around. He heard pleas in Chinese but had no power to help anyone. He bumped into a broken spar and held on for dear life.

The rope around Hiroki's waist chafed his skin and he trailed blood in the green water. A vision of sharks passed through his mind, but he realized he had nothing to fear. Not with all those smooth, glistening bodies floating around for any man-eaters to feed on. He reached out and touched the bodies that passed. They were warm, but dead. The thought of letting go and joining them tempted him.

Then the rope tightened around his waist and he was pulled towards shore. He let go of the spar and was dragged backwards, bumping another body.

Xu gasped for breath. 'Save me,' she cried.

Hiroki gripped the girl's arm with all his strength, believing her to be the only survivor of the *Maria-Luz*.

That night, William Whittefield and John Mung met with the Kobe Club president in his office.

'Two hundred and eighteen women and seventeen crewmen from the *Maria-Luz* are dead,' James Alburg said. 'Thirty-two girls, two crewmen and Captain Emilio Belviso reached shore alive. The captain is downstairs. He thought our red and white K.C. flag meant Knights of Columbus, and he sought refuge here.'

'Peru doesn't have diplomatic relations with Japan,' Mung said. 'That captain isn't covered by the rules of extra-territoriality. He falls under Japanese law. As representative of his imperial majesty's government, I request that Captain Belviso be turned over to me. He'll be tried in a Japanese court.'

'Do you want justice, Mr Mung?'

'That is correct, and I'll see Belviso gets it.'

'Let the Kobe Club handle this,' Alburg said. 'In a moment I'll go downstairs and hear the charges. I'll listen to the witnesses and allow Emilio Belviso to defend himself. Then I'll hang him.'

'The Japanese army and police displayed courage and discipline today,' William said to Mung. 'Not one drop of white blood was spilled by your men. For you to hang Belviso would negate everything you've accomplished up to now. Let us handle this. You want to do away with the treaties forced upon Japan. I think I can promise the backing of the Kobe Club to achieve that end.'

'I guarantee it,' the Kobe Club president declared.

Mung leaned forward, his intense dark eyes fastened on James Alburg. 'The Japanese army and navy will remain in Kobe until you keep your word. If you don't, I'll order them to take Belviso by force if necessary, and damn the consequences!'

Alburg extended his hand to Mung. 'Your military may leave at dawn. That's when the master of the *Maria-Luz* will hang.'

'Pure conjecture on your part, Lieutenant Shibata,' Count Hideyoshi said. 'The fact is Mung sent the army and navy to Formosa and I cannot contact them. For the moment we are blocked. But I have agents in the fleet. We shall soon know its location and take appropriate action.'

The young officer remained silent. Since his appointment as personal aide to the chairman of the newly established Military Expansion Committee, he had learned when to speak and how to please. He placed a cup of tea before the count.

'No moves against Korea will be considered by Parliament until General Nogi and Admiral Takamora return,' Hideyoshi said.

'Mung is a petty, old quill-pusher who knows how to manipulate the bureaucracy to his own advantage,' Shibata said.

'Well put, Lieutenant. You turn a pretty phrase.'

'I would prefer to turn Mung's scrawny neck until it snaps.'

'Really now.' Hideyoshi looked up from his desk. 'I tried to kill the fishmonger several times twenty years ago. I hoped he would die in retirement.'

Blood pounded in Shibata's head. Here is the opportunity I have been waiting for, he thought. To enter into a conspiracy with one of the most powerful men in the empire. 'Mung's death can be arranged,' he said.

Hideyoshi leaned back. The green light from the lampshade reflected in his dark eyes. 'How many men have you killed?' he asked.

'Two,' Shibata said. 'During my officer's training course another candidate insulted my family. The second was an enlisted man who attacked me. In both cases I performed Giri. My revenge was pure. The name of my ancestors remains untarnished. Both attackers are destroyed.'

A metallic smile creased Hideyoshi's pockmarked face. 'Liar,' he whispered. 'Shibata, you are an accomplished liar. The fellow officer you killed held your gambling marker. You and your friends attacked him in the street. Your debt disappeared with his body. The enlisted man was another story. He expired from excessive punishment administered by you.'

'The man attacked me!'

'He rejected you as a lover.'

Shibata's head drooped, his shoulders slumped. He heard the count stand and come out from behind his desk. He felt a hand on his shoulder, but was too frightened to look up.

'A man who bends the truth can be useful to me,' Hideyoshi said. 'I did not select you to be my aide because of one piece of information you brought me.'

Shibata felt the hand move from his shoulder to his neck. The fingers brushed his hair and entered his collar. They prised open the front button, lifted his chin and caressed his throat.

The two men's eyes met and the count smiled. 'You have what westerners call an aquiline nose. It is quite attractive.' He ran his hands over Shibata's broad shoulders.

A thrill of triumph ran through Shibata's body. His heart swelled. More opportunities for advancement were available than he had ever imagined. He opened the buttons of his tunic as he spoke. 'My friends will help me finish Mung.'

'What are friends for,' Hideyoshi said, removing the young man's jacket.

Noriko turned her face to the open window. She sniffed the balmy air with its scent of spring. White and pink plum blossoms coloured the palace gardens. Tomorrow's weather will favour Shimatzu's wedding, she thought. She had received the approval of the Emperor's master of protocol for her innovations. For the first time, a shrine would be used for both ceremony and entertainment.

Noriko was more certain about the wedding than of her feelings for Hiroki. Newspaper reports told how he had organized the rescue of slave girls from the *Maria-Luz*. The articles referred to him as the only bright light in an otherwise tragic event brought about by greed. Hiroki's heroism had been given more space on the front pages of the nation's newspapers than the clean-up of Kobe and the death of the Iron Duke.

Gin-ko had read Noriko the full-page eyewitness account, and taken her to view the photographs at the Reuter's News Agency office in Tokyo. Noriko shivered at the memory of two dead white men in the first photo. Others, of young, nude bodies tumbling in the surf and floating face down in the water, had horrified her. The photographer had framed one picture with a row of bodies on the wet sand in front of happy villagers carrying away wreckage of the *Maria-Luz*. The photo of Emilio Belviso hanging from a street lamp in front of the Kobe Club, his hairy belly exposed, made Noriko feel that some form of justice had been done.

There were many pictures of Hiroki – entering the water, fighting the waves. A separate sequence, entitled 'The Rescue', showed Hiroki being struck by a wave while clutching a naked girl. His right arm was outstretched, his hair matted over his face. The rope had slipped down around his powerful thighs. She could see a dark circle where it had cut into his waist. His manhood was exposed and Noriko looked at it, feeling warm with her thoughts. She remembered their first meeting, their walk in the imperial gardens. She had thought about him a great deal, even fantasized how it would feel to have him touch her.

The last photo in the sequence had kept Noriko's attention. Stumbling from the surf, Hiroki clutched the naked, unconscious girl to his body as if he would never let her go. Noriko turned from the window and huffed at her jealousy. She shifted unconsciously to relieve the warmth in her loins.

Other pictures of Hiroki showed him being honoured by her father in Tokyo's Ueno park. Crowds of people sought his autograph before his ascent with foreigners in a hot air balloon.

Noriko knew Hiroki would be present at the American bachelor party hosted by William Whittefield for Shimatzu. Invitations to the event had been sought after by the most influential people in the capital. No one knew what a bachelor party was, only that the son of the former American ambassador was the host. Noriko's father was also excited. He had twice mentioned that Hiroki would be there with his brothers. He repeated Hiroki's name a third time and smiled in a curious way as he was leaving. Noriko shook her head and sighed. Men fight, eat and make love, but never seem to share the warmth and affection a woman cherishes, she thought. They are always so busy proving themselves to others. She tapped her foot. If only I was acquainted with Shimatzu's bride, I would give her a bachelor party too.

The newspaper stories about Hiroki capped the Kobe success and relegated the attack on the Japanese embassy in Korea to the third and fourth pages. Expressions of gratitude and praise for the actions of Hiroki and the Japanese military were still arriving from western ambassadors, businessmen and clergy, from as far away as India. An atmosphere of euphoria filled the capital. For the present, Count Hideyoshi's cry for revenge against Korea was given scant attention. The holiday mood of the Plum Blossom Festival, the bachelor party and wedding were infectious. People were happy. They dressed in gay colours, smiled more than usual and bowed lower than required.

Under the pretext of wedding invitations, Mung had summoned high-level Black Dragons from as far as Southeast Asia and Siberia. Feeling that Hiroki's actions in Kobe had earned him special consideration, Mung allowed his grandson a seat at his side. For three days they listened to reports from senior Black Dragons with operatives from Java to the Bering Strait.

Now, before they set out for the bachelor party, the Black Dragon wished to test the young man. 'Condense and evaluate the reports and opinions you have heard while sitting at my side!'

Hiroki had prepared for this question. 'The focus is on Korea,' he said. 'The Chinese have blocked a Russian foothold there. General Li's expansion of the Penyang fleet to bases in Hankow, Canton and Tientsin poses a serious threat to Japan. China's purchase of warships from Germany and Great Britain increases the danger to us. Li's fortification of Port Arthur and the Weihaiwei naval base in the north outflanks our navy. The threat from China replaces that from Russia.'

'How do you suggest we react?' Mung asked.

'Prepare for war with China.'

'So. You agree with Count Hideyoshi.'

'No, sir. He speaks of Korea. That is a restricted view. A move against Seoul must lead to war with China. Hideyoshi thinks only of the first step. I think of the second.'

'Let us anticipate a third step,' Mung said. 'If we were to throw China out of Korea, would that create a power vacuum in the region?'

'Yes, sir.'

'What happens in a vacuum?'

'Nothing,' Hiroki said.

'Nothing, until the seal is broken. Then the closest things around are sucked in. Which, in this case, would be Russia as well as Japan. I fear Russia more than China and Korea combined. The new Czar Nicolas is weak, but his army is strong. His wife Alexandra is the dominant personality. She controls the Russian monarch and promotes an aggressive foreign policy in the Far East.'

Hiroki remembered his father's comment that Mung was overly impressed by western military because of his American contacts as a young man. He made no comment.

'Your father brought word that Russia has borrowed heavily from France to expand her navy,' Mung said. 'In return, the czar signed a mutual defence pact with the French against Germany and Austria. In that there is a glimmer of hope for us. Do you see it?'

'Excuse me, Grandfather, but I do not.'

'In the event of a European conflict, Russia's attention would be focused west instead of east.'

Mung saw a glazed look in the young man's eyes. One

105

never knows how fast a sailboat will go until it tips over, Mung thought. I have surpassed Hiroki's ability to grasp the effects of international events on Japan. At least he is man enough to admit he does not understand. Aloud, Mung said, 'My approach is to make limited preparations for the defensive war, and pray it never comes. The German generals say it takes seven times the men to overrun a defensive position than to hold it. Let the Europeans spend seven times more than us. Our manpower, knowledge and money will be used to build a strong economy. War is wasteful.'

Light returned to Hiroki's eyes. 'Sir, I respectfully submit that you cannot prevent a war with Korea and China. I was born and educated in Seoul and I travelled in China. General Li has brought together the nationalistic elements in both countries. There will be other incidents such as the burning of our legation. The Japanese man they killed was my karate instructor. I worked with him in training Koreans, the Special Forces who support Japan against China. We had many street fights with Sugyup, the Korean nationalist organization. They want war, and a war with Korea is a war with China. In addition, there are many Japanese who want war. Count Hideyoshi is ready to lead them. Your position of peace is pressured from both sides. I do not see how it can succeed.'

'I have plans to avoid war,' Mung said. 'If your father completes his mission and we round up the Formosan bandits, the hot-bloods in Tokyo will be satisfied and the Koreans given cause to consider the striking power of Japan's navy. I am trying to ensure a positive conclusion to negotiations with the Chinese over the Ryukyu islands. If Japan's right to Okinawa is recognized by Europe, it will bring honour to our military, pride to our people and give me time to influence western countries into aborting the unequal treaties with us. For that I need Lord Malcolm Cade's help.'

'Grandfather, I must disagree with your conclusion.

106

Most Japanese do not only want to end these treaties. They desire to test themselves in combat against other nations.'

Mung smiled. 'You would have made a wonderful samurai, swaggering here and there with your two swords. But those times are gone. The present-day samurai's dedication must be directed to commerce. The warrior code must be applied to expanding our industry, merchant fleets, and earning foreign currency.' Mung looked at the wall clock. 'Now we must leave. It may not be long before you have a bachelor party of your own. Let us enjoy Shimatzu's before that.'

Chapter 12

Dressed in buckskin and a racoon hat, William Whittefield stood at the entrance of the garden restaurant to welcome the guests. Geishas lined both sides of the path. Each ambassadorial staff arrived dressed in their traditional costumes. The Hawaiian delegation, led by the six-foot-eight-inch King Kamehamea III, danced a hula to the beat of their own drums all the way up the path and into the garden. When a German maiden lit a pipe and adjusted a pillow in her bosom, the geishas realized the women were men in dresses, rouged cheeks and fancy wigs. The Japanese girls were crippled with laughter. Their attempts to maintain decorum were shattered as each new group arrived.

'You should have told us,' Mung said to William. 'We would have worn kimonos instead of tuxedos.'

'Surprise is an essential part of a bachelor party. You should know that Marquis Inei is already inside.'

'He is not yet the marquis,' Mung said. 'If it is permissible, Hiroki will stand with you. Please inform him when Lord Cade arrives. I must speak with the Englishman.'

'Of course,' William said, motioning them inside.

Mung and Iyeasu entered the garden, a large lush green square lawn surrounded by hedges sculpted in the shapes of wild African animals. Lanterns in the plum trees shaded the blossoms into a rainbow of pastel colours. Elegant dwarf trees in pots were artistically placed and illuminated by electric lights. Kimono-clad girls served drinks and food for both Japanese and western tastes.

'Why did you protest the use of Inei's new title of marquis?' Iyeasu asked.

'He may not want to take it at the new price,' Mung said. 'I do not wish to embarrass the man.'

'You would attach additional conditions the night before the wedding? Inei will call it blackmail.'

'Not if I can show him how the Ineis can serve the Emperor and become the richest family in the empire. Certain events have taken place that make his cooperation imperative.'

'May I listen to the negotiations with him?'

'As adviser to the Emperor, you must. I apologize there was not time to inform you in advance. Hopefully, Lord Cade will join us.'

'I am as interested in that meeting as in the party.' Iyeasu looked around. 'Where is Shimatzu?'

'My three grandsons are bringing him now.'

Trumpets blared and drums rolled as the American marine band struck up a Sousa tune. Led by Yaka, flanked by Uraga and Hiroki, Shimatzu was marched to the centre of the green square.

The three brothers stepped back as William Whittefield came forward. He signalled for a chair and motioned Shimatzu to be seated. The young man adjusted his steel-rimmed spectacles, pushed back his coat-tails and sat rigidly straight.

'Ladies,' William cleared his throat, 'and gentlemen.' He pointed at the bridegroom. 'I present to you the honoured guest for this evening, Shimatzu Ishikawa!'

Men bowed. The 'ladies' curtsied and cavorted. The Japanese threw their hands to their mouths in an attempt to hide their laughter at the exaggerated prancing of some of the 'ladies'.

'We are here tonight to bid farewell to another bachelor who is to join the ranks of happily married men.' William stepped back and one burly 'lady' from the Russian embassy chased her mate onto the lawn in front of Shimatzu and promptly threw him down. Their skit raised gales of laughter and applause.

'A toast to the groom,' William called.

Glasses were raised and downed.

William introduced Mung and Inei. He toasted them and the bride. 'To Hiroki Ishikawa, hero of Kobe,' he called out.

Everyone drank once more. A warm glow settled over the party. The band played loud foot-tapping music.

A buckskin-clad guest spoke to the band leader and the music stopped. 'Attention!' the American called.

Other Americans stiffened. They formed ranks and tramped around the square, moving closer and closer to Shimatzu. Two men lifted him off the chair onto a blanket.

'Hip, hip, hooray!' Shimatzu was thrown high in the air.

'Hip, hip, hooray!' Shimatzu flew up again.

Up he went once more, and was placed back on his chair – dishevelled and disoriented.

A light projector focused on a large white sheet draped over the far wall. The electric lights were dimmed and lanterns near the sheet removed.

'Honoured guests,' William said. 'Two years past, the American laboratories of Thomas Edison in New Jersey solved the problem of cinematographic reproduction. This year in Paris, France, the Lumière brothers projected the first pictures that move. Courtesy of the French embassy, I present those pictures to you now!'

An electric motor whirred. A bright light focused on the white sheet. Black and white lines were followed by a man who walked across the screen in jerky movements. He stopped, faced front and his lips moved.

A sigh of wonder swept the rapt audience. They watched spellbound as a steam engine puffed into view. They laughed when escaping steam startled the man. He connected the engine to several freight cars, then climbed on top of the last car and whirled his hand in a circle. The

110

train moved backwards along the tracks, approaching a tunnel, but the man looked straight ahead, his back to the underpass. Tension grew in the audience as the train approached the black hole and the man came closer and closer to being knocked off.

'Jump, you damned fool!' an American in the audience shouted.

Several Japanese stood up, bowed and invited the man to descend. Just a moment before the train reached the tunnel, the screen went dark. Cries from the audience were cut short when the man appeared on the screen again, unhurt. He bowed, and introduced two other men who also bowed. Every Japanese in the audience and many of the Europeans stood and bowed as the lights came on.

'The two gentlemen on either side of the actor are the Lumière brothers,' William said. 'I am certain we shall hear more of them. And we shall see other pictures that move.'

The band struck up a soft exotic Middle Eastern melody.

'Tonight, for your edification and pleasure,' William announced. 'From the far-off land of Arabia where the art of feminine, seductive dancing has been perfected to arouse men's passions, I present – Fatima!'

A voluptuous, barefooted woman in low-cut gold halter, see-through silk balloon trousers and finger cymbals, danced to the centre of the lawn. Her arms, legs and smooth body moved languidly in time to the haunting music. She danced provocatively close to Shimatzu. She pulled him to his feet and led him after her.

'He dances as stiffly as that man in the moving pictures,' someone in the Italian delegation called out, and everyone laughed. Shimatzu danced the woman over to the Italians. They surrounded her as he returned to his seat.

'Tonight I am hosting this party in honour of the Ishikawa and Inei families,' William announced. 'Moryiama Ishikawa, or John Mung as he became known in America,

111

lived as the son of my grandparents and a brother to my father. In honour of my parents I wish to pay tribute to a person who has made relations between my people and his so beneficial to both. Tonight each embassy will perform traditional folk dances in honour of the groom, his family, the bride and her family. The senior ranking guest, King Kamehamea III of Hawaii, will lead his delegation. We are all obligated to join them in the hula.'

The solid beat of Hawaiian drums filled the garden. The big king led the groom and the two fathers to the native dancers. The three Japanese made a giggling attempt to sway and stomp to the Hawaiian music, but soon begged forgiveness from the king. He stepped to the side with them to watch the dance.

'Can you arrange for me to speak privately with the first adviser to the Emperor, Iyeasu Koin?' the king whispered to Mung.

'Hiroki, escort Count Iyeasu to the last room on the left side of the building,' Mung said. 'I will escort the king.'

'I would like you to remain with us,' the king said to Mung with a smile. 'I know you also advise the Emperor and are aware of the contract labour negotiations between our countries.'

'I am honoured.' Mung bowed. He turned to Mr Inei. 'Please excuse us for the present. I would like to speak with you later.'

In the private room, Iyeasu addressed the Hawaiian king. 'Sake is a beautiful gift from Heaven. It expands the heart, lifts the soul and improves one's health.'

'I prefer that Japanese whisky,' the king said, and poured himself a water glassful. He swallowed half the whisky and smacked his lips. 'How is it that within such a short time the Japanese have been able to produce excellent Scotch whisky, build ships and railroads?'

Iyeasu held up his hands and stepped back. 'We are far

from being a modern country, your highness. Japan is a long way behind the West.'

'Do not play the humble Oriental with me.' The king thumped his chest. 'I am not one of those whites to be tricked. You have industrialized faster than China, Indonesia, India and everyone else in Asia.'

'Yet we have inflation, food shortages and unemployment,' Iyeasu said.

'A temporary situation brought about by a 12 per cent population increase within thirty years,' Kamehamea said. 'In Hawaii the land is so fertile you can stick your finger in the ground and watch it sprout roots. Still, my people are dying from syphilis and alcoholism, and we lose thousands to emigration every year. Plantations, business and industries are owned by whites. The Americans are conspiring to take over Hawaii while my people sit on their arses and do nothing.' The king finished his drink. 'Tell a Hawaiian to go to school and he takes his outrigger to look for a bunch of fish.'

Mung laughed.

'I do not understand,' Iyeasu said.

'A bunch of fish is called a school in English,' Mung said.

'How did you get your people so educated so quickly?' the king asked.

'The Emperor issued an edict,' Mung said. 'There shall hereafter be no illiterate family in any community. Nor shall there be an illiterate member of any family of the empire.'

'The people are performing Chu by studying,' Iyeasu said. 'They repay his imperial majesty by carrying out his will. It is the same regarding work in the civil service, the army or private business. A Japanese dedicates himself to fulfilling his given role in life.'

The big king looked wistfully into his empty glass. 'I wish I could issue edicts that would be carried out. In

Hawaii before every edict there must be a luau. When the party is over everyone is too drunk to remember what I said.' He filled his glass again. 'I am king because no one else in Hawaii can hold his liquor better than me. Now what about the contract labourers? I need people like yours who will work but not steal my country.'

'Your ambassador's request is under consideration,' Iyeasu said.

'For three years it has been under consideration,' Kamehamea retorted. 'Thousands of unemployed Japanese could find work in Hawaii. It would relieve the overcrowding in your cities, reduce pressure on your food supplies and be a source of foreign income. They would be paid in US dollars.'

'The bodies of Chinese slave labourers fertilize the cane fields of Hawaii,' Mung said. 'In Kobe 220 Chinese girls died on a ship taking them to the whorehouses of Peru. We will not prostitute our women nor sell our men into bondage.'

'White men bought, sold and worked the Chinese to death.' Kamehamea held out his massive arms. 'Look at the colour of my skin. We are brothers in flesh and blood. I will care for your people in Hawaii. Send responsible men to report to you if I do not keep my word.' He threw back his head and tapped his chest. 'I want Japanese, not whites in Hawaii! I want to establish a confederation of Pacific island states! An alliance between Japan and Hawaii would be a good start. I propose a marriage between my son and Mutsuhito's daughter.'

The two Japanese gaped at the Hawaiian. Neither had ever spoken the Emperor's name and here was a foreigner proposing a marriage to the descendant of the Sun Goddess Amaterasu-o-mi-Kami. It was beyond their ability to comprehend.

'Are you insulted?' Kamehamea asked.

'No. No,' Mung stammered, glancing at Iyeasu. 'We are amazed at the scope of your plans. A confederation of Pacific island states to hold off the Americans.'

'America has not followed a policy of imperialism in the Far East,' Iyeasu said. 'They have not imposed unequal treaties on China or Japan.'

'That is until now,' the king said. 'The US State Department has begun to work through white planters in Hawaii and Samoa to establish them as island states in the American union.'

'But the Germans are holding the Americans back in Samoa, as the French are in Hawaii,' Mung said.

Kamehamea shook his head. 'My spies report the Germans and Americans have agreed to share governorship of Samoa for the present. The French have already accepted ten million US dollars from American businessmen for rights to the Panama Canal and for not opposing the US takeover of Hawaii.'

'I know that President Grover Cleveland refused to annex Hawaii last year when the white planters imprisoned Queen Liluio-kalani,' Mung said. 'He set her free.'

'President Cleveland is under great pressure. There is mass unemployment in America. Two weeks ago he used troops in Chicago to shoot down railroad strikers. He will not be nominated for a third term in 1896. We have two years to form a confederation. Once the Panama Canal opens, the Americans will pour through into the Pacific from their east coast cities. They already are advancing across the Pacific from California and will soon be camping on Japan's doorstep.'

'I cannot pretend to give you the slightest indication of Japan's position in regard to a Pacific island confederation,' Iyeasu said. 'Such a proposal will have to be examined and discussed in depth.'

'What about the contract labourers?' the king asked.

'On that we shall act immediately,' Iyeasu said. 'A test

115

group of one thousand will be sent to Hawaii. If it goes well, more will follow.'

'Good. Now I can return to the party for some serious drinking.'

Hiroki entered the room after the big man left. 'I did not wish to interrupt. Lord Malcolm Cade has arrived.'

'First invite Mr Inei to meet with me,' Mung said. 'Wait ten minutes, then ask Lord Cade to join us.'

Hiroki bowed and went out.

'Did you expect the proposal of a confederation of Pacific island states?' Iyeasu asked Mung.

'We have always spoken of Japan as leader of the peoples of Asia.'

'Yes, but the king is too far ahead of his time,' Iyeasu said. 'Japan must look to the Asian mainland first.'

'What do you think of Kamehamea's proposal of marriage between a Hawaiian prince and the Emperor's daughter?'

'I refuse to even comment on it,' Iyeasu said, rolling his eyes. 'Tell me more about Mr Inei.'

'A banker out of a family of rice brokers. They say he stacked his pennies as a child, saved his yen as a boy and now collects gold bullion and silver coins earned from his factories and merchant fleet. He founded Japan's indigo-dyeing industry, the first silk reeling plant, and outlined the foundation of Japan's treasury. Inei has helped more than a hundred peasant entrepreneurs to establish successful companies in finance and industry. He is a patriot with a beautiful daughter whom my son will marry tomorrow. Tonight I shall push Mr Inei's concept of Chu to the limit.'

A short powerful man with a ruddy-cheeked peasant face entered the room. 'Gentlemen, we missed you at the festivities,' Inei said. 'They are quite unusual and entertaining. It is the first time I have seen westerners unbend. They actually have a sense of humour.'

'I hope you brought your sense of humour to this room,' Mung said. 'In ten minutes Lord Cade will join us. I wish to inform him you will put up your business holdings as collateral against a fifty-million-dollar loan from Great Britain.'

'In addition to converting my industrial plants to weapons production and allowing my merchant ships to be armed?'

'Yes.'

Inei scratched his chin. 'My daughter's wedding is becoming more expensive than I expected.'

'Until now we have spoken in terms of millions of dollars regarding your businesses. I am certain you have conceived of hundreds of millions in export-import. I foresee Japan reaching one thousand million dollars in trade by the mid-twentieth century. That is only fifty years away.'

'Sir, if the house of Inei forfeits on a fifty-million-dollar loan, my family will be poor for eternity.'

'You will be serving the Emperor. If a financial failure occurred, it would be your fault.' Mung produced an envelope bound in red ribbon with the imperial seal affixed. 'This confirms your place in the house of lords with the title of marquis. It also contains an imperial commission to establish the First National Bank of Japan. In addition, you will name the next manager of Japan's national treasury. Not contained in this envelope is a promise I now make verbally – a Japanese bank to be established on Formosa. Its primary task will be the unification of Formosan currency. Appoint my son Shimatzu head of this bank and you will earn ten million dollars the moment he sets a favourable exchange rate for the yen.'

'How can you be certain China will allow a Japanese bank on Formosa?' Inei asked.

'My son Udo sent word that the Chinese Prince Kung is prepared to accept a bribe to grant the bank charter. The Formosan bank will enable you to exploit trade and industrial development in Formosa, southern China and the South Sea Islands. To do that you will have to establish a commercial bank with branches in Tokyo and Nagasaki, under a different name of course. The charters for the commercial banks will be available when you are ready.'

Iyeasu and Inei stared in unabashed awe at Mung. The merchant bowed deeply. He touched the imperial seal on the envelope to his forehead. 'Sir, if a Japanese fisherman and a lowly rice merchant can accomplish this plan of yours, the rising sun will one day illuminate the four corners of this earth.'

Mung bowed. 'The marriage of your daughter to my son is a signal for the economic expansion of Japan to begin. Prior to your entrance into this room, the king of Hawaii made us a proposal to form a confederation of Pacific island states. I see Japan eventually managing the entire Pacific in harmony with its more backward inhabitants.'

'Then why prepare for war?' Inei asked.

'That has to do with my brother Hideyoshi and me,' Iyeasu said. 'I believe overseas investments such as yours and the government's must be protected by guns. Hideyoshi prefers the occupation of other countries to ensure foreign markets and access to natural resources.'

'Your factories will soon be exporting weapons, Mr Inei,' Mung said. 'There can be great profit in that if you produce a high-quality product.'

'I shall see to it,' Inei said.

There was a knock on the door. Hiroki entered and announced, 'Lord Malcolm Cade, British plenipotentiary of the Far East.'

A short wiry man with a large head of flowing grey hair framing a suntanned face, entered and returned the bows of the three Japanese. 'My congratulations to the fathers-in-law to be and to the Emperor's adviser,' he said. 'May you all be blessed with health, happiness and fair weather.'

'Shall we drink to that?' Iyeasu asked.

The British nobleman threw up his hands. 'No, thank you. I must keep my senses. King Kamehamea has been trying to convince me to visit Honolulu. I drank too much with him.' Lord Cade looked at Mung. 'I would like to congratulate the director of the Department of National Decorations for beautifying Kobe. Her majesty's government is impressed with the discipline shown by the Japanese troops and police. And with the heroism of your grandson.'

Mung bowed.

'This is the hero of Kobe,' Iyeasu said, beaming at Hiroki. 'It is possible this young man may become my son-in-law.' Iyeasu saw the shocked expression on Hiroki's face. 'Have I misunderstood? You did agree to a mi-ai with my daughter?'

Confused at the attention focused on him, surprised by having his plan for revenge on Noriko put to the test so quickly, Hiroki searched for the correct response. 'I . . .' He swallowed and began again, 'Yes sir, I asked Father to arrange the mi-ai.'

'Your father shall be away for some time,' Mung said. 'I will make the arrangements. Now go enjoy yourself. Learn what is done at a bachelor party.'

'That boy will sire sons to be proud of,' Lord Cade said. 'Your message indicated important matters to be discussed, Mr Mung.'

'Please be seated, your lordship,' Mung said. 'Marquis Inei has been appointed to form and head the First National Bank of Japan. He wishes to borrow fifty million dollars from Great Britain. His personal holdings in Japan exceed that sum. They will be put up for collateral.'

'What would this loan be used for?' Lord Cade asked.

'To purchase two of your newest battle cruisers and twenty of the most recently built torpedo-boats. The kind your naval advisers are training our men on.'

'This would be a financial coup for Britain. What must I do to obtain it?'

'Help us in negotiations for Okinawa with the Chinese Prince Kung.'

'He is a blackguard who cannot be trusted.'

'That is why I come to you,' Mung said. 'My son Udo has prepared a bribe for the prince. We would like to insure it. The forthcoming military operation against the Formosan pirates is as follows ...'

As Mung spoke, Malcolm Cade was formulating his own plan.

'I will help you keep Prince Kung to his word,' Lord Cade said. 'However, in the negotiations I would suggest that you make three demands: one, Japanese sovereignty over Okinawa; two, twenty million dollars in reparations for the dead fishermen; three, instead of banking rights, demand that China cede the island of Formosa to you.' The Englishman watched the reactions of the Japanese, certain they had no idea his intention was to use Japan to gain part of China for England.

'The Chinese will never agree,' Mung said. 'Our bribe is not that large.'

'You can accept the banking rights on Formosa instead of the island itself. It will allow Prince Kung to save face.'

'Will you grant the loan?' Mung asked.

'If you are successful in Formosa, I guarantee it. Five torpedo-boats will be waiting for you in Canton. The rest to be delivered at a later date.' He pointed at the bottle of Suntory whisky. 'I will now have that drink to toast a successful venture in Formosa and a wonderful wedding tomorrow.'

Chapter 13

Before dawn, Mung and Shimatzu left the palace by rickshaw. A Buddhist priest waited for them at the water's edge in Tokyo harbour.

'Today you will be married,' Mung said. 'Tonight I sail for Okinawa and then Formosa. It is fitting that we celebrate the ceremony of the dead together.'

They watched the priest place several wicker baskets woven in the shape of boats near the water. Each one held a candle in the centre. The baskets were filled with fruit, biscuits and sweetmeats. The priest lit the candles and chanted prayers as Mung set the first of six baskets afloat. He recited the names of his parents and of the father of his first and second wives, whose family name he carried. He recited the name of his first son, Yoshida, and watched as the boats began to sink.

The candles were snuffed out by the water and Mung intoned, 'I send these offerings to you on the other side of the river. It is my wish that you spend eternity in paradise among the enlightened ones. I entreat you to help me pass peacefully from this world of confusion to that of blissful order when my time comes.' He pressed his palms together, bowed and clapped once to send his prayers on their way.

Shimatzu stepped forward and launched boats for his grandparents, his mother and his namesake, Lord Shimatzu Nariakira.

Mung watched the sun's rays illuminate a line of clouds on the horizon, seeing in them the silhouettes of thousands of celestial warriors charging ahead of the rising sun. He shivered and turned back to his son and the priest. They were watching Shimatzu's baskets. Mung looked up again but the ethereal army was gone.

'It will be a beautiful day for the wedding,' Shimatzu said.

Mung paid the priest and joined his son in the rickshaw. 'I must tell you that if events go as planned, your father-in-law will be appointed director of Japan's treasury. You will be assigned to manage Japan's first bank in Formosa.'

'But we have no control over what occurs in Formosa.'

'Have no fear, we will. Reports from Udo are quite positive. His men are in position to capture the bandits. A bribe has been paid to Prince Kung. Your task will be to regulate Formosan currency and set an exchange rate favourable to the yen. Inei will guide you in this and other commercial enterprises. Do as he says regarding financial matters, and always place my Black Dragons or Udo's Genoysha men in key positions to gather information. I will supply you with people especially trained to evaluate reports that come to your office from our agents in southern China and the South Pacific. The Black Dragon intelligence system has become so large, I have had to reorganize it on the Prussian system of bureaux and geographical divisions. Udo will be based in Korea and control operatives in northern China, Mongolia and Manchuria.'

'Are your priorities still economic and industrial, Father?'

'I hope we can return to that, but China, Korea and Russia are expanding their navies. Military information must now be given first preference. Remain alert for commercial ventures abroad and at home. I still believe we can win by peace what others hope to achieve in war.'

'There was no choice but to invite Count Hideyoshi,' Gin-ko said. 'He is one of the most influential men in government.'

'I hear that he did not attend the bachelor party last night,' Noriko replied.

'The American did not invite him. I fear Hideyoshi will repay that slight to William Whittefield's sorrow. But I think it is not Hideyoshi who disturbs you. It is his aide Shibata, and the others who will accompany the count to the wedding.'

'Does Hiroki know how the incident in the Imperial Hall of Martial Arts came about?' Noriko asked.

'My son has been the centre of so much attention since the *Maria-Luz* incident, there was not time to tell him. I know his father and grandfather spoke to him of the mi-ai.'

'I agreed that my father should arrange Hiroki's and my viewing of each other,' Noriko said, with more optimism than she felt.

'I am pleased.' Gin-ko began to rise and fell back. 'So ungracious of me.' She blushed.

Noriko helped her sit up. 'Are you ill?'

'It is nothing but a slight dizziness brought on by the pressure of the wedding.' Gin-ko shook her head. 'Your father is most pleased about the mi-ai. He wishes Hiroki to carry your family name. Udo and I agree. I think you know Mung loves you as a daughter.'

Now Noriko blushed, and felt dishonest. She had decided to comply with the traditional arrangement, then politely but firmly decline to see Hiroki again after their first official meeting.

'Give me your hand,' Gin-ko said. 'We shall have a final check of the preparations at the shrine.'

'You should rest.'

'I wish Udo was here. I promised he would attend his foster son's wedding.' Gin-ko took Noriko's arm. 'I would like to see how the flower arrangers contrasted the old rikka style with the new moribana. It should raise some eyebrows among local practitioners of the art.'

'Mung asked for a theme of traditional combined with

123

modern,' Noriko said. 'I hired my own teacher to supervise. She is the most skilled ikebana artist in the capital.'

'And your arrangements for the wedding are so well planned. They carry the theme through the decorations, food and music.' Gin-ko smiled and colour returned to her face.

The two beautiful women in their bright kimonos mounted the ancient stone steps to the Kan-eiji shrine. Plum blossoms provided a soft pink and white background for the ancient dwarf pines whose emerald-green branches still glistened with morning dew. The geishas Noriko had chosen for their grace and beauty were setting the cloth-covered tables for the hundreds of guests soon to arrive. In the centre of each table were two flower arrangements in the contrasting styles.

At the top of the stairs, Gin-ko leaned on Noriko's arm. The young woman looked questioningly at her companion and the older woman looked away.

'I admire the beauty of the flower arrangements,' Gin-ko said. 'Tell me about them.'

'The newer rikka style incorporates colourful western flowers introduced to Japan in the last few years, but the symbolism of both forms remains the same – our world below, Heaven above and humanity between. The Buddhist cosmology is represented in each branch and depicted in the balance between the container and the plants.'

'The guests will soon begin to arrive,' Gin-ko said. 'I think this wedding will dictate a new style for years to come. It would be good to rest before the ceremony.'

Noriko took Gin-ko's arm and led her to a room where she could lie down.

'I would like to stay with you, but I am responsible for last-minute wedding preparations,' Noriko said. 'I will return in a short while.'

Gin-ko was already asleep as Noriko went out of the door.

In keeping with tradition, the bride and groom and their families prayed at different shrines. Kazumi Inei returned home to dress in white, the clothing of a corpse. She bade farewell to her parents and broke a teacup at the front door, a spell to ensure she would not return. She then followed a procession of family and friends who carried gifts from Shimatzu, Mung and her parents to the shrine. Kazumi mounted the stone steps and met Noriko and Gin-ko at the top. They escorted her to a room where she changed into a colourful kimono, a large white, wide-brimmed hat and obi to match. Her cheeks were rouged, eyebrows pencilled and her body perfumed.

Shimatzu made his appearance before the assembled guests in a brown silk kimono and short ebaori jacket embroidered with intricate designs for good luck. He was escorted by his three foster brothers and his father to a seat at a low table in front of the shrine. Gin-ko joined Mung as Marquis Inei, his wife and family escorted Kazumi to a seat opposite Shimatzu. Noriko signalled to a girl in a royal blue kimono. She shuffled forward and placed three cups of graduated sizes and three sake flasks on the table between the bride and groom.

Shimatzu lifted a flask with both hands and filled the first cup. He presented it to Kazumi. She touched the cup to her lips three times. She filled the second cup and offered it to him. He touched his lips to the sake three times. The final cup was shared three times each.

Then the bride and groom stood and walked together to the Shinto priest who waited near the great bell of Kan-eiji. Family and friends followed. The priest purified the couple by chanting prayers and waving incense. He invited the deities to intercede on their behalf.

Kazumi and Shimatzu each dropped a coin near the priest's feet. He turned, took hold of the thick hemp rope and swung it. The bell tolled, alerting the gods, and the bride and groom bowed. Each said a silent prayer and clapped once to send it on its way to Heaven. The families exchanged congratulations. Guests lined up to wish the couple well.

The joyful, deep-throated chant of fifty male dancers approached. The muscular bare-chested men trotted forward in time to a drum and flute. They danced as they came, taking turns at whirling and throwing a tall, heavy pole decorated in leather, gold and silver with the shrine's symbols. They twirled it high into the air, caught it and threw it up again.

A Buddhist priest came forward and read sutras. He was followed by a famous Tokyo songstress who accompanied herself on a samisen. Drinks were served and the guests were invited to partake of the food on the tables.

Mung took Gin-ko, Kazumi and Shimatzu aside. He bowed deeply to the bride and groom. 'My wife Ukiko died giving birth to Shimatzu,' Mung said to Kazumi. 'Gin-ko and Udo were with her. I was far away in the north.' He turned to his son. 'Your mother wanted you so much she ordered the doctor . . .' Mung choked. He looked to Gin-ko and his eyes pleaded.

'Your mother ordered the doctor to save her baby at the risk of her own life,' Gin-ko said. 'Knowing she was dying, she had me promise to hold you up so she could see you. She opened her eyes, looked at you, smiled, and passed away.'

Mung cleared his throat. 'There are few things in this life I need apologize for. But in the first two years of your life, I refused to see you, Shimatzu my son. I was angry at the loss of your mother. Gin-ko and Udo cared for you when I could not.' Mung turned to Gin-ko. 'Then this beautiful woman who raised you grew angry with me. She put you into my arms against my will. In that moment I knew why your mother had smiled. From that time I loved

126

you as she had. If I have hurt you, I ask your forgiveness.'
Mung bowed.

Shimatzu and Kazumi bowed deeply to Mung. 'I am proud to be your son,' Shimatzu said. 'My wife and I will raise our children to honour you and our ancestors.'

Mung signalled to Noriko and she brought forward a large cloth-bound package. Mung handed it to Shimatzu. 'Because I could not be with your mother during her pregnancy and she did not expect to survive the birth, she had three portraits made of herself during the nine-month period. You look very much like her. I believe she truly died happy knowing I would see her in you.'

Before Shimatzu could reply he was whisked away by Yaka, Uraga and Hiroki to join the dancers. Kazumi took the package from Mung. She bowed to her father-in-law. 'I shall hold these for my husband. I hope to be as brave as the mother who bore him, as good as the mother who raised him and as honourable as the father who conceived him.' She bowed again and returned to her parents.

'The day is quite a success,' Iyeasu said to Mung.

'Your daughter is to be congratulated.' Mung bowed to Noriko. 'If you marry into my family, you can arrange your own ceremony.'

'A marriage to Hiroki would continue our family name,' Iyeasu said to his daughter. 'But of course you will make up your own mind.'

Noriko's legs felt weak. Despite all the joy around her, she was empty inside. Her obligation to her father required she marry Hiroki. She knew her father had not meant to put her in this position, but unless he or Hiroki did something negative she could not refuse the marriage without shaming the two families. Honour and tradition required she accept Hiroki if he wanted her. Noriko wondered how her father and Mung, two intelligent men, could be so wrong in their evaluation.

Shimatzu and his three brothers broke away from the

dancers. They wiped sweat from their faces and accepted food and drink from the geishas. After a few minutes Yaka and Uraga charged back into the whirling crowd.

Shimatzu took Hiroki aside. 'I heard what happened at the Imperial Hall of Martial Arts.' He watched Hiroki turn beet red. 'You have no reason to be ashamed. You acquitted yourself so well that karate will be introduced as a new discipline in the hall. The senior instructor has asked if you would consider teaching.'

'I fought a woman,' Hiroki mumbled.

'You and Noriko were tricked into fighting. Shibata and everyone else in the hall knows that if Noriko was not a woman she would be a kendo instructor.'

'Are you telling me Noriko did not know it was me she was fighting?'

'That is correct. Shibata told her someone challenged the women. That if their champion lost, they would all have to leave the hall forever.'

Hiroki felt as if a weight had been lifted off his chest. 'Take me to see her,' he said.

'Is that Udo's son talking to the groom?' Hideyoshi asked his aide.

'Yes, the one who fights women and loses,' Shibata said.

'He did quite well at Akahasi beach.' Hideyoshi purposely baited Shibata. 'An informant told me Hiroki called you a putrid drop of scum scraped off a shithouse floor.'

The young lieutenant paled. His lips quivered and his breath whistled through his teeth like the hiss of a snake. He doubted the insult was true but could not question his superior, nor disregard the slur to his family without losing his position as aide to the count. He began to tremble. Spittle appeared at the corners of his mouth.

Hideyoshi put a cup of warm sake into Shibata's shaking hand. 'Did you know Hiroki's mother was a whore?'

Hideyoshi said. 'I do not exaggerate. Prior to the closing of the Yoshiwara, she was the most sought-after courtesan in that district of prostitutes. Her mentor, who has since died, was chief Yakuza of Tokyo.'

Shibata gulped the sake. 'You mean the leader of the tattooed men?' he said. 'She was owned by criminals?'

'She had their protection. In the crook of her left elbow Hiroki's mother has a small yellow butterfly tattoo. Why not discuss it with your fellow officers. Together you may think of a way to discipline that loudmouth who has maligned your family.'

Noriko's back was to Hiroki as he and Shimatzu approached. He admired her powder blue kimono with the delicate gold flowers. It was bound by a soft grey obi.

'I would like to re-introduce Hiroki Ishikawa,' Shimatzu said. 'You two met in the palace and on the nine metre square.'

Noriko returned Hiroki's bow. 'Is it true you did not challenge me as a way to keep women from the Imperial Hall of Martial Arts?' she asked.

Hiroki's heart became a balloon lifting his spirits. He was gloriously happy. 'I went to the hall to see you.'

'To fight me?'

'No, no! It was all a terrible mistake!' Hiroki heard himself sounding foolish but could not stop his mouth. He saw her smile and felt hurt. 'Do I amuse you?'

Noriko placed her fingers between her breasts. 'The last time we met you punched me.'

Hiroki stepped closer and Noriko felt the same magnetism as at their first meeting.

'Have you ever seen the pictures of Hell in the Buddhist temples?' Hiroki whispered. He tapped his chest. 'That is where I have been since that day I struck you. I cannot describe my horror when your mask rolled off.'

Once again Noriko experienced Hiroki's charm and

innocence, and she felt fear. 'Look,' she pointed, 'my father has challenged your grandfather to a paper duel.'

'Shall we have a mi-ai?' Hiroki asked.

Noriko pretended she had not heard. 'Let us watch. My father already has charcoal and rice paper.'

Guests closed in around the two men. Hiroki and Noriko found a place at the rear, near the steep entrance steps.

'Freeze,' Iyeasu said, and Mung stood still. Iyeasu sketched Mung's face in caricature. Each stroke of his charcoal elicited sighs of admiration or raucous laughter. He magnified the bent nose, the high cheekbones and bold eyes with heavy, sharp, angled lines. He finished with a flourish and presented the cartoon image. People behind Mung giggled and laughed at the accurate representation in caricature.

Everyone fell silent as Mung accepted the charcoal and paper from his old friend with a smile. He began to sketch in soft, rounded lines, stroking in large puffed cheeks, a button nose and heavy jowls that everyone recognized as belonging to the English ambassador's bull-dog. They laughed and applauded when, with two bold strokes, Iyeasu's wide, cherubic smile appeared on the caricature.

Hiroki grinned at Noriko. 'I believe your father has suffered at the hands of my grandfather.'

'They should sketch your mother, the whore,' Shibata said. 'They could put a for-sale sign under it.'

Hiroki whirled around. He pushed Noriko aside and was immediately surrounded by five army officers. Noriko hurried off to find Hiroki's brothers.

'Do you pimp for your mother?' Shibata asked, feeling the dagger in his jacket sleeve. One move from Hiroki and he would stab him.

Hiroki remained rigidly still. 'I will kill you,' he said in a low voice that shook with anger. 'But not here at Shimatzu's wedding. Leave at once!'

'If you are ashamed because your mother worked the Yoshiwara for the Yakuza, why not kill her!'

'A lie,' Hiroki cried. The officers tightened their circle around him but he saw only Shibata's leering face.

'The yellow tattoo on your mother's arm is the Yakuza protection sign for working women,' Shibata said.

Hiroki's fist struck so quickly that Shibata's knife fell to the ground. The snap of bone in his long straight nose was audible. He staggered backwards and rolled down the steep stone steps.

The officers pounced on Hiroki and he went down under their weight. Fists punched at him from all sides and he could not move. Then Yaka, Uraga and Shimatzu were pulling the army men off him. The two groups separated, glowering at one another.

One of the lieutenants pointed to the injured Shibata sprawled halfway down the steps. 'Why do you strike a man for speaking the truth? Your mother was advertised in the Yoshiwara for three years.'

Hiroki crouched to attack but was held by Mung's voice.

'My daughter-in-law is among the most honourable women in the empire!' Mung pulled out his Colt.44 and pointed it down the steps at Shibata. 'Take that piece of slime and leave before I kill you and him too!'

Ten Black Dragons surrounded the four officers and pressured them down the steps. Mung's glance over the heads of the crowd caught Hideyoshi's wicked grin. He itched to kill the man but knew he would keep his promise to the deceased Lord of Mito, Hideyoshi's father.

'Attend to your bride,' Mung said to Shimatzu. 'Go directly to my palace apartment,' he ordered his grandsons. 'You are all leaving Tokyo!' He saw a glazed look in Hiroki's eyes. 'Did you hear?'

The young man nodded. His thoughts were of the yellow butterfly on his mother's arm. She had told him that one day he would know the story of that tattoo.

131

Chapter 14

'Is it true?' Hiroki asked.

His brothers looked at each other but remained silent.

'Is it true about Mother?' Hiroki persisted. 'She does have a yellow butterfly tattoo on her arm.'

'That was Wada Zenshichi's way of protecting her,' Yaka said. 'Mother saved his life.'

'Is it true he was chief of the tattooed men?' Hiroki demanded.

'You do not understand,' Uraga said. 'Twenty years ago the Yakuza rescued Father and Grandfather in a battle at Tamieka Pond. Wada Zenshichi helped Grandfather escape to Hokkaido. It was information from the Yakuza that saved Sapporo from being burned and pillaged by pirates.'

'My mother . . .' Hiroki gulped. 'My mother was a whore in the Yoshiwara?'

Yaka grabbed Hiroki. 'Never use that word about our mother!'

Hiroki's eyes went flat, his voice low and dangerous. 'Take your hands off me or I will break you!'

Uraga forced his way between his brothers. It was Yaka, the elder, who stepped back.

'You grew up in a different culture at a different time,' Yaka said.

'He is correct,' Uraga said. 'Our mother was the most celebrated courtesan in Tokyo. You have lived away from Japan all your life. That incident in Kyoto with the Japanese girl shows your ridiculous attitude towards sex.'

'Prostitution is outlawed in Japan,' Hiroki said.

'To satisfy the Christian clergy,' Yaka said. 'The Yoshi-wara was closed to impress them. It was part of the treaties Japan was forced to sign. But there are gay houses in every city and village in the country. In Tokyo the same Christians who demanded the laws be changed are among the best customers in the bordellos.'

Hiroki bit his lip and shook his head from side to side. 'Did our mother work in the Yoshiwara?' he asked.

'The circumstances,' Yaka said. 'You do not understand the circumstances.'

Hiroki raised his head. 'I will learn the circumstances from her.' He brushed his brothers aside and stalked from the room.

Noriko and Gin-ko witnessed the confrontation between Hiroki and Shibata, and the older woman had fainted. Noriko, with the help of three Black Dragons, hurried Gin-ko to her father's palace apartment. She had summoned his personal physician.

Gin-ko sipped a cup of green tea. She was pale and weak, but in control. 'Did you know I was a courtesan?' she asked.

'Your story is one of the most romantic I have ever read.' Noriko moved closer to Gin-ko. 'I saw the play three times. My mother took me when I was a little girl. She cherished your friendship.'

'Your mother, Princess Atsu, was a very special person.'

'Mother told me you were the first woman she wrote about in her Book of Good Deeds, and the only woman to be recorded twice.'

There was a knock at the door. 'That must be the doctor,' Noriko said.

'I prefer not to be examined by anyone.'

The door opened and Hiroki entered. He looked down at his mother. Seeing how pale she was, he believed it was because of her guilt. 'It is time to tell your youngest son about the yellow butterfly,' he said.

'I was wrong not to explain sooner,' Gin-ko said. 'I kept putting it off and then suddenly you were grown.'

Noriko put her arm around Gin-ko's shoulders. 'It is not the time to discuss this subject with your mother.'

Gin-ko patted Noriko's hand and looked up at her son. 'I waited too long with you, but my past is not a secret to Shimatzu or your brothers.'

'It appears your Yoshiwara days were not a secret to anyone but me,' Hiroki said. 'Was Father tricked too or did he have more money than your other clients?'

'That will be enough!' the stern voice said from the doorway.

Hiroki whirled.

Mung's grey hair bristled, his eyes shot fire. 'Down on your knees before this lady!'

Hiroki was confused. 'I am the one betrayed, yet everybody is against me.'

'Down on your knees! I, the Black Dragon, command it!'

Hiroki trembled. He saw his mother's pleading eyes looking up at Mung, and sank to the floor, not understanding why he was forced to kowtow.

In a faint whisper, Gin-ko said to Mung, 'For my sake, please do not hurt him. He has suffered enough.'

'Bow your head before this lady who birthed such an ignoramus as you,' Mung ordered.

Hiroki looked up into his grandfather's face and saw contempt. Tears streamed down the young man's cheeks and he threw himself forward. The sound of his head striking the floor shook the two women.

'I will not order you to apologize,' Mung said. 'That must come from your heart. Get up and get out! Wait at the harbour master's office! You will receive orders! Go!'

The doctor stood aside as Hiroki hurried past him from the room.

Mung looked at the doctor. 'Who is ill?' he asked.

'Noriko thinks I am because I fainted,' Gin-ko said. 'It was the strain of the wedding and excitement at the celebration.'

Mung turned to Noriko. 'Please stay with my daughter-in-law.' He addressed the doctor. 'If anything is wrong I want to know how long it will take you to make it right!' He bowed to Gin-ko. 'Take care of yourself. You are very close to my heart. Do not worry about Hiroki. I will resolve the matter.'

The doctor slid the door closed behind Mung and approached Gin-ko. She pointed her fan at him. 'If you intend to report your findings to Mung or anyone else, I will not permit you to examine me.'

The doctor looked at Noriko, who signalled with her eyes he should agree.

'Madam, if you desire privacy it shall be as you wish,' he said. 'It appears to me you already know something about your condition or you would not make this stipulation.'

'You may examine me,' Gin-ko said, staring straight ahead.

Twenty minutes later the doctor accepted tea from Noriko. He sipped loudly, composing his thoughts as the two women watched him. He put down the empty cup and looked at Gin-ko. 'I can only confirm what your previous doctor must have told you.'

'Cancer of the lymph glands?' Gin-ko said.

'I am certain that you have felt the growths yourself.'

'How much time do you think I have?'

'When was this first diagnosed?'

'Three months ago in Seoul,' Gin-ko said. 'I wanted a Japanese doctor to confirm it but have not had the time. The Korean doctor said I had two weeks to a year to live.'

Noriko swooned. The doctor passed a phial under her

135

nostrils and her head jerked away from the smell. She sat up straight and apologized to Gin-ko.

'You must remain strong if you wish to help this lady,' the doctor said.

'I could not think to impose such a hardship on the girl,' Gin-ko said.

'You must allow me to help you,' Noriko pleaded. 'I will be strong. I promise.'

'I do not wish anyone to know,' Gin-ko said. 'That would pain me more than the disease.'

'You can depend on me,' Noriko said.

'I vouch for this young woman,' the doctor said. 'I brought her into this world and watched her mature. You can find no better. She accomplished wonders bringing Mung back to health.'

'Alas, I will not recover,' Gin-ko said, taking Noriko's hand. 'I hope to trust you with my youngest son's happiness for the rest of your lives. But you must know it will not be easy looking after me, or Hiroki.'

Noriko smiled weakly, more concerned with the increasing entanglement towards marriage with Hiroki than nursing Gin-ko.

'What a disgusting appendage that is on the front of your face,' Hideyoshi said. 'It looks like a balloon.'

Shibata licked his lips. 'The doctor predicts the swelling will go down in a day or two. The blackness around my eyes will take longer.'

Hideyoshi pushed himself back from his desk. 'I never would have thought a nose could look like that. Turn towards the wall map. I would rather not see it.' He saw the young man tremble with rage and was pleased. 'You will leave for Hankow on the first available boat! Put your finger on the map at Shanghai! Follow the Yangtze river up-country into central China past Nanking! Hankow is another arsenal in General Li's string of fortified naval

136

bases. It is located at the confluence of the Han and Yangtze rivers.'

Shibata had heard enough. 'My career is ruined,' he cried, dropping his hand from the map. He turned and advanced on Hideyoshi, his face a distorted mask of hatred. His shoulders hunched and he slammed his balled fists on the desk. 'Hiroki Ishikawa will die!'

'From the description of his talented hands, I think it is fortunate you fell down the steps when you did. He could have killed you.'

'I will not go to Hankow or anywhere else until I have my revenge!'

'You will do as I order!' Hideyoshi said. 'I am the White Wolf!'

'First I will listen to the death rattle in Hiroki's throat! I can hardly see around my own nose. Every second it reminds me of my shame. I will kill the bastard, then commit seppuku for disobeying you!'

Hideyoshi leaned forward and put his hand on Shibata's. 'The doctor told you the swelling will recede. The pain will be forgotten and your family honour will be redeemed.' He squeezed Shibata's hand. 'You cannot touch Hiroki now. My agent reported that he awaits a ship for Korea in the harbour master's office.' Shibata tried to pull away and Hideyoshi tightened his grip. 'Attack that office and you will fail! You would be recognized!'

'I am not afraid to die.'

'Of course not. But are you courageous enough to live?' Hideyoshi caressed the younger man's hand. The distorted nose disgusted him but he smiled into the pain-filled eyes. 'If you murder Hiroki now, it will reflect directly on me. It would retard our plans for Korea. The White Wolf Society and the future of a greater Japan would be in jeopardy.'

'I cannot allow the Ishikawa family to walk away without some form of retribution,' Shibata said.

'You are like the warriors of old,' Hideyoshi said. 'But death, no matter how glorious, is not the answer in this case. I want you to live.'

'For what?'

'For revenge against Hiroki, against the westerners, against those Japanese who would stop Japan from achieving her destiny, her glory, her rightful place as a world leader!'

'What can I do!'

'Assassinate Mung,' Hideyoshi said. 'No one will make the connection between you and him. Then you will go to Hankow.'

'What is there in China for me?'

'The Green House and a new future!' Hideyoshi leaned forward over his desk and put his face close to Shibata's. 'The Green House is the secret training centre for those White Wolves chosen to organize spy networks outside the country. Upon completion of the course you will be assigned an area in accordance with the talents you display. Funds will be made available. You will be free to rise to your potential. It is like being commissioned feudal lord, in secret of course. You can become as powerful as you are talented.'

'Why is this training centre in Hankow and not Japan?'

Hideyoshi sighed. 'We Japanese are fettered by centuries of tradition and moral upbringing. But away from our homeland, all moral restraints are off. What takes place in the Green House cannot be practised in Japan – the use and abuse of men and women of other nationalities. This can be the greatest advance in your career. Kill Mung! Go to Hankow and plan how to kill Hiroki! Become as influential as you are inventive!'

Shibata stepped back from the desk and began pacing the floor.

'Mung will visit Hiroki in the harbour master's office before the ship sails for Korea,' Hideyoshi said. 'A clerk there is an agent of ours. He will inform you of Mung's movements. Gather your friends. Ambush the fishmonger!'

'I would prefer more time to plan the attack.'

'There is no more time!' Hideyoshi slammed the desk. 'Mung sails tomorrow for a rendezvous somewhere in the Pacific with General Nogi and Admiral Takamora. It must be done tonight!'

Chapter 15

Mung entered the harbour master's office on the promontory overlooking Tokyo bay and a clerk immediately
cranked his telephone handle three short and two long.

In the duty room of the White Wolf Society, five men
waited near the telephone. 'That is our signal,' Shibata
said. 'Mung has arrived. After he sends Hiroki aboard the
Korean ship, he will return alone. Then we ambush him.
Prepare yourselves!'

Each man examined his pistol.

'If I die before using this,' Shibata held out a traditional
samurai short sword, 'use it to cut off Mung's right hand
and cleave his skull down the middle. Stick the sword in
his chest! That is the traditional punishment for traitors.'

The four men bowed, and followed Shibata to waiting
rickshaws. They were drawn in single file through the
empty streets, unaware they were being followed.

Shibata dismissed the rickshaws at the port and led his
men up the road towards the promontory and the harbour
master's office. At a bend in the path, they took cover on
either side.

A little way behind, Uraga whispered to Yaka and
Shimatzu. 'What are they doing out here? I thought we
would catch them in the port area.'

'We cannot approach closer without being seen or heard,'
Yaka said.

'I think they are after my father,' Shimatzu said. 'He
had planned to see Hiroki off, then return home. But, as a
safeguard, he decided to embark with Hiroki. They sail on
the harbour master's pilot boat to board the Korea-bound
ship on its way out of port.'

'Is Mung going to Korea?' Uraga asked.

'He will direct the ship to rendezvous with the Saeki mailboat to the Ryukyu islands,' Shimatzu said. 'General Nogi, Admiral Takamora and the fleet are on Okinawa. From there they will sail to Formosa.'

'We must wait here until Shibata realizes Mung is not returning,' Uraga said.

'He should as soon as he sees the running lights of the outbound ship,' Shimatzu said. 'Then he and his friends will have to come back past us. The insult to our mother will be avenged!'

In the harbour master's office even the ringing telephone did not wake Hiroki Ishikawa.

'Your ship is casting off now,' the harbour master said to Mung. 'We had better start down to the pilot boat. You will be picked up next to the number one buoy at the harbour entrance.'

'Hiroki, wake up.' Mung shook his grandson. 'It is time to leave.'

The young man opened his eyes. In the harsh light of the overhead electric bulb his grandfather's face appeared severe, although his eyes were forgiving.

Mung placed a case into Hiroki's hands. 'Read this, about your mother. We can talk about it aboard ship. Quickly now, follow me.'

The moment Mung, Hiroki and the harbour master left the building, the White Wolf agent exited by the opposite door. He hurried down the path to warn his colleagues that their quarry was escaping.

Shibata signalled to the other side of the path, pointing to the oncoming figure. The clerk was ten feet away when Shibata jumped up and pointed his pistol. 'Die, Fishmonger,' he cried, and all the guns fired. The clerk was dead before he fell, but muscle spasms kept his body jerking. The five circled him and continued shooting.

'Enough,' Shibata ordered.

'What should we do now?'

All stared at the still figure lying face down on the ground. They looked at each other. Suddenly Shibata's followers turned and fled down the hill.

Shibata removed his short sword from its scabbard and hacked off the dead man's right hand. He turned the body over to position the head so he could split the skull, and looked into the face. It was not Mung. He turned to flee, but from the path below heard shots. Shibata ducked behind a bush and peeked out. His four friends lay dead. He dropped to his knees, body trembling.

Voices floated up from below. 'Where is he?'

'Not this one either.'

'They are looking for me,' Shibata mumbled. Shaking too much to stand, he crawled over the mutilated body of the clerk. He scratched and scrambled his way up the path on all fours, towards the lights of the harbour master's office.

Aboard the Korea-bound ship, Mung and Hiroki were billeted in separate cabins. Mung restricted Hiroki to quarters until he had read the material in the writing case.

The first day passed. The young man only stared at the teakwood box. He placed his food tray on it, and left everything untouched. On the morning of the second day, he put his breakfast tray on the floor and opened the case.

A note from Mung lay on top. 'Your mother is one of the finest and bravest people I have ever known. The sacrifices she made for her parents, Japan and the Emperor are common knowledge to most Japanese through the books, plays and poems you will find here. Your mother is a legend in her own lifetime. That she did not tell you of her past was not from shame, but because of her humble nature. Your father is the one who told your brothers, and they

142

accepted it. I have seen lords bow before your mother. The Emperor's sister, Princess Atsu, wrote about her in the Book of Good Deeds. I suggest you begin there.'

Hiroki twice withdrew his hand before he summoned the courage to pick up the book. When he did, he found it was not indexed. He scanned through heroic, noble and self-sacrificing deeds of many men before he found his mother's name:

Gin-ko Ishikawa, born 1852, Kagoshima, fiefdom of Satsuma, southern island of Kyushu. Former courtesan, Yoshiwara, Tokyo. Married 1873 to Udo Ishikawa.

In Kagoshima an assassination attempt was made on the life of Gin-ko's mother-in-law, Ukiko Ishikawa, who was eight months pregnant. They were attacked by three Yakuza, led by one known to the police as the Golden Lizard. Gin-ko positioned herself in defence of her mother-in-law. She distracted one of the assassins by throwing her knife, which enabled her husband to kill him. Another attacker knocked the unarmed Gin-ko aside and was killed by her husband. But the dead man fell across the pregnant Ukiko, causing the immediate onset of a premature delivery. Under these harrowing conditions, Gin-ko assisted the doctor in the difficult delivery of the child, Shimatzu. The mother died with Gin-ko's promise to raise the boy as her son. Two Yakuza and Gin-ko's aged female guardian died in the attack.

Gin-ko Ishikawa's second commendation is for her support of the men of Sapporo, on the northern island of Hokkaido. In the winter of 1874, Baron Benzowsky led a fleet of Russian pirates into Sapporo harbour to burn, pillage and raze the city. The fortifications of the defenders were inadequate, their cannon antiquated and outnumbered. When all appeared lost, a cold wave forced the pirates to abandon their ships. They took to the ice and attacked the city. Although in her final month of pregnancy, Gin-ko Ishikawa armed the women of Sapporo with sharpened sticks and led them to face the enemy. This action so encouraged the men of Sapporo, they went out onto the ice and defeated the pirates.

Hiroki closed the Book of Good Deeds carefully. The woman he had only thought of as his loving mother was becoming larger than life to him. He went on to read poems written for her, newspaper articles praising her as Japan's most valiant woman.

He began to read the summary of a play that depicted his mother's childhood in Kagoshima:

Her father, a gentle person, physically weak and easily influenced, makes foolish investments. His life savings, home and property are not enough to satisfy his debts. He and his wife are sent to prison. Gin-ko, although only sixteen, realizes her father's poor health will not see him through the sentence. She goes to the Yoshiwara and sells herself to a house of prostitution for the money to release her parents. They are freed, and supported by Gin-ko, who goes on to become the most celebrated courtesan in Tokyo. Her father, who never fully recovers from his prison experience, dies when Gin-ko is nineteen. Her mother passes away shortly after. Immediately Gin-ko ceases her activities in the Yoshiwara, and makes arrangements to enter a Buddhist monastery as a nun. Udo Ishikawa, son of the Minister of Maritime Services, meets Gin-ko through his adoptive mother. He follows Gin-ko to Kagoshima, courts and marries her. In the final act of the play, the bride and groom make a formal visit to the mother-in-law and the Yakuza attack takes place. The play ends with Gin-ko holding the newborn child over its dead mother, vowing to raise the boy as her own.

Tears coursed down Hiroki's cheeks. He replaced the scroll in the writing case and left the cabin to seek Mung.

'Grandfather, may I keep the stories about Mother?' Hiroki asked.

Mung waved his consent.

'I am still confused,' Hiroki said. 'In these last hours of reading I peered through a window at a person I love very much, and I saw her as great. But I also saw that she performed indecent acts.'

'You and I have a problem,' Mung said. 'We were educated by Christians. That makes it difficult for us to understand the Japanese concept that sex is not sinful. My western upbringing in Massachusetts complicated matters for me when I returned to Japan. At least I grew up here.

144

In that, I have an advantage over you. In my fishing village sex was not hidden, whether it took place inside or outside the family. When my mother had her monthly cycle, she selected a woman for my father. Saiyo, my first wife, and her sister, Ukiko, both selected women for me. I chose to abstain because of my Christian upbringing, but I know that sex is more open, healthier and enjoyable in Japan. What Christians call sin, we Japanese take as a natural course of human needs. Incidents of rape are almost unheard of here. There is the annual Penis Festival at the Tagata shrine. And the Ososo Matsuri, the Vagina Festival, at the Inuyzana shrine. Sexual intercourse was a form of prayer in an agricultural society such as ours once was. We seeded the ground for food, and our women to perpetuate our race. Industrialization is changing our lives and morals.' Mung smiled at Hiroki. 'I gather you too have had a change of heart about your mother.'

'I would like to write and apologize to her,' Hiroki said.

'Do it after breakfast. I will mail it from Okinawa. This ship will not touch shore until it reaches the Korean port of Inchon. You must be starved. You have not eaten in twenty-four hours.'

Hiroki was warmed by the thought that his grandfather cared enough to have him watched so closely. He bowed. 'Thank you for your patience and understanding. There are questions I have about my assignment in Seoul.'

'Over breakfast,' Mung said.

At three that afternoon the rendezvous was made with the Saeki mail-boat in the Bungo strait. A longboat was lowered for Mung.

Hiroki bowed to his grandfather and handed him four letters. 'For my mother and brothers.'

'I am pleased you thought of them,' Mung said. 'I had

hoped you might find some words for Noriko. It is permitted before a mi-ai.'

Grandfather wishes me to marry her, Hiroki thought. I want to marry her. I am certain I have given her sufficient cause to deny my suit, but I owe it to the old man to go through with the mi-ai, even if I am rejected.

Mung turned to the officer in the longboat. 'I will be a few moments.' He led Hiroki to the bow of the ship and put his arm around his grandson's shoulders. 'Your mother is ill,' Mung said.

Hiroki looked into his grandfather's eyes and saw pain. He was afraid. 'What is wrong?'

'Your mother is dying of cancer.'

'But that cannot be,' Hiroki said. 'She never told me anything.'

'She thinks no one else knows. I kept it from Shimatzu and your brothers. I am obliged to inform your father when we meet in Formosa.'

'I must go to her and apologize.'

'You cannot,' Mung said. 'She wishes no one to know. That is why I allowed you to write the letter before telling you. If you had known, she would have sensed it.'

'Who will care for her? How much time does she have?'

'She has the finest physicians in the empire. Noriko is with her. The last thing I did before leaving was to arrange for her doctor to consult with the surgeon general of the American fleet. Everything possible is being done.'

'My assignment in Korea, will it be finished before Mother . . .' Hiroki could not go on.

'No one knows exactly how long these things take. But you must see your mission through. It is Chu, an obligation to the Emperor.'

Tears welled up in Hiroki's eyes. He opened his mouth to speak and choked. 'I must tell her I am sorry,' he gasped.

Mung tapped the letters. 'You already have. If you

need a source of strength to help you carry on, read the stories again.'

Hiroki drew himself up, and bowed. 'Grandfather, I thank you for allowing me the privilege of serving the Emperor. And the opportunity to bring honour to our family.'

Mung stepped back and smiled. 'As a boy I learned an American whaler's cry that was only given when a great whale was sighted. Town-ho! We would gather in the bow and watch the majestic creature swim through the water. No matter how many times I heard the cry or saw a whale, I never ceased to be thrilled by one of God's special creations. Grandson, I look at you now and I am proud. Town-ho, young one.'

Chapter 16

Weeks had passed since Mung's arrival in Okinawa. The troops had been drilled in manoeuvres based on information sent by Udo from Formosa. Naval commanders had trained their crews in landing procedures and ship-to-shore artillery support. The captains had familiarized themselves with charts of the waters around Formosa. Now, the five-ship flotilla cruised a mile off the Formosan shore with lights out, waiting for a rendezvous. Mung looked forward to seeing Udo.

At 2 a.m. a sampan bumped the side of the flagship and Mung heard steps on the boarding ladder. He saw the officer of the deck salute.

Captain Togo strode onto the deck, marched directly to Mung and bowed. 'Sir. We are prepared to attack the pirate compound tomorrow night.'

'I expected Udo.'

'He had last-minute arrangements to attend. He looks forward to seeing you and hearing about his son's wedding.'

'I have much to tell him,' Mung said. 'Come with me, Captain Togo. Admiral Takamora and General Nogi await your report.'

In the ship's stateroom, the four men sat around a table covered with charts.

'These are street guides to the city of Pingtung,' Togo said. 'The others are harbour maps with the buoys marked to guide you to the landing spot in the port. There are no fighting ships, Chinese or western, in this area.'

'Where are the pirates?' Takamora asked.

'There are two hundred armed men in a compound next to a Buddhist temple. Here,' he pointed to the map. 'Udo bribed the contractor in charge of temple repairs. If our plan is correctly implemented, we should take the pirates by surprise. When I signal Udo, wooden steps will be set against the wall bordering the compound. Tunnels are already dug and the wall has been weakened in several places to allow our troops to break through. The pirates will be celebrating in honour of their chief, with large quantities of opium and alcohol supplied by Udo.' Togo handed around another set of detailed maps. 'These are diagrams of the compound.'

'Before we look at these, are we agreed to attack tomorrow night?' Mung asked.

Nogi and Takamora nodded.

Togo addressed the chiefs of staff. 'Please have the maps copied for your infantry officers and ships' captains.'

'You are to be commended for thorough preparations,' Nogi said.

'These are Udo Ishikawa's plans,' Togo replied. 'I have been aboard the flagship of the Chinese Penyang fleet as a waiter in the officers' mess.' He saw the startled expressions and added, 'It was arranged by Udo through a Chinese tong chief. Everything and almost everyone in China is for sale. Prince Kung is in Amoy waiting for you to negotiate and give him the remainder of his bribe. I overheard a Chinese naval officer say the English Lord Cade visited the prince.'

'The Englishman is on our side,' Mung explained. 'If we are successful in Pingtung tomorrow night, we should have an easy time of it in Amoy.'

'What else have you learned of the Chinese navy, Captain Togo?' Takamora asked.

'The enlisted men are well trained by German naval advisers, but morale is low. The officers are mostly ineffective aristocrats who purchased their rank from politicians. Admiral Ting Ju-Chang, brother of General

Li Hung-Chang, is a dedicated officer who hates Japanese and whites. He refers to us as dwarfs.'

'You heard him say this?' Nogi said.

'In the officers' mess,' Togo answered. 'We must soon war with China. I beg of you to give me command of a fighting ship. I will sink them before they run up their battle flag!'

'But what of the new warships and the expanded Penyang fleet you reported on several months ago?' Mung asked.

'The three battle cruisers are new to the Chinese navy, but they are only reconditioned French warships with the original armour plate and cannon. The new repeating 20mm British naval shells we have ordered will pierce them.'

'How can that be?' Takamora asked. 'Those ships, even if reconditioned, should carry the latest equipment. I have the plans and a copy of the sales contract. The documents were purchased from the French by the White Wolf Society.'

'Chinese politicians pocketed the money,' Togo said. 'The ships delivered were not what the Chinese paid for. Someone was bribed. Corruption of Chinese politicians and high-ranking military men is driving Admiral Ting and General Li mad. Most of the sailors in the Penyang fleet have not been paid for months because the politicians are pocketing the money. The little cash that filters through is taken by the officers. To stop mass desertions, Admiral Ting has ordered his captains to run private ferry services to earn money for their crews.'

The three older men were aghast. 'Ferrying people with fighting ships?' Nogi said.

'Livestock and farm produce also,' Togo replied.

'Gentlemen, I believe Captain Togo has earned the right to command a fighting ship,' Mung said. 'But if my plans are successful, he will never have to use it in action.'

'I will grant the captain a small fighting ship,' Takamora said. 'He shall command the twenty new torpedo-boats we have ordered from England. Captain Togo, you are hereby appointed commander of the newly formed Torpedo-boat Squadron with the rank of commodore. You will proceed to Canton and take possession of the first five torpedo-boats in your new squadron.

'The small torpedo-boats carry two rapid fire 20mm cannon in addition to the latest English shallow-draught one-ton torpedoes,' Takamora said.

Togo bowed. 'They called us dwarfs.' He grimaced. 'But we shall be twenty sharks against that fat-bellied blowfish when the time comes.'

'It is time to review final preparations for the landing in Pingtung harbour,' Mung said.

The following evening fifty of Admiral Takamora's marines, dressed in civilian clothes, landed outside Pingtung and made their way to designated points around the pirate compound. At the stroke of midnight, the marines set up roadblocks to stop anyone from approaching.

Udo had bribed the harbour master and local police to act as guides for Nogi's landing force. They waited in the darkness of a cloud-covered sky with several Pingtung policemen.

'It is after midnight,' Udo said. 'Where are they?'

'The ship is blacked out,' Togo replied. 'We will not be able to see them until they are upon us.'

At 1 a.m. the Chinese harbour master's pilot boat pulled in. 'So sorry to say your flagship has run aground.' He smiled, pointed into the darkness towards the northern end of the port and giggled. 'Your fleet is lost.'

'Have they put any troops ashore?' Togo asked.

'A few, but they cannot find themselves on the maps. You had better hurry. They are frustrated and angry.'

Udo, Togo and the police guides jumped aboard the pilot boat. Even in darkness, the harbour master knew exactly where to steer.

A nervous Japanese guard shouted at the approaching boat until Togo called the password. He and Udo were taken aboard the grounded flagship, where Mung, Takamora and Nogi waited on deck.

'The harbour master assures me the ship is in no danger,' Udo said. 'In the morning high tide will float you off. You can send the men ashore from here in longboats. I have guides to lead them.'

'Prepare to disembark,' Nogi roared to his officers.

'Somone had better lead us,' Takamora growled. 'I cannot see my hand in front of my face.'

'We are already an hour past our scheduled attack time,' Udo said.

'Keep calm and to your plan as much as possible,' Mung ordered. 'Do not allow anyone to panic! We want as little bloodshed as possible!'

Togo bowed to Mung and Udo. 'The longboats are lowered. We must go!'

'I am a bit old for this,' Udo mumbled. He stepped into the waiting rickshaw, and raised his arm. The column of five hundred Japanese soldiers trotted behind the rickshaw through the streets of Pingtung, headed towards the Buddhist temple.

At 5 a.m. the troops were finally in position.

'Let us get this circus over with before anything else goes wrong,' Udo growled.

At Togo's signal, men lowered themselves over the temple wall. Others crawled up out of the tunnels. They knocked out the last stones in the wall barring their entrance, and achieved a complete surprise. Japanese soldiers prodded pirates awake with fixed bayonets. The opium and alcohol had done their job.

When the sun brightened the city of Pingtung, 194 bandits were lined up in the compound.

'What the hell you doing this for?' the pirate chief, a big-bellied Mongol, demanded. He threw a pouch of gold at Udo's feet. 'If that's not enough, tell me how much you want.'

'We are taking you and your men to the Chinese mainland to stand trial for killing sixty-three Ryukyun fishermen.'

'That was six goddamned months ago,' the Mongol shouted. 'And what's a few fucking Ryukyuns to China! You got more people than you need!'

'We are not Chinese,' Udo said. 'You are being escorted by the imperial Japanese army, the first time in three hundred years we have landed on foreign soil! If your men do not march quickly to our ships, you will all go down in history as the first to be killed by our troops!'

In Admiral Takamora's stateroom, Mung addressed the four men responsible for planning and implementing the Pingtung operation. 'Before General Ryochi Okuda died, he evaluated his military career as having accomplished more by mistake than on purpose. We can apply his statement to the action in Pingtung.'

'Admiral Takamora and I accept responsibility for the mistakes,' General Nogi said. 'They were due to our inexperience. We were not aware of the detailed information required for such an operation. Things such as tides, currents and weather conditions did not seem important because we had steamships. You were correct to tell Count Hideyoshi we were not prepared for ship-to-shore transfer of troops. Without the assistance of the Black Dragons on shore, and if the town elders of Pingtung had not directed their villagers to help our grounded flagship off the mud flat, the entire operation would have been an unmitigated disaster. It is clear our intelligence-gathering organizations should be expanded, and our military must study the principles of modern warfare.'

'I agree we should prepare for a defensive war,' Mung said. 'But it is wasteful to fire bullets when words will do.'

'We respect your opinions despite having been on opposite sides of the conference table,' Takamora said. 'It is your naive concept that Japan can grow economically without military conflict that puts us in opposition.'

'How long would negotiations take?' Nogi asked.

'Prince Kung is anxious,' Udo replied. 'He is in debt and does not want General Li or Admiral Ting involved before he signs the agreement.'

'Could the Dowager Empress annul the treaty?' Nogi asked.

'She would lose her part of the squeeze,' Udo said.

'Do you mean the Empress receives a percentage of the bribe?' Takamora asked.

'She is our guarantor,' Udo replied. 'The old woman is building a new summer palace. She is also in debt.'

'Where is the Chinese sense of national pride?' Nogi said.

'The rulers of China are Manchus,' Udo said. 'Chinese nationalistic movements do exist – led by sons of middle-class merchants. One of the most popular groups is called the Harmonious Fist. They are also known as Boxers. They seek to eject foreigners and reorganize their government. It is said the Chang brothers secretly support the Boxers.'

'China's political arena sounds like a snake pit,' Nogi said. 'Admiral Takamora and I will gladly leave the negotiating to you two. We shall see to re-evaluating ship-to-shore landing procedures on foreign soil. If those bandits had been armed and alert, our bones would be bleaching in the mud of Pingtung harbour.'

Chapter 17

Aboard the Japanese flagship on the way to Amoy in the Formosan strait, Udo slept for twenty uninterrupted hours. Then, at breakfast, Mung told him of Shimatzu's bachelor party and wedding, but did not mention the incident between Shibata and Hiroki. Mung dreaded telling Udo about Gin-ko's illness, but the time had come.

'Is something troubling you?' Udo asked. 'If it has to do with the negotiations, be at ease. The latest report from the tong chief indicates things are in order.'

'It is not that,' Mung said. 'It has to do with Gin-ko's health.'

'Is she alive?'

'Your wife is very ill. Count Iyeasu's personal physician diagnosed cancer throughout her body.'

'Is she alive?' Udo asked again.

'Yes, but time is short.'

'I had hoped to be with her at the end.'

'You know!'

'The Korean doctor told me,' Udo said. 'Gin-ko and I discussed the situation. She is more frightened of pity than death.'

'You are two brave people,' Mung said. 'I think of Gin-ko as my daughter. It is not fair!'

'The gods are not concerned with justice,' Udo said. 'They demand duty, honour and sacrifice.'

'What can I do?' Mung asked.

'Gin-ko worries most about Hiroki. He needs a strong hand to guide him. His physical and intellectual talents are obvious. Because of his quick wit and mature manner, most people forget he is only twenty years old. Gin-ko worries

155

his impatience with others will lead him into trouble. She loves Yaka and Uraga but feels confident they are steady young men who will find wives and travel a relatively straight path in life.'

'Gin-ko would like to see Hiroki married, is that it?' Mung said.

'For two weeks after we learned of Shimatzu's wedding it was like a miracle. She had no weakness or dizzy spells. It would set her mind at ease to see Hiroki wed to the right woman.'

'What is your opinion of Noriko?' Mung asked.

'You know her better than I do. Is she a strong personality? If not, Hiroki would walk all over her. He was that way as a child. Very headstrong. The type of child who ages parents quickly. He tried walking when learning to crawl and ran when learning to walk. Whenever we heard him say "Whoops", we knew he had smashed something or hurt himself.'

'Very few people frighten Noriko. She will be a good match for Hiroki and Gin-ko's wish will come true. The moment these negotiations are complete, you and I will take the fastest boat in the fleet for home. If the bargaining is a protracted affair, I will send you back on a private ship. I want you to be with your wife.'

According to Mung's request, only he and Udo received Lord Malcolm Cade, unaccompanied, aboard the Japanese flagship cruising outside the port of Amoy. Long ago Mung had discovered that Englishmen are formal in the presence of their countrymen. On their own, he had found, they have a sense of humour, are more open and likely to reveal themselves.

'Did Prince Kung mention contact with the tong chief of Amoy?' Udo asked Lord Cade.

'He spoke of the tong chief's offer of a three-million-yen bribe. I advised him to demand four. That will leave the Amoy tong-men one million yen of the five you gave them.'

'If Prince Kung agrees to a cash indemnity to cede the Ryukyus and grant banking rights on Formosa, we will be satisfied,' Udo said.

'But you should ask for more concessions, then allow Kung to save face when you take less,' Lord Cade said.

'Our request shall be as you suggest,' Mung said. 'But tell me what kind of person this Chinese nobleman is.'

'He looks like a popeyed sallow-faced tadpole,' Lord Cade said. 'But do not underestimate him. He is a thirty-year survivor as Tsungili Yamen, a title comparable to the head of Britain's foreign office. Prince Kung's duration of tenure in Chinese politics is considered extraordinary. His philosophy is simple – kill all potential enemies. And it has worked for him.'

'Where will the negotiations take place?' Mung asked.

'I have arranged for the prince to board a German cruiser in this port. You will board a French man-of-war. The talks shall take place aboard both ships. The French and German consuls will act as mediators and guarantors to the agreement so that international recognition of Japan's rights to the Ryukyus can be immediate.'

'Will you be present?' Udo asked.

'I have personally intervened on Japan's behalf,' Lord Cade said. 'More involvement by me or my subordinates would be overly conspicuous. We seek a quick solution to a problem which has already been resolved.'

'Are the negotiations just a formality then?' Udo asked.

'We British have a saying. One must put on a good show.'

'But will Britain join France and Germany in recognizing Japan's rights to the Ryukyu islands?'

'The moment Prince Kung signs, England's approval is automatic. If, as you say, Russia and America have agreed

157

to acknowledge Japan's rights, then your Emperor will soon own several additional islands.'

Mung and Udo stood on the quarterdeck with Takamora and Nogi, watching the Formosan pirates trail after their sullen Mongol leader. The bandits were led off the warships and onto Chinese barges manned by soldiers from the Amoy garrison.

'I am glad to be rid of them,' Takamora said. 'This ship is not meant to be a troop carrier.'

'Sir, a French launch is coming alongside,' the officer of the deck reported.

'That is for you two,' Nogi said to Mung and Udo. 'But I feel uneasy about pulling our ships out during the negotiations.'

'The westerners guarantee our safety,' Mung said.

'My fastest ship will remain to patrol the mouth of the harbour,' Takamora said. 'We shall take advantage of the British offer and refuel at Foochow. It will give me an opportunity to see Admiral Ting's naval base. We should return in two days with our coal bunkers full and prepared for a straight run to Tokyo.'

Neither Nogi nor Takamora mentioned the message they had received from Hideyoshi, their first contact with the White Wolf since leaving Kobe. Based on the count's instructions, they would delay Mung whether he succeeded or failed in the negotiations.

Mung and Udo were piped aboard the French frigate and hosted by the captain to a sumptuous meal. Launches from the German and French ships shuttled back and forth across Amoy harbour, carrying greetings from the Chinese, the Japanese demands and questions of clarification.

'A Chinese court will judge the Formosan pirates and implement justice,' Prince Kung wrote. He made mention of Mung's demands that reparations be paid for the dead

158

Okinawan fishermen. It was a positive step towards recognition of Japan's rights to the Ryukyu islands.

The next morning at 6 a.m., the harbour master's signal gun boomed over Amoy harbour. It was followed by the sounds of kettle drums, cymbals and trumpets. Mung and Udo joined the French captain on the bridge. The noise grew louder and crowds of people swarmed down to the docks. A column of soldiers appeared flanking the Formosan bandits.

'They are parading the pirates through the city,' the French captain said. 'I have witnessed this type of execution before.' He pointed to the southern end of the port. 'They will take them to that beach.'

'What are the pirates carrying?' Mung asked.

'Their own crucifixes,' the captain replied. 'Their hands are tied to the crossbars. Holes will be dug in the sand, the men will be strangled, then the crucifixes set in the holes. The bodies will be left to rot.'

'If I were a captive I would offer some form of resistance,' Udo said. 'To die fighting is better than helping your executioners.'

'If you count the pirates, I am certain you will find less than the 194 you captured. The Chinese take several the night before and practise their torture methods in front of the others. Then they offer the condemned men opium. Those prisoners you see are in a dream-world.'

'They are going to wake up dead,' Udo said.

'I would prefer not to watch the execution,' Mung said, and went below-deck.

Hours later Udo entered the cabin. 'It is over. The shore line has a new forest of dead men.'

'I would prefer another solution to stop bandits from terrorizing innocent people,' Mung said.

'I would have displayed the bodies in all the ports the pirates raided.'

'I sense Prince Kung is rushing to conclude these negotiations before General Li or Admiral Ting are informed.'

'Something else is happening,' Udo said. 'The German consul's launch went ashore for Prince Kung. He is aboard the German cruiser. The French and Russian consuls are aboard too.'

'The Russians? Why are they involved?'

There was a sharp knock on the door.

'Gentlemen, you have been invited by the Tsungili Yamen to a meeting,' the French captain said. 'I believe Prince Kung wishes to accelerate the pace of these negotiations. Are you prepared to leave now?'

'I request that my son Udo be sent ashore,' Mung said. 'He is not well.'

'The ship's surgeon is at your service,' the captain said.

'My son is accustomed to the Oriental art of acupuncture. He suffers from a chronic back condition that responds well to that form of treatment.'

'As you wish,' the captain said. 'I will wait on deck.'

The cabin door closed and Udo turned to Mung. 'What is it you wish me to do ashore?'

'I was testing to see if we are prisoners. In addition I want you to contact the local tong chief and find out whatever you can. Especially why the Russians are involved.'

'Be careful in the negotiations alone,' Udo said.

The German officers and men in formation on the cruiser's deck saluted as Mung was piped aboard. The captain personally escorted Mung to the stateroom where the British, French, German and Russian consuls sat on either side of a long table. At its head, on a chair raised several inches higher than the others, sat Prince Kung. Lord Cade's description of the Chinese nobleman was accurate – the sucked-in cheeks, shaven forehead and bulging eyes reminded Mung of a newborn tadpole. His black silk robe was embroidered on the shoulders to make him appear broader. Mung bowed.

The prince motioned Mung to a place at the opposite end of the table. Mung took his seat, wondering why the British consul was present. Lord Cade had said he would not be represented.

'Gentlemen, I have the honour to present the Tsungili Yamen, Prince Kung,' the German consul said. He introduced Mung next as the personal representative of the Emperor of Japan, then presented each consul.

'Sir,' Prince Kung said to Mung, 'how is it you appear alone at these negotiations? And you have come to this table without a copy of your country's demands or my recommendations.'

All eyes turned on Mung.

'Your excellency, my son, who acts as my deputy, went ashore to be treated for a persistent malady,' Mung said. 'He seeks the help of the able Chinese practitioners of acupuncture. We Japanese are aware that the root of all Asian medicine is to be found in the academies of China.' The prince nodded his approval at the compliment and Mung added, 'I have memorized the necessary documents.'

'In such a crucial negotiation you would trust your memory?' the prince said.

'I am sixty-seven years old and it has never failed me yet.'

'Very well.' The prince looked around the table. 'Please turn to page five, paragraph three.'

'The English translation begins with a reference to China,' Mung said. 'China shall recognize Japan's rights to the entire length of the island of Formosa, which is known as extending from the southern end of Swatow to the northern end of Foochow on the mainland. Chinese vessels in distress shall be afforded landing rights to make repairs, take shelter and purchase food. They are to leave as soon as possible.'

'Remarkable,' the British consul said. 'The reading is exactly as I have it.'

Mung's recital of the Japanese translation was confirmed by the prince's interpreter.

'I cannot speak Chinese, but I have the ability to recall the characters,' Mung said.

The prince pointed at his interpreter and the man placed a writing kit before Mung. All at the table watched the brush flick back and forth, up and down the page. The interpreter compared the characters to the original and nodded to Prince Kung.

'I would not have believed any man could have such faith in his memory,' the prince said. 'Mine is influenced by my expectations.'

'I was born with this ability,' Mung said. 'It is always there.'

'Even so, I prefer not to put too much of a strain on your ability to recall,' the prince said. 'The main points of your demands are that China cede control of the Ryukyu islands, of Formosa, and that we pay Japan a twenty-million-dollar indemnity for the deaths of sixty-three Ryukyuns.'

'That is my country's position,' Mung said.

Prince Kung smiled and his bulging eyes rolled. 'Let us discuss these issues.'

Back aboard the French warship, Udo found Mung alone in his cabin staring out the porthole. 'Is something wrong?'

'I am not certain,' Mung said, turning to face Udo. 'The Chinese accepted all our demands,' he said in a bewildered voice. 'They have given us Formosa! The westerners smiled and confirmed Japan's sovereignty over Okinawa and Formosa, plus the twenty-million-dollar indemnity to be deposited in the British bank at Hong Kong!'

Udo's eyes opened wide. 'I sensed something was going on, but never expected this. How can they give away so much, so quickly.'

162

Mung shook his head. 'I do not know. Most of the time was spent on ceremony and congratulations. Prince Kung listed our demands, I confirmed them and he said they are acceptable. The documents were signed exactly as we presented them. I was in shock. The French captain led me back here by the hand like a child. I have been watching for the return of our fleet.'

'They arrived three hours ago and are hove to outside the harbour.'

'I must talk with Takamora and Nogi to see if they can make sense of what has happened. Did you contact the tong chief?'

'Yes. He said Lord Cade offered Prince Kung a loan of twenty million dollars to pay our demands. In addition, he bribed the prince with another million dollars above the four million yen we put up so China would cede every point to us.' Udo let out a deep breath. 'I almost called the tong chief a liar.'

Aboard the Japanese flagship, Mung addressed General Nogi and Admiral Takamora. 'I went to meet Prince Kung with a fear of being hoodwinked. I returned with everything and feel as if I have been swindled. We only asked for Formosa as a bargaining point suggested by Lord Cade.'

'From what Udo said, it appears to be Lord Cade who manipulated the negotiations from behind the scenes,' Nogi said.

'How do the English benefit from lending money to China and Japan?' Udo asked. 'What do they get from our control over the Ryukyus and Formosa?'

'I do not know,' the general said. 'But when the time is right, I am certain Lord Cade will inform us. For now, you are both to be congratulated.'

'When the copies of the signed treaty are completed,' Mung said to Nogi and Takamora, 'I would appreciate having you both examine them. Udo and I will take the original back to Tokyo on the fastest ship in the fleet.'

'That will be the one patrolling the harbour entrance,' Takamora said. 'General Nogi and I will peruse the documents and hopefully gain some insight into Lord Cade's motives. We shall meet in Tokyo. We wish you a safe journey.'

Chapter 18

Hankow, China

'Strip,' the colonel ordered.

Shibata removed his shirt, shrugged off his shoulder braces and let his trousers fall.

'Underwear too!'

He stood naked before Colonel Honjo.

'If given a geographical choice to set up a spy network, where would it be?' the colonel asked.

'Manchuria borders China, Korea, Inner Mongolia and Russia,' Shibata said. 'Manchuria is the place from which to control those areas and stop the czar's army.'

'Do you expect the Russians to invade China?'

'They have already moved south from Vladivostok and will branch out along the route of the Trans-Siberian railway.'

'Very well,' Honjo said. 'During your time here in the Green House you will study Russian, Chinese and Mongolian.' The founder and chief of the White Wolf espionage school walked around the naked young man. 'You are well-muscled and sufficiently endowed between the legs. I hope there is more between your ears. Some women could find your wrinkled nose attractive. Are you interested in men?' Colonel Honjo slapped his riding crop against his leg and growled, 'Answer without hesitation!'

'I like women and have had sex with men,' Shibata said.

'Good. We shall teach you how to compromise both. You are here to learn the art of espionage, go into the field, apply your knowledge and instruct others. My students must be observant of everything, under any conditions! Treat nothing as trivial! Act without morals or scruples! Never, ever lie to me!' Honjo whipped the riding crop across Shibata's bare back, raising a red welt on the smooth skin.

'I situated the Green House in China for a purpose,' the colonel said. 'You will do things here that are unimaginable at home. You will learn to take advantage of men and women of every race. You will be exposed to all forms of sex in combination with drugs. You must learn how not to succumb! You will be taught how best to use these weapons against our enemies. Your training will begin every afternoon at three and end at midnight, seven days a week for eighteen months. From six every morning you will have lessons in observation, shorthand, codes, languages, cartography and photography.

'You should know that your decision to kill Mung was most influential on your recommendation to the Green House. The attempt was amateurish but your escape, leaving your dead friends behind, is the sign of a good agent. A spy is a survivor, not a hero.'

The door opened and a beautiful redheaded Caucasian woman entered, followed by a petite young blonde girl. Their long silk robes revealed the contours of well-formed bodies. They stood before Shibata but did not look at him.

'This young blonde miss is from Russia,' Colonel Honjo said. 'She was purchased as a virgin especially for an occasion such as this. Greta,' he touched the other woman's shoulder with the riding crop, 'was abandoned in Hankow by a German sea captain. The ladies are here to entertain you.' The colonel turned and strode from the room.

Shibata saw the two women's eyes begin to examine his body. The younger one stared wide-eyed at his resting penis. Greta looked at it as if at a piece of meat for sale on a butcher's block. She stared into Shibata's eyes as she dropped her robe. Her body was chalk white, the pubic hairs curly red. She brushed the long pink nipples of her small breasts against his nipples, and looked down.

Shibata's penis stood out from his body. Greta flicked the head with her long fingernails and he stumbled backwards to get away. She muttered something in German, then turned and pulled the robe off the girl. The young blonde shivered. She tried to hide her body. Shibata saw fear in her eyes.

Greta put her arms around the girl and hugged her, rubbing their bodies together. The girl struggled until she broke away. Her breasts heaved with the effort. Her small round stomach moved in and out over the silky golden hairs nestled between her milky-white thighs. The German woman grabbed the girl's arm, twisting it and pulling her close. She bent her head and suckled the young one's breast.

Shibata's golden rod throbbed. The blue vein pulsated down its length. He stepped behind Greta, kicked her legs out from under her and threw her aside. The blonde girl looked up at him with gratitude. Babbling in Russian, she leaned down to pick up her robe. Shibata grabbed her by the hair and pulled her to him. Her white skin was burning hot against his flesh. He pushed her down on the floor and spread her legs. The beautiful eyes stared, the mouth gaped as he pushed between her thighs and entered her body with a great thrust. She was tight. Like a charge of electricity, he knew he had a virgin. He pinned her shoulders to the floor. The more helpless the girl seemed, the more he desired her. He pressed forward and she screamed. His blood boiled. He drove his golden rod in and the girl screamed again, her face a mask of agony. Shibata laughed and rammed deeper. He withdrew almost the entire length and saw blood on his foreskin. In a frenzy of pushes and stabs, he plunged into the young girl again and again, and finally reached her most sensitive place. Her vagina secreted the honey-like fluid and her body worked in time to his. He climaxed with a shudder but his rod still throbbed. He withdrew from the honey-pot, threw the girl over and slipped back into her from behind. Greta caressed his testicles and it was good. He would have her later.

'Stand up and dress yourself!' Colonel Honjo threw a robe at Shibata.

He staggered to his feet, put on the silk dressing-gown and looked for the women.

'They performed their duty and left,' Honjo said. 'They compromised you, Mr Smart-arse Lieutenant. It is 9 a.m. and your first lesson was to begin at 6. Have a cigarette and sit down!'

Shibata accepted a cigarette with a wooden mouthpiece. He took a long pull, held the smoke in his lungs and let it out slowly. 'Sir, I respectfully ask you to excuse me,' he said, wondering at the strangely sweet smoky taste. He inhaled again. 'In the future I shall always be in control.' He saw the master spy smile. Shibata was about to learn that Honjo's happiness came from the misery of others.

'The little girl was not a virgin,' Honjo said. 'The blood and the hymen you so gloriously ruptured were fake.' He handed Shibata several photographs of him performing cunnilingus on the blonde while the other woman worked on him. 'If that little girl had as many cocks sticking out of her as she has had stuck in her, she would look like a porcupine.' Honjo leered. 'How much would you pay me not to send these photos to your family?'

Fear gripped Shibata's heart, yet his body felt strangely relaxed. He smiled at the colonel. 'A porcupine you say. Would you really show these awful pictures to my family?'

'You responded to those white women as most Orientals do. Let me tell you, it is all up here.' Honjo tapped his head. 'Orgasmic intensity has nothing to do with the colour of one's skin. It is related to expert lovemaking.'

Shibata leaned back. 'Orgasm has to do with this,' he

168

pointed between his legs and chuckled, 'not this,' he tapped his head.

The riding crop whistled through the air and caught Shibata on the shoulder. He shrugged it away but tears filled his eyes. He puffed on the cigarette. 'Why did you do that?'

'If you think with your cock instead of your head, you are worthless to the White Wolf Society and to Japan. An observant agent would have noticed that the young woman's pubic hairs are golden yellow. In blondes they are usually brownish. She dyes the hair with peroxide.' Honjo whipped Shibata again. 'Remember, nothing is trivial!'

Shibata let the sweet smoke drift out of his open mouth. He knew the colonel was giving him a lesson, but could not understand the point. The door opened and Honjo smiled again. Two Chinese girls carrying a cloth bag entered, followed by a tall effeminate white man dressed in a woman's robe.

Shibata heard Honjo's words as if from far away. 'For the second time in less than twelve hours you are compromised. The cigarette you cannot stop puffing contains an opium pellet in the mouthpiece. These three will punish you for your mistakes. I leave the method up to them. If you err again, they will be punished by me.' The colonel turned and left the room.

The two women disrobed and took a black leather contraption with buckles from the bag. The man sashayed towards Shibata. He was thin but big-boned, with rouged cheeks and coloured lips. He dropped his robe and Shibata saw his erect golden rod.

'Stay away from me,' Shibata shouted. He attempted to stand and could not. He fell off the chair and tried to crawl away but his legs tangled in his robe. The man behind him yanked the robe away. Shibata was naked and alone with these creatures.

* * *

169

'I am pleased to see you back in Tokyo with better news than I could have hoped for,' Count Hideyoshi said. He beamed at General Nogi and Admiral Takamora. 'How did you gain so much for just the lives of sixty-three Okinawan fishermen?'

'Mung is responsible for this success,' Takamora said. 'We had little to do with the negotiations.'

'No need to publicize that.' Hideyoshi smiled.

'Yes, there is,' Nogi said. 'We left Mung behind as you ordered. Not to steal his honour, but to prevent him from using this success to forestall preparations to invade Korea.'

Takamora stepped closer to Hideyoshi's desk. 'The general and I believe this success can be used to inspire support in Parliament and from the public for the Korean venture.'

'Our agents report General Li and Admiral Ting have sent additional troops to Seoul and ships to Inchon harbour,' Nogi said. 'Takamora and I are more convinced than ever that control of Korea is necessary for Japan's security.'

'So it is,' Hideyoshi said. 'And it shall be as you say. Mung will be given credit for the negotiations.' I know enough newspapermen to minimize Mung's role in the affair, he thought. 'But,' he pointed at Nogi, 'it was your troops who captured the pirates.' Hideyoshi pointed at Takamora. 'It was your ships which transported them to China without bloodshed. These things must also be told if we wish to recruit volunteers for the Korean expedition. How did you succeed in delaying Mung?'

'I put him and his son on the fastest ship in the fleet,' Takamora said. 'But it had been on patrol outside Amoy harbour during the negotiations and had not refuelled with my other vessels.'

'How long before Mung does reach Tokyo?'

'Five days.'

'Let us make good use of that time,' Hideyoshi said, cranking the telephone. 'Duty officer, this is the White Wolf,' he said into the receiver. 'There is a list of every member of Parliament in your card file. They are all to be notified to hold themselves ready for a special session of the National Diet tomorrow! Notify every newspaper that General Nogi, Admiral Takamora and the head of Japan's Armament Commission, Count Hideyoshi Koin, will be at the Yasukune shrine in two hours to make an important announcement!'

'Sir, is it war?' the duty officer asked.

'Not yet, but let us hope it will be soon. Send a man to sound the shogun's great war gong! Wake Tokyo! Japan is rising from a three-hundred-year sleep!' Hideyoshi replaced the receiver and looked up at the two senior officers. 'Twenty years ago was the last time the war gong sounded. The western naval fleet sailed into Tokyo harbour and destroyed our fortifications. They sank our ships and sullied the honour of Japan. Giri, gentlemen. Revenge, whether it takes twenty years or twenty hundred years. As long as there is an Emperor, there is a Japan. As long as there is a Japan, there will be Japanese to maintain our honour. Very soon we shall sail out of Tokyo harbour to begin the conquest of the Asian mainland. Then,' he stood up, 'then the westerners should beware the fiery rays of the rising sun!'

The three men faced the imperial flag and bowed.

Chapter 19

Imperial Palace, 7 June 1894

'Your father, Count Iyeasu, told me how well you have cared for my wife,' Udo said.

'Gin-ko's spirit keeps me strong,' Noriko said. 'It is a privilege to be with her.'

'May I see her now?'

'She is resting.' Noriko saw the concern in Udo's face and hastened to say, 'Your wife often goes shopping with me. She is an excellent cook and we share the housework.'

'I thought she was restricted to her room.'

Noriko smiled. 'Gin-ko is quite persistent. She will be most pleased to see you.'

'Have Yaka and Uraga visited their mother?'

'Every day until the return of the Formosan expedition, although since then they have been busy. Everyone is excited. The newspapers mention Mung and the wonderful treaty he negotiated.' Noriko saw Udo glance at the closed door. 'You may enter,' she said. 'Gin-ko will enjoy opening her eyes to you.'

Udo bowed so deeply that Noriko blushed. He rose up and said, 'When my youngest son returns there will be a mi-ai. I do hope Hiroki finds favour in your eyes.'

Noriko bowed and smiled weakly. She quietly slid the door open, and closed it behind Udo with her thoughts on the inevitability of having to marry Hiroki Ishikawa.

Udo approached Gin-ko. She slept on her back, the quilt drawn up to her chin. Her face was thin, her skin had a translucent quality. He admired her beauty, and listened to her shallow breath whispering through delicate lips. He could hardly distinguish the outline of her body under the

172

quilt. The desire to touch her and feel her warmth sent his hand forward. He gently rested it against her body. He gazed at her high forehead, arched brows and thin straight nose, remembering their first meeting on the Ginza. The love lion had clawed his heart the moment he saw her. Gin-ko, the most famous courtesan in the Yoshiwara. He had escorted Ukiko, Mung's second wife, and Gin-ko to a Kabuki theatre and acted like a love-struck country boy. He had risked his life to see her again and spent a night in the Tokyo jail because of it. Few people ever forgot the story of the valiant courtesan, twice mentioned in the Book of Good Deeds. Fewer yet knew that he had owned and managed a bordello in Canton for the Black Dragon Society and was considered a consummate lover. Udo laughed to himself. Tears ran down his cheeks. Nothing in his sophisticated experience had prepared him for Gin-ko. It was the difference between sex and love. He had never again been with another woman.

Udo felt a touch on his hand and he looked down. Gin-ko's beautiful tapered fingers intertwined with his. He looked into her anxious dark eyes.

'Do not weep,' she whispered. 'Come under the cover and let me hold you.'

Fully clothed, Udo slipped under the quilt. He pressed himself against his wife and embraced her. She pulled his face into the curve of her neck and he sobbed in great gulps.

Gin-ko caressed him. 'We must talk of our love,' she crooned. 'We must make plans.'

'The lights have burned steadily day and night in the palace, the Parliament and government buildings since word of the Formosan treaty reached Tokyo,' Iyeasu said.

'I was surprised by the enthusiastic reception at the dock,' Mung said.

'Takamora and Nogi may have left you behind, but

173

they publicly credited you with the success of the negotiations.'

'Do they still plan to invade Korea?'

'I have managed to hold them and Hideyoshi off in Parliament until your return. The members of both houses wait to hear you. There is a demand for a large indemnity from Korea for attacking our legation there. Others wish to use the twenty million dollars from the Chinese to sponsor an invasion of Korea.'

'Where exactly do you stand?' Mung asked.

'Show me how to halt the Russians from moving south through Manchuria into Korea. Or how to stop the Chinese from controlling Seoul and hopping the one-hundred-mile gap to Japan. Then I, and most others, will vote against the Korean adventure.'

'Can you see any connection between the Russian and Chinese moves into Korea and Lord Cade's bribing of Prince Kung?'

'The British are inscrutable,' Iyeasu said. 'What appears logical to them makes no sense to me. The English lord is no fool. He will want something in return from either China or Japan.'

'Or both,' Mung said. 'The American whalers I sailed with had a saying about the game of poker. To win you must know when to bet, when to hold and when to fold up and run.'

'Which method do you prefer now?'

'I choose to hold. The Englishman must come to me.'

'And in ten hours you are due to appear before Parliament. It will be like trying to stop a team of wild horses. Your success in Formosa has given our people a taste for the Korean venture, and Hideyoshi is fanning the flames. I suggest you rest until then.'

The two friends parted. Mung took a hot bath, ate a light meal and went to sleep. It seemed as if he had just closed his eyes when he was awakened by the sound of his door sliding open. He reached for his Colt .44 as two figures came through the door.

'Grandfather, it is Yaka and Uraga.'

Mung slipped his weapon under the quilt. 'Turn up the lamp.'

He admired Yaka in his army uniform and Uraga in navy blue. 'Very impressive. I am pleased to see you both.' He looked from one grandson to the other. 'I must tell you about your mother.'

'We know of her condition, but Mother is not aware we know,' Yaka said.

Mung doubted that. His daughter-in-law was the most sensitive person he had ever met. Mother and sons would go on pretending that all was well. Would it not be preferable for them to be able to talk about the truth? he thought. Mung realized the young men were looking at him expectantly.

'Grandfather, do you hear it?' Uraga pointed to the window.

Mung rose. 'You have caught me out. My excellent memory stays but my ears are deserting me.' He walked to the window and his skin prickled. The hair on his arms stood up. 'It is the great war gong of Tokyo.'

'Admiral Ting has devastated Nagasaki port,' Uraga said. 'Eighty people are dead and more wounded. The harbour area is burned.'

'Why would the Chinese fleet attack?' Mung asked.

'Reports to army intelligence indicate Admiral Ting took revenge for Prince Kung's extreme generosity to us in the Formosa agreement. Ting left an ultimatum. Either we renegotiate within a month in the neutral capital of Seoul, or he will burn the entire city of Nagasaki to the ground.'

'There is more,' Uraga said. 'Hiroki's last report to Black Dragon headquarters indicates a large number of Koreans are prepared to rebel.'

'To overthrow King and Queen Min?'

'The Chinese forced the king to send the Russians out of the capital. Many government bureaucrats and officers in the Royal Korean Army and Navy were being bribed by Russian gold. General Li and Admiral Ting stopped the corruption but antagonized some powerful people in the Korean government.'

'Things are happening too quickly,' Mung said. 'I need more time to prevent war.'

'Time is a luxury you do not have,' Iyeasu said as he entered the room. 'The Emperor has summoned his ministers to an emergency meeting. You and Hideyoshi will be questioned, and a decision made regarding war with China.'

'Am I to be held responsible for the raid on Nagasaki?' Mung asked.

'The majority of those who want war consider you a greater hero because of Nagasaki.'

Mung looked at his grandsons and saw the war fever in their eyes. It would be difficult to convince the ministers that peace was a sensible alternative. 'Boys, tell your father to take charge of the Black Dragon headquarters here in the palace,' he said. 'While I am closeted with the ministers, he must direct all agents to gather information relative to our landing troops in Korea.'

The Meiji Emperor's handcrafted golden throne rested on a raised platform covered in red velvet. It stood under a gold-embossed canopy supported by two silver lances. Iyeasu stood to the Emperor's right, the master of protocol to his left. Hideyoshi and Mung stood on either side of the dais, facing General Nogi, Admiral Takamora, and behind them the government ministers at attention in two rows of ten facing the Emperor.

'On 6 June 1894, Admiral Ting Ju-Chang led seven ships of the Penyang fleet into the port of Nagasaki,' the master of protocol announced. 'Chinese and Korean troops landed, eighty-one Japanese were killed and twice that number wounded. The governor of Nagasaki was dragged from his home and warned that if a delegation was not sent to the neutral city of Seoul within one month to renegotiate the recently signed Formosa agreement, Nagasaki would be levelled.'

The Emperor nodded to Iyeasu and the round man stood up. 'A full-scale debate in the National Diet could take two months or be decided in two emotional minutes,' Iyeasu said to the ministers. 'The Emperor asks you to consider the facts in the cold light of reality. Does the Chinese action in Nagasaki constitute a declaration of war? What should Japan's reaction be?' He turned to his left and nodded. 'Count Hideyoshi Koin will speak first.'

'There is no question that the attack is a clear act of war and should be answered in kind,' Hideyoshi said. 'Korea, not China, will be the battlefield. The Penyang fleet is based at Inchon. Korean soldiers took part in the attack on Nagasaki. General Li Hung-Chang is in Seoul with only two thousand troops. If we invade Korea now, we shall gain international recognition for our venture in light of the Nagasaki massacre.'

'Why fight China on Korean soil?' the Emperor asked.

'Sire, Japan's survival depends on our dramatic achievements overseas,' Hideyoshi said. 'Our population increase has been so great that within twenty years we will not be able to feed one fourth of our people unless we secure foreign colonies. If other nations control Japan's food supplies and our access to natural resources, we shall become their slaves.' His eyes swept the ministers and returned to the Emperor. 'The decisions made today reflect on the honour of our ancestors and the survival of our people.' He looked across the dais at Mung. 'For decades we have been told to imitate the West and modernize. Imperialism is a part of modernization.

Every major western nation employs cultural, economic and military imperialism. Now, when we wish to expand Japan's economic and military foundations abroad, there are those who speak against it.' Hideyoshi turned to Nogi and Takamora in front of the dais. 'Our military system is based on the Prussian model. Count von Moltke's dictum should be kept in mind. Perpetual peace is a dream. War is an element in the order of the world as ordained by the gods. Without war the world would stagnate. Von Moltke was correct. Scientists talk of survival of the fittest. We are the fittest in Asia and it is time we took our rightful place of leadership of the coloured peoples of the world. Sire.' Hideyoshi bowed to the Emperor. 'Our military can defeat the Chinese, the Koreans and some day the Russians. Your majesty, if a man raises a warning in time of peace, he is usually ignored. If he sounds the alarm in time of war, it is too late. I would rather be called a fool than a leader who failed to prepare his people to fight those who so blatantly attack us!'

In all the years Mung had known Hideyoshi, he had never heard him present so emotionally powerful and well thought out a speech. Mung thanked the gods that the Emperor had decided to circumvent the National Diet. In Parliament Hideyoshi's speech would have surely resulted in a declaration of war. Mung realized that unless he dissuaded the ministers, war was inevitable.

Iyeasu indicated it was Mung's turn to speak. He stepped forward. 'Prepare for war and seek peace.' Mung let a moment of silence emphasize his words. 'Voluntary interaction with our Asian neighbours is preferable to fighting them. A premature attack could mean disaster. Catastrophic consequences are a distinct possibility if the western nations intervene against us. The Europeans must be neutralized before any move can be made against China or Korea.

'At first glance the attack on Nagasaki appears to be a wanton act of war. But a second look reveals something else. It is no secret that I bribed Prince Kung. General Li and his brother Admiral Ting are angered by that. They cannot discipline or even admonish the prince, so they vent their rage against Japan. Our military described the attack on Nagasaki as a riot. It was a controlled riot, specifically limited to the harbour area. No big guns were used. Only the port was damaged. Admiral Ting's demand to meet in Korea reduces the possibility of friction between Japan and China. I accept Count Hideyoshi's prediction of starvation and unemployment if we do not secure overseas markets and natural resources. But these can be achieved by peaceful trade, as they were by the great mercantile nations of Great Britain, France and Spain.' Mung turned to face the Emperor. 'Sire, I negotiated one successful agreement with the Chinese. I humbly ask permission to try again. If I fail, there is no alternative but war.' He bowed and resumed his place.

Nogi and Takamora were called on to discuss military preparedness. Mung had spoken to both men prior to this meeting and reminded them of the fiasco on the mud flats of Pingtung harbour. 'I need time to seek a peaceful solution,' he had told them. 'You need time to prepare your forces.' Neither man had responded.

Now, Nogi said, 'The imperial army has six active divisions. Some time ago I instituted a military training programme for volunteers to be instructed at local army bases around the country. Within a month these militia units could be activated into eleven more divisions.'

Mung's heart fell. One month was not enough time. His only consolation came from the frown on Hideyoshi's face.

'The imperial navy has been training three crews on every ship in hopes of an expanded fleet,' Takamora said. 'However, the new Torpedo-boat Squadron and Marquis

Inei's merchant fleet, which is needed to transport the army, have not yet been integrated into our plans. A landing in hostile waters against heavily armed forces will require a minimum of two months' preparatory time.'

Mung thanked the gods for the mud flats of Pingtung harbour. In the ensuing debate he pressed for six months to negotiate a peaceful solution. Hideyoshi called for an immediate declaration of war.

The final decision taken by the ministers was to recommend a bill in the National Diet to expand the army and navy. Mung was given three months to convince the Chinese to pay an indemnity for Nagasaki and the Koreans to make compensation for the burning of the Japanese legation.

The Emperor stood. 'Let us make every effort to effect a peaceful solution. But if it is war, let no man turn back until the battle is won.'

'So it is ordered, so it is done,' the leaders of Japan intoned.

Chapter 20

Iyeasu accompanied Mung from the ministerial meeting to the Black Dragon headquarters in the palace. They entered an ante-room to the office from which the imperial intelligence service was directed.

Mung looked at the closed door and sighed. 'Once that opens, I will become caught up in events again. The damage in Nagasaki must be assessed. Then on to Korea for the negotiations.'

'You cannot prevent war,' Iyeasu said.

'Admiral Ting's reason for calling us to Seoul may well be to avert a confrontation. An incident on Korean soil would not involve Chinese civilians. It could be localized. The Chinese may prefer to negotiate rather than fight.'

'We have no sizeable military presence in Korea,' Iyeasu said.

'I have asked William Whittefield, Lord Cade and the Kobe Club to intercede with the Korean monarch. Hopefully a battalion of Japanese soldiers will be allowed to enter Seoul as protection for our legation. Then our troops would number half the Chinese force.'

'The Chinese control the Korean king and queen. They will not agree.'

'If King Kojong does agree, it means the Chang brothers gave him permission and they want peace.'

'How can you compensate the Chang brothers for Prince Kung's bribery and at the same time satisfy Hideyoshi who wants war?'

Mung walked to a world globe and spun it until he found Formosa. 'I could return this island to the Chinese, except for banking rights which is all we originally expected. In return the Chinese might allow a strong Japanese presence in North Korea along the Yalu river. That would stop the Russians from moving south. The westerners are desperate to keep the czar's fleet from a year-round ice-free port in the Pacific. They would help pressure the Chinese.'

'Do you think Hideyoshi and his faction would be satisfied to sit on the banks of the Yalu river?'

'Not for long. Manchuria is controlled by warlords who have asserted their independence from Peking. I doubt the Chang brothers would object if our troops moved out from bases along the Yalu to contest the Russians over Manchuria. They might see it as a strategy to weaken us and the Russians.'

'Too complicated,' Iyeasu said. 'In addition, the Chinese must pay for their attack on Nagasaki.'

'Through the Kobe Club and Lord Cade, I hope to circumvent the Chang brothers and approach the Chinese Empress with another bribe. China has already paid us fifteen million dollars more than we expected. Let us consider ten million as the indemnity payment for Nagasaki. Via the westerners, we could give the Empress the remaining five million as a bribe.'

'Our politicians and military have already counted the entire amount as theirs. Some compensation must be paid for the Japanese dead or it will remain a stain on our national honour.'

'The bribe to the Empress could include the condition of convincing the Koreans to make a generous indemnity payment for the burning of our legation. It would be understood as a way for China and Japan to save face without conflict.'

Iyeasu smiled, and he bowed. 'My friend, if I had a hat I would take it off to you. Whether this will work is another question.'

'I must keep trying for peace while our military and my agents prepare for war.'

'Your two sons in military intelligence believe we can defeat China and Korea.'

'Hot blood clouds one's vision,' Mung said.

'Nogi and Takamora are not youngsters. They claim we have the power to break Europe's control of all of Asia. Korea is only the first step.'

'I agree that Japan needs to expand. But cultural and economic imperialism is preferable and more productive than military domination of other countries.'

'I am afraid I agree with Hideyoshi in this. The West will not permit us to colonize other Asian nations without a fight.'

'They recognized our rights to the Ryukyu islands and Formosa,' Mung said. 'They will be morally bound to accept our sphere of influence in Korea, and later Manchuria.'

'Do not depend on European morality. From the pulpit they preach turning the other cheek, and from the podium it is survival of the fittest. Morals are those actions which enable a people to survive.'

'Are you saying no one is to be trusted?'

'The European economy is built on the backs of their colonies. They will not take kindly to competition from Orientals.' Iyeasu glanced at his watch. 'I cannot wait much longer for William Whittefield.'

'He should be here any moment. He can take you directly to Parliament in his rickshaw. That will save time.'

'I doubt we will have an opportunity to kill Mung before he boards the ship for Nagasaki,' the young army officer said.

'Are the White Wolves in position outside the palace?' Hideyoshi asked.

'All is ready. I saw the American on his way to join Mung and your brother.'

183

'My father disowned Iyeasu years ago. People think we are still related because the Emperor conferred the title of count on both of us.' Hideyoshi walked out from behind his desk to the wall map. 'Actually Iyeasu's death might cause more of a nationalistic backlash than Mung's.'

'What if the American is in the way?'

Hideyoshi recalled the embarrassment of not being invited to the bachelor party William Whittefield gave for Shimatzu. 'Throw the bomb,' he said. 'The more confusion the better.' He handed the young officer a pamphlet. 'Be certain this is found at the scene. Tomorrow I will have people in the streets distributing them.'

William bowed, then shook hands with Iyeasu and Mung. 'I have just come from the British embassy. Lord Cade has convinced the Germans and French to join him in approaching the Dowager Empress to keep the Chang brothers from declaring war on Japan. They'll submit your proposals to retain only banking rights on Formosa, a Japanese presence along the Yalu river and payment of a Korean indemnity.'

'Where does America stand?' Iyeasu asked.

'The United States remains neutral. Unofficially the Kobe Club will join Lord Cade in seeking a peaceful solution.'

'Will the Kobe Club be able to supply the weapons we requested in the event of war?' Mung asked.

'Easily,' William said. 'We were surprised at the limited amount of small arms, ammunition and artillery ordered. It appears Marquis Inei prefers to manufacture those weapons rather than purchase them.'

Mung turned to Iyeasu. 'Please be certain Marquis Inei is able to make delivery in case of war.'

'I will speak with Nogi and Takamora tonight, and tomorrow with Inei.'

'I asked Lord Cade if he is working for the Chinese or

the Japanese,' William said. 'His answer was typical of a European aristocrat. The notion of a gentleman working for an Asiatic is preposterous, he said. I represent England!'

'Then why did he bribe Prince Kung with a million dollars of his own money?'

'Kobe Club members think the loan to the prince was in exchange for two more British trading ports in China. Cade will want at least one each in the Ryukyus and Formosa from Japan. The extra bribe is still a mystery.'

'What do the westerners think of Japan's chances in a war against Korea or China?' Iyeasu asked.

'They believe you will lose,' William said.

'What is your personal opinion?' Mung asked.

'That everyone is in for a big surprise,' William said. 'Kobe Club agents report from the English sailors training your new Torpedo-boat Squadron in Canton that your men are quick to learn and the hardest workers they ever met.'

'They should be,' Mung said. 'Every trainee is an officer above the rank of first lieutenant.'

'I regret that I must be on my way,' Iyeasu said.

'Would you please give the count a ride to Parliament House?' Mung asked William.

'It is an opportunity to discuss specifics regarding the reduced weapons orders from our military,' Iyeasu said.

'It is my pleasure,' William said.

Mung watched the two men leave, the tall American and the short, round Japanese. He opened the connecting door and summoned Udo from his desk.

'Very crowded in there,' Mung said.

'I will tell them to keep quiet,' Udo said.

Mung dismissed the idea with a wave of his hand. 'How is Gin-ko?' he asked.

'I expected worse and wish for better.' Udo watched Mung massage the stump of his wrist, then rub his bent nose. He had known the Black Dragon long enough

185

to recognize the signs. 'Gin-ko knows I must go to Seoul.'

An expression of pain and relief crossed Mung's face. 'You are the most qualified person in the empire.'

'Gin-ko wishes to accompany me. Queen Min is her friend. I told her it is impossible.'

'Noriko will continue to look after her,' Mung said.

A distant thud sounded from the window and the curtains puffed inward.

Udo glanced at the window but made no mention of the disturbance. 'It is fortunate you convinced our military not to go charging off to war. The Chinese fleet sailed from Nagasaki to the Bungo Strait and set a trap for our navy. What does crossing the T mean?'

'Naval parlance for an ideal position from which to attack a column of enemy ships. Whoever crosses the T has an immense advantage. His ships fire from the flank position. All his guns aim at the first line of enemy ships, which can only bring their forward guns to bear.'

The door burst open. William Whittefield's face was ashen, his clothes soaked in blood. He saw the shock in Mung's eyes. 'Not me,' he said. 'It's Iyeasu. Someone threw a bomb into my rickshaw. I jumped out, but Iyeasu didn't move fast enough and his leg was blown off!'

'Is he alive?' Mung asked.

'He was. I stopped the bleeding with a tourniquet. Soldiers helped me bring him here. His personal physician is with him.'

Mung turned to Udo. 'Help William. I must go to my friend.' He started for the door and stopped. 'William, send for the best American naval surgeon!'

Three Japanese doctors were crowded around Iyeasu when Mung entered. He was relieved to see the large stomach rising and falling, and knew his friend lived. He knelt down and took Iyeasu's hand.

'I am still here,' Iyeasu whispered.

Mung nodded and looked at the doctors.

'We have stemmed the bleeding,' Iyeasu's personal physician said.

'Have you experience with amputations?' Mung asked.

'A limited amount.'

'I have invited an American naval surgeon. He may be more familiar with this type of injury.'

'Father!' Noriko burst in and ran to Iyeasu's side. 'What have they done to you?'

He turned towards his daughter but the smile on his lips faded. His eyes fluttered and closed.

'Do not die, Father! Please!'

'He is resting,' the physician said. 'It is due to loss of blood.'

'Where is his wound?'

The doctor looked at Mung, then to Noriko. 'Your father's leg was severed above the knee.'

The girl staggered and Mung caught her. He lowered her to the tatami mat.

'I am sorry to be a nuisance,' Noriko whispered. 'I will just rest here a moment.'

'We are going to anaesthetize the leg,' the physician said.

Udo appeared at the door, followed by Yaka and an imperial guard. He called Mung from the room.

Yaka handed Mung a pamphlet. 'This guard found it on the body of the dead assailant and brought it to army intelligence. No one else has seen it.'

'I examined the body,' Yaka said. 'He was shot in the back by his own men. It appears they wanted us to have the pamphlet, which calls for an immediate declaration of war on China and Korea.'

'This is to be kept a secret,' Mung said. 'Find the printer, destroy the press, burn the shop and isolate everyone connected with it!' He addressed the guard. 'Your quick thinking will be rewarded. Bid your family farewell! You will accompany my son Udo to Korea!'

A tall leather-faced American in navy blues hurried towards Mung, followed by an orderly carrying two wooden cases. 'Sir, I'm Charles Tate, surgeon general of the Pacific Fleet.'

'Come inside,' Mung said. 'I'll translate for you.'

'Please bring a table,' the American said. 'I find it hard to kneel and work. I need more light.' He glanced down at Noriko. 'Is she a patient?'

'She felt faint,' Mung said.

'Please have her rest somewhere else,' Doctor Tate said.

'I will see she is taken care of,' Gin-ko said.

Mung turned in surprise at the voice. Udo and Yaka stood behind her dumbfounded. She turned to them. 'You two can help Noriko to my room.'

Iyeasu's physician whispered to Mung, 'Allow her to do what she is able. Cancer patients often improve when concerned for others.'

Doctor Tate pointed at the silvery needles protruding from the stump of Iyeasu's leg. 'Are these acupuncture needles?'

'They're to anaesthetize, slow the heartbeat and relax the patient,' Mung said.

The doctor made a thorough examination of the wound. 'Please inform my honoured colleagues I will explain as I work,' he said to Mung. 'High-impact injuries are my speciality, but if the physicians have suggestions I would be pleased to hear them.'

The three Japanese physicians bowed after Mung's translation. Doctor Tate signalled his orderly to open the wooden cases. They were lined with bottles, clamps and rows of bright steel instruments. The orderly slapped a scalpel into the doctor's hand. The American leaned over Iyeasu's leg and began to operate.

'I am cutting away the flesh in preparation for reducing

the amount of bone in relation to the muscle and skin around it,' Mung translated. 'This will prevent the bone from pushing through the skin in the event the patient will graduate to an artificial leg.'

'Will he survive?' Mung asked.

'The man's will to live and God's plans will determine the outcome,' Doctor Tate said. 'Bone saw, please.'

Chapter 21

Hankow, China

The three-storey Green House had been purposely built on a rise overlooking the Hankow naval depot. The White Wolves kept watch on the Chinese navy and sought out certain officers to influence.

Inside the building, coloured bars of light from a stained-glass window caught dust particles floating gently down to a table between two men.

'Sit!' Colonel Hanjo said.

The sinews in Shibata's neck quivered, his lean cheekbones protruded and his eyes burned with fervour. He had vowed to establish the best record ever achieved in this school and this was his first meeting with the master spy since his initiation.

'Certain people are born to be agents,' Honjo said. 'The species is rare. You, Akichi Shibata, are one of those to whom espionage comes naturally. We have seen that you can work alone, have shed the few scruples you had, and are quick to learn. In two months you have surpassed your instructors' predictions. Your level of the Chinese language is such that lessons will be discontinued and more time given to Russian and Mongolian. Your request to be indoctrinated into the tenets of the Muslim religion shows an innate grasp of an agent's purpose – to become part of the people on whom one spies. Religion will soon become an integral part of our curriculum. We plan to send people to Rome, India and Mecca to study.'

'Thank you,' Shibata said, bowing until his head touched the floor. 'How long before I take my place in the field?'

'Do not rush the learning process,' Honjo said. 'This is

the place to make mistakes. Outside it could cost your life. You were assigned to coerce Commodore Hung-Ta. What have you accomplished?'

'In two weeks he has been my guest three times. Tonight will be his fourth visit to the Green House.'

'What are his preferences?'

'Whisky, young large-bosomed white women and an occasional pipe of opium.'

'Is he a deviant?'

'Not yet,' Shibata said. 'That is part of my assignment. I was instructed to work him slowly. He is kept supplied with your special cigarettes. Tonight I hope to have him participate in one of our sex shows.'

'I would like to see animals used.'

Shibata shook his head. 'At this point I believe Hung-Ta would be repulsed by such a display. He is one of the better Chinese officers in Hankow.'

'A Chinese fleet killed many Japanese and burned the port of Nagasaki. The Black Dragons learned that Admiral Ting has set a trap at the Bungo Strait for our navy. In seven days three cruisers and a troopship are leaving the Hankow naval base. I wish to know their destination.'

'Hung-Ta would have that information,' Shibata said.

'I prefer to have Hung-Ta alive for use in the future. But if he must die, be certain it is after he has given you the information we need.'

The excitement in Shibata's heart did not show in his face or the sound of his voice. He had learned to conceal his emotions. He already knew exactly how he would break the Chinese commodore. 'I will need the largest room in the Green House and twenty people.'

'Sounds like a major show.'

'You will have the information you seek before the sun rises.'

'I shall be watching,' Honjo said.

* * *

191

'Shibata, you are young, and are bright and quick to learn,' Commodore Hung-Ta said. 'Why did you leave Japan to pimp in China?'

'My country is backward,' Shibata said. 'Compared to China, we are primitive.' He packed an opium pipe and passed it to the commodore. 'I do not intend to remain in the Green House longer than it takes me to make enough money.'

'Have you considered the military?' Hung-Ta said. 'I could find a place for a good officer.'

'I come from a family of merchants. In Japan that is considered only slightly higher than dog shit.' Shibata poured another glass of whisky.

The commodore loosened the buttons of his uniform and drank. 'I have read about social reforms taking place in Japan. Your government is encouraging industry and private business.'

'But an aristocrat would never invite a merchant to his home, or introduce him to his daughter.'

'I would not introduce a horny young fellow like you to my daughter.' Hung-Ta laughed. 'Is it time for this show you promised?' He patted his stomach. 'My belly is full.' He held up the pipe. 'My feelings are good.' He pointed to his crotch. 'My golden rod is prepared to do battle.'

'Tonight you are scheduled to be an observer. Of course if you wish to participate in the performance, it can only enhance your enjoyment.'

'Onward!' Hung-Ta threw his arm around Shibata's shoulders.

The young Japanese led the Chinese officer to a large room with soft lights and sweet-smelling incense.

'I cannot see their faces, but the people standing in the shadows appear to be naked,' the commodore said.

'They are here for your pleasure,' Shibata said. 'Have another pipe. It will set the mood.'

Hung-Ta settled down onto a pile of silk cushions and

sucked in the opium. He watched a large Mongol with shaven skull and long black pigtail step from the shadows into the soft light. The Mongol had massive shoulders, with gnarled muscles in his hairy arms and legs. A beautiful, full-breasted nude white woman stepped into the light next to him, holding a flask of sweet oil. She approached the naked Mongol and began to anoint his body.

'If he touches her without your permission, the other men around the room will bind and whip him,' Shibata said.

'You mean I am in control of that beast?'

'It is part of your entertainment.'

'Fascinating. The woman is expert in tantalizing him with her slow rhythmic massage.'

The Mongol's body gleamed with a sheen of oil. The light played on his quivering muscles.

'His erection is huge,' the commodore said. 'I would like to see him take the woman.'

'You have the power.'

'Not just yet. She is stroking his golden rod and his eyes are about to pop from his head. Listen to his breathing.'

A lute began to play and the woman stroked the Mongol in time to the music. His mouth opened, he spread his muscle-corded arms, threw back his head and howled. Then he grabbed the woman by the neck and pulled her to him, crushing her body to his.

Shibata signalled and several naked men leapt from the shadows. They separated the pair and held the struggling Mongol.

Five young women, one more beautiful than the next, stepped into the light and slowly disrobed before the commodore.

'You may have them all,' Shibata said.

'At this moment I feel I could take them all at once.'

'Enjoy yourself. I am taking the Mongol's partner.'

'What about that poor bastard?' Hung-Ta asked. 'His golden rod is like a tent pole.'

'My men will force him to watch me and his woman. When we are ready, he will be the final entertainment of the evening.'

Shibata dropped his robe and went to the woman. He positioned her in front of the raving Mongol and began to stroke her.

From a viewing port overhead, Colonel Honjo could see that Shibata's caresses were mechanical. He was paying little attention to the woman and less to the wild-eyed Mongol. He watched the women undress Hung-Ta and massage his body with oil. The Chinese naval officer grew frenzied. He did not see Shibata signal to a pair of brawny men. The girls scrambled away from Hung-Ta as the two approached from behind. They twisted the Chinese officer's arms behind his back and forced his face into the floor. Two girls jammed a large cushion under his stomach.

'What is going on?' Hung-Ta shouted. 'If this is part of the show, I am not amused!'

From the viewing port, Honjo watched his protégé swagger before the victim. 'I wish to know everything about the troopship and her escorts,' Shibata said. 'They leave in seven days. You will tell me where, when and why those ships are going!' He cradled his golden rod in front of the commodore's eyes. 'This is what I will use to push the information out of you.' He moved behind the struggling man.

'You fucking no good Japanese freak bastard!' Hung-Ta screamed as Shibata entered him. He bucked, pulled and twisted, to no avail. Shibata climaxed and withdrew. He grabbed the officer by the hair, lifting his head to look into his eyes. Hung-Ta spat into Shibata's face.

'You stupid son of a bitch!' Shibata wiped away the spittle. 'There are ten more men waiting to take you. We will continue hour after hour, day after day. But first,' he raised his voice, 'let the Mongol loose!'

'Three battle cruisers will escort the troopship *Kowshing* with two thousand men aboard,' Shibata told Honjo at breakfast. 'The ships will refuel in Shanghai, then sail from the East China Sea into the Yellow Sea. They will raise the Mokpo light on Korea's southern tip and turn north. The troops will disembark at Inchon and march overland to Seoul.'

'For what purpose?'

'Supposedly to support the Koreans against a possible rebellion by the Tonghaks, a religious group dedicated to overthrowing the monarchy. But the Korean king agreed to a battalion of Japanese troops to guard our legation in Seoul and the Chinese general wants the two thousand men aboard the *Kowshing* to offset our battalion. When the Chinese cruisers complete their escort mission, they will join Admiral Ting's fleet to patrol the sea between Japan and Korea.'

'Your information indicates Admiral Ting will soon be gone from the Bungo strait and our navy can move south.' Honjo spread a map on the table and pointed. 'Here on Tsu-shima island, near the southern tip of Korea, is where Commodore Togo is training with five new torpedo-boats. He is close enough to the Mokpo lighthouse to intercept that convoy.'

'We are not at war,' Shibata said.

'The White Wolf will decide that. Is Hung-Ta alive?'

'The commodore is so full of opium, it will be at least two days before he is fit to return to duty,' Shibata said. 'But I own him. He will find out whatever we must know.'

'Get the exact route of those ships, the thickness of their armour plate, range and number of guns! Knowledge of the location of powder magazines on the cruisers would also be helpful to our navy.'

'I would like to point out that five torpedo-boats are no match for three heavy cruisers.'

'Get that information as soon as possible! Togo and his Torpedo-boat Squadron will worry about the odds. Hideyoshi may wish to sacrifice the little boats to create an incident. It will not take much to start a war.'

Chapter 22

The Imperial Palace, Tokyo

'Conditions to avoid war are better than I thought,' Udo said. 'The Dowager Empress has all but abandoned the Chang brothers in Korea. They have free rein, although no money. The Chinese government is raising an army of eleven divisions for the Tarim basin area. The Russian army has taken Bukhara, Samarkand and Tashkent. A rebel named Yakub Beg, with secret backing from the British, has established an independent Muslim state in the Tarim basin. The Empress wants Yakub Beg dead and the Russians out.'

'The Chinese army will have to cross a thousand miles of mountains and desert to reach that area,' Mung said. 'Korea is closer and far more productive. Where is the logic?'

'The official reason given for moving against Yakub Beg is reverence to imperial Chinese ancestors,' Udo said. 'Because previous Emperors ruled those territories. Unofficially it allows the Chinese Empress, Prince Kung and court officials to steal more money from the government.'

'So much graft and bribery would have ruined a smaller country long ago,' Mung said.

'It could be to our advantage. General Li and his brother petitioned Peking to forget the Tarim expedition. They want to secure Korea against us and Manchuria against the Russians. The general has borrowed from the Shansi banks to purchase weapons. He has spent his family's fortune to buy several wool mills and rent farmland. To supply his army with food and clothing, he has put most of his soldiers to work in the fields and factories, retaining only the best sixty thousand men under arms.'

'That is a quarter of his reported strength,' Mung said. 'What about their navy?'

'Admiral Ting is using some of his ships as ferries to earn money to pay his men. Three new battle cruisers were put into service from the Hankow navy yard. Still, I think the Chang brothers will be more open to negotiations now than before their government abandoned them.'

'Hiroki has reported a minor rebellion by the Tonghaks. How do you think that will affect the Chinese and us?'

'Tonghaks began peacefully by asking for a change in the corrupt Korean land and food administrations,' Udo said. 'They believe in Christ, Buddha and a variety of demons, and do not have clear objectives. We have Genoysha agents in their organization; one is a priest. We should be able to influence certain segments of the Tonghaks.'

'I want it quiet in Korea,' Mung said. 'It appears to me, from Korea's agreement to a battalion of our troops in their capital, that General Li wants peace.'

'Yes, but I feel Admiral Ting would prefer war.'

'Has General Nogi accepted my suggestion?' Mung asked.

'Yes. The battalion to be stationed in Seoul is made up of officers and senior non-coms. Portable film-developing laboratories and hand-printing presses have been supplied to each company commander. Every man has a camera and maps, and is assigned a specific area to scout. In the event that we do invade Korea, those men will be able to guide our forces. They embarked yesterday and I leave tomorrow morning for Seoul.'

'Go to your wife now,' Mung said. 'I will visit her before I depart for Nagasaki.'

'You will see an improvement in her. She has taken charge of Iyeasu's recovery, pampers Noriko and has even gained back some weight. But I remind you to be wary of Hideyoshi. I expected he would make an attempt on your life, not his brother's. I have had men guarding you.'

'Without my knowledge?'

'They will accompany you to Nagasaki. Farewell, Father. We shall meet again in Seoul.'

Udo entered the room on tiptoe. Gin-ko put a finger to her lips and motioned towards the great mound under the blanket. Iyeasu was asleep. 'He is stronger,' she whispered, leading her husband from the room.

'And you?'

'I am fine. Iyeasu and I have begun to speak of the future. The most difficult thing for him is the strict diet the American doctor has prescribed. Iyeasu must lose weight before he can use an artificial leg.'

'How is Noriko reacting?'

'It disturbs us both when her father complains of aching and itching in the leg that has been amputated. The American doctor calls them phantom pains. He says they will disappear.'

Udo took Gin-ko in his arms. 'I came to tell you I must leave.'

'Do we have time to be together?' she whispered.

'Several hours.'

'Then let us make them memorable. I will ask Noriko to relieve me here. You and I shall go to the pillow. It has been too long.'

Udo kissed Gin-ko's forehead. 'You should save your strength.'

'For what?'

'For me.' He held her close. 'I need you.'

Gin-ko clasped her husband to her so he would not see her distress. She wanted to cry out to him to stay with her. To tell him how much she would need him when the end came. But she forced gaiety into her voice. 'It is possible your golden rod holds the cure for me. I need the memories to carry me when you are away.'

'Please,' Udo whispered, trembling. 'Please do not die.

199

You are my strength, my life, my love. I cannot live without you.'

Noriko sat on the balcony of her father's room and watched the rising moon. Gin-ko had confided to her that Yaka and Uraga had engaged a nakoda to arrange marriages for them. They had requested that their mi-ais be held at the same time as hers with Hiroki. Then the two brothers had come to her. They wanted a triple marriage ceremony while their mother was still alive. Did Noriko agree?

'It is worse now than before,' Noriko said to the man in the moon. 'It is not fair. You took my father's leg, you will soon take Gin-ko's life, and I will be imprisoned forever in a marriage to Hiroki. We are all good people. Why must we suffer? I may not be as worthy as the others, but do I deserve to be married to him?' Tears ran down her cheeks. 'I am bound by tradition to say yes,' she sobbed. 'There is no choice for me, but I must confide in someone. I think the gods are coarse and crude.'

A light tap on the door preceded Mung's entrance. Noriko dried her tears and led him onto the balcony.

'How is your father?' he asked.

'He will recover, and in time return to his duties. The Emperor has visited twice. He sends correspondence for my father to evaluate.'

'I will forward reports from Nagasaki and Seoul.'

'Pain disrupts his concentration, but he refuses opiates.'

'It is better that his mind is occupied with other things than his injury,' Mung said. 'Tell me about yourself.'

'I am fine.' She smiled. 'Gin-ko takes care of me like my mother. Her recovery is amazing.'

Mung had just learned from the doctor that Gin-ko's improvement was temporary. He looked up. 'The moon appears to be smiling on us. It is a good omen.'

'Yes,' Noriko replied, thinking that the man in the moon

was really laughing at them. The doctor had also told her that Gin-ko's recovery would not last.

'Tell your father I will stop in Nagasaki to view the port's destruction. I am due in Seoul on August fifth, two weeks from today.'

'Father will be disappointed not to have spoken with you.'

Mung looked at the great mound under the blanket. 'He is my best friend. Forgive an old man his sentimentality. Japanese men do not embrace.' Mung faced Noriko. 'If I could hug you, would you embrace him for me?'

Noriko came into Mung's arms and put her head on his shoulder. 'He never hurt anyone,' she sobbed. 'Why did they attack him? They must be punished!'

Mung held the girl in his arms and looked up at the moon again. In his heart he beseeched the gods. 'Bless this girl. Make her marriage to my grandson long, happy and fruitful.'

According to his instructions, Udo was awakened at 4 a.m. He looked into his wife's face and brushed his lips to her forehead. He had caressed her and felt her ribs, hipbones and the points of her beautiful shoulders. She was so thin. Now she slept, her saintly face in repose. 'I love you,' he whispered softly to her. 'Please wait for me.'

During the night Gin-ko had asked Udo's promise not to take his life when she was gone. He had responded with his tender lovemaking. Now she breathed evenly, hearing his whisper but answering only in her heart. 'I love you, my beloved. Hurry back.'

Gin-ko heard her husband rise from the sleeping mat. She opened her eyes to gaze at his lean sinewy body in the moonlight. Tears blurred her vision. She hoped he would retain a good memory of her. She had used the last of her energy during the night and now had not the strength to rise.

She closed her eyes as he leaned towards her and whispered his last goodbye. 'You are my life.'

Outside the palace gates Udo ignored the rickshaw men. He walked alone, moving quickly through deserted streets, away from the harbour and towards the Ginza. He passed the Nō theatre and stepped into the entrance of a bonsai shop.

A man waited in the shadows. 'Follow me,' he said.

It had been twenty years since Udo smelled the dampness inside the darkened shop. He walked up the wooden stairs to the attic. 'Should I strip?' he asked his guide.

'You are an honoured guest. It is not necessary.'

A single lantern lit the attic room. Seated on either side of a long table were six bare-chested men, their bodies covered with intricate tattoos.

At the head of the table sat the chief Yakuza of Japan. He bowed to Udo. 'Two decades ago you came to us for help.' He placed a scroll on the table and pointed to it. 'It is written that you and your father, Moryiama Ishikawa, kept your vows. That you honoured Wada Zenshichi, the past master of the tattooed men. How may we serve you?'

'I seek revenge against Count Hideyoshi Koin and Lieutenant Akichi Shibata.'

'Our activities may be outside the law, but we rarely resort to violence,' the chief Yakuza said.

'I wish to kill these two men myself,' Udo said, placing five pouches on the table. He opened them as he had done twenty years before and tipped them over, one after the other. Gold dust spilled out in gleaming piles that sparkled in the lamplight. 'Shibata is presently out of the country. Hideyoshi is protected by professional guards. I wish to know how to evade those guards. If I should be killed, I must be assured both men will die in the style meant for traitors.'

'Is this in payment for the attempt on Mung's life at the harbour master's office?'

'That alone would be sufficient reason,' Udo said. 'But I seek retribution for the public insult to my wife at the wedding of Shimatzu Ishikawa. It is Giri, my social obligation, to see these men die.'

The chief Yakuza entered into discussion with the tattooed men at the table in their secret language. A scroll was brought out and referred to. Udo waited.

Finally the chief said, 'It is written that Mistress Gin-ko carries the sign of the yellow butterfly here,' he pointed to the crook of his left arm. 'The mark of Wada Zenshichi's protection binds us. Your wife once saved my predecessor's life. I am honour-bound to protect her reputation.' He pointed to the five glittering mounds of gold. 'Take those with you. We shall hire ninjas, professional assassins, to plan the death of Count Hideyoshi, and that of Akichi Shibata when he returns to Japan.'

Udo bowed. 'I thank the Yakuza for their honourable suggestion, but I must kill these two men myself if possible.'

'And if you die first, we shall see that it is done,' the chief Yakuza said.

Udo bowed again. He was soon on his way to the ship bound for Inchon and his meeting with the Korean king in Seoul.

Chapter 23

The artificial pond in front of the house reflected plum trees laden with fruit. Mung sat in the lotus position on the portico, studying the ruins of Nagasaki port. Children passed by, giggling on their way to school, but a stink of burnt flesh, rotting fish and charred wood hung in the air. A haze of soot still hovered over the city. Mung strained to keep his emotions in check.

A forty-foot navy coal-tender entered port at full speed. Disregarding the harbour master's caution signal, it made directly for the remains of the municipal pier. An army and a navy officer leapt ashore before the ship was docked. Mung saw the soldiers who met them point up the hill to his lodgings. He uncrossed his legs and prepared to receive the messengers.

Yaka and Uraga bowed. 'Grandfather, war seems certain,' Yaka said.

Mung saw the excitement in their eyes and heard it in their voices. He needed an unemotional report. 'How is your mother?' he asked.

The tension left the young officers and understanding filled their eyes. They bowed again.

In a calmer tone, Yaka said, 'Mother is the same. She tends Count Iyeasu and pampers Noriko.'

'How does the girl cope with her father's injury?'

'Very well,' Uraga said. 'She has agreed to a triple mi-ai. When Hiroki returns we hope to make the arrangements for Mother to see her three sons wed. That would make her happy.'

'Are the young women you chose from good families?'

'Mother and Count Iyeasu approve,' Uraga said. 'They spoke to the marriage broker. We have seen photographs and shall meet the girls at the mi-ai.'

'We hope to have a memorable wedding,' Yaka said. 'Possibly a victory celebration at the same time.'

His grandsons were bursting to give him their news and Mung wanted to hear it. 'What are your orders?' he asked.

'We are bound for Tsu-shima island with orders for Commodore Togo!' Uraga said. 'His torpedo-boats are to shadow the Chinese troopship *Kowshing* and her escorts from the Mokpo light to Inchon! The two thousand Chinese soldiers aboard the *Kowshing* are bound for Seoul! It is a violation of General Li's understanding with our ambassador to Korea!'

'Who issued your orders?' Mung asked.

'The new Minister of War, Hideyoshi Koin,' Yaka said.

Mung took a deep breath. 'How did Hideyoshi become Minister of War?' he demanded.

'Grandfather, you know that public opinion was aroused by the news of Admiral Ting's raid on Nagasaki,' Yaka said. 'Then embellished stories of the Korean attack on our legation in Seoul were recirculated by the newspapers and in pamphlets by Hideyoshi's followers. Parliament was caught up in the war fever and voted a 150 million yen military budget, with Hideysohi as Minister of War!'

'That sum is twice the annual operating cost of the entire government!' Mung said.

'There was not a dissenting vote in either house,' Yaka said. 'Everyone remembers how much income your Formosan agreement brought us. There are predictions of more from your forthcoming negotiations with the Chinese in Korea.'

'Did the Emperor make his views known?' Mung asked.

'Count Iyeasu was too ill to present the Emperor's opinion,' Uraga said. 'One of Iyeasu's supporters represented him, and barely prevented Hideyoshi from taking over the Black Dragons and Genoysha.'

Mung felt as if he was running downhill out of control. 'You once told me that neither Hideyoshi nor military intelligence knew of Genoysha's existence.'

'The White Wolf Society is larger and more efficient than we thought,' Yaka said. 'When word reached Iyeasu of Hideyoshi's attempt to gain control of the Black Dragons, he had himself carried into Parliament. He was able to convince the members that you are the most qualified person to coordinate military and civilian intelligence. That is why we have come to you. You will begin receiving copies of all intelligence reports from the military and the White Wolf Society.'

'Grandfather, you should have seen Hideyoshi's face,' Uraga said. 'He turned purple. I thought he was about to have convulsions in Parliament.'

'They spoke openly about the Black Dragons, Genoysha and the White Wolves?'

'It was even in the newspapers,' Uraga said.

Mung laughed from the belly and his grandsons winked at each other. They had heard stories of their grandfather's western-style laugh. For the first time they were seeing it and his straight white teeth.

'I am supposed to lead the country's secret service and they publish it in newspapers?' Mung said. 'They probably listed our agents' names too.'

The young men smiled. 'Of course not,' Uraga said. He handed Mung a sheaf of papers. 'These are reports from military intelligence and Colonel Honjo in Hankow. General Nogi and Admiral Takamora will arrive soon. You must brief them.'

'Why here?' Mung asked.

'Nagasaki is to be the forward command post if we

206

invade Korea,' Yaka said. 'General Nogi has seventeen divisions. Marquis Inei's ships have begun to transport them south.'

'Our father reports from Seoul that the Royal Korean Army was defeated by Tonghak rebels,' Uraga said. 'A later message from Hiroki says General Li's Chinese troops waited until the battered Korean army retreated, then moved in and slaughtered the Tonghaks. After the massacre, General Li reaffirmed Korea's status as a tributary state under the protection of China.'

'That alone is a cause for war,' Mung said. 'The defeat of the Korean army means that nothing stands as a buffer between China and Japan.'

'Be assured that with all the differences between our military and civilians in Parliament, if Japan fights we do so as a united people,' Yaka said.

'If it is war, we must be victorious!' Mung said. 'A loss would make us another vassal state of China's, or indebted servants to the Europeans! Even if we were to win, Japan could become a pauper state!'

The fire in their grandfather's eyes reminded Yaka and Uraga of books they had read and stories heard about him leading the Satsuma riflemen against the shogun.

'Our troops in Seoul will be in danger if war is declared!' Mung said. 'Take pigeons aboard your ship for your father in Seoul and me here in Nagasaki! Make your rendezvous with Togo and his squadron! If hostilities break out, let those birds fly! Notify your father to use every means to keep the Koreans and Chinese off balance! The Black Dragon commands it!'

Yaka and Uraga bowed. 'So it is ordered, so it is done.'

Three hours after the coal-tender cleared port, the first contingents of army and navy headquarters battalion landed at Nagasaki. Tents were set up and a forward base of operations established. Mung was impressed with the efficiency and discipline of the Japanese military, although he doubted their ability to defeat China. But the people of Nagasaki believed. They cheered and they cried. They blessed the troops who had come to redeem the honour of Japan.

Mung sent coded messages to his agents in the Far East and Europe. They were to prepare for war. He received word from navy intelligence that Admiral Ting had divided his Penyang fleet to reinforce the Weihaiwei naval base on the tip of the Shantung peninsula and Port Arthur on the Liaotung peninsula. The Japanese navy was now outflanked in the Yellow Sea. An attempt to land at Inchon would be perilous.

Admiral Takamora and General Nogi arrived in Nagasaki with half the Japanese fleet and seven troopships. They were shadowed by Lord Cade's flagship. The Japanese responded to a message from the Englishman requesting that the two chiefs of staff and Moryiama Ishikawa meet with him and the ambassadors of Germany, France and Russia in his stateroom.

'Sirs,' Lord Cade said. 'My colleagues,' he pointed to the three ambassadors, 'will not agree to Japan's attempted annexation of Korea or any part of it. Other European countries, not represented here, also support China's traditional role in Korea.'

'We have no designs on Korean territory,' Takamora said. 'But we cannot allow raids on our homeland to go unanswered. You saw Nagasaki port. Admiral Ting and part of the fleet that raided this city are at Inchon now. General Li influenced the attack on our legation in Seoul. Japan desires an independent Korea. China wishes a vassal state. How can Europeans, who preach the rights of man, be against a free Korea?'

'The Canton odds-takers are giving seven to one in favour of China over Japan,' the Russian ambassador said.

'I wager ten thousand yen on Japan,' Nogi said. 'Would you care to cover it?'

'General Nogi, sir,' the German ambassador interrupted to prevent an argument, 'Japan is outnumbered and outgunned. Invading Korea is like trying to sting a turtle through its shell. The body is Korea, the shell is China.'

'Allow us to convene an international peace conference in Seoul,' Lord Cade said.

Nogi tapped his chest. 'We shall have direct talks with the Koreans and the Chinese! That is how business is conducted between equals!' He turned towards Mung. 'The Director of National Decorations will soon go to Seoul and arrange these discussions!'

That night, Mung and Lord Cade met privately in an evacuated area of the port. British marines and Black Dragons kept watch.

'Sir, you confuse me,' Mung said. 'You bribed Prince Kung with your own money so he would pay us a larger indemnity in Formosa. Your men stirred up Yakub Beg and a Muslim revolution in the Tarim basin, which drew troops and money away from General Li and Admiral Ting. Why all this help for Japan while proclaiming support for China to your European allies?'

Malcolm Cade lifted his chin. 'I am for England, first, foremost and always,' he said. 'I wish to block the czar's navy and merchant marine from a warm-water port on the Pacific.'

'Then why are you here with the Russian ambassador trying to stop us in Korea?'

'I am here to watch him, Mr Mung, not to stop Japan. The moment your forces gain a foothold in Korea, England will recognize that area as within your sphere of influence. That is a new geopolitical term meaning an area vital to your strategic interests. Would that be satisfactory to your government?'

'If we invade, it would be most acceptable.'

'Important enough for the Japanese military to maintain a line along the Yalu river and the Liaotung peninsula to keep the Russians out?'

'Your companions told us how outmanned and outgunned we are, with the odds running seven to one against us,' Mung said.

'The odds will be ten to one when news reaches Canton that Admiral Ting has reinforced the Port Arthur and Weihaiwei naval bases. You have also been outmanoeuvred. The Chinese navy now controls the Yellow Sea and approaches to Inchon.'

'Why do you make such an offer of friendship if Japan is going to lose the war?' Mung asked.

'The Kobe Club does not back losers,' Malcolm Cade said. He lit a cigar and puffed smoke into the warm night air. 'Alburg and Whittefield lead the toughest, shrewdest business group in the Far East. They rarely misjudge. The Kobe Club is counting on high returns from supplying the Japanese army and navy abroad. Reports from my officers training your men on the torpedo-boats and two battle cruisers claim the Japanese sailors are very good.'

Mung realized he had been purposely given privileged information from the British intelligence service. 'I am pleased to hear someone besides a Japanese speculate on the possibility of our defeating China.'

'The Chinese crews are disgruntled, underpaid, impressed seamen,' Lord Cade said. 'Their officers' corps is corrupt. The troops at Port Arthur are hired mercenaries led by a local warlord. I doubt men like those will stand up to hot lead and cold steel. If your soldiers are as good as your sailors, the Chinese will run.'

'I bow in appreciation for this information,' Mung said. 'Yet the odds remain heavily weighted in favour of China and Korea.'

'You have no other option but to fight,' Lord Cade said.

'If you do not, Prince Kung and the Dowager Empress will sell Korea to the Russians. Then it is only a matter of time before you are invaded by China, Russia, or both.'

Mung sighed. 'I have set myself the task of preventing war, but it appears I am the only one who seeks peace. You have my word that if Japan fights and wins in Korea, I will press for our troops to hold back the Russians.' He made no mention of Hideyoshi's plan to use the Yalu line as a base from which to invade the mineral-rich territory of Manchuria. He decided to up the stakes in this international game of politics. 'If Japan is to guard the Liaotung peninsula against the Russians, we would want to control it and Port Arthur.'

Malcolm Cade clasped his hands behind his back and whistled softly as he paced the dock area. He stopped, about to remind Mung of his debt over the Formosan treaty, then conceived a broader, more comprehensive plan to extend Britain's holdings abroad. He whistled louder and walked faster before he turned back to Mung. 'In the event that Japan takes my advice and is successful against the Chinese in Korea, Britain will support your claim to the Liaotung peninsula as part of your compensation for Admiral Ting's attack on Nagasaki.'

'What is your price?'

'To hold Port Arthur you must take the Chinese naval base at Weihaiwei. Cede it to Britain. Between us we would control the Yellow Sea.'

Mung immediately understood the Englishman's plans and lost his poker face. 'We would control the Pohai strait,' he said in a hoarse whisper. 'It commands the sea route to the Chinese capital of Peking!'

'And the northern capital of Mukden.' Malcolm Cade smiled. 'Very astute, Mr Mung. Is Japan mature enough to assume such responsibility?'

Mung let out a long breath. 'Maturity is not the problem.

My priority is a peaceful solution, and you tempt me to ignore it.'

'The peace option no longer exists.'

'In that event, Japan must win the war,' Mung said. Although he had not believed it possible, Lord Cade's suggestions could give Japanese forces a limited victory in Port Arthur, and a better bargaining position in Korea. Now Mung began to pace back and forth, using his infallible memory to recall Shimatzu's explanations and implications of recent international financial transactions in Europe. He stopped and looked at the Englishman. 'We are both assuming many things over long periods of time. There is one fact that makes it impossible for Japan to benefit from a war. Win, lose or draw, we would be bankrupt. Even if we did succeed, it would be economically impossible to maintain a military presence along the Yalu and Liaotung lines.'

'I assumed you would have learned a lesson from Prince Kung,' Malcolm Cade said. 'Japan must look on war as a business venture. Force the Chinese to the negotiating table and I will back Japan's claim for an indemnity large enough to offset the 150 million yen your Parliament voted for war.'

Mung determined to position the Englishman so he could play the ace Shimatzu's information had given him. 'No matter how successful Japan might be against China, we would be too disorganized and exhausted to stop the czar's army in so short a time. The Russians would push our army aside and take Korea.'

'Britain will not commit troops on the Asian mainland. We are spread too thin in India.'

This was what Mung wanted to hear. He played his son's financial ace. 'Have British bankers persuade the French government to call in its overdue loans to the czar for the Trans-Siberian railroad. It would retard Russian military activity in Manchuria for years.'

212

'My God, man!' Lord Cade grasped Mung's hand. 'That is quite brilliant! Where did you get such an idea?'

'My son studied international finance abroad.'

'Your son has just paid for his education ten times over and has probably saved Japan several army divisions, a couple of battleships and the invasion of your islands. I will see that Russian credit is cut if I have to strangle the French finance minister myself!'

'And I shall be in Seoul on August fifth to attempt a peace treaty.'

The Englishman ground out his cigar and said, 'Having failed that, inform your military the shore defences at Weihaiwei and Port Arthur can only fire seaward. Their guns cannot be turned.'

'But the British designed those fortifications. They supplied and installed the big guns.'

'We set up the situation for the possibility of having to attack those bases ourselves. From the land side, of course.' Lord Cade smiled. 'Now be a good fellow and win the war.'

Chapter 24

'Do we fight?' Commodore Togo asked.

'The Black Dragon will attempt to keep the peace while we prepare for war,' Yaka said.

'Are those my orders?' Togo asked, nodding to the envelope Uraga held.

'Yes, from Minister of War Hideyoshi Koin. Your squadron is to shadow the troopship *Kowshing* and three battle cruisers from the Mokpo light up the coast to Inchon! If fired upon, attack!' Uraga handed Togo the envelope.

'We now have ten torpedo-boats,' Togo said. 'Escorts protecting a troopship will shoot at so many unidentified vessels.'

'I believe the Minister of War knows that,' Yaka said.

'How are we to intercept this Chinese fleet?'

Uraga pointed to the envelope in Togo's hand. 'Colonel Honjo of the White Wolf Society guarantees that information. Admiral Takamora believes you will be the first Japanese in action against a foreign force. The Black Dragon considers it a suicide mission and warns you not to shoot first.'

'We are ready to die,' Togo said. 'Even more so are we prepared to win.'

'Against three modern battle cruisers?' Uraga said. 'They are just a foot shorter than battleships.'

'Come with me,' Togo said.

On the catwalk overlooking the dock, Togo pointed at the ships in his squadron. 'Look. The British gave us the best equipment they had. The boats have new water-tube boilers and will make twenty knots. Each carries two 20mm rapid-fire cannon with new armour-piercing shells. According to intelligence, they can penetrate the largest ships the Chinese have.' He indicated the nineteen-foot cylinders strapped to either side of the torpedo-boats. 'Those are the latest Whitehead, shallow-draught torpedoes, driven by compressed air. Speed thirty miles an hour, range one thousand yards. Each carries two hundred pounds of high explosives.'

'I too am a naval officer,' Uraga said. 'Those Chinese cruisers will blow you out of the water before you get within five miles of them. Their guns are so big they do not have to hit your boats. The concussion from the shells will split your wooden hulls.'

'I will attack at night,' Togo said. 'In the dark it will be possible to move in close.'

'Even with Honjo's information, you cannot be certain to find and track them in the dark.'

'I have two more ships than before,' Togo said. 'We will fan out across the *Kowshing*'s route. Your coal-tender can take up station on the picket line with my torpedo-boats.'

'You spoke of a second ship,' Yaka said. 'Is that it?' He pointed to a sleek, low silhouetted forty-five-foot three-masted steam sailer.

'That is my command craft,' Togo said. 'Colonel Honjo bought her with his own money from the British navy. I call her the *Naniwa*. She mounts two sixty-pound and two twenty-pound swivel guns fore and aft. I have added four rapid-fire 20mm cannon. It will not sink the Chinese battle cruisers, but can certainly draw their attention while my torpedo-boats get the *Kowshing*.'

The two brothers looked at each other, then at Togo. 'We respectfully request permission to be aboard the *Naniwa* when you meet the *Kowshing*,' Yaka said.

'One of you has a ticket,' Togo said. 'The other must command the coal-tender, observe the action, get away and report.' He bowed to Yaka. 'If it is war, there will be enough fighting for you on land with the army.'

Yaka bowed. 'I regret I will not be with you in the first foreign action of the imperial navy. Good luck.'

Seoul
They had slipped into Genoysha headquarters at five-minute intervals – three Black Dragons, two army officers, the Japanese ambassador to the Korean court and Hiroki Ishikawa.

'Gentlemen, we are ordered to seek peace and plan for war,' Udo said. 'The Chinese now control Kyongbok palace and hold the Korean monarchs captive. King Kojong and Queen Min are hostages of the Chinese General Li. Our army in Seoul is outnumbered five to one by the Chinese forces.'

'I understood our army numbered 60 per cent of the Chinese in Seoul,' the ambassador said. 'That was the agreement.'

'More than half our men are out on reconnaissance,' Udo said. 'They are mapping and photographing the terrain all the way north to the Yalu river. If our army invades, those men will act as scouts and guides.'

'What plans are there to protect Japanese civilians if war does break out?'

Udo nodded to his son to answer.

'All non-combatants will prepare a change of clothes and enough food and water for five days,' Hiroki said. 'In the event of hostilities, they are to assemble at our army base here in Seoul. No Korean spouse or child of a mixed marriage will be allowed within the camp perimeter.' Hiroki paused. He knew of Black Dragons and army officers married to Koreans. When there were no objections, he continued speaking. 'The Special Forces, made up of pro-Japanese Koreans and led by Genoysha agents, will harass the enemy outside the army base. Survivors of the

Tonghak rebellion have been organized by a priest who is a Genoysha man. They will disrupt enemy communications and transportation in the event of war. Tell your people to disregard stories of the devil who inhabits telephone poles and lines and is upsetting the geodetic balance of yin and yang in the earth. Our priest's vivid imagination has convinced the Tonghaks in the hills.'

Udo stepped to a wall map of Korea and instructed the group for the next two hours. He made no mention of the daring plan he and Hiroki had devised to thwart the Chinese, based on the military power of the Min family and the queen's anger at the Chinese for confining her to quarters.

30 July 1894

The men of the Torpedo-boat Squadron watched the horizon and the setting sun, concerned that after dark they could miss the *Kowshing*. Commodore Togo perched in the crow's-nest sixty feet above the *Naniwa*'s deck. Binoculars in one hand, telephone in the other, he studied his boats' holding station in a line twenty miles long, thirty miles off the Mokpo lighthouse. He glanced at his watch. 'Twelve minutes to dark,' he mumbled. This far out to sea he had expected to sight the *Kowshing* two hours earlier, with confidence that his formation would not be sighted. His boats were too small to be seen by the enemy at this distance. And with the hard coal they burned, they left no smoke trail when running slow.

Uraga's voice came over the telephone. 'Number one boat is signalling!'

Togo focused on his most southerly boat and read the heliograph message. 'Contact two points off the port bow.' He shouted into the telephone, 'Plan Z for zebra! Execute!' Below him he heard his heliograph clicking orders for the squadron to form up behind the *Naniwa* at slow speed.

'There they are,' he muttered. 'Four smoke trails against the orange sun.'

The glare of the setting sun dimmed. In its last glow he made out the Chinese formation – a giant troopship surrounded by three big battle cruisers, one forward and one on either side.

The sun slipped behind the horizon and it was dark. Togo put the binoculars away. He did not expect to see the Chinese convoy again until it made the port turn and ran north up the Korean coast. Then it would be silhouetted by the Mokpo light. He swung his leg over the edge of the crow's-nest and began to climb down.

Out in the night, one after the other, the four Chinese ships turned on their lights. Sixty feet above the deck Togo swayed back and forth in shock at the unbelievable breach of Chinese security. The *Kowshing* looked like a small city moving through the dark.

Togo climbed down and addressed his men. 'Our squadron is formed up behind the *Naniwa*! The Z plan is in effect! Estimated time of contact with the Chinese convoy is 23:30. We react only if fired upon!'

Uraga, standing beside the commodore, knew boat four had drawn the lucky number to make first contact with the *Kowshing*. If fired upon, as they all hoped, it would attack the port-side battle cruiser. The *Naniwa* would engage the point cruiser. The third Chinese fighting ship would be screened from the action by the *Kowshing* itself.

'Our guns are for the cruisers,' Togo said. 'They are not large enough to sink them, but able to disrupt their aim. Our torpedoes are for the troopship. She is an unarmed converted English freighter. We all know from Colonel Honjo that the *Kowshing* is carrying wagons, supplies and weapons, in addition to men. Her powder magazine is full of ammunition. The white paint spilled down her port side marks the powder magazine.'

A cup of sake was placed in Uraga's hand.

'For the Emperor and victory,' Togo said. 'Kampai!'

The officers drank.

'Keep the cups,' Togo said. 'If the Chinese do not shoot, we can get roaring drunk and fill them with tears of sorrow. If they open fire we shall perform Giri for Nagasaki. Then get roaring drunk and fill the cups with tears of joy.'

The Mokpo light swung through the dark in an arc that silhouetted the Chinese fleet. Togo and Uraga stood on the *Naniwa*'s quarterdeck. 'The *Kowshing* is a giant,' Uraga said.

'And lit up like an English Christmas tree,' Togo replied. 'Westerners claim Orientals are cowardly, indecisive and stupid. The Chinese officers called us dwarfs. But the next few minutes will prove just how big we are. A successful torpedo run requires accurate positioning, correct launching speed and cool judgement.'

Uraga remained silent. He and every man in the squadron knew they were about to write a new chapter in Japanese history.

The crew of boat four prayed to the gods to be fired upon. They had sworn a blood oath to sink the Chinese battle cruiser by ramming their torpedoes into her. Each crew member had bound a cloth around his head bearing the words 'To the death'.

Togo looked at the Chinese convoy, then back to his watch. He dropped his pointed finger. 'Now!'

Twin white rockets whooshed off the *Naniwa*'s deck. Boat four answered with two green rockets, and darted forward at full speed. Other boats in the squadron fired rockets to alert and intimidate the Chinese.

'Listen,' Togo said. A deep mournful sound rolled over the Yellow Sea. He grabbed Uraga's arm. 'The *Kowshing*'s foghorn! And those shrill whooping sirens are the call to battle stations aboard the cruisers!'

'Their lights are still on,' Uraga said. 'Look. There go their flares.'

'Half speed ahead and man battle stations,' Togo ordered.

The ship moved faster.

Togo whirled on Uraga. 'You did not sound battle stations!'

'The men have been at their guns since we sighted the enemy, sir.' Uraga took off his cap. On his forehead he wore a red bandana with black letters.

'To the death,' Togo read. He looked around at his crew. All had removed their navy caps and wore red bandanas. The commodore took off his cap and flung it over the side. 'Have a bandana brought up for me!'

Flares floating above the Chinese ships spread a circle of harsh white light around the convoy. Japanese torpedo-boat four charged into that light and the deep sound of the *Kowshing*'s foghorn stopped. The wail of the shrill sirens faded into eerie silence and the torpedo-boat raced across the smooth silvery water.

Suddenly the cannon of the lead Chinese cruiser spat flames, followed by a horrendous roar. The broadside was the signal for the Chinese fleet's attack. Uraga grasped the *Naniwa*'s rail as she went to full speed and swung to port. He saw giant shells bracket boat four. Not one landed within fifty feet, yet the small boat was blown out of the water.

'Gunners, mark your targets,' Togo shouted through his megaphone. 'Gun captains, fire when ready!'

The two sixty-pounders and the twenty-pounders aboard the *Naniwa* roared. More Chinese flares rose into the air.

'Helmsman, keep us out of that circle of light,' Togo ordered. 'Uraga, enter into the ship's log that on 30 July at 23:34 hours, Chinese warships off the Mokpo light fired on us without warning or attempt at identification!'

The *Naniwa*'s guns roared again.

'A hit,' Uraga shouted, pointing to the orange light blossoming on the fantail of the lead cruiser.

The first wave of three torpedo-boats raced by the *Naniwa* into the attack. 'Banzai!' her crew bellowed.

The Chinese point cruiser fired at the *Naniwa*'s gun flashes and a freight train seemed to roar overhead. Uraga ducked. The sea erupted two hundred yards behind them. A moment later the *Naniwa* shuddered and was showered with sea water as shells exploded on the starboard side.

Uraga wiped salt water from his eyes. 'Can they fire and load so fast?' he shouted.

'We are fortunate,' Togo answered. 'Both cruisers are shooting at us.' He pointed to the second wave of three torpedo-boats passing by into the attack. 'They will have a better chance.'

The *Naniwa*'s guns fired again and Togo shouted to the helmsman. 'Come about! Take us into that ring of light! I want to keep both those battle cruisers shooting at us!'

'We hit the lead cruiser again,' Uraga shouted. 'The fools have still not blacked out their ships.' He was slammed against the quarterdeck rail and fell to his knees, drenched with sea water. Under him the old ship shuddered. Its hull had sprung leaks in numerous places.

Blood ran from Togo's nose. He pulled himself up from the deck. His ship had been bracketed by the big shells, but still she answered the helm and charged towards the point cruiser. He watched the first three torpedo-boats open fire with their 20mm guns on the port-side battle cruiser. The new armour-piercing shells tore the thin iron plate apart, creating havoc amid the Chinese crews on deck. The forward gun compartment was set ablaze and the gunpowder inside caught fire. A moment later a loud explosion blew the entire gun turret off the bow and into the sea.

The cruiser's big guns elevated to fire at the *Naniwa*, but the Chinese gun captains were distracted by 20mm shells sweeping their decks. The first three torpedo-boats flew past the cruiser's bow without a shot being fired at them, heading towards the *Kowshing* that loomed like a mountain half a mile away.

According to plan, to avoid being blown out of the water from behind by the cruiser's starboard guns, the torpedo-boat captains launched their first torpedoes at eight hundred yards, and raced on towards the *Kowshing*. At five hundred yards, boat one launched its second torpedo. The captain of boat three went in at two hundred yards, let go the long metal tube and spun the wheel. His boat heeled to starboard and he watched the white water torpedo trail race directly at the paint mark on the *Kowshing*'s side. Three explosions rocked the big boat before the last torpedo slammed in just below the powder magazine, breaking the big ship's back. Torpedo-boat number three had two men blown over the side. Another was killed below-deck when a twelve-foot piece of the *Kowshing*'s hull plate pierced the torpedo-boat's stern and she sank.

With the primary target destroyed, two of the boats in the second wave turned back and attacked the port-side cruiser. The third boat charged through wreckage, through the bodies of two thousand Chinese troops, and engaged the third cruiser on the far side.

Yaka had observed the battle. He ordered the coal-tender to Pusan and sat down to write his report. 'Chinese opened hostilities off Mokpo light. The *Kowshing* and one battle cruiser are down. Second cruiser abandoned and sinking. Third cruiser escaped. Our losses: three torpedo-boats, twenty-five men. Squadron returning to base for repairs. I sail for Pusan to prepare for the landing of our troops. Dai Nippon banzai! Long live a great Japan!'

At dawn, Yaka went to the stern of the ship and released the pigeons for Mung in Nagasaki. Ten minutes later he set birds free for his father in Seoul. 'It is war.'

Chapter 25

In his mind's eye Hiroki saw Noriko sitting across from him at his grandfather's dinner table. Her smiling face. Those beautiful shoulders. He had felt their power on the kendo square. He remembered her slim figure, dainty walk and the graceful sweep of her neck. He recalled her soft eloquent voice reciting the history of each viewing place in the Emperor's garden. He wished to be with her. To tell her what was about to happen. Every Japanese would be affected by his actions in the next few hours.

His father re-read Yaka's message, then held it up. 'Activate your Special Forces,' Udo said. 'You will enter the Kyongbok palace unarmed. If possible I want the Koreans on our side. We war against the Chinese.'

'Will the Black Dragons and Genoysha be involved?' Hiroki asked.

'Only those already inside the palace. The White Wolf Society and military intelligence will be coordinated through Mung in Nagasaki. I have called up every agent in the Far East.'

'My Special Forces are standing by,' Hiroki said. His years of preparation, planning and training yearned to be tested. Thoughts of Noriko were gone. He could not keep the excitement from his voice. 'Do we wait for a formal declaration of war?'

'That is for the politicians,' Udo said. 'We cannot afford to lose the element of surprise. No one else in Korea knows the fate of the *Kowshing* and her escorts. But I should think that two thousand drowned Chinese soldiers are as strong a declaration of war as can be given.'

'The balloon is ready,' Hiroki said. 'Are the new American field telephones in operation?'

'Didn't you trip on the communication wires inside this compound?'

'I meant outside. To make contact from the palace.'

'Everything is in order,' Udo said. 'Remember to keep your Korean Special Forces from entering the queen's apartment. They must believe she supports us. That there is a chance to escort her from the palace to our compound, although there is actually no way to free the king and queen. Keeping the queen hostage in her apartment will neutralize the Korean army long enough for our troops to land unopposed at Pusan. Queen Min is the key to our success! You know what to do if the Chinese try to recapture her!'

'Yes, but what about our nationals?'

'After you and your men enter the palace, I will call them in. Should something go wrong, try to make your way to Pusan.' Udo looked into his son's eyes. 'I have had to kill people who were not strangers, but it was never personal and I never suffered an afterthought.'

'I will do my duty,' Hiroki said.

Hiroki left the army compound and made directly for the Special Forces camp. Guards at the main gate saluted him. He waved to the men inflating a small hot air balloon. Fifty Koreans, wearing loose-fitting white canvas karate uniforms, stood at attention. Their five Japanese officers saluted and Hiroki bowed. He had trained with many of these men since childhood, handpicked and drilled each one especially for this operation. All were blood relatives of the powerful Min family, loyal to the queen and expert in the art of unarmed combat.

'The time has come to free Queen Min,' Hiroki declared. 'Chinese warships opened fire on Japanese ships in the Yellow Sea. Tomorrow, August first, war will be declared between China and Japan. The outcome will determine Korea's future. Your country will either remain a vassal state to the corrupt Chinese empire or become a free and independent nation guided by Japan. Tonight's venture could influence the outcome of the war and future of your people.' He shouted the question his men had been asked every day for years. 'Are you prepared to fight for your country?'

The response came back with unbridled emotion. 'We are ready to fight! To die for a free Korea!' The men of the Special Forces raised their arms. Their fists were gnarled from years of pounding into sand and gravel, against wood and stone.

Hiroki returned their salute. 'Our primary objective is to free Queen Min from her Chinese captors! She will be taken to the Japanese compound, from where she will call on her people to rise! A smaller unit will attempt to reach King Kojong! I have men in position to stop any Chinese spies who might observe our approach to the palace!' He pointed to the balloon. 'That will be used at the palace's south wall as our signal to go over the north wall!'

Kyongbok Palace, 9 p.m.
A Special Forces man lit the fuse leading into the basket under the balloon. As it began to rise, other men let the guide ropes slip through their hands. The hot air balloon floated up and was secured just above the twenty-foot-high stone wall. Others lit star rockets and strings of firecrackers, throwing them over the palace wall as they ran.

On sight of the balloon on the opposite side of the palace, Hiroki led his men up and over the north wall. On the inside, two Genoysha agents led them at a run across the parade ground towards the palace kitchen. A quarter of a mile away the balloon exploded in a spectacular pyrotechnic display and the palace guards ran towards the explosion. Hiroki and his men approached the building and burst inside, startling the few kitchen workers.

'Line up against the wall and remain silent,' Hiroki ordered.

'They are unarmed,' the cook called to his workers. He seized a cleaver.

Hiroki scaled the butcher block and kicked the cook in the stomach. The round man doubled up and crumpled to the floor. The others had not moved.

'Group B, go!' Hiroki shouted.

Fifteen men left the kitchen for the king's apartment. Hiroki and the remainder followed the second Genoysha man. They hurried through corridors and up the stairs to Queen Min's apartment.

Hiroki and the guide turned a corner ahead of the others and crashed into three Chinese guards. Before the startled guards could even lower their rifles, the men behind had disarmed them with swift karate blows.

'The next turn to the right,' the Genoysha man said, and dashed ahead.

The guards in front of the queen's door heard running footsteps and levelled their rifles. The Genoysha man turned the corner and all four guards shot him. Hiroki leapt over the riddled body. He kicked one guard in the groin and knocked out a second with a snap punch to the forehead. He pushed up the rifles of the third and fourth guards as they pulled their triggers. Shots ricocheted off the stone walls and the Special Forces men swarmed over the Chinese.

Hiroki knocked on the queen's door. He waited. His men stared at the door.

A thin, small voice came from inside the royal apartment. 'Password, please.'

Hiroki recognized the queen's voice. 'I am Gin-ko's son,' he answered.

Again they waited expectantly. There was a click of a

key and the snap release of a latch and bolt. The door opened a crack.

Hiroki leaned forward and looked into the heart-shaped face of Queen Min. She wore bright red lipstick with rouged cheeks, and a high black hairdo. She peeked out at him. 'Yes?' she said.

'Your highness.' Hiroki bowed. 'As representative of his imperial majesty the Emperor of Japan, I am privileged to bring greetings and offer you his protection.'

'There was to be no killing,' Queen Min said.

'Those shots were fired by the Chinese guards.' Hiroki signalled and the four were brought around so the queen could see them. They were bound, gagged, but still alive.

'You and your men are unarmed?' the queen asked.

'As you requested,' Hiroki said. 'Are you prepared to leave?' His mission was to get into the apartment and isolate the queen.

'Not until my husband arrives. You may enter.' She opened the door.

Hiroki stepped inside and the door slammed behind him. He looked into the barrels of two hunting rifles held by the queen's elderly body servants.

'Raise your hands,' the queen said. 'My men will search you. In the meantime, tell me about your mother. Is she well?'

'My mother is quite well,' Hiroki said, spreading his legs. 'She attended a wedding just before I left Japan.' The servants were older men. The one who searched him grunted as he bent. The other seemed more frightened of the weapon he held than of the visitor.

'Her Korean physician thought she was quite ill.' The queen's red lips puckered. 'I am pleased he was wrong.'

'I was not certain you knew of her condition, your highness. The last communication from Tokyo indicated my mother was doing as well as can be expected.'

The servants stepped back and the queen nodded at

them. 'Had my men found a weapon on your person, your condition would have been dead,' she said to Hiroki. 'And I would have sided with the Chinese. Where is King Kojong?' she demanded.

'Pardon me,' Hiroki said. He moved to the window, at the same time keeping his eyes on the old men. He drew the drapes back and placed an electric lamp on the sill. 'If I raise this lamp three times, a message will be sent to your family and the Min generals that you request Japan's assistance to expel the Chinese invaders.'

'Raise that lantern once and I will tell my men to shoot!' the queen said. 'I make no commitments until the king arrives! It was not our agreement to ask Japan to expel the Chinese! Your country is to be given favoured nation status for freeing my husband and me from the Chinese.'

It had been a mistake to ask the queen to sanction Japan's armed intervention, but the light in the window was the signal that Hiroki held the queen hostage. His father would take care of the rest. He had only to wrest the shotguns from the two old men and bring his Japanese officers into the apartment.

Loud voices in the hall and pounding on the door diverted the attention of the two servants. Hiroki stepped by the queen and kicked the first man's arm. He squeezed a pressure point below the other's elbow. Both weapons fell to the floor.

Hiroki drove his callused fist down and splintered a small table into pieces. 'Queen Min, order your servants to stay back or they are dead!'

'Are you my protector or my enemy?'

The pounding on the door grew louder. Hiroki bent his knees, cocked his fists and advanced on the two frightened old men.

'They will do as you say,' the queen whispered. 'I fear I have made a mistake in trusting the Ishikawa family.'

Hiroki opened the door to three Japanese officers. They

rushed in and locked the door behind them. 'Report,' Hiroki ordered.

'General Li's troops have taken the king from the palace. Twelve of our people were killed trying to get into his apartment.'

'What of our Koreans outside this door?' Hiroki asked.

'They are unaware of what is happening.'

Hiroki heard the queen pick up the telephone. He leapt across the room and snatched it from her.

'Yes, your highness,' a man's voice said. Hiroki stared at the receiver. 'Does your highness wish to make a call?' He was about to put down the telephone and rip out the line when he had an idea. 'This is the Japanese ambassador speaking. I am dining with the queen. It is necessary for me to speak with Mr Udo Ishikawa at the Japanese compound.'

'One moment please.'

Japanese compound

'Send runners to the Min family elders and generals!' Udo handed the messenger several envelopes. 'Tell them we have saved the queen! They are to keep all Korean troops in their barracks until further notice!' He motioned the messenger on his way and called three other Black Dragons into the room. 'My son has signalled that the queen is his hostage. Hiroki's life may depend on how quickly you kill the three conservative Korean ministers who back King Kojong. Our people saw the Chinese take the king from the palace. The Korean cabinet has been called to emergency session.' The telephone rang and Udo picked it up. He listened to the voice and gasped. 'Hiroki! Where are you?'

'With the queen in her apartment. With telephones so new here, I suppose they forgot to cut them off. I can see from the window that the Royal Korean palace guards are being marched away by General Li's men. Chinese units are surrounding the Korean army barracks outside the palace wall. We are trapped here. Chinese soldiers are forming up on the parade ground just below the window. I assume we shall soon be attacked, and the only weapons we have are two shotguns.'

Udo looked up from the phone and shouted, 'Colonel!' The commander of the Japanese forces hurried into the room. 'How many men can you put under arms immediately? They must run from here to the palace and overcome three hundred Chinese.'

'Our seven hundred can take three thousand Chinese,' the colonel said. 'Rumour has it they called us bowlegged dwarfs.'

I cannot return to Japan and tell Gin-ko Hiroki is dead, Udo thought. 'Enter the Kyongbok palace,' he ordered, making the first decision ever for his personal benefit. 'Stop the Chinese from taking Queen Min! Protect my son!'

The colonel began shouting orders before he was out of the room.

'Hold out as long as possible,' Udo said into the telephone. 'Now let me talk with Queen Min.'

Hiroki asked the queen to come to the telephone but she refused. 'She will not speak with you,' he said to his father.

'Never mind,' Udo said. 'Barricade yourself in that apartment! The Japanese army is on its way.' He heard no response from his son. ' Are you still there?'

'Yes, Father. Do you have the feeling we are changing history?'

'You are making history! Be there when I arrive and we shall write it together! I am on my way!'

Udo hung up the telephone and scribbled a message. He handed it to his orderly. 'Send this to the Black Dragon, but first get me a rickshaw! I am going to war!'

Chapter 26

'We cannot allow ourselves to be distracted by rumours of a western conspiracy against us,' Nogi said. 'There is a war to fight with China.'

'My thoughts are on negotiating the peace,' Mung said.

'Not if we lose.'

Mung turned to Takamora. 'I want it noted in the minutes of this meeting that my agents report that Russia, France and Germany cut communications with the British simultaneously with China's declaration of war against us. Those three countries called in our ambassador in Seoul about the sinking of the *Kowshing*. They say we violated international law. I believe they are conspiring against Japan.'

'Do you think they would attack us?' Nogi asked.

'It would take two months for their military to prepare,' Mung said.

'We are ready now,' Takamora said. 'The invasion of Korea has begun.' He walked to the wall map. 'I have ordered Togo's Torpedo-boat Squadron to rendezvous with me at sea. We will escort Marquis Inei's troopships to land at Pyongyang, the provincial capital of northern Korea. Hideyoshi's White Wolves report the main body of General Li's army is camped there. They have old weapons and poor discipline. In addition, many senior officers are in Peking on holiday.'

'I assumed you would plan to attack Seoul first,' Mung said.

'The Korean capital will fall by itself if we defeat the Chinese in the north and the Korean army in the

231

south at Pusan. Your Black Dragons have provided us with excellent information about Pusan's fortifications, its harbour and weather. Udo learned well from our Formosan fiasco.'

'He and Hiroki are still surrounded in the Kyongbok palace.'

'Many men will make sacrifices before this is over,' Nogi said. 'It is a time to show courage, gain honour and serve the Emperor. If Udo can keep the Chinese and Korean armies in Seoul for another twenty-four hours, it will be too late for them to send reinforcements to Pyongyang or Pusan to oppose our landings.'

'Are you still in telephone communication with Udo?' Takamora asked.

'Through Yaka in Pusan,' Mung said. 'This should be him now.' He snatched up the telephone on the first ring.

'Grandfather, our engineers have spliced the telephone lines,' Yaka said. 'You can speak directly with my father in Seoul.'

'I am here,' Udo shouted over the static.

'What is the situation in the palace?' Mung shouted.

'Confusion. The Chinese fear that if the queen is harmed they will have to fight us and the Koreans.'

Mung repeated Udo's words aloud.

'Tell him that possibility should be considered,' Nogi said. 'But he must keep the Chinese and Korean armies in Seoul.'

Mung repeated Nogi's order into the phone.

'There may be another way,' Udo said. 'The Tonghaks have attacked government offices and Korean army troops on the outskirts of Seoul. I have made an offer to have our soldiers in the palace join with an equal number of Korean troops to subdue the Tonghaks. If that is accomplished, General Li would then allow our civilians to be evacuated on ships bound for Japan. After they have departed, I shall release Queen Min. It should take at least seventy-two hours.'

'I thought the Tonghaks were on our side,' Takamora said.

'They are religious fanatics who are anti-everyone,' Mung said.

'How long can Udo keep General Li's troops immobilized?' Nogi asked.

'Three to five days,' Udo told Mung.

'Can Udo confirm Colonel Honjo's report of a ten-ship Chinese fleet in the Yellow Sea?' Takamora asked.

Mung repeated the question and Udo's reply. 'Admiral Ting now has twelve ships in the Yellow Sea. Two new seven-thousand-ton battleships have joined his North Sea Squadron. They are at Weihaiwei naval base. Another twenty ships are in Port Arthur.'

'If they catch us at sea as we did the *Kowshing*, it will be a disaster,' Takamora said.

'If we do not act as boldly as our men surrounded in the Kyongbok palace, we deserve to lose,' Nogi said. 'Tell Udo and his son to proceed with their plan.'

Mung replaced the receiver in its cradle. 'The line is dead.'

It was the third day locked in the royal suite with Queen Min. The more numerous Japanese troops had surprised and overwhelmed the three hundred Chinese soldiers in the palace compound. They had charged into the palace itself but were now surrounded by General Li's Twenty-first Division and other Chinese units. Hiroki had not been sleeping well. He looked up from his sleeping mat and watched his father at the queen's writing desk. A pile of crumpled writing paper lay at Udo's side. He rested his writing brush and held up a document to the morning sun.

'Can I help?' Hiroki asked.

233

'Does this appear official to you?'

Hiroki rolled off the sleeping mat and peered at the paper. 'It looks impressive.'

'Does the signature match these?' Udo handed over several proclamations and requisitions written by Queen Min.

'Yes, but will the Korean generals accept the queen's declaration of war on China without hearing it directly from her?'

Udo glanced at the two Japanese guards standing before the closed door of the queen's bedroom. 'You must convince the Min family it is a possibility.'

'But I wish to remain here with you,' Hiroki said.

'You are more important outside. If General Li keeps his word and allows our soldiers to fight alongside the Koreans against the Tonghaks, I want you to slip out with them and deliver this letter to the senior Min general.' Udo took the queen's seal from a desk drawer and affixed it in three places as he had seen on the other documents. 'This should keep the Koreans in place for a while longer. I doubt they will fight the Chinese or move south against us without speaking directly to the queen. The Chinese will be forced to keep the Twenty-first Division in Seoul watching the Koreans and us.'

'Once our soldiers leave the palace, the Chinese could easily break into this apartment,' Hiroki said.

'They outnumber us and could do that now. I made it plain to General Li that if they try to take the queen before our nationals are evacuated, I shall kill her.' Udo pointed to the letter in his son's hand. 'Do your duty!'

There was a knock on the door and a voice called, 'Sir, the Korean general invites our men for breakfast before we leave to fight the Tonghaks.'

'If something happens to me, try to get to your mother,' Udo said. 'You are her favourite. I want you to know that she and I both approve of Noriko. I doubt you could find a better wife.'

234

Hiroki bowed. 'I will do as you say.'

'One more thing,' Udo said. 'At breakfast, let the Koreans eat first. They may try to poison our men.'

Nagasaki

'Sir, please pick up phone three. It is Count Iyeasu.'

Mung picked up the telephone and heard Iyeasu's voice. 'The Emperor, Parliament and all Tokyo are anxious. People have been in the streets throughout the night waiting for news. Our forces should have reached Pusan three days ago, and Pyongyang a day before that.'

'The Chinese have cut all internal communications and destroyed our underwater telephone cable from Pusan to Nagasaki and Hiroshima,' Mung said. 'The last pigeons flew in with old messages from Hiroki. The Tonghaks were wiped out and our nationals are on their way home. Queen Min was released into General Li's custody. She is with King Kojong.'

'Did Udo get out?'

'Yes. He is with Hiroki and our soldiers. They returned to their military compound in Seoul. No news from Takamora or Nogi.'

'The war could be over and we do not know it,' Iyeasu said. 'The Emperor wishes more attention paid to military communications in the future.'

'There is nothing to do but wait. I will notify you as soon as I hear something.' Mung hung up the phone and lay down to sleep.

Six hours later he was wakened by a telephone operator. 'Sir, it is the Kobe Club president.'

'Congratulations,' James Alburg said. 'My agents in Pusan report your forces routed the Royal Korean Army. They are in full retreat towards the capital.'

'What details do you have?' Mung asked.

'Your ships entered Pusan harbour at dawn without interference. My agents say your army scouts stationed

235

in Korea provided your company commanders with maps, photos and detailed plans of the Korean army's disposition. There was a fierce six-hour battle on the outskirts of Pusan. Then the Koreans broke and ran for Seoul.'

'On the Emperor's behalf I thank you for informing us,' Mung said. 'I will relay the information.'

'The Europeans thought the Chinese would eat you alive,' Alburg said. 'But at the Kobe Club we felt differently. Your military has vindicated our confidence.'

'There is still no word from Pyongyang.'

'That will take time. By ship it is a thousand miles further away than Pusan.'

'Thank you again. The Kobe Club will be remembered fondly in the history of our people.' Mung carefully replaced the receiver. Everyone in the room stared at him. No one moved. He realized they were waiting for him to speak. 'A complete victory in Pusan,' he said softly.

The room erupted. Men came running from other offices to hear the news. It spread through the building, to the army camp and into the city. The people of Nagasaki cheered. Mung would have liked to join them but was still concerned for the second invasion force. He telephoned Iyeasu in Tokyo to tell him the news of Pusan. Minutes later Tokyo's ancient war gong sounded and the capital exploded with joy.

Twelve hours later there was still no word from Pyongyang. The national euphoria had peaked. An exhausted population held a second vigil. And twenty-four hours later there was still no word. The mood was sombre. The defeat of the imperial fleet became a sobering possibility. Streets emptied. People stood in long lines at temples and shrines to pray for the men who were to have landed in northern Korea.

Thirty-six hours after word of the Pusan victory, again Mung arose from his bed to answer the telephone.

'William Whittefield here. I have news of Pyongyang.'

Mung's stomach lurched. 'Good or bad?'

'You've done it,' William shouted. 'Nogi's troops landed and advanced in tight formation. Although outnumbered, they drove the Chinese from the provincial capital. General Li is regrouping his men along the Yalu river and Nogi is going after them.'

'How long ago did this take place?'

'Seven days. Did you receive my messages?'

'Nothing arrived,' Mung said.

'Then you don't know about Admiral Ting and his fleet. That could spell disaster for the imperial navy.'

The men in the operations room saw the smile on Mung's face fade. They watched him frown and replace the receiver.

'General Nogi has taken Pyongyang and is moving north to the Chinese–Korean border,' Mung said.

The men held their breath in anticipation of the bad news. They silently followed Mung to the wall map.

'Admiral Ting left the Weihaiwei naval base to trap our fleet in Korea Bay,' Mung said. 'He has twelve ships, including the two seven-thousand-ton battleships. We have only eleven small craft. The Chinese outnumber, outweigh and outgun us.' He pointed on the map to Mukden, Antung and Yingkow. 'On land, General Li has activated his reserves here, here and here. Two hundred thousand men are moving to trap General Nogi at the Yalu river. I have no contact with our agents to warn either Nogi or Takamora. Release only the news of Pyongyang to the public!'

For a short while the people of Japan again rejoiced in news of victory. Then tension grew once more as the nation waited for word from the north. In Nagasaki especially fervent prayers were offered for the defeat of Admiral Ting's squadron.

18 September

Mung was alerted by the harbour signal gun. From his

237

office window he saw one of Togo's torpedo-boats careen into the harbour at full speed, firing bursts from its two 20mm guns and sounding its shrill steam whistle. An outgoing freighter responded with a deep-throated foghorn. One after the other, ships large and small greeted the torpedo-boat. The men in the office crowded behind Mung at the window.

'They fly the victory flag,' came a voice from over Mung's shoulder.

Mung could see a smaller flag under the Emperor's rising sun banner, but could not make out its design or colour. As others around him began to celebrate, Mung thought it strange to be most concerned with the realization that he needed spectacles.

'We have won,' a young lieutenant shouted. 'Sire, we have won!'

'On land or at sea?' Mung asked.

'I shall find out.' The officer raced from the office.

Mung watched crowds pour down to the dock. Temple gongs sounded. Christian missionaries rang their church bells. He saw the lieutenant returning with a young naval officer. They were followed to his office by everyone in the building. People tried to push in to hear the news.

The naval officer stood in front of Mung and bowed. It was Uraga. Mung's face lit up.

'Grandfather, Admiral Takamora has defeated the Chinese North Sea Squadron in Korea Bay! Everything came in fours. It took four hours to defeat them, four of their ships went down and four were damaged. Admiral Ting escaped with four ships to Weihaiwei naval base.'

'What of ours?' Mung asked.

'Except for minor damages, the imperial fleet is intact.'

There was stunned silence in the crowded room. Then Mung stepped forward to embrace his grandson and the

238

room erupted with chanting. 'Banzai! Banzai! Dai Nippon banzai!'

'Let him tell how it happened,' someone called out.

Mung's heart filled with pride for his grandson and his country.

'They had larger ships,' Uraga said. 'But our weapons, armour and tactics were superior. The Chinese came after us like cavalry in a line abreast. Admiral Takamora signalled for our fleet to divide into two columns and surround them. Once in range, our ships could fire at all of theirs, but only their ships on the outside could shoot at us. It was those outside ships that were sunk or damaged. The others escaped.'

'Where is our fleet now?'

'They have Admiral Ting bottled up in Weihaiwei and the rest of the Penyang fleet blocked in Port Arthur.'

'Is there word from General Nogi?' Mung asked.

'One success after another,' Uraga said.

'We heard about his victory at Pyongyang,' Mung said. 'Then there were reports of 200,000 Chinese troops marching to trap him at the Yalu.'

'He defeated them several days ago.' Uraga saw the stunned expressions on his grandfather's face and the men around him.'I thought you knew. The entire Chinese army along the Yalu is in retreat. General Nogi sent three flying columns forward to take Mukden.'

Mung grabbed his grandson by the arm and pulled him to the wall map. He pushed men out of their way with the stump of his left arm. 'It is 150 miles from the Yalu to Mukden! That city has over a million people! What does Nogi think he is doing?'

'Grandfather, I do not believe General Nogi intends to stop at Mukden. He signalled my father to activate all our agents on the route from Mukden to Peking.'

'Has the man gone mad?' Mung gasped. 'He cannot take the capital of China!'

239

'Grandfather, we are blessed from heaven by the divine leadership of his imperial highness, the Emperor. We can do whatever he orders.'

'I doubt the Emperor thought of Mukden or Peking.'

'It is only three hundred miles between those cities,' Uraga said.

'With several million Chinese blocking the way.'

'We shall fertilize the countryside with the bodies of all who oppose us!'

Mung ignored the simplistic army slogan. 'Where is your father?'

'Near Inchon with Hiroki and Yaka. They are safe.'

Mung reached for the telephone and dialled. 'Fukoku kyhoii,' he said when Iyeasu answered. 'Do you remember that battle cry? Rich country, strong army?'

'Lord Hotta shouted it before committing seppuku,' Iyeasu said.

'Hotta sacrificed his life for mine. He threatened that if I ever faltered in my duty to Japan, he would rise from the grave and haunt me. After you have reported to the Emperor, please send someone to Hotta's grave to read aloud Uraga's battle report.'

'You can do that yourself,' Iyeasu said. 'The Emperor summons you back to Tokyo to work with Hideyoshi on a negotiated settlement with China. Lord Cade has arrived here with word from Peking. Your son and grandsons are summoned to Tokyo also. The Emperor wishes them to be with Gin-ko. She is dying.'

Chapter 27

'I would rather marry a pig or a Pantagruelian,' Noriko said, repeating the phrase an American girl at school had used. She giggled as she arranged a spray of wild flowers in a bamboo vase. She had no idea what a Pantagruelian was, but she was angry with Hiroki. Since his letter from the ship, his mother had not heard from him. *If he really wants to marry me, he should have sent me a letter.*

'Are you smiling because of the mi-ai?' Gin-ko asked.

'I fear the strain of the ceremony will be too much for you,' Noriko said.

'Today I am strong. Stressful moments will come again when Hiroki arrives. You should leave and prepare yourself for the mi-ai. He would be shamed if you are present when he apologizes to me.'

'Do you wish me to escort you to the ceremony?'

'My husband will do that.' Gin-ko smiled at the thought of Udo. She shooed Noriko on her way.

Noriko waited for Hiroki in the corridor. She had planned and practised her words to him a thousand times. Then, when he finally turned the corner, the sheepish look on his face disconcerted her. She grew angry at feeling pity for him. He deserved being unhappy. Instead of her suave, cynical, prepared speech, Noriko burst out with words she had not intended. 'Your mother is dying!'

Hiroki flinched and lowered his eyes. 'I know.'

'She believes you and your brothers are unaware of her condition. If you cause her more pain, I will not marry you!' Noriko removed her mother's small dagger from her obi. 'In samurai times this was meant for wives to kill themselves rather than face shame.

I will take my own life before marrying you if you hurt her!'

'My grandfather told me of the love and care you have given my mother,' Hiroki said. 'I am, and shall always be in your debt. I have come to apologize to her before the mi-ai. I hope you will look on me with favour and we will be married soon.'

'My father wishes our marriage. He wishes you to carry on our family name.'

'I will proudly accept the name of Koin and bring honour to it and our children.'

'Then it is my On to your mother and my father to marry you,' Noriko said. She flinched at the hurt of her words reflected in Hiroki's smooth, strong face.

'If it were not for your obligations, would you consider me?' Hiroki asked.

He saw Noriko's beautiful lips tighten and the bright dark eyes look beyond him.

'I also have an On to my family and will marry you for the help you have been to my mother, and to my grandfather when he was ill,' Hiroki said. 'There is the obligation to the Emperor to combine our family fortunes and political power for the good of Japan. But if none of these reasons existed, I would still seek you as my wife.' He watched for her reaction but Noriko appeared unaffected.

'Uncle Mung and my father will not attend the mi-ai,' she said. 'They are meeting with Lord Cade and Count Hideyoshi.'

Hiroki turned and went to his mother's door. Noriko watched him go down on his knees. He opened the door and crawled through on his belly. As she walked away she was again angry at herself for pitying him.

'You will make your mother cry,' Gin-ko said. 'Rise up and let me hold the hero of the Kyongbok palace.'

Hiroki went to his mother on his knees. He opened

242

his mouth to speak and a great sob retched up from his chest. His body shuddered. His mother was a frail image of her former self. Her eyes were large, her face thin and her jet black hair, although perfectly combed, was dull and lustreless.

She reached out and he buried his face on her shoulder. 'I am so sorry, Mother. Please forgive me. I should commit seppuku for my behaviour to you.'

'To learn of my past as you did was indeed a shock. Your reaction was predictable.' Gin-ko stroked her son's head and patted his back as she had when he was a baby. 'Soon you will marry and learn that sex and love are separate things. When they are combined, as they have been with your father and me, it is the most beautiful gift the gods have given to humanity. It is something to nurture in your marriage. Noriko is a wonderful young woman. We have become close friends in these last months. I have an On to her which I find difficult to resolve.'

Hiroki sat back on his heels. 'Mother, is it possible I could repay this obligation for you?'

The conversation was moving as Gin-ko had planned. She looked into her son's eyes. 'It may be too much to ask of you. As a young, virile man you may not be able to comply.'

'Please, Mother,' he pleaded. 'If you have ever given me any gift, allow me to fulfil this On for you. I will meet every obligation you have to Noriko.'

'She has given so much of her time and energy into making these months pleasant for me. She took care of your grandfather, which would have been my duty had I been here. I wish to make her happier than most Japanese women for the rest of her life.'

'Exactly what I want for her,' Hiroki said.

'Then you are in love? It is not like your brothers' arranged marriages?'

'I loved her from the moment we met.'

243

'You take after your father. The love lion tore his heart too. With me it was different. At first I thought your father was a country bumpkin. How wrong I was. He has made me supremely happy. I would like the same for Noriko.'

'Mother, tell me what to do.'

'It would be naive to expect that in your years together some annoyance and petty arguments will not strain your relationship. That cannot be avoided.'

'Is there a special way to maintain harmony in the home?'

'Sex,' Gin-ko said. 'More arguments have been worked out in bed than over tea in rational conversation. In Japanese society it is accepted the husband will have one or more concubines. In this I believe the Christians far more advanced. Their religion requires sexual loyalty. Nature's forces naturally draw men and women together. You cannot continue to be angry while embracing. Your father and I have found it so. Neither he nor your grandfather had concubines or went to the pleasure houses. Ours has been an ideal marriage under difficult conditions. I would like Noriko to enjoy life with a faithful husband.'

'I do so swear that from the day of our marriage I shall sleep with no other woman but my wife.'

'I would prefer your vow to begin today, from her acceptance of you at the mi-ai.'

'And so it shall be,' Hiroki said, and bowed. 'Thank you, Mother. Our first girl child shall be named for you.'

Gin-ko handed her son a package. 'This is a rare thing. Most pillow books illustrate and explain how women can pleasure men. This was written two centuries ago by an expert in the art of lovemaking. It tells the male how to pleasure a female. Love Noriko with your heart, your mind and your body, Hiroki my beloved son.' She held out her arms and drew him to her.

His eyes filled with tears.

'Go to your brothers and prepare for seeing the prospective brides. Your father will escort me.'

Hiroki touched the book to his forehead. He bowed and left the room.

Mung and Iyeasu were on their way to the meeting with Hideyoshi and Malcolm Cade. Iyeasu dragged his wooden leg. His crutches tapped a steady beat on the stone floor of the imperial palace. He had not lost weight and his movements were slow.

'My daughter and Gin-ko have become very close,' Iyeasu said.

'What is my daughter-in-law's present condition?' Mung asked.

'The woman has steel in her spine and courage in her gut. She gave me the will to live when I lost my leg. But she has no control over the disease that eats away at her. There are periods when she can walk unaided, but they become fewer and farther between.'

Mung sighed. 'I hope she can endure the strain of the mi-ai. It must be difficult for Noriko too. She nursed me, you and now Gin-ko.'

'The doctors do not give Gin-ko more than a month of life,' Iyeasu said. 'But I must ask you to put your thoughts of her aside. We turn our attention to my brother. He is now the most powerful man in Parliament. If there was an election, he would become prime minister.'

'Without the Emperor's blessing?'

'We have a democratic state and Hideyoshi controls it. He has taken credit for building up our military by pushing bills to finance the war. This, he claims, led to our victories in Korea.'

'Are the people aware that Nogi is stalled on the road to Mukden? He is taking more casualties from disease than from the enemy. The latest reports indicate he is low on ammunition and supplies.'

'What of the Kobe Club's guaranteed delivery?' Iyeasu asked.

'They have kept their agreement and supplied our forces in the south,' Mung said. 'There we have taken every objective from Pusan to Seoul. But Marquis Inei miscalculated our needs in the north. He assumed his factories could meet the army's requirements. The war came sooner and is more intense than he expected.'

'You had asked me to question Inei because the Kobe Club felt their orders were too small.'

'That was the evening you lost your leg,' Mung said. 'The question was forgotten in the course of events.'

Iyeasu lowered his chin and shook his head.

'There is nothing to be done about that now,' Mung said. 'Possibly Lord Cade has a solution.'

Hideyoshi was already seated at the table with Malcolm Cade when Mung and Iyeasu entered. 'I have requested from Lord Cade to forgo formalities and speak directly to the point,' Hideyoshi said.

Mung and Iyeasu nodded their agreement.

The Englishman leaned forward and said, 'Japan is either on the verge of a great victory or a disastrous defeat. No one in the West believed your armies could take Korea, cross the Yalu or bottle up the Penyang fleet.'

'If we are so successful, where is the disaster?' Iyeasu asked.

'In your success,' Malcolm Cade said. 'Your military is over-extended north of the Yalu. They need weapons, ammunition and winter supplies. The Manchurian winter will kill Nogi's army. He cannot reach Mukden before the freezing cold sets in. In the spring General Li will pour one million men down the Mukden road, over the Yalu river and sweep your army from Korea into the Yellow Sea.'

'Where will the Chinese supplies come from?' Mung asked.

'The Russians,' Hideyoshi said. 'My White Wolves report

the monk Rasputin has encouraged a secret agreement with Peking.'

Mung frowned. 'Colonel Honjo was to send all information to me. I was not informed of this!'

'Gentlemen, you can sort out your differences another time,' the Englishman said. 'I have a proposal to ensure your victory.'

'Sir, you were quite enthusiastic about your ability to have the French call in their loans to the Russians,' Mung said. 'Now we find the czar will supply arms to China.'

'I did what I promised,' Malcolm Cade said, fixing each man at the table with his hard grey eyes. 'I had an agreement with the French finance minister, but obviously pressure was brought to bear on him. Something has happened between France, Russia and Germany, which neither I nor my intelligence service can fathom. It is another reason for Japan to end this war quickly with a victory.'

'Can you give us that victory?' Iyeasu asked.

'Two of them.' The Englishman grinned.

'Will the Chinese negotiate?' Mung asked.

'After your success at Pyongyang and the Yalu, the Chinese requested a loan from Britain. I will approve it on condition there is peace between China and Japan. That will help bring the Chinese around. Prince Kung and the Empress will be delighted to discuss a settlement for Port Arthur and the Weihaiwei naval base. A bribe will assure favourable terms for Japan.'

'What will Britain gain?' Mung asked.

'Japan will give us the Weihaiwei naval base and all of the Shantung peninsula, which will be ceded to you by China. You will keep Port Arthur and the Liaotung peninsula. Between us we shall control the Yellow Sea, the Gulf of Pohai and all water approaches to Peking, the capital of China.'

'And what indemnity will the Chinese pay us for peace?' Iyeasu asked.

'I have not thought that out yet but be assured Japan will be well compensated, which will put Peking further in our debt. Britain wishes special trading privileges in Shanghai and on the Yangtze river for providing these banking services.'

'Why are you so certain we can take Port Arthur and Weihaiwei?' Mung asked.

'Because we trained and equipped your navy and know it is better than the Chinese navy. Your troops are now battle-tested. The soldiers guarding Port Arthur were hired from a Manchurian warlord. If you cannot beat them, you can always buy him.'

'There is something else,' Hideyoshi said. 'The British designed and built both Chinese naval bases. They purposely set the big guns only to fire seaward, in case they would have to capture those bases.'

Mung caught Lord Cade's frown. Obviously he and Hideyoshi had been conferring. The lord seemed to be revealing his intelligence secrets to quite a few people.

'I have forwarded the plans of the two naval bases to General Nogi and Admiral Takamora,' Hideyoshi said. 'They are ordered to attack both bases from the land side.'

'But the Emperor has not approved such a plan,' Iyeasu said.

'The Emperor only sanctions government,' Hideyoshi replied. 'He does not control it.'

'We overthrew the shogun to restore the Emperor to power,' Mung said.

'But you are the one who insisted on a democratic form of government. I opposed it.' Hideyoshi sneered. 'And now I find it quite convenient.'

'Japan's internal political arguments should not impede its decision making,' Malcolm Cade said. 'If your troops north of the Yalu freeze to death, you have lost the war. Pull them back before winter sets in and take those two

Chinese bases. I promise the peace settlement with China will repay your cost of the war, give you control over Korea and a sizeable chunk of China.'

'If I understand correctly,' Mung said, 'Count Hideyoshi has already used his power as Minister of War to attack Port Arthur and Weihaiwei. What I would like from Britain is a mutual defence pact. We support you against Germany, France and China. You support us against Russia and China.'

The three Japanese watched the Englishman. If he agreed, it would mean recognition of Japan as an equal by the most powerful nation in the world. It would be the first time a white, Christian nation had done so with a non-Caucasian state.

'The time is not appropriate,' Malcolm Cade said. 'Let us postpone discussion of an Anglo-Japanese alliance until after you have taken Port Arthur and Weihaiwei.'

Chapter 28

Even with the Ishikawa family reunited, the mi-ai was a subdued, melancholy affair. Gin-ko was happy to see Yaka and Uraga pleased with their prospective brides, but she was ill and the ceremony was hurried. The three brothers took leave of their parents and future in-laws. Each walked away with his young lady, followed by a matchmaker.

Noriko turned onto a stepping-stone path to a bench under a maple tree and Hiroki followed, admiring her every move. She sat on the stone bench and gazed up at the red, gold and bronze leaves. He moved closer to the bench and her cheeks flushed.

The sunlight played on Noriko's glossy black hair. Hiroki saw her dark bright eyes change from soft sable to hard ebony. Her jaw was set, her lips thin. 'Why are you angry with me?' he asked.

The question startled her and she turned her shoulders, revealing the nape of her neck. Hiroki looked into the back of the brocade kimono and desired her.

'Everything comes too easy for you,' Noriko said. 'You do not walk, you strut as if you own the earth and expect everyone to do for you. There are obligations one accrues. It is as if you do not understand the concept of On.' She saw him flinch and for some unknown reason felt compelled to hurt him more. 'You have been blessed with a superior intellect and physique. You accomplish easily what others must strive for. Yet you do not appear grateful.'

'To whom?' Hiroki asked. He tapped his head and chest. 'Am I guilty for that which my parents bestowed on me?'

'You take everything for granted.'

'I will not take you for granted.'

'Do you agree that I will study, do social work and continue my kendo lessons?' Noriko asked.

'If it does not upset the harmony of our home and the raising of our children.'

'How many children?' she pouted.

'How many do you wish?' Hiroki smiled but Noriko frowned. 'I like children,' he said. She looked away and he added, 'You will have servants.'

'I have done well until now without servants. I will manage the house and tend my own children.'

'Do you think you could love me?' Hiroki asked.

Noriko felt a shock in the pit of her stomach. She had an urge to reach up and stroke his smooth strong face. To touch his neck muscles and the tendons that blended into broad shoulders. Sexual desire came upon her again and Noriko was angry at herself for allowing it to surface. 'Shall we marry?' she asked.

'There is little choice,' Hiroki said. 'We are both honour bound to do so.' He turned to the marriage broker and said, 'We agree to a wedding.'

'The mi-ai went well,' Udo said. 'Gin-ko was able to make it through the ceremony. She is resting now.'

Iyeasu bowed, and congratulated Udo and Mung. 'We shall be in-laws. When and where is the wedding?'

'The other families agree to Gin-ko's request that it take place here in three weeks,' Udo said.

'Accepted,' Iyeasu said.

'With your permission we wish to restrict the ceremony and celebration to immediate family.'

'Your father and I had big plans, but we understand,' Iyeasu said.

'Gin-ko does not have much time left,' Udo said. 'I wish to be with her as much as possible.'

'We will try not to disturb you,' Mung said. 'Only give

251

us your evaluation of what we have told you about our meeting with Lord Cade and Hideyoshi.'

Udo wished to ask how Mung, who had lost his wife, and Iyeasu his leg because of Hideyoshi, could bear to sit in the same room with the new minister of war. He turned his thoughts from his personal feelings. 'It appears the Englishman and Hideyoshi have some secret understanding. It may have to do with the Russians, French and Germans who have become very cold towards the British in Tokyo, Seoul and Canton. Our agents are unable to provide more information. I believe Lord Cade's tactics are sound. Pull Nogi's troops back across the Yalu before the snow flies. Send him and Takamora to take Port Arthur and Weihaiwei. We need the guns, ammunition and supplies stored in Port Arthur.'

'Remember Formosa,' Mung said. 'Admiral Ting will be expecting us this time.'

'Not from the land side,' Udo said. 'Father, you have greatly underestimated our military. The battlefield successes in Korea were not luck or favours from the gods. Our men have the Kruger repeating rifles that do not jam in mud or dirt. Our night attacks on land were coordinated with the new field telephones. The Black Dragons, White Wolves and Genoysha agents supplied detailed maps and photographs to our army. They personally led our men over unfamiliar terrain. In some cases our agents sabotaged Chinese communications and bridges, and burned their supplies. Seventy of our men are undercover among the Chinese mercenaries at Port Arthur. In Weihaiwei there are twenty Black Dragons prepared to meet and lead our troops in the land assault. We have the original plans of the naval bases, their harbour charts and locations of their floating mine-fields. We intend to foul their drinking water and cause delays and disruptions in communications and supplies.'

'The intelligence services have laid a solid foundation

for our success,' Iyeasu said. 'If we take those bases, the Chinese will certainly sue for peace. It must be done soon. We are short of money and supplies.'

'There is one disturbing point,' Udo said. 'Hideyoshi has promoted Colonel Honjo to general and recalled him from Hankow to Tokyo. Honjo is one of the most dangerous men alive. He is certain to be involved with Hideyoshi's plans to become prime minister.'

Hankow

General Honjo clapped Shibata on the shoulder. 'We are both leaving Hankow. I travel to Tokyo, you to Manchuria.'

'The remainder of this war will be fought on the Shantung and Liaotung peninsulas. I could be useful there.'

'The Chinese are already beaten and too stupid to surrender,' Honjo said. 'The next war will be against the Russians and the stakes will be Korea, Manchuria and the northern territories as far as Siberia. I am sending you out of the Green House to prepare the way. You have from three to ten years to lay the groundwork for our invasion of Manchuria. I want you to emulate the successes of the Black Dragons in Korea. The next time our armies cross the Yalu I want them to take Mukden, Vladivostok and half a million square miles of Manchuria.'

'Has my request for a pharmaceutical laboratory been considered?' Shibata asked.

'Your opium-based wonder-tonic will be made and bottled here in Hankow, as well as the Golden Bat cigarettes. Supplies will take about a year to reach you. Use the time to travel through Manchuria. Make connections. Pay Chinese, Mongols and Russians to act as your agents. There is a quarter of a million yen in our Shansi bank account for you to draw upon.'

Shibata bowed. 'I will prepare the way for the imperial

army. When you move into Manchuria it will fall like a ripe plum into your hand.'

Honjo smiled. He picked up his riding crop and slashed at Shibata's face. The younger man blocked the general's arm and, in one smooth motion, twisted it behind his back. 'My judo instructors were efficient,' Shibata said.

'Good,' Honjo said. 'Release me! Stand at attention!'

Shibata dropped his hands and stepped back. The general walked around him as he had done that first day in the Green House.

'You have been the perfect candidate,' Honjo said. 'No one, I repeat, no one has ever come close to the ratings you received from your instructors. Have they told you that?'

'They have been most complimentary.'

'And rightly so.' Honjo smiled. 'Especially after the sinking of the *Kowshing* and your new information about the Russian, French and German plans for China.' He stopped to face his protégé. 'Close your eyes! Hold out both hands! I have a present for you.'

Shibata obeyed the orders and waited expectantly.

'Your one weakness is over-confidence,' Honjo said. 'Lying, stealing, even murder come easy to you. Never rely on others! You will work alone and must always have complete control of any situation! Trust no one!'

Shibata heard the riding crop cut the air. It swung up in a vicious cut between his legs and he jackknifed. He crashed to the floor doubled up, retching in pain.

Honjo stood over him. 'This is my gift to you, Akichi Shibata! Your final lesson! Never put yourself in a vulnerable position, no matter who asks it!' He crouched near the writhing man. 'The Green House is certainly not named for the colour of the building. Like a horticulturist, I cultivate, breed and grow deadly bastards here. You are my best specimen yet. Never trust anyone!' Honjo saluted with the riding crop. 'Good luck with the Manchus.'

*   *   *

254

'Tonight may be the only time we have to celebrate before our wedding,' Yaka said to his brothers. 'Father and Grandfather are busy with the war. Shimatzu is in Formosa. They are not available to host a bachelor party as grand as Shimatzu's for us. As older brother, I propose to host our own private bachelor party. Follow me!'

Uraga and Hiroki trailed after Yaka to Tokyo's water-front. They went from one western bar to another, drinking and looking for Europeans who knew what a bachelor party was.

'None of these blokes will join our celebration,' Uraga said.

'What is a bloke?' Yaka asked.

'I heard Hiroki say it,' Uraga said. 'Pick his head up off the table and ask him.'

Yaka grabbed his brother's collar and pulled him upright in the chair. 'I am awake and I heard the question,' Hiroki said. He pointed to a big Swedish sailor at the bar. 'A bloke is a guy. Like that one.' He waved his hand at the other sailors in the bar. 'They're all blokes,' he said in English.

The big Swede took up his tankard of beer and came to the table. 'Who's calling who a bloke?' he asked in broken English.

'Do you want to join our bachelor party?' Uraga asked.

'I'm not political,' the Swede said.

Other sailors drifted towards the table and surrounded the brothers.

'We three are going to marry,' Yaka said.

'Each other?' the Swede asked. He translated his joke for his mates and they laughed.

'Be my guests,' Yaka said. 'Bartender,' he shouted, 'bring drinks for my friends!'

'No Jap buys me a drink unless I buy him one first!'

Hiroki sensed danger and realized his brothers were unaware of the sly looks passing between the sailors.

'We shall drink with you and buy the second round for everyone,' Hiroki said.

'Better yet, let's arm wrestle for each round,' the Swede said.

'What is arm wrestle?' Uraga asked.

The Swede pulled over a chair and plopped down. He planted his elbow in the centre of the round table. Opening and closing his big hand, he said to Uraga, 'Take a grip. When I say go, press the back of my hand to the table.'

Uraga's hand was lost in the Swede's big hairy mitt. The blond giant promptly slammed Uraga's hand to the table. Only then did he say, 'Go!'

The sailors roared with laughter. 'Now you can buy us all a drink,' the Swede shouted.

Yaka placed his elbow in the centre of the table. 'I am the older brother. It is my place to redeem the honour of our family.'

The Swede put his elbow up. His hand towered over Yaka's.

Yaka pulled his hand back. 'This time someone else will say go.'

'Bartender,' the Swede called. 'Get over here! This little heathen son of a bitch has learned something about arm wrestling.' He turned and stared Yaka in the eye. 'Double or nothing!'

Yaka nodded at the bigger man. Their hands touched. 'Go,' the bartender shouted.

With ease the Swede pushed Yaka's hand backwards and pressed it flat on the table. 'Two more rounds for everyone,' the Swede shouted. 'The Japs are paying.' He downed a tankard of beer and a glass of whisky. Then he pointed at Hiroki. 'What about you?'

'He is our little brother,' Uraga said.

'Looks bigger and stronger than both of you.'

'Double or nothing,' Hiroki said.

The blond giant grabbed another tankard of beer and

quaffed it in one long gulp. He put his elbow in the centre of the table.

'Bartender, bring four more rounds and charge it to this big, dumb Swede,' Hiroki shouted.

'Who you calling dumb?'

'The one who is going to pay for seven rounds of drinks for everyone in this bar!'

'It ain't going to be me,' the Swede said. He rolled up his sleeve, flexed his muscles and moved forward on his chair. 'Come on, Jap, take a grip.'

'Do you have the money to pay if you lose?' Hiroki taunted.

'I never lose!'

'The money.' Hiroki smiled.

'Who'll back me?' the Swede shouted, and his friends showered money onto the table. He cleared a space in the middle.

Hiroki saw the big man move forward to the very edge of his seat. His cheeks were blazing red.

'Take a grip, Jap! I'll put your hand through the table!'

Hiroki concentrated on the distance between him and the wooden rung on the chair between the big man's legs. As their hands met, Hiroki shouted, 'Go!' and karate kicked the chair out from under the Swede. The blond giant slipped into a squat position, off balance and locked in a struggle of strength.

Hiroki watched the red in the seaman's cheeks spread up his face and down his neck as his bent legs began to tremble. Hiroki believed time was on his side, but the big Swede had muscles like steel cables. Their two hands quivered in the centre of the table. Hiroki closed his eyes and focused all his power into his shoulder, forearm and hand. The seaman's body shook with the strain of maintaining the squat position, and suddenly his legs gave way. As he fell backwards, Hiroki jammed the big hand to the table.

Yaka and Uraga jumped up to congratulate their brother

257

and he hurried them past gaping seamen towards the front door. Behind them there was a great roar. The crowd parted and the big Swede charged after them, swinging his fist. Hiroki ducked a round-house right. He turned sideways and drove his foot deep into the pit of the big man's stomach. The Swede doubled over. His head came up with puffed cheeks and his lips opened. As he spun around he spurted beer over those near him. His friends shouted protests and beat him to the floor. The Swede crawled under a table.

The three brothers ran out of the bar, laughing as they sprinted from the dock area. No one followed and they stopped to catch their breath.

'Little brother,' Uraga panted, 'I am glad you were with us. We have heard stories about the round-eyes' fondness of brawling. I was not prepared for it.'

'I have a reward for little brother,' Yaka said. 'Follow me!'

'Where are you taking us now?' Hiroki asked.

'To the ladies in Lotus House,' Yaka said. 'It is only fitting after a mi-ai to seek female companionship. Who can wait three weeks to satisfy his golden rod?'

'I cannot go,' Hiroki said.

'Little brother, this time there is a beautiful Chinese girl waiting for each of us.' Yaka grinned.

'No,' Hiroki said.

'Do you now think of Chinese girls as your sisters too?' Uraga asked.

Hiroki shook his head.

'Do you have the pox?' Yaka asked.

Hiroki had thought to keep it secret but soon realized his brothers would not be satisfied until he explained. 'I have taken the obligation of Mother's On to Noriko. Mother requested I follow Father and Grandfather's example.'

'An obligation to be celibate except with your wife?'

Hiroki nodded and his brothers shivered. 'I am glad I will not marry for love,' Yaka said.

'It worked for our parents,' Hiroki said, and wondered if Noriko would ever love him. 'You two go on. I have some reading to do.' Perhaps his mother was correct. Through the pillow book he might learn to bewitch Noriko.

Chapter 29

2 October 1894

Two months after the sinking of the *Kowshing*, Admiral Takamora's ship entered Tokyo harbour with the victory flag flying. The great bronze war gong was sounded and official celebrations commenced. Shrines, temples and government buildings were gaily decorated. Organized parades were joined by spontaneous groups of people in festive clothing carrying banners and flags.

In the great hall of the National Diet the Emperor sat on his golden throne. Members of the House of Peers, House of Commons, Cabinet and Privy Council were in attendance. Everyone awaited the war report in silence.

General Nogi strode to the podium. His deep voice boomed like an artillery piece. 'Due to the glorious guidance of the Emperor,' he bowed, 'the skill of our elected leaders,' he bowed to the members of the Diet, 'and to the energetic labour of our people, Japan is about to take her place among the modern nations of the world. The Chinese, who have dominated Korea for centuries, refused to negotiate with our government. Admiral Ting referred to us as dwarfs and opened fire on our torpedo-boats in the Yellow Sea.' The general jammed his fists into his hips and threw out his chest. 'They spurned diplomatic relations and declared war,' he bellowed. 'Sirs, the Chinese made a mistake. We crushed their allies in the Korean regular army. We chased them from the Pusan peninsula to Seoul. Then we ran the best Chinese regulars across the Yalu river.

'I allowed King Kojong to return unharmed to the Kyongbok palace, but in spite of that his family killed Queen Min. They burned her alive on the parade ground before the eyes of the Royal Korean officers' corps, for her cooperation with Japan. That was when we intervened. The Japanese imperial army now controls the Kyongbok palace and the Korean houses of Parliament. I have appointed a new king more disposed to a democratic form of government under our guidance. Japan must take on itself the responsibility of guardianship of the Korean kingdom until such time as it is fit to rule itself.'

Mung adjusted his new steel-rimmed spectacles and focused on members of the general staff sitting up front. They were aware that Queen Min had been killed because of the confusion created by Udo's forged orders. Once again Mung disapproved of his adopted son's methods. However, he had to admit the sweeping victories were in part a result of Udo's actions.

Nogi continued with his report. 'Japan lost 1,005 brave men on the battlefield, and 4,900 were wounded. The Chinese suffered fifty times our casualties. It will take them years to recover from the defeat of their armies.' He nodded to a murmur of approval of the low casualty figures.

Mung's Black Dragons had reported over 15,000 Japanese dead from disease and the winter cold along the Yalu, but these had not been counted as battlefield casualties. Most members of the Diet were former samurai who considered it a disgrace for a soldier to die in such a manner.

Nogi bowed to Takamora. 'We are an island nation. Control of the seas must always be uppermost in our minds. It is fitting that the commander of our imperial navy should continue this report.' He stepped back.

Takamora bowed to the Emperor and addressed the assembly. 'At the outset of this war, China had sixty-five fighting ships against Japan's thirty-two. We were outgunned in the Bay of Korea, but we succeeded in sending Admiral Ting's fleet running for cover to Port Arthur and Weihaiwei naval bases. We blockaded both bases, the Chinese challenged us with their torpedo squadrons, and in one glorious night of battle we destroyed them.' Takamora bowed to Nogi and faced the assembly again. 'The army and navy cooperated to attack both Weihaiwei and Port Arthur. While navy gunboats engaged Chinese fortifications, our transports landed the imperial infantry behind them. Our troops captured the bases and turned the Chinese guns on their own ships in the harbour. We sank, destroyed or captured every Chinese vessel.' He stood still for a moment, then said, 'China no longer has a navy! The Penyang fleet does not exist! I sent Admiral Ting's battle flag to the people of Nagasaki to show them Giri has been done! The honour of our people, our nation and the Emperor has been upheld! Our ancestors, who died on the shores of Korea four hundred years ago, have been vindicated!

'Two days ago Admiral Ting surrendered to us and then shot himself. China rightfully fears our troops could take Mukden and march on Peking. They are suing for peace. It is only fitting that our Minister of War Count Hideyoshi Koin be invited to address this assembly. He is the man of foresight. He, more than any other, persuaded us to pass the largest military budget in our history. This is our man of vision who foresaw our victories on land and sea!'

The members of the Diet erupted in wild cheers and applause. Top hats were flung into the air as Hideyoshi Koin walked onto the dais and bowed to the Emperor.

'My brother is taking every advantage he can,' Iyeasu whispered to Mung. 'He was not scheduled to speak.'

'He deserves recognition,' Mung said. 'He had more confidence in our military than I did.'

The members of Parliament settled back into their seats to listen to the first minister of war of the modern state of Japan.

'In ten days Lord Cade, the British Plenipotentiary

of the Far East, will escort General Li Hung-Chang to Shimonoseki for negotiation of a peace treaty,' Hideyoshi said.

Mung turned to Iyeasu. 'Why was I not informed?'

'I met with the Emperor just before this meeting and he did not know either. My brother has guaranteed himself a place in any negotiations. Hideyoshi is now too big a hero for the Emperor to reprimand.'

'This must be the connection Udo suspected between Cade and Hideyoshi,' Mung whispered. 'Honjo's arrival could be related.'

'Possibly so,' Iyeasu said. 'Nogi and Takamora are giving all the honours to Hideyoshi. The military may want the Englishman's backing when they fight Russia.'

'Fight Russia? Are they mad?'

'You know the plans exist.'

'So did Icarus' scheme to fly,' Mung said.

Hideyoshi's thin high voice carried to the rear of the great hall, swelling hearts with pride. 'The westerners thought we would be defeated. The Chinese were certain of it. Even some Japanese were unsure. Those who doubted know little of our country, nothing about the will and the spirit of the Japanese warrior!'

Men in the assembly straightened their backs and preened.

'We are successful because we are directed by a god come to earth.' Hideyoshi bowed to the Emperor.

Mung stood with every man in the Diet and bowed. 'Your brother will be the next prime minister of Japan,' he whispered.

'If so, I will break my word to his imperial majesty and kill Hideyoshi. He cares little for the Emperor and nothing for the people. Only for himself.'

Mung stared at his friend hunched on his crutches. This short, square man had stood on principle before, knowing he would be renounced and disowned by his father for what he believed was right for his country. Iyeasu would truly kill his brother if necessary.

'General Nogi and Admiral Takamora, come forward,' the Emperor said.

The two men stepped to the centre of the dais next to Hideyoshi.

The Emperor smiled and announced, 'General Nogi and Admiral Takamora, you shall be awarded the Grand Cordon of the Chrysanthemum, and receive all rights, stipends and pensions due the recipients of Japan's highest honour. And from this time forth you have both become titled counts in the Empire of the Rising Sun.' He looked at Hideyoshi. 'Count Hideyoshi Koin, you will be raised to the rank of marquis and take your place as a permanent member of the Privy Council.'

Mung glanced at Iyeasu.

'The Emperor could not avoid it,' Iyeasu said. 'Hideyoshi is too popular. But I believe the closer Hideyoshi is to his imperial majesty, the greater opportunity the Emperor has for control over him.'

'Minister Moryiama Ishikawa and Count Iyeasu Koin,' the Emperor called out. 'You, who were instrumental in negotiating the favourable treaty for Okinawa and Formosa, will join Marquis Hideyoshi Koin, Counts Nogi and Takamora in the Shimonoseki negotiations with the Chinese General Li and British Plenipotentiary Lord Cade.'

General Honjo's shaven skull reflected the overhead light in the private reception room.

'You look uncomfortable in that tuxedo,' Hideyoshi said. 'It appears your shoulders will burst the seams.'

'I am filled with pride.' Honjo bowed. 'You are certain to become the next prime minister.'

'Let us hope so.' Hideyoshi beamed. 'The Emperor has summoned me and the others going to Shimonoseki.'

'Before you see the Emperor, you should know that Lord Cade has already squeezed the Chinese dry. Japan will be paid even more than we thought. General Li is now a puppet in the Englishman's hands. The Dowager Empress fears an uprising of Chinese peasants if negotiations are drawn out. She wishes the talks finished quickly.'

'Who are the main agitators among the Chinese people?'

'The Harmonious Fist Society, referred to as Boxers.'

'Can we utilize them?'

'I already have people in their organization, and some of their leaders are being trained in the Green House.'

'Good. We must discuss that later. Now what about Lord Cade?'

'He awaits confirmation of your intent to maintain a Japanese force along the Manchurian border and prevent the Russians from obtaining a warm-water port in Korea.' Honjo placed a letter in Hideyoshi's hand. 'He asks you to sign this.'

Hideyoshi read the letter and smiled. He took out his official seal. 'Of course this agreement will remain secret from our governments.'

'It is between you and Lord Cade.'

'I will need a new seal for the rank of marquis,' Hideyoshi said, pressing his stamp on the letter.

'There is little the Emperor can deny you at this time,' Honjo said. 'Your popularity is too great. I have a request of my own.'

Hideyoshi preened. 'I am now in a mood to dispense favours.'

'I wish to control education in Japan,' Honjo said. 'It is a plan I have worked on for years, and the time is right. The minister of education died recently and the position stands open. Ask for one of your supporters to be appointed education minister, a weak man I can influence.'

'What is your plan?'

'If Japan is to become a world leader and maintain her status, we will eventually have to fight the Europeans. To win, we must shape a state personality bred to obey. Buddhism and Shintoism are already incorporated into the school system. We will use them to focus on the Emperor as the authority, and not on the law. Although constitutional government suits our purposes now, we must be able to circumvent the system in order to control it.'

'And if we insulate the Emperor from the people, we will control him too,' Hideyoshi said.

'It will take a generation before we see results,' Honjo said. 'But if we institute the Prussian educational system and have every school teach the same lesson throughout the country on the same day at the same hour, then I guarantee a population that will obey. They will be taught that every army officer, policeman and government clerk is an extension of the Emperor. That to disobey them would be to defy his imperial majesty. The younger generation will learn to conform.'

'You will be a great asset to me here in Tokyo,' Hideyoshi said. 'I promise that you will control education and I will rule Japan. We shall discuss this further at the victory dinner after my meeting with the Emperor.'

Mung and Iyeasu stood on the balcony of the imperial reception room and watched the fireworks over Tamieka Pond. Another spectacular display of star rockets burst over Tokyo harbour. Red, gold and silver showers of light poured over Yokohama. The capital and all Japan were celebrating victory on this unusually warm October night.

Mung held out an envelope to Iyeasu. 'I received this after our audience with the Emperor. It is from Shimatzu in Formosa.'

'Tell me what it says. I am too exhausted to read.'

'Do you want a chair?'

'If I sit down, I will never get up,' Iyeasu said.

266

Mung cleared his throat and began to read, 'The Black Dragons report that Lord Cade has forced the Chinese to pay Japan 230,000 taels of silver and confirm Formosa and the Pescadore islands as ours.'

'Where in Buddha's name are the Pescadores, and how much is a tael of silver worth in yen?'

'There are two and a half ounces of silver in a tael,' Mung said. 'I do not have my abacus but it should amount to almost twice our estimated cost of the war. The Pescadores are located between Formosa and the Chinese mainland. There is more in the letter. The Chinese will also concede the Port Arthur and Weihaiwei bases on the Liaotung and Shantung peninsulas.'

'My word,' Iyeasu said. 'I would not have asked for half the money or one third the land.'

'Our agreement with Lord Cade is to hand over Weihaiwei and the Shantung peninsula to him.'

'What about Korea?'

'We already occupy and govern Korea,' Mung said. 'China will recognize it as being within our sphere of influence.'

'Why should the Chinese accept such harsh terms?'

'Shimatzu writes that Britain will lend China the funds for the indemnity,' Mung said. 'Prince Kung and the Empress have received bribes from us. Remember, the ruling family in China are Manchus, more concerned with their ancestors and Manchuria than with the Chinese mainland. Shimatzu feels we should complete the negotiations and return from Shimonoseki in time for our children's wedding.'

'I have the feeling Hideyoshi is controlling all these events,' Iyeasu said.

'He is carrying us and Japan forward on the crest of a wave.' Mung pointed to the sky rockets over the harbour. 'Your brother has much to celebrate. Do you know why he wants the education ministry?'

'You can be certain it is to serve his purpose, not the people's.' Iyeasu swung away on his crutches. 'I must sleep before boarding the ship for Shimonoseki. Let us hope the wave we ride does not come crashing down and destroy everything. My brother is noted for that.'

Chapter 30

23 October 1894

Mung stood before Japan's legislature two days after the Shimonoseki agreement had been signed. He bowed to the Emperor, to members of Parliament, and began the speech that would propel him to national fame.

'Your imperial majesty. Honoured members of the Diet. Marquis Hideyoshi Koin, Counts Iyeasu Koin, Nogi and Takamora should all be here at the presentation of this report. Unfortunately they have been taken ill from food poisoning. I can assure the members of Parliament of the four men's speedy recovery,' Mung said, although he was not certain. On the return voyage from Shimonoseki, three sailors had died and half Takamora's crew were stricken with the disease. None had eaten the same food as the officers. The Emperor had instructed Mung to minimize the illness, concentrate on the success in Shimonoseki and take as much credit as possible for the negotiations. From his sickbed Iyeasu had agreed, calling it the perfect opportunity to block Hideyoshi's drive to become prime minister. With the Emperor's approval, Iyeasu's assistant had written Mung's speech.

Now Mung went on to recite the speech from memory. 'The war with China has served two purposes. It ends the Chinese threat to our islands from Korea, and has restored the integrity of our people. We are no longer a country of feudal fiefdoms. We are a modern nation. This conflict has energized our people to unite against a common enemy. In doing so we have forged the foundations of a twentieth-century nation. From this day forward Japan must be acknowledged as a major military power in the Far East!'

Mung was uncomfortable sounding like Hideyoshi, yet the words were effective. He felt power over the audience. Every member of the National Diet remained perfectly still. They waited for him to continue.

'An international diplomatic revolution is already under way as a result of our victories on land and sea. The British were first to act on our behalf. At Shimonoseki they dictated terms for us which the Chinese accepted. France, Germany and Russia have also responded to the new reality of an awakened Japan. They have formed a mutual pact to cope with our new geographical acquisitions and political successes. The United States and all Europe must now re-evaluate their policies in Asia and the Pacific. They are well aware that 70 per cent of the world's population resides in China, India and the Far East. More than two-thirds of the world's peoples are non-Caucasian. By virtue of our nationality, religion and recent victories, Japan is the natural choice to lead the Oriental nations into the twentieth century. No foreign country thought we could defeat the Chinese army and her Korean allies. The West must reassess Japan's place in the scheme of world politics.'

Next Mung would reveal the final agreement with China, and he was saddened. General Li Hung-Chang had been a puppet at the negotiations, accepting the terms as the bribed Chinese royal family in Peking had instructed. Li signed the agreement and departed Shimonoseki a broken man. Li and his brother Ting had been among the few aristocratic Chinese patriots. The corrupt and antiquated political system in Peking had ruined both men. Now reports from Canton and Hankow told of the Boxers, a new generation of Chinese who opposed their corrupt government's dealing with Japan, and were leading public protests against the treaty.

Mung's prepared speech did not hint at his regret. He modulated his voice to rise and fall in a pattern that pumped pride into the hearts of his listeners. 'The terms of the Shimonoseki agreement are as follows: Japan will receive 414 million yen, three times our total military budget for the entire campaign.' He heard members of Parliament suck wind through their teeth. Most would never learn that part of the money was to be used to maintain a military force along the Yalu. It was one of Lord Cade's conditions.

'The Japanese values of bravery, perseverance and self-sacrifice on the field of battle and at home are responsible for our victories.' Mung again felt Hideyoshi's words coming out of his mouth. There was no denying their effect. Row on row of men seated before him were mesmerized. 'This was a war of justice. It was our duty to the Asian people to bring freedom and human rights to the oppressed of China and Korea. Peking has paid for the harsh treatment of its citizens. In addition to the 414 million yen indemnity, China has ceded us Weihaiwei naval base and Shantung peninsula, plus Port Arthur naval base and the Liaotung peninsula. General Li Hung-Chang confirmed that Formosa and the Pescadore islands are under Japanese rule. China renounces the tributary status of Korea and recognizes Japanese guardianship over that country to establish a free and independent state. Japan will also be allowed the use of seven new trading ports on the Chinese mainland. This includes special privileges to establish non-taxable industries there.' Mung bowed to the Emperor. 'Your imperial majesty, Japan now holds colonies on the Asian continent as a first line of defence against any aggressor. You ordered our armies to march. We obeyed. Japan is victorious!' He turned back to the members of Parliament and bowed. 'If you agree to these terms, the war with China is over.'

There was absolute silence in the great hall. No one moved. Mung looked from those seated before him to the Emperor and back again. In three short months his country had gained two hundred thousand square miles of land, three times that in fishing grounds, enough money to pay its debts, modernize its industries and redeem the honour of its ancestors who had failed in Korea four hundred years before. Yet no one responded. Again Mung looked to the Emperor. His imperial majesty stared straight ahead.

An old man whom Mung recognized as a former prince of Choshu, stood up and bowed to him. In the hushed silence, his voice echoed. 'Thank you.'

There was a great rustling as everyone in the hall stood and bowed. Someone began to clap and others joined. A tumultuous cheer was followed by chanting and applause. Young men rushed onto the speaker's platform, raised Mung on their shoulders and marched him around the hall. Young and old followed as Mung was carried out of the National Diet to the Yasukune shrine. Prayers of thanksgiving were offered to the gods, and the Shimonoseki accord was made public.

The next day Mung's picture appeared on the front page of every newspaper in Japan. Foreign correspondents wired the story around the world.

'Hermit Kingdom Ends Its Isolation.'
'Japan Imitates The West.'
'Japan - The Newest Imperialist Nation In The World.'

Toyko's largest daily carried Mung's photograph under the caption 'Moryiama Ishikawa, Hero Of Formosa, Hero Of Shimonoseki And Grandfather Of Three Grooms At Tomorrow's Wedding.' Members of the royal family, Parliament and industry all vied to cover the cost of an elaborate wedding, but Mung and Udo politely rejected the offers.

'The Ishikawa family requests donations in honour of the triple wedding be made towards the welfare of wounded soldiers and families of the dead. The wedding ceremony will be a private affair as the mother of the grooms is ill.'

Udo sat at his wife's side with the shades drawn. Gin-ko had fallen asleep holding his hand. She never complained, but when they lay close at night he felt her shudder and heard her moan in her sleep. He had bathed and clothed her in preparation for the doctor's visit. After her bath he carried her to the sleeping mat. 'I thought I had more time,' she had whispered.

He looked down at her drawn face. He watched her chest rise feebly in shallow breathing. Her body was thin, her face pale, yet the abscesses on her legs and the lesions over her hip appeared to be healing. Udo did not understand. The doctor had told him this healing was part of the process of dying. He thought of the power he had, the important men he could call upon. And yet there was nothing he could do for Gin-ko. No one who could help. Not even the prayer notes he had purchased by the basketful.

He had gone to see a Protestant missionary. 'When you are sad, come to us,' the missionary had told him some time before. 'We will pray for you.'

The missionary's prayer was an honest one, Udo thought, and repeated it to himself. 'Oh God, Thy will be done. Spare Gin-ko, for she is sorely needed by me and our children. If not, please release my wife from her suffering. Take her peacefully and in tranquillity to Thy kingdom.'

Udo remained sitting with Gin-ko's hand in his, remembering how he had fallen in love with her at first sight. Yet that love, which burned his soul and seared his mind, was anaemic compared to the love they shared through the years. He bent his head and listened for her breathing, but it had stopped. His heart jumped, his body turned to stone. Then he felt her grip on his hand tighten. She sighed and began breathing again.

'Gods, if you want her, take her peacefully,' Udo whispered. 'Only let her see her sons married.'

There was a tapping at the door and Gin-ko tugged

at his hand. 'I am here,' he said. 'It is probably the doctor.'

'I was having a dream,' she said. 'I was at a Kabuki theatre. The actors wore masks but I could see behind them. They were all people I knew who have died. Little Mother greeted me. And Ukiko was there.'

The knock on the door was repeated. 'Come in,' Udo said, grateful for the dim light. His cheeks were wet with tears.

Gin-ko released his hand. 'You wait outside while I am being examined.'

Udo nodded, and left the room.

The doctor reached for the electric lamp. 'Please, do not turn it on,' she said.

'I must see you.'

'There is no improvement and will not be any. I only ask that you prescribe something to give me strength for the wedding tomorrow.'

'I advise you not to attend,' the doctor said. 'Save the little strength you do have.'

'For what? I wish to leave my husband, my sons and their wives with a good memory of me.'

The doctor remained silent.

'Please,' Gin-ko said. 'I have tried not to be burdensome or demanding. I want my children to think I am feeling well so they can enjoy their wedding and the bridal night.'

'Honourable lady, you have been a pagoda of stone,' the doctor said. 'Everyone has derived strength from you.'

'Then help me maintain my dignity.'

The doctor bowed. 'I shall come to you an hour before the ceremony. Take some goat's milk to line your stomach. The stimulant is powerful.'

'Father, you are not getting out of that bed until you are fully recovered,' Noriko said.

'I have only one child and tomorrow I will see you married!'

'Your brother and many others are close to death from this influenza that was first diagnosed as food poisoning. You could suffer a relapse. I was speaking with a chef about tomorrow's wedding arrangements and he suddenly began to shiver. They had to carry him to his room. It is hard to believe how quickly it strikes.'

'It happened to me like that,' Iyeasu said, touching his big stomach. 'It took five men to carry me to my cabin on the ship. My muscles ached. I could not get warm.'

'Have some more soup.'

'If I hold the soup down, will you return my crutches?'

Noriko crossed her hands and pursed her lips.

Iyeasu took up the soup bowl. 'We shall let the doctor decide about tomorrow.'

Noriko smiled when her father drank the soup. 'The doctor is in awe of you,' she said. 'He will obey your orders.'

'You will soon be taking orders from your husband.'

'You can talk lying down,' Noriko said. She tucked the quilt around her father.

'If your mother was here, there would be no need for me to tell you anything. She would have taught you about the relationship between husband and wife.'

'Mother left me her pillow books.'

'It is not sex I refer to. It has to do with the obligations of a wife to a husband. You have received the most liberal education a modern Japanese woman can. Now I wonder if I was correct to encourage it.'

'Yes, Father. I thank you for it. How I wish I could take my downtrodden sisters by the hand, lead them into classrooms of higher learning and brighten their lives with knowledge, as mine has been.'

'Yet a woman's destiny in Japan is to live in her husband's shadow and submit to him in all things.' Iyeasu hesitated

275

a moment. He looked at his daughter and she lowered her eyes. 'The life's work of a woman is obedience,' he said. 'She must observe the rules of society. She must avoid extravagance, act according to her station in life and above all, obey the rules. Jealousy and discontent must be avoided.'

'Father, you forgot to mention not to slander or act silly.'

'Those you never did and never will do. I am proud of you. Your mother and I were proud when you were born. I cannot remember ever being disappointed in you. The blessing I wish for you is to be loved as I loved your mother.'

Noriko was relieved to hear a knock at the door. She put the subject of love and Hiroki from her mind.

'This is more like a hospital than the imperial palace,' the doctor said. He took both Iyeasu's wrists and checked his pulses. 'You look better than your brother. Hideyoshi still has fluid in his lungs. If he does not die of the influenza, his rage at Mung's popularity will kill him.' The doctor smiled. 'You will be up and around soon.'

'Then convince my daughter to return my crutches in time for tomorrow's wedding.'

'That could be a bit early,' the doctor said.

'It was not a request, it is an order,' Iyeasu growled.

'Oh Father, you always do that when you want your way,' Noriko said.

'I will give you a similar but milder dose of a prescription I have prepared for Gin-ko,' the doctor said.

'How is she?' Noriko asked.

The doctor shook his head. 'If she survives the wedding, it will be a miracle.'

Chapter 31

The Koin family shrine was located in an old graveyard not far from the imperial palace. A five-foot bronze miniature of the Great Buddha of Kamakura sat on a moss-covered stone inside a gazebo. His future wife would come here this morning as part of the marriage ceremony, and Hiroki awaited her. From across the road he watched her walk daintily on her wooden clogs through the rain.

Noriko went to the shrine's well and performed the symbolic ritual of purification by rinsing her hands and mouth. She then entered the gazebo and rang the bell for the attention of the gods. She meditated, bowed her head and clapped once to send her prayers to those who dwell beyond the clouds. In addition to the prayers for her father and Gin-ko, she begged not to disgrace her family by being divorced. She vowed to obey her husband and conform to his ways. She wished for many children to love. 'I need love,' she said aloud as she began to open her umbrella.

Hiroki came running through the rain and into the gazebo.

'You startled me,' Noriko said.

He pointed at her fingers. 'You have a kendo grip on the umbrella. Are you going to trounce me again?'

Noriko looked down at her hands and Hiroki laughed. 'I came to ask if your father needs help getting to the ceremony, and to explain about my mother. We must pretend we know nothing of her illness.'

Noriko cocked her head. She wanted to tell him how sometimes he could be so caring, but most often he strutted about like an old samurai lording it over everyone. She looked at the Buddha, recalled her vow and lowered her eyes. 'Thank you, but my father will be fine. And your mother will take medicine before the wedding to give her strength.'

'I really came to talk with you,' Hiroki said.

'It is bad luck.'

'Today is Friday the thirteenth. Westerners think that is bad luck. I believe people make their own luck.' He motioned to the Buddha. 'Our gods are as helpless as the Christian god they hang on the wall.'

'What is it you wish to say?'

'My brothers selected their wives from photographs. After the mi-ai they agreed to marry. It is different with us.'

'Yes, you knocked me unconscious.' Noriko frowned.

'Only after you beat me with the kendo stick.' Hiroki pointed to his nose. 'It still bleeds when I sneeze.'

Noriko laughed and Hiroki was delighted. It was the first time he had seen her happy since they met. 'Although our wedding was not arranged, it was assumed,' he said. 'Your father, my grandfather and parents all wished us to marry.'

'It is a bit late to change things,' Noriko said, fearing he wished to cancel the wedding, and becoming confused by her own reaction.

'If it had not worked out this way, I would have courted you,' Hiroki said.

'Perhaps you are grateful to me for nursing your mother.'

'My regard for you came before that.'

'You knew of the years I helped your grandfather,' Noriko said. 'This must be a great On for you.' The moment the words were out of her mouth she realized why she was always so angry at him. 'Do you feel obliged to marry me?'

'Yes,' Hiroki said.

Noriko's spirits sank. The deep dark secret in her heart

278

was a fear of being married to Hiroki because he was obligated. Now he had admitted it. She opened her parasol between them to hide her tears. 'I thought so,' she murmured, and started to leave the gazebo.

'The obligation I have is to my heart, Noriko. It is not an On to my parents or my grandfather. I love you.'

Noriko stopped in the middle of a puddle. She whirled on her wooden clogs, letting the umbrella fall to her side. The great weight lifted from her heart and she bowed. 'I love you,' she sobbed. 'I will be very happy to be your wife if you accept me.'

Hiroki grinned. His eyes twinkled. He leapt from the gazebo, slipped and fell into the puddle at her feet. Looking up with a silly grin, he said, 'I will always try to impress you. If I appear ridiculous at this moment, please forgive me. I love you with all my heart.'

Their eyes met and they laughed together.

Mung's uninterrupted twelve-hour sleep and Udo's warning still did not prepare him for Gin-ko's appearance. Her high cheekbones protruded under red-rimmed eyes. Her hands rested limply on the blanket. Udo sat at her side with his arm supporting her in a sitting position.

'You are shocked,' Gin-ko whispered.

'Forgive me,' Mung said. 'I should have come sooner.'

'Please sit close to me. My request is rather presumptuous and my voice not strong.' Gin-ko ran her tongue over dry, cracked lips.

Udo dabbed gently at her mouth with a damp cloth. He held her more firmly.

'My dear daughter-in-law,' Mung said. 'Say what you will. If it is within my power, consider it done.'

'I ask . . . I ask that after the wedding ceremony you use your position as Black Dragon to send our sons and their wives away from Toyko.'

'Are you strong enough to attend the ceremony?' Mung asked.

'The anticipation has kept me alive these last days,' Gin-ko said.

Mung looked to Udo, who nodded.

Gin-ko glanced up at her husband, then at Mung. 'We have discussed this, and both agree. The doctor will give me a stimulant before the wedding to see me through the ceremonies. I doubt there will be much time after. Could you make the travelling order for the children immediate? I do not wish their first days of marriage to be spent in mourning.'

Again Udo nodded his assent to Mung.

'I had thought to give my grandsons and their brides a gift of foreign travel in the spring,' Mung said. 'I want Hiroki to study lighter-than-air travel.'

Gin-ko reached out and touched Mung's hand. 'Please do not send Hiroki up in a kite again.'

'No kites,' Mung said. 'I speak of gas-filled balloons. They are so safe that one day the skies will be filled with them.'

Colour entered Gin-ko's face. 'Remember the hot air balloon in Hokkaido?'

Mung smiled and took Gin-ko's hand. 'The Vulcan pirates shot a hole through it and I disappeared into a snowdrift.'

Gin-ko rested her head on Udo's shoulder. 'Yes. Udo and Danjuro pulled you out of the snow. Do you think I will meet Danjuro?'

Mung caught his tongue. He had been about to remind her the Mito giant was dead, and then realized Gin-ko knew that. He stood up. 'Rest easy. Immediately after the ceremony your children will collect their belongings and leave Tokyo. A ship bound for Hawaii departs this evening. They will all be on it.'

Udo rested Gin-ko's head gently back on the pillow.

'Mung and I have some business to discuss. I will return shortly.'

Outside the room they spoke in whispers. 'The boys will be upset not to be with their mother,' Mung said.

'I also wish them to leave,' Udo said. His body began to shake.

Mung embraced his adopted son. 'Be strong,' he whispered. 'Be strong. I will do as you ask. Is there anything else you wish?'

Udo opened his mouth but then shook his head. 'I must go back inside. The doctor will come soon to administer the stimulant. It could be dangerous.'

Mung faced the three young couples seated before him. The grooms looked handsome in their new kimonos. The brides were striking with their rouged cheeks, sparkling eyes and upswept shiny black hair. They waited for the patriarch of the Ishikawa family to speak.

'Soon we shall join your parents for the abbreviated formalities of the marriage ceremonies,' he said. 'Normally the proceedings take place over several days or months, but we do not have time.' Mung looked into the eyes of each of his grandsons. 'Your mother is dying.' He was proud that all three controlled their emotions, for he would test them to the limit. 'Your mother and father request that you not be here when she . . .' Mung cleared his throat. 'You will leave Tokyo! Immediately after the wedding you will board ship for Hawaii!' He looked at the brides-to-be. 'At the mi-ai, the obligations of your husbands to the Black Dragon Society were explained to you. Not long ago this would never have been discussed with a wife, or even mentioned in public. Recently our parliamentarians have seen fit to comment about Japan's patriotic societies. Newspapers, domestic and foreign, revealed our work during the Sino-Japanese war. Thus I feel obliged to inform the three brides of their husbands' next assignments. Tonight you will all sail for

Hawaii!' Mung handed Yaka an envelope. 'These are your instructions. From Honolulu you and your bride are to sail to Germany!' He handed the others their envelopes. 'Uraga, you and your bride go to France, Hiroki and Noriko to the United States!'

The three brothers bowed. 'So it is ordered, so it is done,' they said in unison.

Noriko led the young women in bowing their acceptance of the orders.

'As there was not time for a bachelor party, consider this trip a different western innovation known as the honeymoon,' Mung said. 'I wish you all good fortune and long and honourable lives. Now let us join your parents and begin the wedding ceremonies.'

Mung was astonished at Gin-ko's transformation. She looked thin, but beautiful. Her dark hair shone. She had used every technique in the art of make-up learned as a courtesan to cover the signs of her illness. Her purple kimono with yellow sash was draped to hide the back of a seat without legs that supported her in a sitting position.

Gin-ko and Udo sat at one end of the table. Mung, the eldest, took his place at the other end. On his right sat the three brides and their parents; opposite them across the long low table were the grooms.

Gin-ko nodded to her sons and they presented gifts to their new in-laws. The brides placed their gifts in front of the grooms.

The usual yuino banquet was represented by tea and rice cakes. Mung noted Iyeasu eating a second cake. The doctor's prescription had worked well for both his friend and his daughter-in-law.

The three brides excused themselves. They returned dressed in white, the symbol of death, and sat opposite their parents with their new husbands to emphasize the breaking of ties with their families. Then the six left to change into colourful kimonos.

'Mother looks quite well,' Uraga said in the men's dressing room.

'It is a special stimulant that has invigorated her,' Hiroki said. 'How can we leave her?'

'The Black Dragon ordered it and Mother requested it,' Yaka said. 'Father also wishes us to go. He spoke to me this morning.'

'When the effect of the medicine wears off, Mother will be worse,' Hiroki said.

'We must respect our parents' wishes and the Black Dragon's orders,' Yaka replied. 'When we return to the ceremony, put on your happy faces. We shall bid our mother farewell with smiles.'

'I am pleased to see Noriko holding up so well,' Yaka said. 'She is like a daughter to Mother. They have spent more time together than we. Take care of Noriko, Hiroki. We love her too.'

'I shall,' Hiroki said.

The brothers returned to sit with their brides for the san-san ku-do. Three wine cups of graduated sizes were placed before each couple. At a sign from Gin-ko, her sons poured rice wine in the smallest cups and served their brides. The young women touched the cups to their lips three times.

Hiroki looked into Noriko's eyes and forgot everything and everyone at the table. He watched her delicate hands pour the second cup. As she presented it to him, their eyes met again. He touched the wine to his lips three times. The third cup was filled and shared nine times each as the brides and grooms silently pledged themselves to each other.

Udo moved behind the couples and placed a government registration form between each. When everyone had signed, he collected the forms. Each groom presented his wife with a ceremonial dagger to protect her honour. Then the wedding banquet began. Waiters brought trays of beautifully decorated food.

Iyeasu cleared his throat for everyone's attention. 'During my years of studying in France and England, I attended several Christian weddings. A favourite toast by the father of the bride was to say, "I have not lost a daughter but gained a son." This is especially true for me.' He handed his son-in-law an envelope and bowed to Udo and Gin-ko. 'With the permission of his parents, I hereby deed all properties, enterprises, titles and wealth to Hiroki Ishikawa upon my death.'

Hiroki bowed to his grandfather, to his parents and to Iyeasu. 'I accept this adoption and the responsibility of providing an heir to ensure the succession of the Koin family name. I will see to the welfare of my wife and your estates. I will honour your grave and those of your ancestors.' He turned to the head of the table and saw a tear spill over the edge of his mother's eyelid. He bowed and tried to speak, but could not. He gathered his strength and cleared his throat. 'Although I take on the Koin family name, I will always fulfil my filial obligations to my parents.' Knowing he would never see his mother again, Hiroki's eyes filled with tears.

'We shall celebrate this adoption with another round of sake,' Yaka said. He began to sing and the others joined in.

Mung saw Gin-ko swoon and catch herself. She patted her husband's hand when he turned to her. Udo nodded to Mung, who signalled for the Shinto priest to enter.

Swinging a smoking censer and waving a willow branch, the priest chanted prayers to purify the newly married couples and implore the gods to bless them. He placed branches of cherry blossoms and pine tied with butterfly bows before each couple – to symbolize fruitfulness, virtue, and remind the husbands and wives of their three, three, nine exchanges of silent vows.

'Gin-ko Ishikawa wishes to say a few words,' Udo said.

For the first time everyone felt free to look at the stately woman seated at the end of the table.

Gin-ko wondered if they could see her weakness. The stimulant was wearing off. 'Men realize the strong influence of women on them,' she said. 'That is why we have so many customs which give husbands dominance over their wives. It is common for Japanese wives to be subordinate in thought and deed to their husbands. Yet there are a few men strong enough, confident enough to share with their wives the good and bad of life on an equal basis. These men are rare. My husband has been one of them.' She looked into Udo's eyes.

Noriko slipped her hand into Hiroki's and squeezed.

Gin-ko turned to her sons. 'I hope you will follow your father's example. My life has been full and enriched by this unusual relationship.' She began to lose focus of the faces down the length of the table and summoned her last reserve of energy. 'To you, young brides,' she looked at Noriko longer than the others, 'loyalty to the Emperor, to your husband, and many joyful moments is my wish for all the days of your lives. May you have children as special as mine.'

Iyeasu bowed his head, then said, 'I speak on behalf of the parents of the brides. We promise to look after your fine sons. We will see they take good care of our wonderful daughters, and our grandchildren.'

Mung stood up at the end of the table and announced, 'Will the brides and grooms please take leave of their parents. This ceremony is concluded.' He was looking at Gin-ko when he said, 'You are going far. Know that our hearts, our thoughts and our love go with you.' He bowed to her.

Udo and Gin-ko remained seated as the guests departed. When they had gone, he signalled the servants to leave also. Gin-ko slumped on his shoulder. 'I am so tired,' she whispered.

Ever so gently Udo picked up his wife and carried her to their room.

Chapter 32

The doctor closed the door to Gin-ko's room. 'There is nothing more I can do. She is sleeping.'

'How much time?' Udo asked.

'Soon.'

Udo removed an envelope from his obi and handed it to the physician. 'Please have this delivered to the bonsai shop near the Nō theatre on the Ginza.'

'I can give you something to relax.'

'No, thank you,' Udo said. He slid open the door and returned to Gin-ko's side. She slept. He went to the window and pulled back the drapes. The golden glow of the sun faded under the skyline. Below the window people walked in the imperial gardens with no idea of what was taking place in the room.

Udo sat at Gin-ko's side and listened to her faint breathing, recalling their life together. In the dark he felt her fingers search for his. They clasped hands but she did not wake. It reminded him of their wedding night. She the famed courtesan. He the founder of the largest brothel in Canton, the man who used women – bought, sold and traded them like cattle. But he had not known how to initiate sex with his wife. Under the blanket that first night, Gin-ko's hand sought his and Udo had wept. He had confessed how lonely he was during the years of manipulating women. Gin-ko wept with him, and admitted her own loneliness despite being the subject of adoration. They had embraced and fallen asleep. Only later did they begin to explore each other, as if uninitiated novitiates in the art of love. Udo had been born anew in his wife's love. The past was forgotten. Their lives had become a discovery of themselves and the world around them.

'Now we go beyond the pale together, my beloved Ginko,' he whispered. 'We shall learn the truth of Heaven, Hell or non-existence.'

Udo's head lowered on his chest and he dozed.

It was dark. Quiet. Udo had lost track of time. He felt the coolness of Gin-ko's hand in his. He listened for the whisper of her breathing and heard nothing. He put his lips to hers and they were cold. He embraced her limp body and, with a catch in his throat, whispered to her, 'Wait for me, dear one.' He placed her hands at her sides.

Udo went to a cabinet and withdrew the long and short swords of a senior samurai and a six-shot Colt pistol. He tucked them in his obi and bowed to his wife. 'I am now free to perform Giri.' He knelt and touched his forehead to the floor. 'I have no life without you, Gin-ko, and no honour without Giri.' He backed out of the room on his knees.

At the west gate of the imperial palace, a man stepped from the shadows. He pulled up his sleeve to reveal an intricate tattoo on his forearm. 'We received your message to put our plan into action. We are prepared to repay the On of Wada Zenshichi to Mistress Gin-ko.' He signalled and a rickshaw appeared from the darkness. 'Ninjas are in position outside Hideyoshi's house. It is only a short way from here. Are you prepared?'

Udo touched his two swords and nodded.

'Please get in,' the Yakuza said.

As Udo mounted the rickshaw from one side, a masked, black-clad figure appeared opposite.

'Have no fear,' the Yakuza said. 'Be seated.'

'Is this the ninja?' Udo asked the Yakuza, but the tattooed man was gone. Udo reached for his Colt .44.

'I am pleased you carry a pistol,' the man said. 'You may need it. Hideyoshi's guards are alert professionals.'

'Are you a ninja?' Udo asked.

'Yes. I am the leader. The rickshaw man is also. He will take us to the main gate of the marquis' house. If we can dispatch the sentries quietly, others will join us to finish the guards on the veranda and inside the house. We will try not to arouse those off-duty people sleeping in the gardener's hut.'

Udo and the black-clad figure were pulled along the main boulevard parallel to the imperial palace. The rickshaw angled across the wide, empty street towards the gate of Hideyoshi's house.

'Put the pistol in your lap,' the ninja said. 'Do not use it unless you are threatened.' He pulled down his mask, revealing the rouged face of a geisha. He put on a black wig and draped a colourful kimono around his body.

Udo felt the rickshaw pick up speed. The driver lowered his head and trotted directly for the closed iron gate. One of two guards behind the iron bars rushed out to meet them. 'Stop there,' the guard ordered, but the rickshaw driver did not slow his pace. Almost on top of the man, he dropped his pulling tongs and leapt towards the gate, thrusting a three-foot sword through the bars and into the throat of the second guard.

Udo was thrown forward. The chief ninja used the momentum to leap on the outside guard. He thrust his finger into the guard's collar and dug his knuckles into the man's neck, blocking his windpipe. The flow of blood to the guard's brain ceased, his body went limp and he fell dead. Udo caught sight of black-clad figures running along the outside wall. They filtered through the gate and disappeared into the darkness of the garden.

'Take your seat,' the rickshaw driver ordered. He picked up the pulling tongs and trotted up the path to the veranda. Udo pulled back the hammer of his Colt.

The chief ninja, dressed as a geisha, resumed his place.

'Remain seated,' he said. 'Let them come to us!' The rickshaw stopped at the bottom of the steps.

The veranda was well lit. Two guards walked down the steps side by side. Suddenly several shiny objects whizzed past Udo's head and the guards staggered. Small gleaming throwing knives stuck in the throat and chest of both men. Black-clad figures swarmed over the dead guards. Without a sound the bodies were pulled aside. Other ninjas worked the outside hinges free from the western-style wooden door.

The chief ninja discarded the geisha costume and gathered his men at the front entrance. He signalled Udo forward as the door was pulled off its hinges. Ninjas rushed in and caught the two inside guards playing Go at a small table. They died quickly and quietly. Ninjas darted past Udo, down the halls and up the stairs. They listened at each door.

Udo was ushered forward to the doorway of Hideyoshi's study. The man he had come to kill was writing in a ledger. The black-clad ninjas stole across the tatami mats and were at Hideyoshi's side when he looked up. Udo had the satisfaction of seeing fear in the pockmarked face a moment before a black-gloved hand clamped over his mouth. Hideyoshi's arms were twisted back. Recognition and terror filled his eyes as Udo approached. Hideyoshi tried to twist away. He kicked, he bucked, and screamed muffled threats. The ninja leader reached past Udo and pressed a vertebra behind the marquis' neck. Hideyoshi stiffened, and collapsed. The two ninjas slapped his face until he regained consciousness.

'Do not kill me,' Hideyoshi gasped. 'What is it you want? I will be prime minister soon. Ask anything!'

'Your death,' Udo said.

'Your father has forgiven me!'

'Mung and Iyeasu would have killed you long ago if not for the Emperor. Your hired killers took your brother's leg

290

and killed Mung's wife. Your man Shibata insulted my wife in public, at your instigation. That is why I will kill you!'

Hideyoshi's head rolled from side to side. Tears streamed down his face. 'I had nothing to do with it. Nothing! I am innocent! Let me apologize to your wife!'

'Yes,' Udo said. 'A good idea. Gin-ko died a short time ago.'

Hideyoshi lurched forward and grabbed for a pistol hidden under the desk top. The two ninjas caught his arms.

'Cover his mouth and place his right hand on the table,' Udo ordered.

Hideyoshi's cries were muffled by the black-gloved hand. Udo took a small knife from his obi and drove it down through the back of Hideyoshi's hand, pinning the hand to the table. Udo stepped to the side and drew his short sword. He watched Hideyoshi's wide, fear-filled eyes, then hacked the hand off at the wrist. Hideyoshi stared at the blood spurting from the stump of his wrist, at the severed hand pinned to the table. He moaned.

Udo stepped in front of him. 'This is the death that Shibata, your lover, prepared for Mung on his return from the harbour master's office! The death of a traitor!'

Hideyoshi watched Udo draw back the short sword once again. His muffled screams came like the yowling of a sick cat through the gloved hand over his mouth. His eyes started from his head.

'You are a traitor to your class, your ancestors and the human race,' Udo said, and drove the sword into Hideyoshi's chest.

The ninjas released their grip and the body arched in the chair. It quivered, then slumped forward. The hilt of the sword protruding from Hideyoshi's chest propped his body over the desk. Udo stepped back and took up his long sword. He raised it with a two-handed grip and split Hideyoshi's skull, leaving the big sword wedged in the bone. 'That is for the honour of my wife, my family and for me!'

The three ninjas walked a stiff-backed Udo to the rickshaw, and escorted him to the west gate of the imperial palace. Once in his apartment, Udo took a bowl of water and a brush from the cabinet. He carried them to Gin-ko and brushed her lips in the last water rite. He put a long white muslin gown over her body, removed her pillow and rested her head in a northerly direction.

Udo dressed himself in a long white robe. He pulled his sleeping mat next to Gin-ko's and placed the cabinet at her feet. He set two lit candles and two incense sticks on either side of two vases. Behind the cabinet, he positioned a small screen upside down. He took a short dagger, the one he had given Gin-ko when they were married, and placed it on top of the rice paper on which he had written his death poem.

'When I gaze to the place where my true love is,' he recited.
'Naught remains but my sob.
When I search for the flower of my heart,
There is no light, no sound.
Death keeps a calendar,
We have a rendezvous.'

Udo pulled open his robe and knelt at Gin-ko's side. He took a deep breath and hardened the muscles of his abdomen. He drove the knife point into his left side, pulling the blade across to the right and turning the point up. Blood poured over his legs. He withdrew the knife and placed it next to the death poem. Slowly he straightened his legs and pulled the blanket up, taking Gin-ko's hand in his, resting his head next to hers. His body trembled, he sighed, and he closed his eyes.

Chapter 33

'We know who killed Marquis Hideyoshi Koin and why,' General Honjo told the army officers gathered in the duty room. 'But the truth does not serve our purpose. The Emperor decreed there will be no more killing between the White Wolf Society and the Black Dragons. His imperial majesty is angered at Mung because his son Udo defied imperial orders. Udo killed Hideyoshi, then returned to his dead wife's side and committed seppuku. The Ishikawas will be buried tomorrow in a private ceremony one hour after Marquis Koin's state funeral. It is a sign of the Emperor's displeasure with Mung and his family.'

'We are obligated to kill Mung and the Yakuza who paid for the assassination,' an officer said.

Honjo allowed others to express their agreement, then cut them short. 'Wrong! You are obligated to serve the Emperor and make Japan the greatest and most powerful nation on earth! Forget a killing contest with Mung, the ninjas or Yakuza! That is my first order as leader of the White Wolf Society! We must find someone to take the marquis' place in the House of Peers. I seek a leader prepared to continue our territorial expansion on mainland China into Manchuria. Someone we can control!'

'Your appointment to the seat can be arranged,' a senior officer said.

'No,' Honjo said. 'I am aware of my limitations. Manipulating people from behind the scenes is my expertise.'

Several names were suggested and rejected. Then a young officer stood up. 'I am an aide to Count Iga Sasaki. He supported Marquis Hideyoshi's policies with votes and money.'

Honjo glanced at the scroll before him. 'I have this Count Iga Sasaki on my list. What kind of character has he?'

'Weak.'

'Good. What are his social habits?'

'He is a spendthrift who rarely sees his family. Enjoys drinking and mildly unusual sex. Enough to embarrass him.'

'He will do. Plan to compromise him further so we have total control! I shall place him in an honoured position at the funeral to show he is to be Hideyoshi's successor. I remind those of you involved with the funeral arrangements to make certain the affair is smooth and impressive! It is to begin at exactly seven tomorrow morning and finish at ten! I also want an observer to attend the Ishikawa funeral and list the names of those who are present!'

'Sir, if the Yakuza and ninjas are not held accountable for the marquis' death, who will be?'

'Udo Ishikawa's father.'

'Sir, I would consider it an honour to kill Mung.'

'Not necessary. Hideyoshi had a plan to disgrace him that involves the Europeans. It will make Mung wish he was buried with his son and daughter-in-law.'

The Buddhist priest left the Ishikawa family cemetery. His prayers for Udo and Gin-ko had been heard only by Mung, Iyeasu, two rickshaw drivers and General Honjo's observer.

Mung and Iyeasu sat down in the nearby gazebo. 'They were a different generation from us,' Mung said, motioning to the freshly dug graves.

The short round man put his crutches at his side. 'I am about their age.'

'Yes, but Udo grew up outside Japan. The Emperor's

restriction to you and me not to kill your brother should have bound him.'

'He did nothing until Gin-ko died,' Iyeasu said. 'Actually I am pleased Hideyoshi is dead. The manner of his death is a fitting message to those White Wolves who tried to ambush you and who caused the loss of my leg.'

'There is a sad beauty in the way Udo and Gin-ko were found, side by side, hand in hand. It explains Udo's insistence that his sons leave Tokyo.'

'Do you think Gin-ko was aware of his plan to join her in death?'

Suddenly the one-ton bronze Buddha on the moss-covered stone began to shake. Mung held onto the gazebo rail for support. Iyeasu clutched the bench. The complacent Buddha flew off its stand and out of the gazebo.

Halfway between Tokyo and Yokohama, Japan's most densely populated area, a crack had appeared in the earth's surface. Crustal distortions moved the eastern layer of the fault zone twenty-two feet north. The release of tension on the western layer caused it to jump thirteen feet south. Within two minutes the wild gyrations of the earth's surface had damaged or destroyed every structure within thousands of square miles of the epicentre. Cooking fires prepared for the midday meal scattered and burned the wooden homes.

Residents along the Pacific shoreline heard the sea hiss outward. Parts of the ocean floor never before seen were uncovered. 'Tsunami!' The dreaded cry went up. People snatched their children and fled inland. Water rushed out of bays, harbours and inlets to fill a newly created rift in the ocean floor, and the tremendous outgoing wave held back the sea. The new underwater canyons filled and the waters grew still. But the sea could not be restrained. It joined with those delayed incoming waves into a massive upheaval. The tsunami surged towards land at two hundred miles an hour. It swept in towards the main island of Honshu and was slowed by volcanic slopes, gaining in height and density. The 150-mile-long wall of water grew to ten, twenty, then thirty feet high at the shoreline. The killer wave moved a quarter of a mile inland and crashed down, its backwash sweeping people, homes, trees, boulders and stone temples out to sea.

Mung's seat was ripped from its foundation and he was flung from the gazebo. The roof crashed down on Iyeasu. Mung jumped up and was thrown down again. He tried to crawl towards the wreckage on top of his friend but was bounced onto his side. He saw houses around the cemetery collapse. Then as quickly as it had begun, the upheaval ceased.

Mung got to his knees. There was not a building standing between him and the imperial palace. A bird swooped down to perch on a crooked tombstone and cocked its head at him, the only moving thing in the graveyard. Mung looked around at coffins spewed up from the earth. Skeletons were exposed – jaws open wide, dark accusing eye sockets and bony outstretched hands protesting their ejection from Mother Earth's womb.

'Get me out of here!' Mung heard Iyeasu's call and saw the collapsed gazebo roof move.

'Are you hurt?' Mung called.

'Not yet,' came the muffled reply.

The debris above Iyeasu will shift if there is an aftershock, Mung thought. He looked for their rickshaw drivers, but they had fled. He saw the White Wolf observer crawl out of a crevice in the ground and run away. Mung peered under the roof. He stretched his arms under the portion above Iyeasu. 'When I lift, you crawl out!'

He bent his knees, straightened his back and used his leg muscles. There was the creaking and splintering of wood. Iyeasu pushed upward and squirmed out on his back. Mung let the roof drop and plopped down on the ground.

'My crutches are still under there,' Iyeasu cried.

'Forget them. I cannot lift that again and you cannot stand to help me. Come away from here!'

'Where will we go? The world is destroyed!'

'The imperial palace still stands. And I can see some buildings and houses beyond it.'

The wail of a child pierced the air. It signalled moans and cries from those trapped in collapsed buildings. Mung ran towards the sound of the child. He stumbled over the leg of a skeleton, caught his balance and hurried on. An unharmed baby sat near the outstretched hand of its mother. Mung cleared the roof shingles from the mother's head but it was smashed and bloody. He hastily covered it up. From all around him came pleas for help.

'Fire,' Iyeasu cried. 'Put that fire out!'

Carrying the child in his left arm, Mung hurried to the shrine's well. It was caved-in. The second well he tried had also collapsed. Cries of trapped and injured people grew louder.

Iyeasu was dragging himself towards the rickshaws and Mung went to him. 'Hold the child while I try to help these people.'

'We are trained to save cities,' Iyeasu said. 'Others must be trusted to help individuals. I wrote Tokyo's fire-fighting manual and fire laws in 1873.' He pointed in the direction of the port. 'Look.'

Mung hefted the baby and gaped at the line of smoke moving towards the city. 'By the gods,' he gasped. 'The wind is behind it!'

Iyeasu dragged himself into a rickshaw. 'Now give me that child! You pull us to fire brigade headquarters. I must tell them to set up at the Eitai bridge.'

Mung handed over the baby and went forward, but found it difficult to move the rickshaw without a left hand to grasp the pulling tong. He took off his jacket and slipped the left tong through the sleeve. He buttoned the front of the jacket, pushed his head into the improvised harness and lifted. They moved away from the cemetery.

The streets lined with small private houses were relatively clear, but as they approached the Sumida river they saw that larger buildings had collapsed across the road. Crevices had opened up and the earth humped ten feet high in some places.

'Keep going to the river,' Iyeasu said. 'It is a natural firebreak.'

Mung's sixty-seven years wore on him and he paced himself, but even at a walk pulling the rickshaw was a strain. Rather than admit physical weakness, he assumed it was mental anguish that sapped his strength. Dead bodies lay everywhere. Wounded and maimed littered the street, crying for help. From the rubble of buildings came the muffled pleas of those buried alive. Debris and broken cobblestones blocked the way. Mung concentrated on the road, forcing himself to disregard the cries. Iyeasu was right. Their duty lay ahead.

They approached the Eitai bridge and the way became even more difficult.

'Stop,' Iyeasu shouted. 'The gods have gone mad!'

They heard a human sound with the quality of a gigantic frightened beast. The hair stood up on the back of Mung's neck. A mass of people was streaming across the bridge, followed by a wall of fire miles long chasing them. Thousands were jumping into the river. Firemen tried to direct the flow of humanity to the wide open area of the military supply depot and public parade ground.

'You cannot reach the bridge with that mob coming this way,' Iyeasu shouted. 'The fire will stop at the river and the panic will decrease. Then we can go forward.'

Mung slipped out of his improvised harness and climbed up into the rickshaw. The fire had caught up with some of the fleeing people. He choked at the smell of burning flesh. Wooden buildings exploded into giant torches even before

298

the flames reached them. The cement casements of the bridge began to crack. The heat buckled metal structures. Paving stones exploded. Like a crazed animal, the fire raged right and left of the river.

'The wind has turned,' Iyeasu cried. 'It is blowing towards the fire! Tokyo is saved!'

'Not on that side of the river,' Mung shouted. 'The smoke is still coming towards us!'

'How can that be?' Iyeasu shouted into what became a roaring gale. He pointed to the dust being whipped around them towards the river, and sheltered the child with his body.

Mung huddled in the rickshaw, his face ashen. He shouted into Iyeasu's ear. 'A heat vacuum! The fire is sucking oxygen into it! That is what is causing the wind! Look at the debris being swept across the river by the suction!'

'The fire has a mind of its own,' Iyeasu shouted above the roar of the wind. 'It feeds itself!'

'Look! The fire brigade flag is retreating from the river!'

They watched the flag atop a long bamboo pole lead the fear-maddened crowd to the open parade ground where tens of thousands had already gathered. 'Why are the firemen giving up?' Mung shouted.

Iyeasu grabbed his arm and pointed, 'Tornadoes!'

'Not in Japan,' Mung said.

'Look! There are two! The beast is crossing the river!'

Mung had seen the big black funnelled windstorms in America but never heard of them in Japan. His mind refused to accept what his eyes saw – two big red funnels, giant cones of fire rising into the sky. They whirled up and over the two-hundred-yard-wide river, scorching and sucking up humans, animals, everything in their path. The sky reddened with burning embers that whirled out of the tops of the funnels and spread fires all over Tokyo. Mung counted four more fire-storms crossing the river further south.

Iyeasu shoved the baby into Mung's arms. 'Get away from here,' he shouted.

Mung pushed the child back and jumped from the rickshaw. He wriggled into the jacket harness and turned the rickshaw around, moving forward at a walk, then at a trot. People began running by him on either side. A woman banged into him, tried to bow her apology and was trampled. His pulling load became lighter. He was being pushed, faster and faster. Crazed people had bunched up behind the rickshaw and were shoving it ahead of them. Mung ran as fast as he could. His legs skipped over the ground. He stumbled and was caught up in the jacket harness, pushed over the cobblestones and through rubble.

And suddenly most of the people were gone. Mung stood up, clothes torn, face bloodied, eyeglasses gone. He turned to Iyeasu and was met by a blast of heat.

'Take it and run,' Iyeasu cried. The child came flying through the air into Mung's arms. Another fire-storm was bearing down on them. 'Run! May the gods be with you!' Iyeasu turned in the rickshaw to watch his death approach.

Mung hugged the child and humped his shoulders. He turned and ran, the heat on his back putting fear in his heart and power in his legs. He passed people who had gone by him.

A sewage ditch angled left of the road and Mung leapt over the edge. He jumped down the slope, sliding into mud, slime and human waste as the giant red cone blotted out the afternoon sun. Others followed him into the ravine from the road. Those who hesitated burst into flames. Mung slapped his hand over the child's mouth and pinched its nose. He covered its body with his and dived into the slimy muck, burrowing down in the filth, away from the heat. He felt the child struggling in his arms but stayed under until the baby started to go limp. Then he turned face up, he and the child gulping the hot air with great gasping breaths. The fire cone had passed them. He tried to clean the baby's face but even the earth had been blackened by the fire. The heat had baked the shallower parts of the sewage canal dry. Smoking bodies lay face down.

'You saved my life!' A young man sloshed through the knee-deep slime to Mung. He took the older man's arm and helped him up. 'I saw you dive in and I followed.'

'Can you help me to the imperial palace?' Mung asked.

'Sir, I think you need a doctor before you go anywhere. Your back is burnt and blistered.'

'Your back also needs attention,' Mung said.

'Yes, but I have fewer years.' The young man bowed.

'Here. Carry the child. The imperial palace is most likely being used as a hospital. What is your name?'

'Taro Kihei.'

'Taro, let us leave this place.'

With the young man's help, Mung struggled up the slope and out of the ditch. He turned in a circle to survey their surroundings. 'Two-thirds of the city is gone.'

'At least there are no more fire-storms,' Taro said.

'Nothing is left to burn. Without landmarks it is difficult to know where we are.' Suddenly Mung realized he was looking at the charred remains of his dear friend, a round form propped up in the ashes of the rickshaw. Mung turned away and gagged.

He began walking in the direction of the palace, followed by Taro carrying the child. They approached the parade ground.

'Sir, look at all the motionless people,' Taro said.

As a sleepwalker, Mung approached the crowded field. The warehouses around it had been burned to their foundations. Nothing remained but thousands upon thousands of people huddled on the green grass. Five hundred by five hundred square yards of humanity massed together. No one moved. No one cried. The bamboo pole of the fire brigade bent gently in the cool breeze that swept the silent field. Firemen crowded around its base – grotesque hunched statues. They all looked upward with the same stare of horror, their mouths open wide.

'Do not go there,' Taro called. 'I think they are all dead.'

'They are not burnt. I must see what killed them.' Mung walked into the square and examined standing, kneeling, crouched bodies. Different faces all expressed the same terror.

'I saw two fire-storms approach the field when I jumped into the ditch,' Taro said.

'There are tens of thousands of people here,' Mung said. He touched the fire brigade commander's shoulder and the body fell, taking a dozen dead firemen down like dominoes. Mung turned and staggered towards Taro and the child. 'You are correct,' he murmured. 'They are all dead.' He felt his legs quiver and his body begin to shake. He saw the ground coming up to his face, then blessed darkness.

Chapter 34

Kobe, 28 October 1894

'It's the reports we haven't received that make me nervous,' William Whittefield said. 'For two days Tokyo has been cut off. Not a whisper from Yokohama, Kanagawa or Chiba. The entire Kanto plain area has been disconnected from the outside world.'

James Alburg lit a cigar and said, 'Nagoya reported earth tremors. Happens at least once a week on these islands. Telephone poles snap and that ends communication for a while.'

'Not for two whole days,' William said. 'Our agents have pigeons for that purpose.'

The harbour signal gun sounded and Alburg looked at the office clock. 'It's only 10 a.m. That gun is supposed to go off at twelve.'

Both men moved to the window. Seven boats with dirt-smudged sails filed slowly into the harbour.

'Those are Toyko boats flying distress flags,' William said.

'There are at least thirty more ships further out to sea. Something's wrong.'

'I'm going down to the dock to find out what's happened.'

'Wait here,' Alburg said. 'If our agents are aboard they'll come to the Kobe Club first.'

An hour later a dishevelled American was ushered into the president's office. 'Toyko is destroyed,' Roger Johnson blurted out. 'There's no food, the people are drinking rain water and they're sleeping out in the open! Tens of thousands died!'

'You're tired and overwrought,' Alburg said. 'It can't be that bad.'

303

'I am shaken, but I do not exaggerate. The quake killed a few thousand. The tidal wave another ten or fifteen thousand. It was the fire that decimated the city. I swam underwater in the Sumida river to the point of unconsciousness. The river became so hot I thought we would boil alive.'

'But Tokyo has the best fire department in the world,' William said.

'They never had a chance.' Johnson brushed his hand over his face. 'The fire brigade set up behind the river. They planned to counterattack the blaze from there. But cyclones of fire jumped the river and spread all over the city. The fire companies were trapped too.'

'Other people must have taken cover as you did,' Alburg said.

'Most of those between the port and the river didn't have time. Many who got over the bridges or swam the river were directed to supposed safety on the public parade ground by the firemen. It was the largest open area without trees or buildings to burn.' Johnson began to tremble.

Alburg shoved a glass of whisky into his hand. 'Drink that!'

The unnerved man swallowed the amber liquid in one gulp. He took a deep breath, then said, 'The ones on the parade field weren't touched by fire or burnt by heat. There were rows and rows of them, all with their mouths open, their eyes looking up.'

'What happened?'

'Dead. All dead. A fireman from Chiba said they suffocated. Fire-storms passed over the open field and sucked away their air.'

'How many?' William asked.

'The police couldn't count everyone. They were too packed together. A ten by ten square yard area was measured, the bodies counted and multiplied by five hundred square yards.' The empty glass dropped from Johnson's hand. He spoke under his breath.

'I couldn't hear you,' Alburg said.

Johnson shuddered and began to weep. 'Forty thousand men, women and children,' he gulped.

'You mean in all Toyko?' William asked.

'No. Only on the parade ground. Forty thousand. And the babies. The little babies with their mouths open.'

William picked up the glass and filled it. He drank half and handed it to Johnson. Alburg took a drink straight from the bottle. The three stood in silence for some moments.

'There was a big aftershock twenty-four hours later,' Johnson said. 'Buildings were still crumbling when we evacuated. There were over two million people in Tokyo when the quake hit. The survivors need help!'

'They'll receive it from the Kobe Club,' Alburg said. 'There are two of our ships in the harbour. The one full of rice was scheduled to go north. The other is loaded with tinned beef, field and medical supplies for the American and English troops in Canton and Peking. I'll send both ships to Tokyo immediately.'

'Let me organize a collection of tents, clothing and medicines from the people of Kobe,' William said.

'Get it aboard within eight hours,' Alburg said. 'We sail then.' He went to his desk and wrote out two cheques. He blew the ink dry and handed them to William. 'These will start a relief fund. Ten thousand dollars from me and ten thousand from the Kobe Club.'

William sat down to write his own cheque for ten thousand dollars. 'We'll contact Shimatzu Ishikawa in Formosa. We need cement, lumber, shingles, nails, tools and any other materials to rebuild Tokyo.'

Word of the disaster spread throughout the empire. The people of Japan, from the frozen island of Hokkaido in the

305

north to the subtropical southern tip of Kyushu, sent food, clothing and medicine. Marquis Inei and other industrialists cancelled foreign shipping contracts and ordered their captains back to the capital with relief supplies.

On the island of Formosa, Shimatzu used the bank's money to buy up all the available lumber. He took options on millions in unharvested board feet of timber. With family funds he purchased three woodcutting mills, ordered them disassembled and shipped to Tokyo. He bought two printing presses and all the paper that could be put aboard a ship within forty-eight hours. He leased the fastest ship in the harbour, packed it full of medicine, food and all the Chinese doctors he could entice aboard with promises of high wages. Shimatzu and his wife sailed for home on the ship.

The American commander of the Pacific Squadron heard of the disaster and ordered two of his ships to escort Shimatzu's vessel and lend whatever assistance they could in Tokyo.

From the four points of the compass, help from Japanese, Americans and Christian missionary groups was on the way. But one hundred and five thousand people had already died in Tokyo within an hour. Fifty-six thousand were injured. The winter rains, cold, and poor living conditions increased the cases of influenza to epidemic proportions. In the next two months twenty thousand more died of respiratory diseases.

'Father, there is a young man with a child he claims is yours,' Shimatzu said.

Mung looked up. 'Taro Kihei,' he exclaimed. 'Please enter and be seated. Shimatzu, this is the young man who pulled me out of the sewage ditch.'

'I heard how you brought my father to the palace.' Shimatzu bowed. 'Thank you.'

'The doctors tended my burns and sent me away,'

Taro said. 'No one would believe the baby belonged to your father.'

Shimatzu bowed again to Taro. 'My family shall always be in your debt. We tried to locate you.'

The young man blushed and shifted the baby in his arms.

'And who has cared for the child all this time?' Mung asked.

'At first I did. He is a very well-behaved baby. I strapped him to my back and worked at the docks unloading the relief ships. Then I took sick with influenza. Women in the tent city near the port cared for him. There are many orphaned babies. Parents died protecting them from the fire with their own bodies.'

Mung saw the emotion on Taro's face. 'So it is a male child,' he said brightly, purposely changing the subject. 'We shall need him to rebuild Tokyo.'

'There will be little for him to do when he grows,' Taro said. 'The streets have been cleared for weeks. Most of the rubble is gone and hundreds of new structures are being erected every day.'

'I am most pleased to hear this,' Mung said. 'As Director of National Decorations, reconstruction of the Kanto plains is my responsibility.' He nodded at Shimatzu. 'My son has done most of my work. I too had influenza and have not left the palace since you brought me here.'

'What did you do before the quake?' Shimatzu asked Taro.

'I followed my father's profession. I am a Confucian scholar and teacher.'

'Where are your parents now?' Mung asked.

'They died in the fire. My sisters, my wife, our house and all our belongings are gone.' Taro held the child closer. 'The baby was a comfort to me. He was someone to love and hold on to. That is why I was tardy in returning him.

When I became ill, I realized I could not take responsibility for him.'

Mung read the sadness in the young man's eyes. 'What do you intend doing now?' Mung asked.

'Eventually I will return to my studies and teaching Confucianism.'

'Does your religion conflict with Shintoism or Buddhism?' Shimatzu asked.

'Some people have made a religion of Confucianism,' Taro said. 'But it is really an ethical doctrine based on the teachings of Confucius, meant to enhance the proper management of society. We stress the individual's responsibility to mankind. The perfecting and preservation of oneself and existing political and religious institutions through education. Confucianism strives to improve society for the welfare of all.'

Mung adjusted his spectacles and rubbed his bent nose. 'Are you interested in the welfare of this child?'

'Very much,' Taro said.

'Would you be inclined to continue caring for him?'

'Yes, but the conditions in the tent city are unsuitable. The child is yours.'

Mung shook his head. 'I found him with his dead mother. Are you prepared to put your Confucian teachings into practice?' he challenged Taro.

'In what way?'

'You said there are other children whose parents died in the quake. Gather twenty more. Start an orphans' home. I will fund it in the name of Count Iyeasu Koin.'

Shimatzu's face brightened. 'I will donate the building materials and supervise construction.'

Mung smiled at his son. 'I am proud of your offer, but if Taro agrees he will oversee building the orphanage. You must leave for England in two days. Lord Cade turned down our request for a loan. Japan needs that money to rebuild Tokyo's industries and keep our people from starvation.' He turned to Taro. 'My son and I assume you will accept responsibility for the orphanage.'

'I am your most humble and dedicated servant.'

'What do you call the child?' Mung asked.

'I did not use a name as I thought of him as yours,' Taro said. 'If you agree I shall call him Iyeasu in honour of the count for whom the orphanage is to be named.'

'That would be most fitting,' Mung said. 'If you wish, I shall adopt you and the boy into the Ishikawa family.'

Taro bowed. 'I thank you for the honour but must humbly decline this most generous consideration. I alone carry the name of Kihei. I wish to adopt Iyeasu.'

Mung turned to Shimatzu. 'Have adoption papers drawn up before you leave. I consider it a family On to sponsor both Taro and little Iyeasu in all their endeavours.' He smiled at Taro. 'Now let me hold that child. If it were not for him, I doubt I would have run so fast or dived so quickly into that ditch.'

As Mung cradled the baby in his arms, he heard loud voices outside his door. He could not know the message he was about to receive would lead to disgrace and set Japan on an unalterable course to another war.

Chapter 35

The Black Dragon messenger waited until Shimatzu, Taro and little Iyeasu were gone before he addressed Mung. 'Sir, the ambassadors of France and Germany have demanded a meeting with our prime minister to discuss Japan's recent territorial acquisitions. They are led by Sergei Witte, Russia's minister of finance.'

'Understandable,' Mung said. 'Those countries have financial and military interests in the Far East. They wish to clarify ours.'

'The Black Dragon office in Formosa reports that German and French troops in China and South-east Asia have been placed on alert. All military and diplomatic leaves were cancelled. German and French warships are being refitted at the Chinese naval shipyard in Hankow.'

'How do you relate these reports to the request for a meeting?'

'It was a demand, not a request. Our Genoysha agents in Vladivostok report that city under martial law. The czar's Black Sea and Baltic fleets have begun to arrive there. Russian troops in Manchuria, Outer Mongolia and Siberia are assembling at ports along the Sea of Japan.'

Mung's knees felt weak as he approached the world globe. He placed his little finger on Vladivostok and his forefinger on Hankow. 'We are caught between them, and out on a limb.' He rapped Korea with his knuckles. 'Our best troops are overseas.'

'More bad news, sir. General Li Hung-Chang has regrouped remnants of the Penyang army in Mukden. And Russian, French and German barges are carrying his soldiers down-river to the major seaports.'

'By the gods,' Mung declared. 'They have four invading armies and three fleets of warships. Where is Lord Cade?'

'Off to India.'

'Damn! I must inform Nogi and Takamora.'

'They are with the Emperor. You, General Honjo and the new Minister of War, Iga Sasaki, have been summoned to an immediate audience.'

'Marquis Hideyoshi would have enjoyed what is about to take place,' Honjo said.

'Are you certain the Emperor will appoint only Mung and the prime minister to negotiate?' Iga Sasaki asked.

'Follow my instructions and you will soon be Japan's next prime minister. Watch my right hand. If it is at my side, speak. If behind my back, remain silent.'

'What if I am questioned and your hand is behind your back?'

'Grunt. Try to appear wise. Say something like, that must be taken into consideration. Or, this should be given more thought. Better yet, shift the question to someone else. Me, if necessary.'

'I have memorized your instructions,' Sasaki said. 'Will the building loan for my villa in Gifu be forthcoming?'

'Do as I say and you will receive the money as a grant, plus an extra bonus of two interesting young ladies from Calcutta. Now let us get on with this.' Honjo led the way to the imperial reception hall.

'Please be seated,' the master of protocol said. He bowed to the Emperor and retired.

'Prime Minister Mori, is the situation as serious as it appears?' the Emperor asked.

'Yes, your imperial majesty. An invasion of Japan is possible.' Mori nodded at Mung. 'The Black Dragon reports Russian, French and German military preparations for war. The Penyang army is forming up along China's east coast.

All Chinese merchant vessels in the Gulf of Pohai are being requisitioned by the imperial Chinese army.'

'Minister of War, what is the disposition of our military?' the Emperor asked.

Honjo put his right hand behind his back and Count Iga Sasaki grunted. 'Sire, the chiefs of staff are better prepared to present a more accurate and detailed report,' the minister said.

General Nogi bowed. 'Your majesty, we have two hundred thousand troops stationed in Korea, along the Yalu and occupying Port Arthur. When we relinquished Weihaiwei naval base to the British, fifty thousand of our men were transferred to Formosa, Okinawa and the Pescadores. There are in excess of a quarter of a million men overseas.'

Admiral Takamora bowed to the Emperor. 'Sire, our navy is spread over tens of thousands of miles to protect the supply lines for our troops and our new colonies.'

'I prefer you do not say colonies,' the Emperor said. 'Japan shall lead these new territories to independence as modern nations.' He leaned forward and spoke softly. 'Can we prevent or repulse an invasion?'

'It would require two months to bring our troops back,' Nogi said. 'There are less than twenty thousand battle-tested soldiers in Japan proper, and the rehabilitation of Tokyo and the Kanto plains adds to our problem.'

'Even if our navy was in position, we are no match for the combined battle fleets of Russia, France and Germany,' Takamora said.

'I suggest we prepare for an invasion at the same time as we meet with the Europeans and hope there is another explanation for the foreign military build-up,' Mung said.

Honjo smiled at Mung, and asked, 'Does the Black Dragon know of the secret Franco-Russian military alliance in the Far East?'

'It appears the secret was well-kept from me,' Mung said.

The White Wolf Society should have shared such information, he thought, grinding his teeth in anger. He noticed Honjo's hand move from behind his back to his side.

'The Black Dragon should have known,' Sasaki said. 'It was this alliance that prevented the British from stopping France's bank loans to Russia.'

Mung watched the light gleam off General Honjo's shaven skull. This man is far more dangerous than Hideyoshi, he thought.

'Prince Kung recently accepted a three-million-rouble bribe from Sergei Witte to oppose Japanese expansion on the continent,' Honjo said. 'Furthermore, the British Foreign Office has rejected Lord Cade's policy of containing Russia in the Far East. London has encouraged Czar Nicolas's moves into Manchuria, thus reducing Russian pressure on India. Lord Cade is at this moment en route to England to convince his Foreign Office to reorder its priorities.'

Mung knew his face was red and could not suppress his anger. Three times in five minutes his competence had been called into question. Now the report he had received about Lord Cade being en route to India was said to be wrong. He watched Honjo's hand come to his side again and heard Iga Sasaki speak.

'Your imperial majesty, it is of the utmost importance that the prime minister be accompanied by the Director of National Decorations to meet the foreign ambassadors,' Sasaki said.

Honjo looked quizzically at Iga Sasaki. 'Does it not usually enhance one's bargaining position if the opposition is outnumbered?' He moved his hand to his side and the minister recited the prepared response.

'Certain demands will be made on the Japanese government by the western ambassadors,' Sasaki said. 'It is the prime minister's duty to face them. It appears these demands are related to the Shimonoseki agreement

313

with China. The Black Dragon was responsible for those negotiations and should attend this conference to defend his gains.'

Nogi stepped forward. 'In that case, Admiral Takamora and I should be included in the delegation. We were as much a part of the Shimonoseki negotiations as anyone else.'

Mung was pleased by the support from the chiefs of staff, but had to agree with Honjo's next words. 'Japan could not afford to lose the finest military men in the empire. If exaggerated concessions were forced on us because of our vulnerability to invasion, Counts Nogi and Takamora would have to resign if they were involved.' Again Honjo smiled at Mung. He and Hideyoshi had known of the triple intervention. The refitting of the French and German fleets in the Hankow naval base had resulted in a wealth of information from the Green House.

'I have decided Minister Sasaki is correct,' the Emperor said. 'Prime Minister Mori and the Director of National Decorations shall be the only ones to negotiate with the Europeans! They must use delaying tactics to gain us time! General Nogi, Admiral Takamora, issue a recall from abroad to all the military units needed to face a foreign invasion! Everyone is dismissed, except Mung!'

As the others filed from the room Mung believed he was about to be stripped of his title of Black Dragon, and he felt relief. The organization was becoming too large for him to direct. He had erred in sending his three grandsons and Shimatzu overseas. With Udo gone he felt isolated, and sensed that Honjo had infiltrated men into the Black Dragon Society and Genoysha.

'I have kept you at a distance since the deaths of Udo and Gin-ko,' the Emperor said. 'But you have been in my thoughts.'

'I am honoured, sire.'

'You are still the only commoner I have ever had a private

conversation with. You think differently from aristocrats.'
The Emperor examined Mung's face. 'With Iyeasu gone,
you must be lonely.

'He was a good friend,' Mung said.

'I miss him too,' the Emperor said. 'If not for Udo's
indiscretion, I would appoint you to the Privy Council as
my personal adviser.'

The former fisherman from Nakanohama lowered his
grey head. 'It is best I not be too close to your imperial
majesty, at least until these negotiations are concluded.
Every time General Honjo smiled, I was shown to have
made another mistake.'

'You and Prime Minister Mori are in a difficult position.
Japan may well be invaded. We need millions of yen to
rebuild Tokyo, millions more to mechanize our industries,
and more still to increase our exports and finance a modern
merchant marine fleet.'

'Sire, do you consider that these objectives take precedence over the new territories we have acquired?' Mung
asked.

'I believe Japan is not prepared for the problems of
administering foreign nationals or managing overseas territories. We do require new trading ports in China. Money
must be pumped into our economy, not out of it. I wish to
end western control of Japan's import–export tariffs. We
cannot expect to govern Korea and parts of China while
the Europeans control our seaports and artificially fix the
price of Japanese gold four to one in their favour. Japan's
currency must be stabilized if we are to become economically independent. For these things I would renounce rights
to Korea, Port Arthur, everything! But I cannot declare that
publicly. Our military victories and your success as a nego-
tiator have so stimulated national pride and imagination
that our people believe we are the most powerful nation
in the Far East.'

'Is the prime minister aware of your views?'

'I have spoken to him on the necessity of equal trading rights with the Europeans in China. He knows I am against the cost of maintaining an overseas army. Our economy needs to be invigorated. We must occupy ourselves with improving Japan, not Korea and China or British interests in Manchuria.'

'Are you saying, sire, you want us to negotiate away our territorial gains?'

'Yes. The Liaotung peninsula, our presence in Korea and along the Yalu. Even the Pescadores and Formosa if you must. Give them back. To prevent war I would relinquish everything, although I cannot say this aloud. You and Prime Minster Mori must make it appear as if the westerners imposed conditions on you.'

'It would make the negotiations easier for us,' Mung said. 'I believe Sergei Witte will demand our withdrawal from mainland China.'

'Yes, but you and Prime Minister Mori may never be forgiven if you capitulate. I cannot support either of you, but I will have my Privy Council vote in Parliament to accept your recommendations of capitulation.'

'Sire, I ask you to relieve me of my position as Black Dragon before the negotiations. I am sixty-seven. You heard my mistakes pointed out. I am too old for the post.'

The Emperor ignored Mung's request. 'I wanted time alone with you because we may never have the opportunity to speak face to face again. Twenty years ago I publicly proclaimed you Shishi, man of high purpose, my personal champion. If you and the prime minister succeed in negotiating the terms I have outlined, both of you will be disgraced. But it will be in Japan's best interests. We must withdraw our military from abroad and protect our islands. Trade off territory for security. The Europeans have put China into debt and control her because of it. I do not want such a situation in Japan.'

'So it is ordered, so it is done.' Mung bowed.

Chapter 36

'Your country has pricked the bubble of Chinese military power,' James Alburg said to the Japanese prime minister and Mung. 'Japan has shown that the Dowager Empress no longer possesses the mythical Mandate of Heaven.'

'In your forthcoming negotiations with the Europeans, Sergei Witte will act as a cutting edge to slice up the Chinese melon,' William Whittefield said.

'Do you mean this triple intervention is a ruse to gain territory for the West?' Prime Minister Mori asked.

'A very thin ruse,' the Kobe Club president answered. 'You relinquished Weihaiwei naval base to England. Prince Kung gave them Burma and the Empress conceded trading rights on the Yangtze. Russia, France and Germany will pressure Peking to cede an equal amount of territory to each of them. To soften the blow on China, the three European allies will force Japan to relinquish the areas you have recently won. When you pull your troops out, the Europeans will take China apart.'

'Have they no feelings of humanity to the Chinese or fairness to us?' Mori asked. 'You say they'll demand we give up our hard-fought gains, then grab the same territories for themselves. Where is the justice?'

'There's a crude American maxim,' Alburg said. 'A stiff penis has no conscience. Russia, France and Germany are preparing to rape China. If Japan gets in the way, she too will be ravaged. Europe's blood is up. Your army and navy stripped China naked. Your military showed how helpless she is, and now the Europeans are panting to take her. They see this as their last opportunity to gain rich colonial concessions in an ever-shrinking world.'

317

'Can we look to America for help?' Mung asked.

'I think not,' Whittefield replied. 'Our president's newly declared Dollar Diplomacy is a tricky way of entering the colonization race. The State Department is looking to acquire Hawaii, Samoa and the Philippines.'

'Do you gentlemen know exactly what Sergei Witte wants from Japan and for himself?' Mori asked.

Alburg and Whittefield exchanged glances. 'If Mr Alburg reveals this information it must remain your secret,' William said. 'The Kobe Club paid handsomely for it and wishes to benefit from the investment.'

Mori and Mung bowed. 'You have our word,' Mori said.

Alburg removed a sheet of paper from his wallet and read aloud, 'France receives Indochina – from Saigon to Hanoi and from Bangkok to Phnom Penh. Russia receives a sphere of influence in Manchuria and Korea. Peking will grant the czar rights to develop railroads, mines and establish tax-free industries in Manchuria. Three months after Japan leaves the Liaotung peninsula and Port Arthur, Sergei Witte's Russian troops will be invited by Prince Kung to reoccupy those places. Germany will take all of Kiachow bay, the port of Tsingtao and trading rights along the Yangtze river. Holland takes the Indonesian islands of Malaya, Sumatra, Borneo, and whatever else is out there.'

'That will put the Dutch only 350 miles from Australia,' Mung said. 'How did they get involved?'

'Holland loaned the czar four hundred million guilders at one per cent interest for Witte's promise of Indonesia. Russia will advance much of the money to China at 6 per cent interest. The remainder is to be invested in extending spur tracks off the Trans-Siberian railroad into Manchuria, down the Liaotung peninsula to a warm-water port and access into the Yellow Sea.'

The discussion was interrupted by the Emperor's master of protocol. Through an interpreter he said, 'Mr

318

James Alburg, Mr William Whittefield, it is time for your appointment. Please accompany me to the imperial reception room. You are to be presented with the Order of the Sacred Treasure.'

Mori held out his hand to the Americans. 'You deserve Japan's highest honour for organizing and managing the earthquake relief fund. Mung and I would like to be with you at this presentation, but we must prepare for tomorrow's meeting with Sergei Witte. Know that you have the heartfelt thanks of the Japanese people.'

The four men bowed and shook hands. 'Are you certain of the information you have given us?' Mung asked the Kobe Club president.

'Yes,' Alburg said. 'We bribed the czar's cousin, Charles. He's usually drunk, but when money is involved he's always prompt and accurate.'

William shook Mung's hand. 'Fare thee well, my friend. I have been recalled by President Roosevelt to be his personal adviser on the Pacific islands and Japan.'

'Perhaps we will meet again one day,' Mung said. 'Give my best wishes to your family.'

William bowed to the prime minister. 'I wish you good luck on your negotiations with the Europeans.' The two Americans left the room.

Mori led Mung to the large wall map. 'It is time to make plans for tomorrow's talk with the round-eyes,' Mori said.

'It should be relatively simple.' Mung waved at the map. 'We give them everything they want.'

Mori smiled. 'You and I may lose face, but let us discuss what we can salvage for Japan's future. I doubt either one of us will ever again be active in our country's political life after these negotiations.'

Sergei Witte sat in a high-backed chair at the head of the conference table. He was flanked by the French and German ambassadors. Opposite the Russian finance minister at the other end of the long, polished table sat the Japanese prime minister and Mung.

'Gentlemen,' Witte said to the two Japanese, 'the governments of France, Germany and Russia respectfully request your country's withdrawal from recently occupied territories on the Asian mainland.'

'By what right or authority do you make this appeal?' Mori asked.

Mung caught Witte's eye signal to the German ambassador and sensed the Europeans had also prepared well for this meeting.

'Japan's control of the Liaotung peninsula threatens Chinese sovereignty,' the German ambassador said. 'Your troops along the Yalu river endanger the stability of Manchuria. Japanese occupation of Korea jeopardizes the political equilibrium of that country as well as the entire region.'

Basic to Mung and Mori's negotiating strategy was their scheme to grant the European demands while appearing pressured to do so. Mung took the first step. 'Gentlemen, since Commodore Perry opened Japan to the outside world some forty years ago, we Japanese have tried to emulate the West. From you we have learned that territorial expansion is a natural right of a developing nation, and necessary for the progress of a modern state.'

'The Oriental has difficulty with the concept of modernization, which dictates constant change,' Sergei Witte said. 'The eastern mind conceives progress in stability, not in movement. You yellow people wish to expand, yet maintain the status quo. This is a conflict between thought and action.'

'I disagree with your conclusion,' Mori said. 'Japan and Europe are not so different in their goals, or their methods. We seek political and economic independence through trade and negotiations, not war.'

'Monsieur.' The French ambassador wagged his finger.

'That is the epitome of naïveté. Those nations who depend on international commerce are by definition at economic war with each other. Immediate success comes over a gun barrel. Long-term accomplishments are achieved down the sights of a cannon. '

'Does this mean that France, Germany and Russia have only a temporary truce in their economic battles?' Mung asked in feigned innocence. He watched the European faces harden.

'Have you read Kipling's new poem "The Ballad of East and West"?', Witte asked. 'There's a line that reads, Oh, East is East, and West is West, and never the twain shall meet.'

Lord Cade had presented Mung with a copy of Rudyard Kipling's book *Barrack-room Ballads*. Mung used his total recall to respond. 'Let us quote Kipling's verse in its entirety, East is East, and West is West, and never the twain shall meet.' He stressed the following lines,

Till Earth and Sky stand presently at God's great
    Judgment Seat;
But there is neither East nor West, Border, nor
    Breed, nor Birth,
When two strong men stand face to face, tho' they
    come from the ends of the earth!

Mung looked directly at each of the stunned European statesmen. 'Are we strong enough to find an equitable and fair solution?'

The German ambassador broke in to protect Sergei Witte from further embarrassment. 'You do not understand, Mr Mung. Japan's presence on the Chinese mainland precipitates the fall of the ruling Manchu dynasty. This would create a radical change in Asia's economic and political development. The resulting chaos would foment international rivalries. This cannot be tolerated!'

Mung adjusted his spectacles and fingered his bent nose. It was his signal to Mori to end the session quickly. 'I repeat the prime minister's first question,' Mung said. 'By what right do Europeans request Japan's withdrawal from territories honourably won on the field of battle and negotiated in a peace treaty between two sovereign states? This is Asia. Japan is the new Rome of the Far East. We shall lead the peoples of Asia, Africa and India!'

Sergei Witte's cold blue eyes settled on Mung. 'Japan is not Rome and you are not Caesar! Japan is exhibiting an inflated sense of power since its recent victories. You must put aside your self-righteous pretensions to leadership of the coloured peoples. You ask by what right we request your withdrawal. By right of might, we demand it!' The Russian finance minister slammed the table. 'Simply!' Witte lowered his voice to a low growl. 'Very, very simply! We are stronger than you! Our armies more numerous and in position to invade Japan!' He leaned back in his chair and waved his hand. 'Your army and navy are scattered from here to hell and back! Take our offer as a realistic evaluation of Japan's military power, or you shall be crushed!'

Mung glanced at Mori. He is either a good actor or badly shaken, Mung thought.

In a low voice the prime minister said, 'Sir, until now you have made us no offer. Only raised your voice in demands which could result either in war or certain disgrace for our country.'

'Evacuate the Asian mainland and you can keep everything the Chinese gave you,' Witte said. 'I will see that the Empress Dowager compensates Japan with an additional thirty million taels of silver for your country's cooperation.'

Mung felt giddy. Everything the Emperor wanted and more was being forced on them. He gained control of himself. He was back in the international poker game and prepared to play a card he had held for two decades.

'Gentlemen, the United States and England have agreed to renounce the unequal treaties forced on Japan forty years ago by western nations. Twenty years ago Russian's Count Muriev signed a letter of intent to that effect. It was part of the Sakhalin–Kuril islands agreement I negotiated with the count. A few months ago the Russian ambassador in Tokyo confirmed Muriev's letter of intent. Mr Witte, if Russia, France and Germany are prepared to give up control of Japan's import–export tariffs and regulation of our monetary system, I can promise speedy agreement.'

Mori impressed Mung as a natural poker player by adding, 'I would prefer time to consider my colleague's recommendations. Japan must retain trading privileges on the Chinese mainland to offset the territories you are asking us to relinquish. We will discuss this further tomorrow!'

For another five days the negotiations continued. On the last day, Sergei Witte held up his hand and pointed at the two Japanese diplomats. 'We will not lose our military advantage by wasting more time! We have conceded all there is! Return to your Emperor. Tell him, your Parliament and your people that if within three days Japan does not agree to withdraw from the Asian mainland, the invasion of your islands will begin!' He stormed out of the room, followed by the other Europeans.

Mung turned to Mori. 'We did it!'

'They did it for us,' the prime minister said. 'Yet, even though we may have saved Japan from invasion and financial servitude, people will label us traitors. We have dishonoured our ancestors by evacuating Korea, the second national humiliation in the history of our country. We shall become known as the pair who did not understand On.'

'I have given directions to our followers in the National Diet,' General Honjo told Iga Sasaki. 'When Mori and Mung present the European demands for a vote, we will all stand with the chiefs of staff and Privy Council. The

Emperor has ordered them to vote for withdrawal. Others in Parliament will be forced to accept the terms.'

'But it is a national disgrace,' Sasaki said. 'So many lives were lost to gain Korea and the Liaotung peninsula.'

'We shall capitalize on Mori's disgrace to make you prime minister. And on Mung's shame to incorporate the Black Dragons and Genoysha under my command. You will appoint me chief of military intelligence when you are head of state. Then we begin planning to defeat Russia.'

Two days later, Sergei Witte spoke with the compassion of a victor to the pair of grim-faced Japanese seated at the conference table. 'Gentlemen, the assassination attempts on your lives after your speeches in Parliament are regrettable, but I am most pleased that Japan has accepted our terms. It is unfortunate that your country's overseas expansion coincided with ours. Europe has a sacred mission to spread western culture, industrial expertise and Christianity to our Asian brothers. Is there anything you wish to add before the official signing of this agreement?'

Neither Mori nor Mung responded. Both men were shaken by the personal abuse heaped on them in Parliament, in the press and on the streets. The second assassination attempt in as many days underscored the deep resentment, bitterness and sense of national shame in Japan. Mung and Mori had been hung in effigy on the Ginza, outside Parliament and on the steps of the Yasukune shrine. Throughout the country western clothing was less in evidence; European eating places were being shunned. The financial relief of not having to support an overseas army and the cancellation of the unequal treaties, so long a rallying cry for anti-western elements, were ignored. The honour of the nation had been sullied. Iga Sasaki called for Giri against Russia, the nearest European nation involved.

Sergei Witte placed five copies of the agreement in front

of Mung and Mori. After each had signed, Witte offered the Japanese the pen that had been used, but they declined. The German ambassador's proposed toast was ignored, and the Japanese took their leave. They returned to the imperial palace protected by fifty Black Dragons and a contingent of imperial guards.

In the imperial reception room, the prime minister presented the agreement to the Emperor. 'Your majesty, it is done as you requested.'

'I shall peruse this document at another time,' the Emperor said. 'Recount the main points for me.'

'Sire, Japan retains undisputed rights to the Ryukyu islands, Formosa and the Pescadores. Our troops must leave China and Korea within two months. In return, the Europeans have renounced their control of our seaports, tariffs and monetary system. In effect we are free of the unequal treaties. China will pay Japan another thirty million taels indemnity, and open seven new ports of trade to us on the mainland. In these port areas we shall have the right to establish non-taxable industries and receive most favourable nation status in commerce.'

For some moments the Emperor gazed at the two men. Then he smiled. 'You have saved Japan! What you two have done is as important as any battle. The future will vindicate your actions. Some may call you traitors, but in truth you are heroes! I regret I cannot proclaim this publicly. I expect that the situation for both of you may grow worse. In the last hour a telegram arrived from Korea. Twenty army and navy officers committed seppuku in order to influence me to negate the tripartite agreement and stop our troop withdrawal from the mainland.'

'Is it a revolt?' Mung asked.

'Apparently not,' the Emperor said. 'It appears the evacuation will begin as ordered. I would like to protect both of you by allowing you to resign and become anonymous, until such time as there will be an understanding of what

325

you have accomplished and right thinking prevails. But alas, I need my prime minister to implement the agreement. You, Mung, have been my eyes and ears since I came to Tokyo twenty years ago. As Black Dragon you enabled me to guide Japan into the modern world. But this mass suicide of military officers makes it impossible for you to continue as Black Dragon. I hope to appease the military by placing all intelligence-gathering organizations under military supervision.'

Mung bowed. 'It has been an honour for me, my ancestors and my descendants to serve your imperial majesty. Sire, I am prepared for retirement.'

'Not just yet.' The Emperor smiled. 'Under that thatch of grey bristles works a brilliant mind and an infallible memory governed by a loyal heart. I need all three. Once you told me that the strength of a modern nation is determined by the level of education of its population.'

'It was my creed as Scholar of Satsuma and when I was appointed to formulate the guidelines for our national education system in 1873.'

'General Honjo now influences national education,' the Emperor said. 'He has instituted an official regime of studies meant to dominate and control the minds of our people. If successful, his militaristic concepts will govern the future of Japanese society, not mine.'

'Sire, Honjo's system stresses reverence to the Emperor,' the prime minister said. 'I assumed this was a positive thing.'

'It is, when power is in the hands of moral men. Honjo intends to isolate me, then speak in my name as the shoguns did to control past Emperors. I am determined to outmanoeuvre his manipulation of our education system by establishing an institution of higher learning – so prestigious that it will influence the curriculum and standard of all lower schools in the country. Where the head leads, the body will follow. Mung, you will be appointed vice-chancellor, responsible for founding the university and setting academic standards. Prince Matsukata, a loyal member of my Privy Council, will be chancellor. His role will be to prevent Honjo and Sasaki from interfering. You will begin by combining the imperial colleges of Kaisei Gakko and Tokyo Igakko to form Tokyo Imperial University. Now, the first problem is funding.'

'Sire, I believe money for the university can be diverted from the profits gained in an exceptional transaction Mung has planned,' Mori said.

The Emperor raised an eyebrow, then nodded to Mung.

'Your majesty, in the small print of the document you hold, Sergei Witte agreed to my request of an advance credit to Japan of the equivalent in roubles to thirty million taels of silver,' Mung said. 'With this credit I approached Marquis Inei. He bought several tons of Formosan gold at the artificially low price set by the Europeans. Tomorrow, when the unequal treaties are officially abolished, we shall do what the Europeans have been doing to us for almost fifty years, sell the gold at four times its value.'

'But no one in Japan or the Far East would buy it,' the Emperor said. 'Not until the repercussions of the cancelled treaties have been evaluated and the gold market stabilizes.'

'My son Shimatzu will sell the gold in London tomorrow, before all this becomes known.'

'How can you communicate so swiftly?'

'Witte is allowing me use of the new trans-Alaskan telegraph line. The Russians have connected their lines with the Americans'. They laid a cable from Vladivostok across the Bering Strait. We have an undersea cable to Vladivostok from Sapporo.'

'But how can you contact London from the tip of North America?' the Emperor asked.

'Via British Columbia, California, New York and the trans-Atlantic cable to England.'

327

'Has a message ever been sent to the other side of the world before?' the Emperor asked.

'Not from Japan,' Mung said. 'But all the equipment is ready, and in theory it should work.'

The Emperor shook his head. 'The world is shrinking. It took Shimatzu ten days to reach London. Now you will send messages to him in hours. When I studied geography, that part of the world we now call Europe was designated on maps by sea monsters.'

'Sire, if this gold transaction is successful, there will be sufficient capital to found a university,' Mori said. 'Mung could be given some positive recognition to offset the negative reaction to our military withdrawal.'

'Not possible,' the Emperor said. 'If the military hears of this money, Japan will soon be on the road to war with Russia. It depresses me that I cannot publicly acknowledge the sacrifices you two have made for Japan.' He turned to the master of protocol. 'Give me your short sword!' The Meiji Emperor took the gleaming steel blade and cut two buttons off his tuxedo. He placed a black bone button in each man's hand. 'This is from the Emperor of Japan, descendant of the Sun Goddess Amaterasu-o-mi-Kami, to his most loyal subjects. This token of my esteem must remain our secret. Be careful. Many have sworn to kill both of you. It may be years before we can meet again.'

21 January 1895

Part 2

Chapter 37

Fairhaven, Massachusetts, 21 April 1902

Hiroki and Noriko Koin had learned to relax in American hotel rooms. Several years of purchasing missions for their government had made them experienced travellers. This time they had left their two boys with friends in Washington DC. The trip was to be a second honeymoon.

Noriko came out of the shower towelling herself and Hiroki, leaning back on the hotel bed, revelled in her beauty. He gazed at her bare legs, the tawny skin smooth and glossy over lean flanks, her full breasts held erect by wide powerful shoulders.

Noriko saw him looking at her and smiled. She wrapped the towel around her slim waist. 'Your golden rod is thinking again. Doesn't it get tired?'

'Not with you looking like that.' He laughed and reached for her.

Noriko slipped away, her dark eyes glowing. 'There is no time for sex before our appointment. Read your grandfather's letter.'

'In seven years we have received seven letters from him,' Hiroki said. 'They always begin by reminding us to observe the Ceremony of the Dead for our parents. Then he tells us how well the university is doing. And about the success of the orphanage.'

'This letter reached us by special courier from Washington,' Noriko said. 'I hope we are ordered home.'

'Not likely. The information I sent about American improvements on Count Ferdinand von Zeppelin's rigid-frame powered airship kept us in Washington an extra year.

I am certain my last report on Marconi's wireless will result in an additional sentence to remain in exile.'

'Why is radio so important if we already have telephone and telegraph?'

'I will never forget the maze of communication wire around the army camp in Seoul. I was able to speak with my father from the Kyongbok palace until they cut the wire. But radio waves are invisible. They cannot be cut or blown up. We can fly kite antennae from our ships and keep in contact with the shore. The people I spoke with at the Edison laboratories in New Jersey say Marconi is correct. That radio waves conform to the curvature of the earth. It means the strength of the transmitter determines the distance of the signals. With a strong enough generator we could talk to people on the other side of the world without a wire.'

'I would like to speak with the children,' Noriko said. 'I worry when we leave them behind. I am also concerned about the difficulty they will have when we finally do go home.'

'We speak Japanese to them.'

'But I prefer their schooling to take place in Japan.'

Hiroki saw the wistful look on his wife's face. 'Call Washington. Talk to them while I dress. Then we shall read the letter.'

Noriko put through the call, then replaced the receiver with a smile on her face.

'Feel better?' Hiroki asked.

'Much. Everything is fine. They have eaten lunch and are about to take their afternoon nap.'

'Why westerners say Orientals are inscrutable I will never know. I could read the relief on your face from here.'

'Read the letter, not my face.' Noriko sat at her husband's side and kissed him. 'Do you always examine the envelope so carefully before opening?'

'I am an intelligence officer. Our security chief in

Washington advised us to take extra precautions. Honjo has our agents reading all the mail from foreign embassies and western military bases before it leaves Japan.' Hiroki broke the seal, unfolded the letter and began to read:

'Dear grandchildren and great-grandchildren, We missed you at the family reunion. Yaka and Uraga returned from Peking in time to visit Prime Minister Mori's grave. With Shimatzu, we numbered four at the cemetery. Since Mori's assassination six years ago, it is only our family who publicly remember him. I remind you both of your obligation to perform the rites for your departed parents.'

'See,' Hiroki said. 'One letter a year that always begins with a reminder of the Ceremony of the Dead.'

Noriko touched his wrist. 'Hold the paper steady. The next line says he wants the children and me home.'

'And I am ordered to Korea,' Hiroki said.

'I will not be separated from you.'

'These are orders.'

Noriko's shoulders set and her eyes narrowed. She silently vowed that she would accompany her husband.

Hiroki continued reading Mung's letter aloud.

'The Europeans did not realize they were doing us a favour when they took the geographical fruits of our 1894 victories for themselves. The lack of territorial responsibility, combined with the indemnity we received and cancellation of the unequal treaties, have propelled our country into the twentieth century like a giant Chinese sky rocket. Tokyo has been rebuilt more beautifully than before. Our national trade figures are forty times higher than ten years ago. Inei's banking genius has trebled our merchant fleets and gained us one of the highest credit ratings in the world. Japan is bursting with economic and military energy.

'The international suppression of the Boxer Rebellion in China affected Japan far more than any other nation. The first organized revolt in Hankow was led by people trained

333

in Honjo's Green House. We supported the rebels until they sided with the Dowager Empress against all foreigners. Then we joined the multi-national force to suppress them. Our intelligence agents in China were the eyes and ears of that force. Our eight-thousand-man élite officers' corps led the expedition into Peking. They outnumbered each force sent by Russia, Britain and France. In newspapers and at the negotiating table the Germans made a great noise about their participation, but in fact they remained in the rear. The Russian General Lineivitch dictated peace terms to the Empress. The Chinese must pay a 333 million dollar indemnity – 30 per cent to Russia, 21 per cent to Germany, France 16 per cent, Britain 11 per cent, Japan and the United States 8 per cent each. Italy, whose soldiers did not even participate, will receive 6 per cent. This unfair settlement, manipulated by the same countries who deceived us before, has outraged our military, our politicians and our people. All have lost respect for western fairness and for their ability in combat. Even evaluations by western military experts admit the Japanese soldier was superior in the field to any other in the Peking operation.

'Our men led the final assault on Peking and suffered the most casualties. Only our soldiers and the US marines did not take part in a rampage or wanton pillaging, rape and murder. The Kaiser had sent orders to give no quarter and take no prisoners, and the atrocities began again when the German contingent arrived. Honjo forwarded a copy of the Kaiser's order to me, in which he refers to Chinese and Japanese as the Yellow Peril.'

Hiroki looked up from the letter. 'I wonder if Kaiser Wilhelm invented the Yellow Peril phrase, or if he took it from America's west coast newspapers.'

'I would like to know why you are being sent to Korea,' Noriko said.

'It must have to do with my knowledge of the language.' Hiroki went on reading the letter. 'The dynamic growth of our country, coupled with the national insults suffered in the latest negotiations and our loss of respect for western military, has created a powder keg in Japan. The Russians lit the fuse last month by occupying Manchuria and declaring North Korea within their sphere of influence. We know Sergei Witte signed a secret alliance with China. Witte is not aware that Lord Cade and I both came out of political retirement to sign a secret Anglo-Japanese alliance. Inform William Whittefield about this. He will know whom to notify in the American government. Tell him the British will use Japan to police the Russians on the Asian mainland. We will use Britain to neutralize the Chinese. If war does break out between Japan and Russia, Britain promises to close the Suez Canal to the czar's Baltic fleet. It will give us another month or so to prepare. This time we have guarantees the French will cut back on Russian loans, thus restricting the Russian railroad building and their purchases of war materials.

'General Honjo requests you join your brothers in military intelligence in Seoul. You are to reactivate and rebuild your Special Forces for purposes of espionage and sabotage against the Russians in Korea. I must warn you to be extremely careful of Honjo and his people. They are loyal Japanese, but unscrupulous. They justify any action, no matter how amoral, by its results.

'Your report on the wireless radio has excited many here. We have seen demonstrations. Nogi and Takamora would like a supply of radios for the army and navy. Ask William to help in securing them, as well as American military observation balloons.

'In light of the unfair treatment accorded Japan in 1894 and because of recent events in Peking, I have reminded the Emperor of Noriko's father's creed, a translated quote from the Latin, *Si vis pacem – para bellum*. If you want peace, prepare for war.'

'The Iron Chancellor, Otto von Bismarck, once told my

father that Japan must never go to war against more than one enemy at a time,' Hiroki said. 'The Anglo-Japanese Alliance isolates Russia in the Far East, and Grandfather accomplished that.'

'I am pleased he is no longer in disfavour,' Noriko said.

'It sounds as if he has a working relationship with Honjo. My grandfather is too valuable an asset to be allowed to sit on the shelf when the country is preparing to fight.'

'When are we to return?'

'Immediately.'

There was a knock on the door and a voice called, 'Marquis Koin? Marquessa? Your guests await you in the lobby.'

'Thank you,' Hiroki called. 'I cannot get accustomed to being a marquis,' he whispered to Noriko.

'William must have registered us with our titles. Could you do my blouse in the back?'

Hiroki moved behind his wife and kissed her neck. 'The buttons, please,' she said. 'It will be wonderful to wear a kimono again.'

'I am sorry that I must leave you and the children, but happy I am returning to active duty.'

Noriko had her own plans but said nothing about them. 'Western women must be contortionists to be able to put their hands behind their backs and close the buttons by themselves,' she said.

Chapter 38

'Marquis, Marquessa,' the mayor said. 'Fairhaven is honoured by your presence, but my wife and I don't know whether to bow, salute or shake hands.'

Hiroki extended his hand with a smile. 'Noriko and I have become comfortable with American greetings, although not with the European kissing of cheeks. We were educated at American missionary colleges, Noriko in Japan, I in Korea.' He shook William Whittefield's hand. 'My grandfather and William's father studied together. They were adoptive brothers.'

'That's why I booked you into this hotel,' William said. 'Fifty years ago it was a seamen's tavern.' He pointed to the reception desk. 'That's part of the original bar. Your tour of Fairhaven begins here.'

'Before it does, I would appreciate your assistance in making travel arrangements to Washington for us as soon as possible,' Hiroki said.

'We hoped to have the pleasure of your company longer than that,' the mayor said.

'My wife and I were looking forward to an extended vacation in Fairhaven, but we've been recalled to Japan.'

'Then you'll be needing accommodations on to California,' the mayor's wife said. 'I am certain William, with his Washington connections, can take care of that.'

'And I will, although regretfully,' William said.

'Good,' the mayor's wife said. 'Now I have a request. They claim each language has its own music. I would like to hear Japanese spoken.'

'I believe you will be disappointed in the musicality of Japanese.' Hiroki laughed. 'It is said that to the western ear

337

our language sounds like a series of grunts and grumbles. But there is certainly no problem. You have an expert in William Whittefield.' He turned to William. 'I assume these people do not understand us?' he said in Japanese.

'Not a word.'

'Good. We need the quickest transportation to the capital to pick up our children, and from there to California. I am ordered to Korea.'

'I assume it has to do with the Russians. I have a message from President Roosevelt for your government.'

'This appears to be a serious conversation,' the mayor said. 'I don't know if my wife heard any music in the language, but I suggest we begin the tour.' He led them outside the hotel and waved his hand. 'The paving stones and concrete piers weren't here in your grandfather's day. Then it was wooden sidewalks, dirt roads and timbered piers. The ships tied up along the quay were mostly three-masted whalers.' The mayor took them across the street and pointed at a large brass plaque embedded in the cement pier. He read aloud:

'From this berth in the year of our Lord 1840, the *J. Howland*, with William Whittefield master, went whaling, and in January 1841 rescued two Japanese fishermen. Shin-ho died. Captain Whittefield adopted Mangiro, christened John Mung, and raised him in Fairhaven. In 1851 John Mung returned to his home islands, where he rose in the service of the Japanese government to a high position.'

The mayor looked up and said, 'Every time we thought to put your grandfather's title on the plaque, we had word he had been given a new one. We are proud of John Mung.'

'It was not always so,' William said. 'Fifty years back few people were aware of Japan's existence. There was a depression in the United States and antagonism to cheap Oriental labour from China. My father rescued Mung from a bitter fight just a few yards from here. Our family always

338

felt it was the fight that caused Mung's return to Japan. The *J. Howland* had been several months at sea when it tied up here. In Hawaii it was the custom for any seaman to buy the service of a prostitute.' William turned and pointed to the hotel. 'Mung went to what was then a water-front bar. He had not yet learned that Americans follow different morals abroad than they do at home. Because he, an Oriental, approached a white prostitute, sailors in the bar beat him up, killed his pet cat and threw him off this pier. My father found him floating face down in the water, almost dead. Not long after, Mung learned that my grandparents had been censured and banned from the church their grandparents founded because he attended services with them. In 1848 he left for the California gold fields, and never returned to Fairhaven. He travelled on to Hawaii and Japan.'

'It appears Mung had a difficult life in Fairhaven,' Noriko said.

'On the contrary. He told me that outside of those two incidents, he has wonderful memories of his years in this city.' William indicated a group of buildings at the end of the road. 'That is the shipyard he and my father worked in during vacations from Harvard High School.'

'It is where he memorized the construction of the first whaler he built in Kagoshima,' Hiroki said.

'Not exactly,' William said. 'Most Japanese learn about your grandfather from legends in children's stories or from the plays written about him. Did you know he is an artist? We have paintings and sketches he made of his whaling trips, and of Fairhaven. During his years at sea he drew sketches of the interiors and exteriors of the ships he worked. He told me those drawings were more influential than his shipyard experiences because he was more mature when he drew them. The modern method of construction made sense with a fixed keel and new sailing methods.'

339

'How old is your grandfather now?' the mayor's wife asked.

'Seventy-four,' Hiroki said. 'And he is still quite active. He claims longevity because of his western diet at an early age. He raises sheep, poultry and wheat at Tokyo University to improve the Japanese diet, and has had some successes in curing rickets. He hopes one day to end the national malady of bow-legged Japanese.'

The mayor looked at his watch. 'We should be going. There are people waiting to meet you.'

'We'll stop at the telegraph office to arrange the transportation for the Koin family,' William said.

'I must also send a telegram to Japan,' Noriko said. 'I wish to receive the reply in California before we board ship. Can that be done?'

'To whom is your telegram?' Hiroki asked in Japanese.

'To your grandfather. I am about to ask my first favour of him. He must give permission for the children and me to accompany you to Korea.'

'That could be dangerous,' Hiroki said. 'I will be travelling much of the time.'

'Your mother travelled with your father through Korea, Mongolia and Manchuria, taking care of Shimatzu while she was pregnant with Yaka. I am going with you!'

Hiroki recognized the set of his wife's shoulders, the determined light in her eyes. 'I will add my request to yours,' he said. 'If Grandfather denies it, I think it will be time for the marquis and marquessa to disobey. As my mother did.'

From the telegraph office, the mayor led them up a wide street of neat houses fronted by white picket fences. They stopped before a tall, white clapboard building with a steeple. The sign read, FIRST METHODIST CHURCH OF FAIRHAVEN.

'Marquis and Marquessa Koin,' the mayor said, 'half a century ago the congregation of this church took part in

340

an unchristian act. They expelled the Whittefield family because of racial prejudice towards their adopted son, your grandfather. We have since made amends to the Whittefield family, and now respectfully request the opportunity to apologize to the family of John Mung.'

Hiroki and Noriko looked at each other and nodded. They followed the mayor into the church. Overhead, the bell tolled.

Inside, a chorus of hundreds of voices blended in serene harmony,

> 'Yes we shall gather at the river,
> The beautiful, beautiful river.
> Yes we shall gather at the river,
> Doing the work of the Lord . . . '

The mayor and his wife stepped aside. William led Hiroki and Noriko down the long aisle between rows and rows of parishioners singing. At the front of the church the minister led them up the steps and behind the pulpit.

The song ended and the minister signalled his congregation to be seated. He addressed Hiroki and Noriko. 'The hymn you just heard was sung by the congregants of the Seamen's Chapel in Honolulu. It was some fifty years ago that Reverend Damon performed the conversion ceremony for your grandfather. When the *J. Howland* returned to Fairhaven, your grandfather and the entire crew walked from the dock to this church as you have done. They thanked God for their safe return. As your grandfather grew to manhood, so did a vulgar prejudice arise in this community. There was unjust anger and deceitful action taken by members of this congregation against John Mung and the family who adopted him. Years ago members of this church apologized to the Whittefields. We now request your help in asking your grandfather's forgiveness for the deeds of our parents. Please inform him that he and his family have been voted life members of this church.' The minister stepped back and motioned Hiroki to the podium. 'We would appreciate hearing your thoughts at this time.'

Hiroki looked to Noriko. She nodded, and he stepped forward.

'Ladies and gentlemen, fellow members of the First Methodist Church.' Hiroki had to wait a full two minutes until the applause died out. Then he said, 'My wife and I are deeply moved by the outpouring of your feelings and the depth of your moral and religious convictions. My grandfather has been granted four more years than the Biblical promise of three score and ten. He is in good health and still tells stories of his life in Fairhaven, always coloured with affection, pride, and most of all, understanding. The racial prejudice grew in Fairhaven as John Mung matured. He was a handsome man and parents feared their daughters might consider an Oriental as a husband. John Mung was one of the youngest men ever to captain a New England whaler. And the only non-white to navigate an American ship back around the Horn. He was elected master of the whaler by its crew, an all-white crew. If Mung was white, he would have been a great catch for some young lady of Fairhaven.'

There was considerable coughing and clearing of throats in the congregation.

Hiroki waited for silence. 'What you do not know is that my grandfather had his own racial prejudices. We Japanese are a proud and tradition-influenced people. John Mung's reason for returning to Japan was because he could not find a Japanese bride in America or Hawaii. A Caucasian would not do for him, and he would not consider a Chinese bride either. He was obligated to father Japanese children who would honour the graves of his ancestors. His anguish at the time of expulsion from this church was not for himself, but for the Whittefield family who suffered because of him. The influence of Fairhaven,

342

Harvard High School and his whaling voyages, allowed my grandfather to return to Japan as the first bridge of modern knowledge into our country in two and a half centuries. John Mung and William Whittefield's father, John, took part in military campaigns in Japan which resulted in the fall of the shogunate and restoration of power to the Emperor. They were instrumental in founding a constitutional monarchy in Japan. The Whittefield family continues to be involved with the democratization and modernization of my country. On behalf of my grandfather, my family and my people, I thank you for this unselfish gesture of brotherhood.' Hiroki sat down to the applause of the congregation.

William stood up to announce, 'On behalf of the Whittefield family and the people of Fairhaven, a museum shall be established in the name of Mangiro, John Mung, the fisherboy who changed the course of Japanese and American history. My grandfather's house, where Mung spent his early years, will be the site of this museum.'

'The City Council has incorporated the cost of maintaining the Mangiro Museum into its budget in perpetuity,' the mayor announced.

Noriko whispered to Hiroki, and he stood. 'In response to the honour of membership you have bestowed on us in the First Methodist Church of Fairhaven, my wife and I will dedicate a wing to the American missionary library in Tokyo.'

The minister stepped forward, 'Every good gift and every perfect gift is from above. Let us pray.'

The congregation bowed their heads in silent prayer. The minister blessed them, and led Hiroki and Noriko back down the aisle to the front door as the congregation sang a hymn.

The Japanese couple stood on the church steps for some time, accepting the good wishes of the parishioners and sharing memories of John Mung with them.

'I have never been so moved,' Noriko said to Hiroki.

'The people were genuinely repentant of their parents' behaviour and concerned for our feelings.'

'They fell in love with Marquis and Marquessa Koin,' William said.

Noriko blushed. 'Do we have time to see the house your family donated?'

'I'm afraid not,' William said. 'We need to talk privately and catch your train. The US State Department has completed your transportation arrangements. Come.'

In the Fairhaven railroad station, the stationmaster placed three chairs around his desk and left the office.

'Grandfather wrote that you would know whom to tell about the secret Anglo-Japanese Alliance,' Hiroki said to William.

'Yes, Theodore Roosevelt. The president wants the Russians out of Manchuria. He believes their occupation of Manchuria and troop movements into North Korea violate America's free-trade policy. Our intelligence service predicts future Russian military expansion on the Asian mainland, and a possible invasion of Japan.'

'Will America support us?' Hiroki asked.

William shook his head. 'Not to the extent of sending troops. I recently drafted a letter from President Roosevelt to Czar Nicolas, requesting the removal of Russian troops in Korea and Manchuria.'

'What results do you expect?'

'None. Roosevelt referred to the Russians in Washington as lying diplomats who make a science of mendacity. In the event of a Russo-Japanese war, the president hopes Japan will win. You are to tell your government that he will smile upon any assistance private American citizens give Japan against Russia. The United States will not interfere if your troops land in Manchuria and Korea. In return, Roosevelt wants no Japanese opposition to our new holdings in the Pacific.'

'You are referring to Hawaii?'

'The Philippines too,' William said. 'Those islands fell into our lap at the peace treaty with the Spanish. Our diplomats still do not know what to do with them.'

US naval officers in Washington had told Hiroki that Manila and Honolulu gave America the two major coaling stations needed for their fleets to control the Pacific. He pictured the map and realized the Americans were halfway to Japan, but his mind rejected the possibility that one day America and Japan might clash. 'I am certain Washington will soon receive Japan's confirmation of non-interference in the Philippines and Hawaii,' Hiroki said. 'I must now ask your help in acquiring military observation balloons for our army and navy.'

'I will personally see to that,' William answered.

Hiroki turned to Noriko and said, 'As the wireless is still in the development stage, I would like to use part of the Koin family fortune to open a factory near the Edison laboratories. To produce and attempt to perfect wireless radios for our military. The Inei family in New York could manage the business.'

'You are head of the Koin family,' Noriko said. 'The decision is yours.'

'I must do it for Japan.'

'I agree,' Noriko said. 'The only problem I see is that the Ineis in New York are silk merchants and bankers. Would they know how to manage such an enterprise?'

'The Inei family will have every assistance,' William said. 'I am certain the American government would help in exchange for reports of your experiences with the wireless in military use.'

The stationmaster returned to the office. 'Sir, the train is pulling in.'

'Thank you,' William said. He turned back to Hiroki. 'All we have discussed will be attended to. I wish you both a swift and safe journey. I send my regards to your family. President Roosevelt also sends his best wishes.

345

He asked me to say, If you want peace, prepare for war.'

Hiroki bowed to hide his shock. It appeared Japanese consular security had been breached.

Si vis pacem – para bellum.

Chapter 39

The Fifth Moon Inn stood outside the city of Mukden on the crossroads to Peking, Korea and Manchuria. It was a long, two-storey building with red lacquered walls and yellow roof tiles that sparkled gold in the sun. The inn's reputation had grown in the past six years. Travellers talked of the quality food, fair prices and charming girls on the second floor. Chinese and Russian militarymen from garrisons around Mukden were always visible. Their officers received a 20 per cent rebate for billeting their men, plus free accommodations on the second floor with a girl who spoke their language, be it Khalka Mongol, Cantonese or Russian.

The Japanese proprietor was considerate, honest and kept a clean house. On this day he stood on the balcony outside his office and watched the Orquen tribesman trot his little Mongol pony towards the corral. Patrons at the inn paid scant attention to the hunter wearing a deerskin hat and jacket, with a rifle slung across his saddle. He passed the reins to a servant and started for the rear of the building.

The proprietor dashed downstairs and bowed low before the tribesman. 'Your room and bath are waiting, sir.'

'As it should be,' Akichi Shibata said, throwing his rifle to the owner. 'I want to know the minute General Honjo arrives!'

'He is already here, and requests your presence after dinner. The general is presently occupied on the second floor.'

The sun had set when Shibata entered Honjo's room

347

carrying a leather briefcase. His powder-blue robe accentuated his lean sunburnt face. Shibata's eyes darted to every corner of the room before he closed the door behind him and bowed. 'General, I am honoured at this visit and trust I can make your journey worthwhile.'

'I was five days on horseback,' Honjo said. 'The roads appear safe.'

'My people were guarding you from the moment you disembarked,' Shibata said. 'Eight years ago, travellers were not so safe. I walked the length and breadth of Manchuria then, selling house wares to women, pornographic pictures to men, and recruiting for my organization. I was in great danger every moment.'

'And how many are now in your employ?'

'Five thousand at full pay, plus eight hundred Japanese agents. I control an additional forty thousand part-time information gatherers.'

'How do you manage to manipulate that many people?' Honjo asked.

'With opium. The medicine my men have been hawking for six years at the weekly markets and fairs is heavily laced with the drug. If people have pain, Green House Elixir will soften it. The Golden Bat cigarettes with the opium pellet in the mouth-piece often gets them started. They keep coming back for more, and the more they need the more information flows in. We push Golden Bats to the workers around Russian and Chinese army camps and power stations. About one in ten labourers employed by both armies is somehow obligated to me.'

'I am impressed,' Honjo said. 'Explain how this system of inns as command posts operates.'

Shibata strutted around the room as he talked. 'I needed centralized locations to receive information, issue orders and distribute the opium. We now have thirty inns in Manchuria and northern China, all located on major crossroads, many like this one near army bases. We train the women to ask questions. A new innovation is to offer jujitsu lessons to army personnel at low cost. With every ten lessons, there is a free afternoon on the second floor. But the most productive method is to bribe post office officials to let us examine the mail. Most people in this area are illiterate. Those who do write, have something important to say. The operation is so lucrative, I would prefer to show it to you tomorrow morning.'

'Very well,' Honjo said. 'Your last report of 175,000 Russian troops occupying Manchuria and North Korea even convinced Mung to prepare for the possibility of war.'

Shibata stiffened. 'I thought Mung was in disgrace.'

'He was. I do not agree with the man's methods, but he is a very talented patriot. He set up and signed a secret alliance with England that isolates Russia in the Far East. When I took over Genoysha and the Black Dragon Society, Mung rendered every assistance. I have kept him informed through the years.'

Honjo saw the look in Shibata's eyes and knew the younger man was thinking he had become soft.

'What about his youngest grandson, Hiroki Koin?' Shibata asked. 'Has he returned to Japan?'

Shibata is not asking a question. He demands an answer, Honjo thought. He has lost respect for me. One day I may have to kill him. But meanwhile, like Mung, Shibata is too valuable. Honjo smiled. 'I sent Marquis Koin to Korea. He is reorganizing the Special Forces and setting up espionage and sabotage units in North Korea.' He saw Shibata's eyes glaze over, his left hand bend inward, his fingers begin to twitch.

'I will have that son of a bitch brought to me,' Shibata growled. Flecks of spittle appeared at the corners of his mouth. 'Where exactly is he?'

'Somewhere along the Yalu river involved in planning the invasion of Manchuria.'

'I will capture and torture him! He will suffer!'

'No!' Honjo shouted, as much to emphasize the order as to bring Shibata back to reality.

'He broke my nose!'

'You will break your vow of loyalty to me and the Emperor if you kill him now! He is needed to set up our spy system in Korea!'

Shibata pulled a pocket mirror from his sleeve and examined his disfigured nose. 'I see this every morning when I awake and every night before I sleep! I see it reflected in the eyes of others! I despise the scum who did it!' He wiped the spittle from his lips.

'Hiroki Koin is as important to the taking of Manchuria as you are,' Honjo said. 'Mukden is the key city in northern China. The easiest way to attack that city is from Korea. Hiroki and his people have gathered a wealth of intelligence for our troops to take Seoul and move north across the Yalu.'

'Is his information as important as this?' Shibata threw down a folder. 'The exact plans of the Russian electrically controlled mine-fields that protect Mukden! In that folder you will see how my agents have installed switches to detonate or render useless most of those mines!' He dropped a second folder on top of the first. 'This is for Takamora. It contains exact charts of Port Arthur's defences. Gun positions overlooking the harbour are designated and drawn with triangulated distances from the buoy at the harbour entrance. Included are the locations of anchored mines and anti-torpedo nets protecting the larger Russian ships.'

Honjo was visibly impressed. 'I believe Togo will be in charge of the battle fleet. He is now an admiral.'

'Then tell Admiral Togo that Admiral Fersen, who commands Port Arthur's naval defences, has a special plan if attacked at night. The Russian has placed powerful searchlights on the hills around the port. He will allow attacking ships to get in close, then turn on the lights and sink them.

Give me Hiroki Koin and I will drop those torpedo nets, mark a path through the floating mine-fields and put out those searchlights!'

'Not now.' Honjo hoped to soothe the half-crazed Shibata. 'Hiroki is too important. You will perform that mission in Port Arthur because I promise you that when this is over, I will personally deliver Hiroki to you.'

Shibata trembled with rage. He threw down a black leather-bound book in front of Honjo. 'This is the official Russian military code book! It contains all Russian naval identification signals!' Tears ran down his cheeks. 'Give me that bastard now!' he stammered. 'I have earned it! I will rape him! I will cut off his balls!' He wiped the tears with the back of his sleeve and choked. 'I have learned to use electric shock. Please let me have him!'

Honjo fingered the black book. He had to divert the maniacal desire for vengeance or Shibata would become useless and Hiroki would be dead. He smiled at Shibata. 'I taught you the brutal approach to vengeance. Now I will teach you the more sophisticated Chinese method of revenge. Strike at the thing your enemy loves most. Break his heart, then later play with his body.'

Shibata stood in the centre of the room, chest heaving, lips sucking air, absorbing Honjo's words.

'Think about Hiroki's family,' Honjo said. 'They are alone in Seoul. He has two small sons and a beautiful wife. Use your imagination.'

Shibata's eyes opened wide, looking at Honjo as if he was a god. His rampaging thoughts of what he could do to Noriko caused him great joy. He licked his lips and murmured, 'His wife and children, you say?'

'We have three days to talk of it. Tomorrow morning I want to see your post office operation and hear about using electricity for interrogation.'

The following morning Honjo accompanied Shibata to a

low-roofed building without windows located two hundred yards behind the inn.

'An hour after the mail is delivered at 6.30 a.m. to the district post office, we have it here,' Shibata said. He opened the building's only door and held aside a heavy black drape for Honjo to enter. They stood in darkness, then went through another black drape.

Fourteen people were gathered around a low flat table with a bright electric light overhead. The door burst open and a man rushed to the table to dump letters from a sack. Shibata and Honjo watched people sort the mail. Certain letters were given to professional openers. The written material was removed and scanned. At tables on opposite sides of the room, everyone appeared to speak at once.

'I do not understand what is going on,' Honjo said.

'My translators speak a total of twenty-one different languages and dialects. There is no time to waste because the mail must be returned to the post office by 10 a.m. to go out on schedule. The letters are sorted according to priority, military and government correspondence first. You saw the letters opened, the material read. Those of substance go to our copiers and then to expert sealers. The envelopes return to the post office exactly as they come in.'

'What are they doing there?' Honjo pointed to the corner table nearest to them. A man read aloud and three women took turns copying.

Shibata listened, then told Honjo, 'The letter is about me. Abdur Rashid Ibrahim is leader of the Tatar Muslims. He has written to a Russian priest named Father Gapon in St Petersburg. They met in Stockholm last year at the Russian Socialist Revolutionary Council meeting.'

'What does he say about you?'

'Nonsense. That I am a man without ideals or morals, but the revolutionary movement can use me to supply weapons.'

'Will you?'

'To the Tatars first. Ibrahim is a warlord who can field a rabble of twenty thousand men behind the Russian army in Manchuria. His fighters are undisciplined but can be used to raid the Trans-Siberian railroad and Russian trading posts along the Tatar strait. I will request that Tokyo send this Father Gapon a shipment of small arms. I doubt he can succeed in a revolution, but he could be disruptive enough to divert a division or two of Russian soldiers.'

'I have read in the newspapers about these socialist revolutionaries in Europe. How much stock do you put in them?'

'The idealists are cannon fodder for the anti-czarist politicians. Fanatics like Father Gapon can be counted on to give the czar a headache, nothing more. Will you approve my request to send him weapons?'

'Yes. Your work in Manchuria is appreciated by our military and our government. Every petition you have made for funds and personnel has been approved. I will see it continues.'

Shibata picked up a translated copy of a letter and handed it to Honjo. 'If Prime Minister Sasaki and the general staff want a war, they should appreciate this.'

Honjo's eyebrows lifted in surprise. 'It is written by General Bezobrazov, the supreme commander of all the czar's forces in Siberia, Manchuria and Korea.'

'Yes. One of our agents is employed as his houseboy in Port Arthur. I have underlined the most important passages. It is addressed to the czar himself.'

'The Far East is still in a state of flux,' Honjo read. 'Determination and military force are necessary to consolidate Manchuria and Korea into your imperial majesty's realm. Without bold action, Russia will be unable to rule the more numerous yellow peoples of Asia, or control encroachment by our hostile European rivals in this area of the world.'

Shibata handed a translated telegram to Honjo. 'We have

listening posts on the telegraph lines too. This is the czar's reply to Bezobrazov.'

'It is desirable for the Japanese to appear to have opened hostilities before you invade Korea in force. However, if their army were to enter Seoul and cross the thirty-eighth parallel, you have permission to attack without a declaration of war.' Honjo studied the message for several minutes, then spoke. 'Nogi planned to take Seoul and march north. But if that is what they are waiting for I will suggest we bypass Seoul, come up the Yalu and attack Mukden from there. Technically that will not violate Korea's neutrality.' He patted Shibata's shoulder and led him from the room, saying, 'Based on what you have already shown me, I want to congratulate and reward you. With the authority vested in me by the Emperor, I hereby promote you to the rank of lieutenant general. I shall put it in writing as soon as I return.' Honjo bowed to his former student. 'I said you were a natural spy-master. Yet you have surpassed all my predictions and expectations.'

'Thank you,' Shibata said. 'I shall continue to press for a high standard of achievement from myself and my agents. I have a personal favour to ask.'

'Name it,' Honjo said.

'I will not go after Hiroki Koin until his usefulness to you is over. Send two of the most accomplished lovers in the Green House, a male and female, to Seoul. I will forward their instructions regarding Noriko. When Hiroki next sees his wife, he will remember his whore mother.'

Chapter 40

Gently tugging a rope attached to a row of twenty wicker baskets suspended from the ceiling, Mung smiled for the photographers in the orphanage's baby dormitory. He put his finger to his lips. 'Shhh. We do not wish to disturb the children.' He handed the rope to a young boy, and led the reporters outside to the garden.

This was the final interview in a series suggested by General Nogi and Admiral Takamora, meant to reinstate Mung's good name in the public's eye. The first article was a re-evaluation of negotiations after the triple intervention. Two well-known political analysts and a Privy Council member praised Mung's success in cancelling the unequal treaties with the West. A feature article by Japan's leading economist examined the country's phenomenal decade of economic growth due to Mung's procurement of favourable nation status with China, new trading posts and the enormous indemnity received from Peking in 1895. Another article told of Mung's agricultural experiments to improve the Japanese diet, and of his influence on national education as assistant dean of Tokyo University.

'Sir, what led you to found this orphanage?' a reporter asked.

'Iyeasu, the boy pulling the rope. And this man.' Mung pointed at Taro Kihei who had walked into the garden. 'Mr Kihei is administrator of the orphanage. He saved my life during the fire-storm of 1894 after I saved the boy from the earthquake. Both lost their families that fateful day. I lost a very dear friend for whom the boy is named and to whom

355

the orphanage is dedicated. Count Iyeasu Koin perished in the fire-storm.'

'Abortions and female infanticide have been an accepted part of Japanese society since recorded history,' another reporter said. 'Have your posters, handbills and lectures reduced the number?'

'No,' Mung said. 'I offered to pay doctors and mothers not to abort, also to no avail. Taro Kihei succeeded. He let it be known that women could leave their babies in baskets by the entrance. We turn the outside light off. They come in the dark. No one sees, no one questions.'

'How many children are cared for here?'

'One hundred and fifty.'

'Why have you taken it upon yourself to change the habits and mores of our people?'

Mung knew the true reason was the influence of his early Christian upbringing, but his response was, 'I am sickened and angered to see fully formed foetuses on city garbage heaps. They were little human beings. It is wrong for parents to kill girl babies. In our modern industrial society, females can be as productive as males. Female infanticide is a carry-over from our former agricultural society when men were more important to survival. This is no longer the case. We are a small nation compared to our neighbours. The Chinese and Russians are far more numerous. We need a larger population.'

'Sir, we know the Russians have occupied Manchuria and sent troops to Korea. Are you advocating more babies in case of a future war?'

'My goal is to save children, educate the young and improve the health of our population. I resigned from politics ten years ago. It would be presumptuous of me to speculate on a conflict with Russia,' Mung said, knowing war was a distinct possibility. For several months now Honjo had assigned a special liaison officer to inform him of Russian activities on the Asian mainland. In addition to

the secret Anglo-Japanese agreement, Mung had also negotiated with the Kobe Club for weapons. He had used his
influence with the Inei financial empire to fund the building
of observation balloons and the import of wireless radios
produced by Hiroki's American factory for the army. This
afternoon, for the second time in recent months, he was
invited to an audience with the Emperor.

Taro bowed to the reporters and looked to Mung.
'Gentlemen, Mr Ishikawa must prepare for a meeting.'
He pointed to a line of nurses carrying baskets of baby
bottles. 'I think photos of the children being fed will appeal
to your readers.'

'The imperial palace,' Mung told the driver. Alone in
the closed coach, he leaned back and stretched his legs,
contemplating the forthcoming meeting with the Emperor.
The newspaper interviews were somehow related to the
growing hostilities between Japan and Russia. Fifty-three
Japanese soldiers aboard a ship captured by the Russian
navy had committed seppuku rather than be taken prisoner. Honjo's liaison officer had told Mung they were
scouts from the Nineteenth Imperial Division on a training
exercise to map landing sites near Vladivostok. Yesterday
Mung had received a coded message from Yaka and Uraga
in Korea. They claimed Honjo ordered the scouting party
to Vladivostok and then had Akichi Shibata in Manchuria
betray them – a diversion meant to stir up the Russians. In
the event of war, Japan's first naval target would be Port
Arthur, fifteen hundred nautical miles away. Mung appreciated the importance of the diversion but was against the
unnecessary sacrifice of lives. With Shibata's vast network
of spies in Manchuria, false plans could have been fed to
the Russians some other way.

The last sentence of his grandsons' message disturbed
Mung. 'It would be advisable to recall Hiroki and his
family to Japan immediately.'

Mung was escorted from the carriage to the imperial reception room where Nogi and Takamora awaited him. They stood on the raised platform on either side of the vacant golden throne. Mung admired the heavy velvet tapestry embroidered with silver and gold that hung behind the throne.

'It is good to have you back,' Nogi said. 'Your Latin message to the Emperor influenced us to request your presence. Prepare for war.'

'If you desire peace,' Mung completed the quote.

'Under what conditions would you take up the sword against Russia?' Takamora asked.

'If I were convinced the czar is prepared to redraw the map of Asia in Japanese blood. My lords, I am seventy-seven. Age brings with it certain privileges. I respectfully ask why I have been summoned.'

'This latest incident of fifty-three soldiers committing seppuku has triggered off the most serious wave of anti-Russian feelings in the country and Parliament,' Takamora said. 'People have not forgotten nor forgiven the Russians for seizing our gains in the Sino-Japanese war. Or how we were snubbed by them in the Boxer settlement.'

'More important, since Honjo has controlled the Black Dragons and other intelligence-gathering organizations, he and Sasaki have isolated the Emperor,' Nogi said. 'His majesty is being manipulated as in the days of the shogun. This is not how the Emperor envisaged a constitutional monarchy.'

'His imperial majesty has influence on the Privy Council,' Mung said.

'In the last few years, members of the Privy Council have felt buried alive,' Nogi said. 'Since Sasaki's overwhelming success in the last election, the national cabinet is referred to as a puppet show run by a puppet. Honjo pulls Sasaki's strings and he, in turn, pulls the strings in the cabinet.'

'With his majority in Parliament, could Sasaki declare war on Russia?' Mung asked.

'The only thing preventing him is the Emperor, Nogi and me,' Takamora said.

'I understood you two were in favour of military expansion to ensure Japan's access to natural resources and overseas colonies as a first line of defence.'

'Correct,' Nogi said. 'But our military is not prepared to take on Russia at this time. The national treasury is low, and you have proved to us the importance of negotiations as a military weapon.'

'What is it you want of me?' Mung asked.

'Delay the outbreak of hostilities by three or four months,' Takamora said. 'If you can give me that much time, I can guarantee victory at sea.'

'I think there is a way,' Mung said. 'But you understand that I will try to achieve by peaceful means what you wish to attain by war. I must have your promise of cooperation.'

'The destructive power of modern weapons has become too great, and devoid of personal honour,' Nogi said. 'I consider it our duty to attempt every peaceful method of resolving our differences with Russia. But Bezobrazov has replaced Witte as the guiding power of Russia in Manchuria, and he wants war.'

'How can you delay the Russians?' Takamora asked.

'William Whittefield informed me that President Theodore Roosevelt wants Russia out of Korea and Manchuria. Roosevelt will send a note to that effect if our government requests it. The American president will also notify Germany that if Kaiser Wilhelm aids Czar Nicolas in a war against Japan, the United States will support Japan.'

'Does Roosevelt know of our secret alliance with England?' Takamora asked.

'I informed him through Whittefield last year.'

'Then the question should be, what can America gain by helping Japan?' Takamora said.

'The Korean, Manchurian and Siberian markets,' Mung said. 'Roosevelt is trying to do for America what Prince von Metternich did for Austria fifty years ago. He is attempting to balance the power in the Far East so the Russians, Chinese and we Japanese will realize that no one can win. His success will create a vast market in the Far East, and Roosevelt intends that America will service that market.'

'It is quite a brilliant concept for a man who pretends to be a cowboy,' Nogi said. 'I should think England would stop the man.'

'Ten years ago they might have tried. Today they are spread too thin. There are still a quarter of a million British troops in South Africa cleaning up after the Boer War. The mutinies and revolts in India and Burma have England's army engaged and their navy racing back and forth to keep them supplied. Roosevelt does not believe we can defeat the Russians. And with America backing Japan, the Russians cannot invade our islands.'

Nogi leaned forward. His jaw muscles twitched, his eyes gleamed. 'Give us four months and we shall defeat the Russians quickly and decisively.'

'First I suggest you grant every request Akichi Shibata makes for aid to the revolutionaries in St Petersburg, Moscow and other large Russian cities,' Mung said. 'Socialist revolutionaries have caused major industrial disruptions requiring large numbers of the czar's best troops to be diverted from Manchuria to police rioting workers.'

'For a man who has been out of power for so long, you are quite knowledgeable,' Nogi said.

'General Honjo keeps me informed,' Mung said.

'It is appropriate for you and Honjo to have this relationship,' Nogi said. 'He and Prime Minister Sasaki are waiting outside.'

The velvet tapestry behind the throne parted and the Emperor appeared. Mung wondered why the Emperor had been listening from behind the curtain. The three men bowed and the Emperor took his seat.

Nogi ordered the master of protocol to summon Prime Minister Sasaki and General Honjo. He waited to speak until they had taken places at Mung's side. 'The replacement of Sergei Witte by Alexander Bezobrazov in Manchuria indicates Russia's intention to invade Korea,' Nogi said. 'The secret alliance between China and Russia implies future cooperation to invade Japan. In case of a land war on the continent, we appear to be outmanoeuvred.'

'And so the Russians believe,' Honjo said. 'But the assumption is wrong. The czar's politicians and military are blinded by their attempt to justify the tremendous expense of men, material and money to complete and operate their rail-lines.' Honjo looked to Mung and said, 'Moryiama Ishikawa saw the advantage of the iron-hulled steamship over the Siberian rail-line twenty years ago when he negotiated away Sakhalin island to the Russians for the Kurils and recognition of Japanese rights to the Ryukyus. Contrary to popular belief, the Russians can move only seven thousand troops a month by rail into Manchuria. Each rail-line is single track. Part of the year they are blocked by snow. Akichi Shibata has sabotage units in Siberia, Mongolia and Manchuria trained and equipped to cut the rail-lines. We should do everything possible to induce the Russians to make a commitment to a land war in Asia. Their army will be left dangling at the end of a six-thousand-mile line of communication and supply which we can sever on command. This strategy places the importance for the outcome of a war with Russia on our imperial navy.'

'The Emperor prefers negotiation to war,' Takamora said. 'General Nogi and I require another four months to prepare the imperial forces to face the Russians.'

Mung saw Honjo's head move slightly towards Sasaki, and the prime minister said, 'The time to strike is now. The incident of the fifty-three martyrs has incensed the public and Parliament.'

The five men looked to the Emperor but he remained rigidly silent.

'The cost of a war with Russia will be astronomical,' Nogi said. 'If we win a military victory and sustain an economic defeat, Japan will lose its momentum towards becoming a major power in the Far East. Time is needed to secure financial support from abroad.'

'The lessons of the tripartite intervention and results of the Boxer Rebellion are clear,' Sasaki said. 'Military weakness in the eyes of the Europeans means destruction and national humiliation for Japan. Military might will gain us respect and economic concessions. A decisive victory over the Russians will result in a large indemnity for Japan. The czar will bear our cost for the war.'

Nogi nodded at Mung. 'Mr Ishikawa has information that America does not wish a decisive victory by either side in a confrontation between Japan and Russia. President Roosevelt favours a balance of power policy.'

'Mr Ishikawa has apprised me of this situation,' Honjo said. 'I appreciate the importance of Roosevelt's planned manipulations. What the Americans, Europeans and many of our own statesmen fail to recognize is that Japan has prepared so well for this war, it will be over within six months, too quickly for anyone to intervene.'

'As prime minister of Japan, I am prepared to go directly from this meeting to Parliament and call for an immediate declaration of war against Russia,' Sasaki said.

'And I will stop you,' the Emperor said.

Sasaki staggered back as if struck. The others sucked wind through their teeth. Since the first shogun, three hundred years before, no Emperor had become directly involved in politics. He used the Black Dragon Society, his advisers and the Privy Council to influence the real rulers of Japan. Even the modern constitution assumed the concept of the Emperor sanctioning government, not directing.

Sasaki bowed low. 'My humble apologies, your majesty,' he stammered. 'My intentions are to strengthen the nation and your position as our divine leader.'

'I understand and appreciate your efforts,' the Emperor said. 'However, past events and present circumstances require me to take an active role in the future course of Japan's relations with the world. Parliamentary decisions are often slow, and sometimes quickly coloured by undisciplined emotion. Prior to the Sino-Japanese war, too much time was wasted in parliamentary debate. I circumvented Count Hideyoshi's legislative influence through my Privy Council and Moryiama Ishikawa, who was then the Black Dragon. People forget that Parliament's hesitation during the Boxer Rebellion resulted in a fiasco by the first international relief force to Peking. Through General Nogi and Admiral Takamora, I again circumvented our national legislature to quadruple the size of our armed forces in the second and successful relief of Peking. More recently, I called upon Moryiama Ishikawa to negotiate the Anglo-Japanese alliance.'

Mung felt uncertain as to the Emperor's reasons for praising him, for revealing his contacts with the Kobe Club and Theodore Roosevelt. He was now positive the Emperor had initiated the press interviews. But for what purpose, Mung did not understand.

'I accept General Honjo's prediction of decisive victory over Russia,' the Emperor said. 'However, General Nogi and Admiral Takamora request another four months preparation time. Marquis Inei, the national treasurer, requires another forty million dollars for the military. Ten thousand horses are on their way from Europe and the Middle East. They will have to be trained and incorporated into our cavalry, artillery and supply units.' The Emperor stopped speaking. For a full minute the room remained silent. The five men before him bowed, and waited.

The Emperor spoke again in a slow, measured tone that carried the weight and authority of the gods. 'Six hundred years ago Kublai Khan twice attempted to invade Japan. His first landing was made with only twenty-five thousand men and was almost successful, due to Japan's feudal lords' inability to take quick, decisive, coordinated action. Our national penchant for a unanimous collective decision almost resulted in a Mongol victory. To save Japan from a second larger Mongol army of 140,000 troops, the Emperor created the post of Tairo, the Great Elder. He was Supreme Adviser to the Emperor, Generalissimo, Commander of the nation's armed forces and Final Arbiter in all affairs of state!' The Emperor of Japan leaned forward and rested his hands on the arms of the golden throne. 'I require the government to accept, without debate, a re-created position of Tairo! One man will have the power to settle internal political and military disputes of our national leaders! His decisions will be undisputed! Tairo will speak for me!'

Mung wondered who the Emperor had chosen, and he heard his name called.

'Moryiama Ishikawa, step forward!' the Emperor said.

Mung's legs shook. For the first time, he mounted the raised platform on which his imperial majesty sat. He bowed low and heard the Emperor say, 'By virtue of the respect you have gained from friend and foe in the half century of service to your country, and for your silent acceptance of undeserved pain, unwarranted public disgrace and personal deprivation in the service of your Emperor, I proclaim you Tairo, Great Elder! From this moment you are my Supreme Adviser! General Nogi, Admiral Takamora, Prime Minister Sasaki and General Honjo are proclaimed your advisers!' The Emperor addressed those four men. 'You will take Tairo's decisions to Parliament, where they are to be approved with a minimum of discussion! Although it will not be officially proclaimed, let it be known that the word of Tairo is the word of the Emperor!'

'Sire, forgive me, but as prime minister I must question the . . . the adaptability of your recommendation,' Sasaki stammered.

The Emperor fixed Sasaki with his dark eyes and spoke softly. 'It is not a recommendation, but an order from your Emperor. In 1874, prior to moving my capital from Kyoto to Tokyo, the Japanese feudal lords were at each other's throats while the Europeans threatened to invade us. To save Japan I sent an emissary to the warring Japanese factions. The emissary carried with him the symbols of my divine authority – the sword, the jewels and the mirror. I ordered the emissary to throw the three symbols into the sea if the feudal lords of Japan did not unite against the West.' The Emperor stood. 'I will destroy the three heavenly symbols and disappear from this earth if my will is not obeyed immediately and without question!' He held out both hands towards Mung and spoke in the archaic, poetic form of Japanese. 'I proclaim thee Great Elder, Supreme Adviser to the descendants of Amaterasu-o-mi-Kami!' He looked to the four other men and ordered, 'Bow to Tairo!'

Mung glanced at the Emperor and also started to bow, but the Emperor shook his head. 'Faithful servant, Moryiama Ishikawa, you were my personal champion with the title of Shishi, Man of High Purpose. With the passing of years Tairo has become the more fitting title. Lead the empire to peace or war. Be aware that victory in whichever you choose is essential for the future of Japan.'

The master of protocol brought forward a mirror and held it before Mung's face. 'Tairo, look at your image and know you are a man in the service of a god!' the master of protocol said. He stepped away and returned with a jewel necklace cupped in the palms of his hands. 'Tairo, observe the reflected light on the walls. If I turn the jewels thus, the images are distorted. If I twist so, we see pleasing geometrical patterns. Always keep in focus what is best for the Emperor, the embodiment of Japan!' He placed an ancient sword in the Emperor's hand and said to Mung, 'The Son of Heaven is your protector!'

Mung bowed, and heard the Emperor instruct the four leaders of Japan. 'The decision when and if to go to war rests with Tairo, the Great Elder!'

'So it is ordered, so it is done.'

Chapter 41

Hiroki Koin decoded the telegram, but did not want to believe the terse message from Yaka. 'Return immediately to headquarters. Noriko attempted suicide.'

He packed his bags and caught the first available train. Alone on the end platform of the rear car of the Seoul express, Hiroki gazed at the low thatched huts and geometrical patterns of rice paddies passing by. He searched his mind to understand Noriko's action. It must be that something tragic had happened to the children. He could think of no other reason.

The train slowed as it entered the suburbs of the Korean capital. The iron brakes squealed and the train entered Central Station. Hiroki swung off before it came to a stop. He pushed through the crowd on the platform and stepped into the first rickshaw outside the station. He was pulled swiftly through the streets, but had to ask the driver to stop at a public toilet when his nerves affected his bowels.

'Please, the bandage stings,' Noriko said.

'It is your tears,' the nurse said, drying Noriko's cheeks. 'A week of crying should have used them all up by now.'

Noriko grimaced as she strained at the cloth binding her hands and legs to the bedposts. Yaka had purchased the four-poster European bed and tied her hand and foot.

'Do not twist your neck while I change the bandage,' the nurse said. 'You will tear open the wound.'

'My husband is coming,' Noriko moaned. 'He will be here soon. Do not let him see me like this! What will I tell him!'

'The scar on your neck is healing. When it is completely

closed, I can show you how to use cosmetics so no one will know it is there.'

'It is the scar on my conscience I need to erase,' Noriko cried. 'I will always know what I have done.' She gasped for breath. 'Where are my boys? My children!'

The nurse cradled her head, soothing her with a soft hand and calming words. 'Do not worry about them. They are well taken care of. You must get well.'

'Where are they?' Noriko screamed.

'You promised not to become hysterical. Their aunt is looking after them in Pusan. I told you that. I will telephone them as I have done every evening, then return and tell you everything they said.'

'Why? Why?' Noriko moaned.

'You do not want your sons to see you like this,' the nurse answered.

Noriko wept with great sobs. 'I want my medicine!' She tried to sit up and was restrained by her bonds. 'I need my medicine,' she whimpered.

'You know the doctor has restricted you to twice a day.'

'I need more! I will be good. Please!'

'It is forbidden,' the nurse said. 'The elixir did this to you.'

Noriko closed her eyes and moaned. 'I did this to myself. Please let me die before my husband sees me.'

'Stop that! The doctor explained to you how those agents addicted you. Your brother-in-law Yaka says you are not to blame. You never had a chance.'

'At least let me have a cigarette,' Noriko pleaded.

'The doctor said only three a day. You have had two and can have a third before you sleep tonight.'

'I need one now, before my husband arrives! Please! Please!'

'Marquessa, do not beg.' The nurse turned away so Noriko would not see her tears. She took a cigarette from the pack, placed it between Noriko's lips and lit it.

After the third puff, the deep-etched lines on Noriko's forehead smoothed. 'It was the medicine, not me,' she murmured, inhaling deeply and drifting back in time to her arrival in Seoul.

The train station was new, colourful and filled with people. Black Dragon and Genoysha families were on hand to meet the Koin family and invite them into the small but thriving Japanese community. Hiroki accepted invitations to Japanese gatherings, but preferred to take a house in a Korean neighbourhood. It was a sign to his Special Forces comrades that he remembered them and his vow to make Korea a better place.

Hiroki hired a Korean couple to tend the household and teach his family the language. It pained Noriko to remember how she had spurned the idea of servants and sent the couple away. She wished to clean her own house and care for her own children.

But shortly after Hiroki left to travel north, she and the children took ill. She needed help. A handsome Korean couple, who spoke Japanese, agreed to live in and tutor the children, all on a temporary basis until she was well.

At first Kim and Woo were efficient, pleasant and unassuming. They protected her from friends who came to call, and brought her a special medicine to bring back her strength.

Noriko had read the label and smiled. 'Green House Elixir, Product of Hankow. For the treatment of unstable meridians. Cleanses linking blood vessels to free the life forces flowing from organ to organ. Rectifies the imbalance of cosmic energy in the body. Restores tchi and the balance between yin and yang.' She was doubtful but agreed to try it.

The children recovered from the illness and returned to school, but Noriko accepted the bed-rest urged on her by the servants. She required larger and larger doses of the elixir, and took to smoking the cigarettes provided by Woo.

Then one day she called for her medicine and Kim entered the room without a shirt. He was a well-proportioned, muscular man. She reprimanded him and he left without a word, taking her medicine with him. Noriko waited impatiently. She called him again. Kim returned to the doorway without his shirt, elixir in hand.

'Why are you not properly dressed?' Noriko asked.

He smiled and held up the bottle. 'Do you want this?'

'Yes. Bring it when you are fully clothed!'

Kim bowed and left.

Again Noriko waited. The children returned from school and Noriko was happy to see them, but she knew they sensed her irritability. 'Go to Kim or Woo,' she said. 'Tell them Mother needs her medicine.' Once more she waited.

Later, Noriko heard the sounds of Woo putting the boys to bed. It was dark when Kim appeared in the doorway, still without his shirt, holding the green bottle.

'I told you to dress and bring that bottle to me,' Noriko shouted.

'Which should I do first?'

'You are insolent! I am the lady of this house! Get dressed and bring my medicine immediately!'

Again Kim bowed and left.

Noriko groped for a cigarette, but the package was gone. 'Woo! Get in here this moment!' She heard herself screaming but did not care.

The beautiful young woman appeared in the doorway. 'Your husband is impertinent,' Noriko said. 'He will not bring my medicine. Please get it for me and tell him to dress properly.'

'Kim is not my husband.'

'But I was given to understand you are married.'

Woo moved to the bed. She smoothed Noriko's hair. She washed and massaged her as she did every day, but did not speak.

'Could I have another pack of those cigarettes?' Noriko whispered.

Without speaking, Woo turned and left the room.

Twenty minutes went by. Forty minutes. An hour. Noriko began having stomach cramps. Her body shook. She ached for the medicine. She shouted, she threw things at the door, but no one answered.

Finally she slipped out of bed and stumbled to the door. The hallway seemed strange, unfamiliar. Noriko realized it had been weeks since she had left her room. Holding onto the walls, she made her way to the kitchen. In the dim light from the hearth she saw Kim and Woo embracing. She knew they were aware of her presence, but they did not stop their caresses. The beautiful girl was naked. Kim wore only his cotton pantaloons, pushed out in front by his erection.

Noriko wanted to order them out of the house but instead heard herself saying, 'My medicine, please give it to me.'

Kim fondled Woo's breasts but he looked at Noriko. He stepped back and took a bottle from a shelf lined with the green bottles. He uncorked the elixir and came close to Noriko. She could smell his cologne. 'I will get a cup,' he said.

Noriko snatched the bottle from his hand and drank.

Kim gently put his hand on hers and pulled the bottle from her lips. 'Too much and you will sleep forever,' he said.

Noriko felt a calming effect flow through her body. Kim's muscular body pressed against hers and she tried to push him away. But her hand slipped off his warm shoulder and fell limp at her side. He put his arm around her and curved his body into hers. She had not the strength to resist. 'Stop,' she whispered. 'Stop this minute.'

His hands caressed her breasts and his lips kissed her shoulders and neck. She felt his hardness against her thigh and watched the scene as if it was happening to someone else. Kim picked her up and carried her to the sleeping mat. He shared one of Woo's cigarettes with her. Noriko drifted lazily in and out of reality as he fondled her. She realized he was naked and his body was magnificently muscled. He was caressing her, doing things with his hands and mouth that attuned her body to his. He took the cigarette from her lips, crushed it out and slowly tore her nightgown down the middle. He covered her face and neck with kisses while his hands moved over every part of her body. He lowered his head and nibbled her breasts. He bit around her navel and moved his head down. Noriko drifted in a sea of pleasure.

The following morning there was a full medicine bottle at Noriko's side. She drank from it and drifted off. When she woke she vaguely remembered kissing the children before they went to school. Woo's cigarettes were there for her use. She smoked, and suddenly it was night. There was a fresh bottle of medicine for her to drink.

Morning and night seemed to come closer and closer together. She measured time by the bottles of medicine, consciously longing for, but relieved that Kim did not appear.

Then one afternoon the bottle was empty. No one answered her call until evening. Kim appeared in the room stripped to the waist.

'My medicine, please,' Noriko said.

Kim pulled the drawstring on his cotton pantaloons and they dropped to the floor. He stood before her, a magnificent man holding out her bottle.

372

'Get out,' Noriko screamed. 'Get out, you pig!' She threw the empty bottle at him.

Alone in the dark, cold and hot sweats racked her body. She shivered, every nerve craving the medicine. She kicked the quilt off. She rose from the bed, took two steps and slumped to the floor. She crawled around the room to find the empty bottle she had thrown, and rolled onto her back, holding it to her lips. She pointed her tongue and licked far into the bottle, tearing her tongue on her teeth, swallowing her own blood. She doubled up with cramps. She shook with convulsions, then lay sobbing on the floor.

Sometime later, Noriko crawled along the hallway to the kitchen. There was the feeling someone was watching, but the kitchen was empty. She gathered her feet under her, clutched the wall shelves and pulled herself upright. Firelight reflected off the neat rows of dark bottles on the top shelf. As she reached up, two hands cupped her breasts from behind. She smelled Kim's cologne. Revulsion and lust went through her at the same time. He fondled her breasts and moulded his body to hers. Noriko took a bottle and uncorked it. She drank as Kim undressed her and laid her down. A cigarette appeared in her hand. Kim drove himself into her on the kitchen floor.

Noriko slept. She lay quietly. Wantonness grew in her as she waited for Kim and the elixir he brought. His sensuous body wove through her dreams.

Every night Kim appeared naked at the bedroom door with a green bottle, and waited until she invited him in. She vaguely recognized that Woo was often in the room, lighting cigarettes, watching the lovemaking.

Then one night Kim stroked her body and Noriko felt nothing. She let smoke curl up out of her mouth and stared blankly at the ceiling. The cigarette was taken from her hand and Woo stood naked over her, inhaling deeply. Woo returned the cigarette to Noriko's lips. Noriko inhaled, then watched Woo puff. The beautiful woman turned

373

slowly, stretching, showing off her splendid body. Then she lay down next to Noriko. Kim pressed his body against Noriko's back. Woo's firm breasts touched Noriko's and Noriko shivered. She was sandwiched between the two warm bodies. Kim's erection pushed between her legs. Woo's tongue moved in her mouth. Woo's arm was around her, their breasts pressed together. Kim's arms were on Noriko's, around Woo. Woo's hand moved between Noriko's legs, fluttery fingers directing Kim's erection into the velvety softness, massaging. Noriko threw her head back and screamed as an orgasm gripped her. She drifted in hazy, drug-induced tranquillity, and the Korean couple used her body to satisfy themselves.

Sometime during the early hours of the morning, in the midst of her dream-world, Noriko's mind became lucid and she paid attention to the whispering.

'Akichi Shibata should be pleased with this report,' Kim said. 'I expect he will want us to expose the marquessa's addiction and perversion. That should hurt her husband, Marquis Hiroki Koin.'

'Can we disappear then?' Woo asked.

'Directly back to Hankow and the Green House,' Kim said. 'We will probably be appointed instructors.'

The two left the room.

Numbed by drugs, revolted by the hideous memory of her actions, Noriko retched. The pain in her heart tore away the misty opium curtain covering her mind and she knew what she must do. Concentrating every ounce of strength through the discipline learned in kendo, she put on her robe, crawled to a cabinet and took out the small dagger Hiroki had presented to her at their wedding. The half-empty bottle near her bed called to her, but she resisted. Crawling on hands and knees, she reached the door and pulled herself upright against the wall. She stumbled down the hall to the far end of the house, where the children slept. She hoped they would never find out about their mother's wickedness. Her legs quivered and she knew if she hesitated it would be too late. The room grew blurry. Tears poured down her cheeks. 'Goodbye, my babies.' She let the scabbard drop and brought the dagger to her throat.

'You cannot see her until after you have spoken with the doctor,' Yaka said.

'Noriko is my wife,' Hiroki said.

'And if you want her to remain so you had better hear me out. In one week she has tried four times to kill herself.'

'Why?' Hiroki demanded. 'Are the children dead?'

'The children are unharmed. They are with my family.'

'Where is Noriko?' Hiroki demanded.

'I will not tell you until you hear the entire story and speak with the doctor.'

'All the way from the Yalu river I kept thinking of your message. I do not have patience. Yaka, please tell me what has happened.'

'That is my worst fear,' Yaka said. 'Your impatience. Mother always said it is your major character flaw.'

Hiroki threw up his hands. 'I am listening.'

'Listen with your heart,' Yaka said. 'Noriko needs your understanding.' He held out a bottle and turned the label for Hiroki to read. 'Have you ever seen this before?'

'Yes. I slipped over the Manchurian border several times. Akichi Shibata's agents use it to debase, corrupt and control Chinese and Russian officials.'

Yaka nodded. 'Shibata ordered two of his people to compromise Noriko. They were outstanding pupils at the Green House.'

Hiroki's knees buckled and he leaned against the wall. In his travels along the Yalu he had learned from Green House graduates of their vicious training, their cruel and perverse conduct against the enemy. He could not speak, only motioned Yaka to continue.

'The agents, a male and a female, arrived in Seoul soon

375

after you left. They poisoned the food Noriko bought in a noodle shop she frequented. She and the children became ill. Noriko hired the couple to work as housekeepers until she was better. The children recovered quickly, but the agents addicted Noriko to this elixir. Then they did as they wished to her.'

Hiroki gulped. 'What was that?'

'Shibata ordered them to disgrace you through Noriko.'

Tears rolled down Hiroki's cheeks. 'Did they hurt her?'

'Very much.' Yaka reached out to comfort his brother. 'Only you can save her.'

'Why did they attack her and not me?'

'You are too important to the forthcoming war with Russia.'

'Let me see Noriko!'

'Not until the doctor speaks with you,' Yaka said.

'When will that be?'

'Soon.'

'Where are the agents who did this?'

'Come, I have kept them on ice for you,' Yaka said. He led Hiroki to an outside storeroom where a Black Dragon stood guard. Hiroki followed his brother inside. There was a large pile of hay in the centre of the room. Yaka pushed off the top layers of hay, revealing the bodies of a naked man and woman lying face up on large blocks of ice. 'They confessed everything under torture,' Yaka said. 'Then I tied them to the ice and let them freeze to death.' He turned to his brother. 'I assure you they suffered for their actions! You must forget them and think only of how to help Noriko! She befriended and nursed our mother to a gentle death. Do not abandon your wife!'

The guard opened the door and said, 'The doctor has arrived.'

'Burn these two pieces of shit and throw their ashes on the dung heap,' Yaka ordered the guard. He escorted his brother back to the headquarters building.

'Some tea perhaps?' the doctor asked Hiroki.

'Sir, I wish to see my wife.'

'And so you shall. But I must warn you that your first meeting will be crucial to her recovery.'

'Now!' Hiroki said. 'I want to see Noriko now!'

'Drink the tea and show respect for your elder,' the doctor said. 'I must explain in detail what happened to your wife and how you can help her. There can be no secrets between you that could later destroy your relationship. I hope you are a strong man.' The doctor indicated that Yaka should leave.

Two hours later, with the cup of cold tea still before him, Hiroki heard the doctor say, 'You may now visit your wife. She is at home.' But Hiroki did not move.

The doctor stood. 'If you cannot find it in your heart to forgive her, do not see her at all. If Noriko perceives disapproval in your eyes, she will eventually succeed in killing herself. We cannot keep her tied up forever.'

The doctor left the room and Yaka entered. 'Are you ready to see Noriko?'

'Tell me how you found out about this,' Hiroki said.

'Your next-door neighbour heard the children crying. She and her husband went into your house. They found Noriko collapsed on the floor in the children's room with a dagger wound in her throat. She was bleeding profusely. She begged the neighbours to protect the children from Shibata's agents who were asleep in the house. The neighbour is one of your Special Forces men. He seized the pair.'

Hiroki looked up at his brother. 'Does Noriko know I am here?'

'I told her you are due to arrive soon.'

'I need to think,' Hiroki said, and left the building.

Chapter 42

Mung left the Emperor's chambers and walked alone to the Yasukune shrine. He had no one but the gods to tell of his appointment as Tairo. He prayed for guidance at the shrine, then returned home to share the wonder with his son and grandsons by mail.

The following days were spent in conference with Nogi, Takamora and members of the Privy Council. Mung was in telephone contact with Inei and by telegraph to Shimatzu in Formosa. He prepared his staff for their first working meeting.

General Honjo and Prime Minister Sasaki made their way to the palace for the first meeting with Tairo.

'We are in a struggle for power with the Emperor,' Sasaki said.

'Use your head,' Honjo snapped. 'The moment his imperial majesty made known his personal involvement, he controlled the direction of the country.'

'Then why has he not done so before?'

'The shoguns and former prime ministers succeeded in isolating the Emperors. In effect they did not disobey, since they heard no imperial commands. But the Meiji Emperor is not one to be silenced. We will have to bide our time. I have influence over those who educate his son. He will be easier to control.'

'I expected you would fight to retain authority.'

Honjo looked out of the carriage window and drummed his fingers on the sill. 'People assume I seek personal power,' he mused aloud. 'Not so. My aim is to mould Japan into a mighty nation.'

'Are you prepared to accept the peace-seeker Mung as Tairo?'

'His last message to the Emperor was to prepare for war if we desire peace. Mung is closer to our position of military expansion than many of the newly elected parliamentarians from the National Socialist Society.'

'But Hideyoshi hated Mung. He paid to have him assassinated more than once.'

'Hideyoshi hated everyone. He never forgave the abolition of the aristocracy, and Mung was the chief architect of the constitution.'

'But Mung is now seventy-seven,' Sasaki said. 'He is hard of hearing and his hand shakes.'

'His mind is as sharp as a samurai sword, and he still remembers everything. The Emperor is correct. We need a Tairo to defeat the Russians. Our constitution requires majority votes on questions that in time of war will demand instant decisions. To win a series of swift victories, we cannot keep telephoning Tokyo for a referendum. Our national desire for a unanimous decision is a weakness. It takes too much time to achieve.'

'What if Mung does find a peaceful way?'

'Simple. He shall be eliminated. Then you, Nogi or Takamora will become Tairo.'

At Mung's insistence, the palace physician had prescribed a herbal stimulant to help him through the crucial meeting. As a result, seated at the head of the long, low table, Mung could hardly remain still. He heard his heart pounding and felt his blood rushing through his veins. He had a tingling sensation in his lower lip and hoped it was not the beginning of another stroke.

Mung bowed to Nogi and Takamora on the right, to Sasaki and Honjo on the left, and said, 'Gentlemen, based on your reports and recommendations I, Tairo, have taken the following steps. My son Shimatzu is on his way to

London to borrow forty million dollars in preparation for war.' He handed a letter to Sasaki. 'Please send this as an official message to Czar Nicolas in St Petersburg, and a copy to Viceroy Bezobrazov in Port Arthur. It is a request for Russia to withdraw her troops from Korea and her personnel from Manchuria. All Russia's mining and milling enterprises now in operation will be allowed to continue. Japan will also have the right to search for and develop natural resources in Manchuria.'

'Do you really expect the Russians to agree?' Sasaki asked.

'President Roosevelt will send a similar message to St Petersburg. He will threaten the czar's Hapsburg cousin Wilhelm, ruler of Austria-Hungary, not to war against Japan or America will side with us. In addition, Lord Cade has this time kept his word. The French government and financiers have stopped all loans to Russia. Czar Nicolas is being pressed to repay his debts. That should retard any immediate Russian military moves.'

'In anticipation of Shimatzu's financial success in acquiring money in London, I would like to train and equip seven more infantry divisions,' Nogi said.

'And I wish to purchase three new English mine-sweepers,' Takamora said.

'And you, General Honjo?' Mung asked. 'What does military intelligence require?'

'The starting date of the war,' Honjo said. He opened a large artist's briefcase and handed out file folders of maps, reports and harbour surveys. 'These were compiled by your grandson Hiroki in Korea, and Akichi Shibata in Manchuria. Both established extremely efficient espionage and sabotage units.'

'I am pleased at the effectiveness of your intelligence organization,' Mung said. 'I also take this opportunity to thank you for keeping me informed during the years I was out of favour. I expected you to oppose me as Tairo.'

'You, sir,' Honjo bowed, 'are one of the founders of the modern state of Japan. Our personalities may clash, in your position I would have done things differently, but I could not have done them better. I support you because the Emperor ordered it, and because of your history of successful failures.' Honjo smiled. 'You think of yourself as a peacemaker, but a survey of your career indicates otherwise. In almost every instance that you attempted to negotiate peace, there have been wars from which Japan has grown stronger.' Honjo held up his hand and ticked off on his fingers. 'In 1854 you supplied modern rifles and artillery that resulted in the fall of the shogun. In 1873 Lord Saga and the Choshu rebels fell to your guns. In 1874 the three houses of Mito faded away. More recently we succeeded over the Chinese in Formosa and Korea. Each of your efforts for peace resulted in a successful war for Japan. I say send your letters to Czar Nicolas. And if the Germans want to fight us, all well and good.' Honjo's eyebrows disappeared in the creases of his shaven head as he leaned forward. 'We shall slaughter the white armies of the steppes and any others who challenge us in Asia!'

Mung was more taken aback by Honjo's evaluation of his career than by the fierceness in the general's burning eyes. Mung pointed to the letter in Sasaki's hand. 'If Russia complies with my request, there will be no war.'

'How would we know if the czar does withdraw his troops?' the prime minister asked.

'The Russians will be monitored in Manchuria by Akichi Shibata and in Korea by Hiroki Koin,' Mung said.

Hiroki walked the deserted streets of Seoul isolated in his thoughts of Noriko's disgrace. She had failed him, his children and their ancestors. Near the outskirts of the darkened city, he was drawn to the light in a Buddhist temple. He entered and sat down at the feet of a large, placid-faced idol. But he had no prayers and the Buddha had no answers.

'A young man who weeps before the statue of Buddha must carry a sorrowful burden.'

Hiroki looked up into the benevolent face of an old priest. A white wispy beard framed his thin features. The priest's eyes reminded Hiroki of Grandfather Mung. They gazed into his heart like a friend wanting to help.

The priest sat at Hiroki's side and looked up at the Buddha. 'I hope you do not ask a stone statue for solutions.'

Hiroki shook his head. 'No,' he sobbed.

'Ask a man,' the priest said.

Tears poured down Hiroki's cheeks. 'How can a husband return to his wife when she has fornicated with another? What will happen to our children?'

The old man drew the story of grief from Hiroki.

'I must kill Akichi Shibata,' Hiroki concluded.

But the old priest would not allow talk of revenge to mask the possibility of a solution. 'Shibata's death is not of major importance. It can be discussed another time. Let us talk of life. Your life, that of your wife and children. To find an answer, you must take a proper view. Only then can you resolve to rectify it in speech and action. I see two choices. Decide either to leave your family or to remain with them. If you continue as head of the household, either you will punish your wife, which in effect punishes you and the children by making a hell on earth for everyone. Or you can comfort and nurse your wife back to health and self-respect.'

'What about my self-respect? I am bound to a woman addicted to opium who invited another man into her bed.' Hiroki retched. He could not even bring himself to mention Noriko and the woman.

The priest was pleased the young man had not yet taken the choice of breaking up his family. He passed Hiroki a piece of root. 'Chew on this. It has a pleasant taste and will relax you.'

Hiroki bit off a piece and chewed. 'What should I do?' he asked tearfully.

'Face the truth,' the priest said. 'Your wife was addicted to opium purposely by others. It was not of her own weakness or desire for the drug. According to what you have told me, the agents were experts in the art of seduction. The cause of your pain is not that your wife was seduced, but that your pride and respect are damaged. This is due to your attachment to a specific code of honour you deem more important than the lives of your family and yourself. This craving to be held in high esteem by others is the source of your pain. It is not your wife's actions. You mentioned that your parents were prostitutes before marriage. Yet they truly loved each other.'

Hiroki did not remember having told the priest about his parents, but it did not seem to matter. He continued chewing on the pleasant-tasting root and his thoughts floated by. The priest's voice seemed to come from far off.

'Fulfil the vow you made to your mother. Love your wife. Care for your children. Join the world of true men. Rest, my troubled friend.'

Hiroki leaned his head back against the wall, and slept.

The elderly man ran a finger into Hiroki's mouth and withdrew the masticated root. 'Dream on, young one. I pray my words have soothed your soul and focused your mind in the right direction.' He turned and left the temple. Having fulfilled his role as priest, he would next report to Korean army intelligence that Japanese agents were in Seoul.

A root-induced dream began with Hiroki's view of his parents. He wished to run to his mother for comfort but his father's stern eyes were an invisible shield that maintained a distance between them. In a most forceful way, they communicated his On to Noriko.

'How can I love her as before?' he cried out.

'Not as before,' his mother answered. 'You will find a greater love.'

'When I touch her, I will know another has done so,' Hiroki sobbed. 'When we make love I will always wonder if she compares me to him.'

'When you caress your wife, search for her heart,' Hiroki's father said. 'No man but you has touched her heart. When you hold your wife, cradle her soul. Only your soul can become one with hers.'

'Be patient,' his mother said. 'Be faithful to your promise to me, and to your On to Noriko.' She faded away into darkness and Hiroki slept.

He awoke on the floor of the temple and looked around. The old priest was gone. People were lighting incense, praying, meditating. Hiroki put down a generous donation. He squinted as he stepped into the daylight, and hurried home.

The sun filtered through closed bamboo window shades, fashioning a design on the quilt of the four-poster bed. Hiroki followed the doctor into the room and the nurse stepped away from the bed. Noriko slept. Nothing the doctor said had prepared Hiroki for his wife's appearance. Bound hand and foot, she lay spread-eagled on the bed in crumpled night clothes. She had lost a third of her body weight. Her eyes were sunken holes with dark rings underneath. Her once beautiful hair was stringy and lustreless. Tears from his eyes splashed onto her thin, drawn face and she looked up. Hiroki saw recognition.

Noriko's eyes widened. 'Noooooo,' she screamed, twisting her head and thrashing her body. 'Noooooo! Noooooo! Do not look at me!'

Hiroki saw the ugly red gash under her chin. 'It will be all right,' he whispered

'What have I done?' Noriko sobbed. Her body convulsed.

384

'Untie her feet,' Hiroki ordered the nurse. He undid the bonds around his wife's hands.

Noriko pulled away from his embrace and slipped off the bed. She scrambled away to huddle with head down, knees up, arms wrapped around her legs in a corner of the room. 'Kill me! Kill me,' she moaned over and over.

The nurse held out a pack of cigarettes to Hiroki. 'These will calm her.'

He snatched the cigarettes. 'Where the hell did you get these?'

'There is a whole crate of Golden Bats in the kitchen,' the nurse said. 'They were here when I arrived.'

Hiroki shook a cigarette free of the pack and broke off the mouthpiece. He turned a tiny pellet into the palm of his hand and held it up. 'Opium. Destroy the entire crate!'

For two days Noriko did not respond in any way to Hiroki. She huddled in the corner or lay face down on the bed.

On the third day, alone with her, he turned his back to pick up a newspaper. Noriko smashed a vase and tried to slash her wrist with a shard. Hiroki dived over the bed and brought her down to the floor. He held her by the front of her quilted robe and lifted her to a kneeling position.

Her head lolled from side to side. 'Hit me. Let me die,' she moaned. 'If you really love me, help me to die.'

Hiroki went down on his knees and embraced Noriko. 'I do love you. I can understand your wanting to die. I will help you kill yourself, on one condition. You must do it in front of the children. I will bring them here.' Hiroki started to move away.

Noriko crawled after him, holding him around the knees with a strength he did not believe she had. Her eyes were wide with stark, primitive fear. Her words came in great gasps. 'No! Do not let the children see me like this! They already saw me with my neck gashed. I pray the memory will not haunt them.'

'Should I bring them to see your dead body?'

'Cremate me. Do not tell them. Please!' She collapsed and sprawled on the floor.

Hiroki knelt and held his wife in his arms. He kissed her cheeks, her head, her lips, and whispered, 'You helped me accept the truth about my parents. If ever our children should learn what happened here in Seoul, you must be the one to answer them.'

'My body craves the medicine,' she whimpered. 'I have seen you sitting on the edge of the bed. You think I am sleeping but I am plotting how to knock you unconscious. I might even kill you to get the medicine.'

'I know,' Hiroki said. 'You cursed me stronger than I thought possible for a lady of breeding.'

'I do not remember that.'

'You have periods of great pain. And you shout.'

'I do not mean it if I curse you,' Noriko said.

'Do you love me?'

Noriko bowed her head. 'Yes,' she mumbled.

'Then do not leave me.' Hiroki grasped her arms and began to weep. 'Please do not leave me. You are not the only one who suffers. I am afraid to be without you.'

Slowly Noriko's arms crept around her husband's neck. 'Tell the doctor I am prepared to cooperate with his treatment,' she whispered.

'It will require complete withdrawal from the opium.'

'Will you remain with me?' Noriko asked.

'Always.'

'Doctor, I cannot bear to watch another moment of Noriko's agony,' Hiroki said.

'These four days of sweating, herbal tea diet and purging of her intestines are necessary to cleanse her body of the drugs. Only then can I begin acupuncture. The objective is to create a free flow of tchi, the vital energy, and balance it rhythmically between and through the large organs. When

386

this uninterrupted flow of tchi is achieved, we enter the final phase of the cure.'

Hiroki stayed at Noriko's side through the remainder of the treatment. At four-hour intervals the doctor placed thirty-six needles into the skin at various points in her body. Two assistants twirled and heated the needles according to the doctor's instructions. At the end of the third day the needles marking Noriko's major organs vibrated continuously and the assistants were no longer needed.

The doctor withdrew the last needle, then picked up a bowl of uncooked brown rice. 'Your wife has not eaten solid food for a week. If she were to try and grind this rice with her teeth, they would break or fall out. If you cannot chew it for her and pass it lip to lip into her mouth, I will ask the nurse to take charge.'

Hiroki took the bowl. 'When will we know if the treatment is successful?' he asked.

'The smooth flow of tchi has been achieved, but it is extremely weak. It must be strengthened by fresh air, good food and exercise. I will teach her yoga and meditation, and give you a list of proper foods.'

'I have received a message ordering me north in a week.'

'Take your wife with you,' the doctor said.

'This is a dangerous military mission. Capture would mean execution. The Russians, in response to a demand from our government, have agreed to withdraw from Korea and Manchuria. I am to monitor that withdrawal.'

'The worst that could happen to your wife if she accompanies you is death. Alone in Seoul she is already dead. It has been your love that saved her, not my medical expertise.'

Hiroki nodded. For the next six days he would follow the doctor's instructions. He and Noriko took longer and longer walks in the fresh air. Some colour returned to her cheeks. She shopped with him and cooked while he read her poetry.

On the seventh day, as Noriko was brushing her hair prior to their morning walk, Hiroki signalled to Yaka outside the house.

There was a knock on the door. 'Please answer,' Noriko called.

Hiroki heard but remained silent in the kitchen. He could see the front door but not be seen. Noriko called him again. When he did not respond, she walked to the front of the house and opened the door. Their two sons, aged six and seven, stood before her. Noriko took a step back and Hiroki thought she might flee, but then she reached out and hugged both boys, raining kisses on their heads and faces, making them wet with her tears. Hiroki dried his own eyes and went to the front room.

'Mother, you are so thin,' the older boy said.

'Your mother has been ill,' Hiroki said. 'She is not completely recovered yet and I must continue to fatten her up. When she is good and plump, I will bring her to you in Japan.'

The boys did not show their disappointment at returning to Japan without their mother, and Hiroki was proud. Yaka had prepared them well.

Noriko looked up to Hiroki. 'Is it another mission?'

'Yes, and you are coming with me this time.'

'In my condition I would only make your task more difficult. I am well enough to look after myself.'

'I need you to look after me.' Hiroki smiled at her. 'It will only be for a month. You and I are going to walk to the Yalu and then sail home to the boys and Japan. I have been commissioned a major in charge of the new Air Reconnaissance Battalion stationed in Tokyo. But more of that later. Today we spend with our sons. Tomorrow we travel north.'

388

Chapter 43

Dressed as Korean merchants, Hiroki, Noriko and five Special Forces guards travelled north from Seoul through the Chang Dang valley, the ancient invasion route to Seoul. Three guards ranged ahead to contact Hiroki's field agents and bring them to his camp after dark. He had planned the journey for reconnaissance and information gathering, as well as to encourage Noriko's recovery.

For a week she rode in their cart more than she walked, but Hiroki saw daily improvement. She began to eat well and sleep less. On the fifteenth day she walked from dawn to dusk, then remained awake late enough to hear a report from a Special Forces agent.

'I believe the Russians intend to invade Korea,' Noriko said before retiring. 'If so, they will certainly not retreat from Manchuria.'

Hiroki looked up from writing and smiled. 'In addition to becoming clear-eyed, with a blush of pink to your cheeks and shiny hair, your mind is alert. What brings you to that conclusion?'

'The few Russian camps we passed were small, yet the soldiers were digging latrines and putting up tents, not taking them down. Yesterday and today we passed Russians stringing telephone wire. If they intend remaining in Korea, as it seems, their route of supply is through Manchuria. They must protect it.'

'You would make a good agent, Noriko. Your observations are supported by these reports.' Hiroki tapped the papers in front of him. 'The Russians have lied to our government. We are near the Yalu and the end of our journey. We should begin to see more Russians and receive more detailed reports.'

'You appear to sleep less now than when we started,' Noriko said.

'No. When we began, you slept most of the day. Now you see more of me.'

'Would you sleep with me?' Noriko asked. 'I will understand if you do not wish to make love. But I need you to hold me.'

Hiroki looked at the ground. 'I wish to sleep with you, although the doctor warned that you may not be ready for intimate relations.'

'I wish to try.'

'Very well,' Hiroki said. He stood at the side of the cart with his back to Noriko.

'Why do you hesitate?' she asked.

Hiroki stripped and slipped between the quilts. Noriko's body was smooth and warm and his immediate erection overruled his plan to move slowly. He clasped her to him. 'I have been with no woman but you and there will be no other,' he gasped. 'It has been months.' He rolled on top of her, thrust violently, and climaxed. 'Noriko, I love you,' he moaned.

She brushed her fingers over his face. 'You need a haircut.'

Hiroki looked down at his wife. 'I need to love you properly.' He kissed her forehead, her eyes and her mouth. He recalled the illustrations and explanations in the pillow book his mother had given him. With patience and tenderness, he devoted himself to Noriko's needs. She did not seem to respond.

'Let us hold each other and sleep,' she said, snuggling close to him.

Hiroki shut his eyes and wondered if they would ever again enjoy the wild unpractised ecstasies of first love.

Noriko feigned sleep, fearing her husband would never

again love her as he once had. She drifted off, accepting that life for them had changed.

During the night, Noriko rose to relieve herself. As she moved from the sleeping quilt, Hiroki's hand shot out and pinned her back down. 'Do not go,' he mumbled.

'I will not attempt suicide,' she said, turning towards him.

He was still asleep, yet he held her in a grip of iron. 'I need you,' he murmured. 'Please stay.'

Noriko wept tears of joy. She soothed her husband until he released his grip on her.

When she lay down again, she kissed his mouth. She ran her lips up and down his body.

'What are you doing?' he asked.

'Making love to the man I married. It will be a mating we shall not forget. Look up at the stars and remember their position.'

Hiroki opened his eyes. 'The sky is cloudy.'

She caressed his golden rod. 'You will soon see the stars.'

The following morning husband and wife were too weary to walk. They rode in the cart and smiled continually at each other.

Shortly before noon, a guard hurried back towards them. He was followed by a tall Mongol on horseback. 'This fellow works for you and Shibata,' the guard said.

'I gave specific orders that all meetings were to take place after dark,' Hiroki said. 'The Koreans have their agents too.'

'Sir, this Mongol stole a letter sent by Eugene Alexiev, first adviser to the czar. It is addressed to Viceroy Bezobrazov in Port Arthur.'

'What does it contain that is so important?'

'The letter is written in French. The Mongol cannot read it.'

'Give it here,' Hiroki said. 'And find out why he did not take it to Akichi Shibata.'

'He told me he followed his grazing herd of horses over to this side of the Yalu river. He was carrying the letter and by chance learned you were in the area.'

Hiroki noted the broken seal on the envelope, and opened it. He passed over a lengthy salutation between noblemen, on to the words of the most influential man in the Russian government.

'We in St Petersburg are concerned because primitive people continue to rule the mineral-rich Far East. The time has come to utilize Russian military might to consolidate Manchuria and Korea into the czar's realm. Domination over the nomadic northern tribes by Mother Russia would be a benevolent and humanitarian act. We shall establish order where there is chaos, Christianity in place of shamanism, and bring enlightenment into a cultural wasteland. Without our conquest of Manchuria, the more numerous yellow peoples would one day pour into Russia and attempt to rule us.

'We have made a secret agreement with Peking. China will allow our development of Manchurian natural resources and encourage the building of parallel industries. The Dowager Empress will accept Russia's sphere of influence in Korea, which is to remain a tributary state to China. This leaves Japan with the only viable army standing between economic, political and military stability in Asia. Our secret service reports the Japanese have two infantry divisions in Korea at this time. One in the south, the other spread throughout the country under the guise of merchants, sailors and craftsmen. You must prepare our northern army for war with Japan. We in St Petersburg will formally declare hostilities on the first day of spring, 1 May 1904. It is reasonable to assume you will have achieved victory before winter sets in. We will then dictate terms to the little yellow men, proceed with the expansion of Russia, and bring progress to Asia.'

Hiroki looked up from the letter. 'It is already 20 December. We must get this to Tokyo.' He called in his men. 'This letter gives the date Russia will declare war on Japan. My wife and I must return home immediately. Have two copies made of the letter! Make preparations to leave in the morning!'

Hiroki walked with the Mongol a short distance away from the camp. 'Would you kill a man for money?' Hiroki asked.

The big Mongol pondered the question, then asked, 'How much money?'

'Enough gold to buy a thousand horses.'

'I have killed for fun, why not money. Who?'

'The White Wolf in Manchuria,' Hiroki said.

The Mongol looked down on Hiroki and purred like a big mountain cat. 'The viper that bites Akichi Shibata will die of poisoning.'

Hiroki placed a pouch of gold in the Mongol's callused hand. 'Go to your horses and think of what I have said. If you agree to carry out my request, I shall give you another pouch of gold. And send two more when you have killed the White Wolf.'

The Mongol opened the pouch and stirred the gold with a thick finger. 'It will be difficult to get close to him.'

Hiroki held out the letter. 'Take this to Shibata! Say nothing of our meeting! He will question you and keep you near while he reseals the letter for Bezobrazov.'

The Mongol hefted the gold in his hand. 'It will take me at least a month to reach Shibata with my herd.'

'Think about it on the way.'

Later that night the camp was awakened by the pounding of horses' hoofs. The Mongol reared his mount to a sliding halt that threw up clods of dirt. He flung a lead rope to

393

Hiroki and shouted, 'I brought five horses. If you cannot ride, you are all dead! A hundred Korean soldiers led by officers of the Royal Korean Intelligence Corps are coming to attack you!'

Hiroki pulled Noriko from under the quilts and lifted her onto the largest, strongest-looking horse. 'Do you remember how to ride?' he asked her.

'The horses in Washington had saddles.'

'One of us must reach Tokyo with the message.' Hiroki handed Noriko one copied letter and kept the other.

'Both of us,' she said.

'This is not the time for discussion,' the Mongol growled. 'Give me the second pouch of gold! Mount up with your weapons!'

Hiroki looked up at the mounted Mongol and the big man grinned. 'You lose it either way. If you do not give me the gold, they will take it.'

Hiroki sprang onto a horse's back. 'You will get it when we reach the road to Chongjin.'

The Mongol shrugged. 'Tell your wife to hug the horse with her legs and hold the mane with both hands. I will lead.'

He took the reins of Noriko's horse and led them single file at a walk, off the main road and into the rice paddies. Water rose up to the horses' bellies. The Mongol's horse scrambled up onto an earthen dike that separated the flooded paddies. He pulled Noriko's horse behind his.

A light drizzle wet the grass and dampened the sound of the horses' hoofs. The moon and stars were masked by rain clouds. After several minutes on the dike in single file, the Mongol dismounted and walked ahead.

Voices in the night moved towards them. Men were splashing through the water in the paddies on the right and left. The five soothed their horses with whispered words and soft caresses as the sounds came closer and closer. Hiroki understood orders in Korean from an officer telling his men to keep a straight line.

Noriko choked back a scream at the sight of the Mongol at her side. He whispered to Hiroki behind her. 'The Korean officers are staying dry by walking the dikes. Their men are in the paddies. Hold tight and get ready to gallop!' The big man swung up onto his mount, unslung a double-barrelled shotgun and moved forward.

A horse behind Hiroki snickered.

'Halt!' a Korean officer shouted, directly in front of Noriko. Her body quivered. 'I heard a horse,' the officer shouted.

'We heard a horse's arse,' came a disguised falsetto from the paddies, and the soldiers hooted.

The Mongol covered the eyes of his animal with his big fur cap. He aimed the double-barrelled shotgun over the horse's ears and pulled both triggers, killing the officer and wounding his aide. Two Korean signalmen were knocked off the dike by the charge of the Mongol's horse.

Noriko dug her hands into the horse's mane. Her legs hugged him with all her strength. There was gunfire to the right and left but she was too frightened of falling to pay attention.

Hiroki kicked his mount forward. He did not shoot for fear the gun's flash would give away their position.

'The road is two hundred yards ahead,' the Mongol shouted. 'Turn right!'

Suddenly Hiroki and his horse were airborne. They flew off the dike, landing sideways in three feet of water. The horse lurched to its feet and Hiroki, with a death grip on the stirrup, was dragged through the paddy. The horse scrambled up another dike, pulling Hiroki over the mud bank and into a flooded paddy. Gunfire frightened the animal and he scrambled up a steeper embankment. A thousand pounds of horseflesh teetered over Hiroki, then gained its balance and pulled him onto the road. He calmed the animal and mounted, shouting for his wife.

'Here! Follow us!' The voice came from Hiroki's right, and two of his men galloped by. He spurred his horse after them.

Several minutes later Hiroki pulled his horse up to keep from ploughing into the group at a small crossroad. He reined in next to Noriko. 'Are you all right?'

She reached out and touched his arm, but did not speak.

'Do not dismount,' the Mongol ordered. 'I am the best horse thief on both sides of the Yalu! I do not intend to be caught by a bunch of dung-eating soldiers! You go straight for fifteen miles with this road! Take the crossroad right to the main Chongjin highway! You will see signs from there. Run your horses until they drop! Then run your feet until you reach the port, or you are dead! Do not let them take you alive!'

'I lost my weapon,' Hiroki said.

'That second pouch of gold for a gun.'

Hiroki flipped a pouch to the Mongol. 'Will you do what I asked?'

The big man tucked the gold into his waistband, and shrugged. 'If I can be certain to get away with it.' He threw Hiroki a pistol. 'Only four bullets left. Tell your men to follow me. We will lead the trackers on a false trail. Ride swiftly!' He pointed to the overhead wire. 'That carries secrets faster than the wind.' He wheeled his horse around and galloped off, followed by the guards.

'Why are you dismounting?' Noriko cried to Hiroki.

'I must destroy that telegraph line or word will get ahead of us.' He climbed the pole, put the muzzle of the pistol to the wire and pulled the trigger. He slid down the pole and mounted, kneeing his horse closer to Noriko's. 'Death could come upon us suddenly. I may not have the chance to say I love you.'

396

'I know you love me,' she answered, and they galloped away.

It was daylight when they reached the Chongjin highway on exhausted horses. Hiroki found a long, straight pole and beat both beasts to keep them moving. 'I would steal fresh horses if there were any in sight,' he said. The only passersby were following slow-moving bullocks pulling two-wheeled carts.

'The poor horses cannot go any further,' Noriko said. 'We have to leave them and walk.'

'It is thirty miles. Can you make it?'

Noriko slipped off the exhausted animal and took the stick from Hiroki's hand. 'This will be my cane. If I falter, you may use it to beat me.'

Rain began to fall and most travellers left the road for shelter. The young couple hurried along through the mud. Darkness fell and they were the only ones still moving.

Sometime before midnight, the rain stopped and they caught sight of the Chongjin lighthouse. Its bright beam swung over the harbour and city every half minute.

'Hurrah,' Hiroki cried. 'We are going to make it. I will carry you if necessary.'

Noriko plodded on, not responding for fear he would hear her teeth chattering.

'Seize them,' a voice shouted, and figures rushed out of the darkness.

Hiroki dropped to one knee and fired, killing two men and wounding one. Another leapt at Noriko brandishing a knife. Hiroki dived between them. He and the attacker crashed into Noriko, knocking her backwards, off the road. Hiroki went down under the man and felt the searing pain of the knife in his side. He heard the blade scrape against his rib cage and smashed the face in front of him with his pistol butt. Two more men dived on top of him, pinning his arms back. The gun was jerked from his hand. He butted his head into one attacker's face and smashed the middle knuckle of his fist into the man's temple. The second attacker drove a knife into Hiroki's left shoulder, then stabbed for the throat, but Hiroki protected himself with his left arm, taking another cut. He drove the heel of his right hand into the attacker's nose, driving the bone up into his brain.

Hiroki tried to squirm out from under the bodies but his left side was numb. Three more men jumped on him. He struck one in the Adam's apple with a wedge punch, and was startled by a familiar bloodcurdling scream – Noriko's kendo battle cry. The female voice froze the attackers as it had Hiroki in the Imperial Hall of Martial Arts. He saw Noriko leap forward with the walking stick held as a kendo sword – a female panther protecting her wounded mate. Her attack was savage, her blows swift. One man on top of Hiroki died with his head bashed in. The last one fled, limping into the darkness.

Noriko rolled bodies off Hiroki. Tears streamed down her cheeks as she tried to stop his bleeding. He wanted to tell her he loved her but had not the strength.

Chapter 44

Hiroki could not see and his left side was numb. It took total concentration to bring his right hand up to his face.

'I will cleanse your eyes,' an unfamiliar female voice said.

'Where am I?'

'Aboard a Japanese ship bound for Tokyo.'

'My wife?'

'Open your eyes now,' the nurse said. She pointed with a damp cloth to the corner of the cabin where Noriko was asleep in a sitting position.

'Is she well?' Hiroki asked.

'The Marquessa has not left this room in two weeks. She changed your bandages, dressed your wounds and would not allow anyone else to feed you.'

'Tell her I love her,' Hiroki whispered, and drifted back to sleep.

The next time he woke, Noriko was at his side. She brushed her lips to his and they gazed into each other's eyes. Both wept.

During the voyage, Hiroki's periods of wakefulness lengthened. He heard from the Special Forces man who had carried him aboard that Noriko had killed one attacker and beat off the last two. Noriko refused to talk about that.

'A Special Forces Agent was in the Korean army telegraph shack when the message arrived for a patrol to search for us,' she told him. 'The man gathered other agents and they found us on the road. The doctor who closed your wounds claims you have more stitches in you than an embroidered kimono.'

Hiroki reached up and touched his wife's face. 'By saving

you in Seoul, I saved myself. I knew the knife cuts were bad and I thought I was dying. I saw you fighting like a wildcat to save me and willed myself to live for you.'

Tokyo

Noriko knelt and put house slippers on Mung's feet. 'It is so good to see you after almost ten years,' she said. 'Hiroki is still resting.' She took Mung by the arm and led him into the sitting room, to a high European chair so he would not have to bend his knees. She moved the hibachi closer to him for warmth.

'How is my favourite grandson?' Mung asked.

'He improves every day. He limps and cannot raise his left arm above shoulder height, but he has full strength in his hand.'

'At least that.' Mung held up the stump of his left arm. 'It can be a nuisance with only one hand.' He leaned forward and asked with concern, 'How are you?'

For a moment Noriko thought Mung had learned about her ordeal. Then his stern old face creased into a broad smile and he adjusted his spectacles. 'I see you are even more beautiful than before. Saiyo, my first wife, was like that. They would come to our house and ask to look at her.'

'Who were they?'

'Friends, neighbours and people who had heard of her beauty.' Mung seemed to drift away into his memories for a few moments. Then he looked up and addressed Noriko again. 'Are you able to tend to Hiroki's needs, the children and this big house without servants?'

Noriko blushed. 'I closed off some rooms and have an elderly couple who come in daily to clean and care for the garden. I prefer to cook.' She knew she would never again employ live-in servants.

'Consider this house yours,' Mung said. 'It is a welcome-home present from me to you and your family. I bought it when I was out of political favour.'

Hiroki stood in the doorway holding the wall for support. 'And now my grandfather is Tairo, the Great Elder, and has permanent residence in the palace.' Noriko started towards him, but he shuffled into the room unaided. 'Let me show that I am fully recovered and able to greet the greatest man in the empire.' He bowed low, and Noriko placed a chair for him close to Mung's.

'I am honoured to have children like you two,' Mung said. 'I would have been here sooner but that letter you brought, written by Alexiev to Bezobrazov, has complicated matters. Many cabinet members wished to declare war after reading that letter. I denied their motion and formally requested the Russians to live up to their promises of withdrawal from Manchuria and the Liaotung peninsula. I included your reports of a Russian troop build-up in Korea. Bezobrazov's answer to our ambassador was that he would not dicker with little yellow monkeys like us. He departed for St Petersburg, leaving behind a General Stossel in charge of Port Arthur.'

Anger flushed Hiroki's face. 'We will show that white baboon how costly it can be to underestimate Japan! When do we attack?'

Mung shook his head. 'Look at you. All cut up from a knife fight and itching for another war. Do not be so anxious.'

'I do not lust for battle,' Hiroki said. 'I have seen the Russian boy soldiers who were forced into the czar's service. They are unprepared, but can be trained if given time. We must strike soon.'

'Nogi and Takamora have requested until March to incorporate our new Ariaka breech-loading artillery, your wireless radios and the new five-cartridge Murato rifles into service. Nogi is training his field artillery to operate with the wireless and long-range cannon. They stationed a forward observer with a wireless radio on top of a hill overlooking the enemy's position. He relays coordinates

401

to the artillerymen, who cannot even see their target. After they shoot, adjustments are made via the radio. The enemy has no idea where the shells are being fired from.'

'I first thought of the wireless in reference to the navy,' Hiroki said.

'And they are making great use of it from ship to ship and ship to shore. General Honjo designed a portable transmitter using pedal power from a bicycle to generate electricity. He has trained hundreds of operators. They are stationed with their families at strategic points along international sea routes such as the Panama and Suez canals, Cape Horn and the Cape of Good Hope. They live there and report by radio to our passing ships. Or to a senior agent in the area who relays the information by telephone or telegraph.' Mung looked around. 'Which reminds me, where are your children?'

'They are receiving tutoring in Japanese,' Noriko said. 'They must improve to keep up at school.'

'Do they speak English?'

'Yesterday I showed them off to Uraga,' Hiroki said with pride. 'I conversed with the boys in English, Korean and Japanese.'

'Excellent,' Mung said. 'It is very important to keep up their language skills. Tokyo has become an international community. There are journalists from all over the world waiting for war to break out. There is one pesky newspaperman from the *New York Journal* who constantly writes derogatory things about Japan, most of them unwarranted.'

'The *Journal* is a muckraking paper,' Hiroki said. 'Its owner, William Randolph Hearst, is anti-Oriental and promotes the Yellow Peril idea to sell newspapers in the United States. He creates fear and antagonism towards Chinese and Japanese by saying they will take white men's jobs. Who is the reporter you mentioned?'

'Jack London,' Mung said. 'Honjo wants to have him

killed in a staged accident. London usually drinks and looks for fights in the bars along the Yokohama waterfront.'

'Killing an American newspaperman is a bad idea,' Hiroki said.

'Especially not Jack London,' Noriko said. 'His book *The Call of the Wild* is this year's American best-seller. I met him in New York when he lectured, and again at a cocktail party. He believes in Nietzsche's idea of the superman and Karl Marx's theory of communism.'

'I am familiar with both concepts,' Mung said. 'They appear contradictory. How does the author equate the two?'

'*The Call of the Wild* is about a dog who, after years of faithful service to his master, returns to the forest and leads a wolf pack against the establishment. The dog represents the superman who unites his oppressed class in a bloody revolution and a bid for freedom against the decadent masters. The moral is that socialism triumphs.'

'The idea of socialism has raised its ugly head here,' Mung said.

'Socialism in Japan?' Hiroki said. 'Unbelievable! We Japanese do what we are told.'

'Japanese extremists are the worst kind,' Mung said. 'In June of this year a large meeting of socialists took place in the Kanda district of Tokyo. They displayed red banners proclaiming Anarchism and Anarcho-Communism. The police warned them it is against the law to demand the removal of the Emperor or the government, but they continued their demonstration and were jailed. Their membership lists were confiscated and mass arrests made. In the search of one home, a young woodworker was found to have explosives, metal containers and instructions on how to make bombs. Honjo employed electric shock torture and a group of twenty-five admitted to a plot to assassinate the Emperor.'

'They should be sentenced to death,' Hiroki said.

'They were hanged,' Mung replied. 'The Socialist movement in Japan is finished. Honjo saw to that. But in doing so he assumed greater control over newspaper censorship and thought control through the education system. The Tokyo police are his private army. His policy of restricting civilian rights is supported by many ministers and members of Parliament, but such a policy isolates the Emperor.'

Noriko served tea and commented to Mung, 'I have heard that you alone stand between Sasaki's and Honjo's control of the Emperor and our government.'

'That is why I was appointed Tairo, but it is an anachronistic position. Our government has become too complex for one man to make it work. Listen to this from Shimatzu.' Mung fished a letter from his pocket.

'Is he still in Formosa?' Hiroki asked.

'His family is there,' Mung said. 'I sent him to arrange a national loan from the British, but their bankers turned down his request. He met with an exiled Russian financier named Jacob Schiff who hates the czar for persecuting Jews. This Schiff took Shimatzu to the United States to raise the money. Let me read what Shimatzu writes from New York.' Mung adjusted his spectacles and cleared his throat. 'Jacob Schiff escorted me into a room where several men were gathered. I later learned that those men control more than 50 per cent of America's wealth. Although Schiff's English is heavily accented, when he spoke the mighty men of industry listened. He told them Japan has a better credit rating than any other country in the world. That Japanese ethics and morals require us to repay our debts rather than sully the name of family, country or the Emperor. He referred to the recent survey which indicates that the level of Japanese education is higher than the average American's or Englishman's. He used, as an example of Japan's potential, our economic recovery after the earthquake, and prompt repayment of debts incurred during that period of rebuilding. Schiff then wrote out a cheque for six million

404

dollars. J.P. Morgan, president of First National City Bank, confirmed that President Roosevelt is interested in keeping the Russians out of Manchuria. Morgan does not think the Japanese capable of defeating Russia, but he feels our army could make the Manchurian incursion unprofitable for the czar. He wrote out a cheque. Next to speak was John D. Rockefeller of National City Bank. He stated it was worth a few million dollars to keep Russia from a warm-water port, and wrote out a cheque. Father, I left that room with vouchers for thirty million dollars!' Mung looked up from the letter and grinned.

'Does that mean I should prepare to join my Air Reconnaissance Battalion?' Hiroki asked.

'You have about sixty days to recuperate, then another thirty to train. I promised Nogi and Takamora that much time. Meanwhile I am hoping to hear news from Manchuria that will avoid a war.'

Chapter 45

The fourth year of the twentieth century was three days old. Icy Siberian winds whipped through Mukden and beat against the walls of the Fifth Moon Inn. Akichi Shibata reread the end of Honjo's message. 'Make ready to cut the stem.' It was the signal to prepare for Japan's invasion of Manchuria.

Shibata had promised Honjo ten years before that the northern territory would fall like a plum when Japanese troops attacked. He sipped a delicate rice wine and pondered the implications, assuming his last message had swayed Tairo to consider war. He had sent detailed information about increased troop trains from Russia to Manchuria, on the expansion of the czar's navy in the Yellow Sea, and Bezobrazov's declaration in St Petersburg that the Chinese provinces of Amur and Kwangtung would fall under the jurisdiction of imperial Russia. These were obvious steps towards the czar's annexation of Manchuria, and the beginning of Russia's drive into Korea.

Shibata motioned his aide closer. 'For us the war has begun. If you thought I worked you hard before, now even you will sweat in this sub-zero weather.'

'What should be done with the Mongol?' the aide asked. 'He is outside.'

'Bring the horse thief in and keep a pistol at his back!'

The Mongol's fur hat brushed the door lintel and he filled the room.

'You are going to be the first casualty of the war,' Shibata said.

'What war?' the Mongol asked.

'You swore the letter from Alexiev to Bezobrazov, which

406

I paid you so handsomely for, was brought directly to me.'

'True.'

'Liar,' Shibata shouted. 'Marquis Hiroki Koin took an exact copy to Tokyo weeks before mine arrived there!' He shoved Honjo's letter in the Mongol's face. 'It says so right here!'

'I cannot read,' the big man said, silently cursing himself for not having killed Shibata as he had been paid to do. He let the knife slip from his sleeve into his hand, and felt a pistol jammed into his back.

Shibata brought up a Luger from under the desk. 'Raise your hands, close your eyes and spread your legs!'

The aide lashed out with his foot into the big man's crotch. The Mongol grunted, doubled over and fell to his knees. Shibata came from behind the desk and shot him once through each shoulder. The knife fell from the Mongol's sleeve and Shibata laughed. 'If I only had time, I would play you like a light bulb with my electrical toys.' He grabbed the Mongol's pigtail, jerked his head back and glared into the hate-filled eyes. 'But lack of time does not mean you will die easily!' Shibata slammed the butt of his pistol into the ashen face. 'Take him out and tie him to that post opposite my window,' he ordered the aide. 'Throw water over him! He will freeze to death slowly!'

Shibata returned to his desk to institute Operation Red Pigeon, the plan aimed at demoralizing and slowing the Russian troops arriving in Korea and Manchuria. His people would initiate acts of light sabotage against the Trans-Siberian railroad and its spur tracks. Derailments, misdirected supplies and fouled drinking water were to appear accidental.

He looked out at the Mongol being tied to the stake and an idea blossomed. Anger would keep the Mongol alive longer, to suffer more. Shibata opened the window and shouted to his aide, 'Piss on the horse thief!' He closed the window, sat down at his desk and encoded his message to Honjo. 'I am preparing the plum to fall.'

'Wish your Uncle Uraga a safe journey,' Noriko said. 'You may salute him.'

The two boys snapped to attention and threw their right hands up to their foreheads.

Uraga solemnly inspected his nephews, then saluted them. 'Would you like to join the navy and wear a uniform like mine?'

They both looked at the floor and remained silent.

'I see,' Uraga said. 'You prefer to wear the eagle wings like your father.'

The boys grinned and bowed. They wished their uncle well and went off to bed.

'Are you leaving tonight?' Noriko asked.

'Yes,' Uraga said. 'I have been assigned chief intelligence officer on Admiral Togo's staff. I expect Hiroki will soon receive his orders.'

'He already has. On the first of February his unit will land at the mouth of the Yalu river.'

'Yaka is chief intelligence officer in that area.'

'Then war with Russia is certain?'

'Almost,' Uraga said. 'It just came over the wireless that our special envoys were kicked out of St Petersburg by Bezobrazov. We recently infiltrated a third infantry division into Korea to offset a surprise Russian invasion from Manchuria. As Tairo, the decision for war rests with Grandfather. I do not see that he has any other choice.'

Mung, cautious of the absolute power of Tairo, had decided to poll the military. He sat on a raised platform flanked by Nogi and Takamora on his right, Sasaki and Honjo on his left. Faced by five ranks of the most senior officers in the imperial armed forces, Mung tried to ignore his feelings of awe. Each man was a hero several times over.

'If it is to be war, we should act as one,' Mung declared. 'Previous to making such a momentous decision, I will ask you to vote. Before my personal envoy was so rudely dismissed from St Petersburg, we learned the czar now considers Manchuria part of Russia. He also wants Korea as a Russian protectorate. Our agents report that Bezobrazov has set up a Special Committee for Far Eastern Affairs. It is charged with the takeover and administration of Korea. In addition, Russia has demanded our withdrawal from Korea. They threaten that Japanese troop movements north of the thirty-eighth parallel will constitute an act of war against the czar. Now, Chief of National Intelligence Service Honjo has requested a few words before the vote.'

Honjo stood up. 'Gentlemen, I remind you it is only one hundred miles from Pusan on the southern tip of Korea to Nagasaki or Hiroshima. We cannot allow the Russians to occupy Korea! In time they would use Pusan to launch an invasion of Japan. I already have thousands of army agents at work north of Seoul. Technically that constitutes a mass troop movement. The Royal Korean Intelligence Corps knows that. The Russian army intelligence knows that, and I am certain the czar was informed of it before he made his statement. In effect, Russia has already declared war on Japan!' He bowed, and sat down.

'Before you vote, it is my duty to remind you of the horrors of war and the disaster and disgrace of defeat,' Mung said. He took the time to meet the eyes of each man standing before him. 'Vote,' he ordered.

'War! War! War! War! War! War! War! War! War! War . . .' The unanimous choice rang from every mouth but one.

'Admiral Togo, you did not vote,' Mung said.

Togo bowed deeply to Mung. 'Tairo, my abstention should be taken as a request to speak before the final decision is made.'

'Do so now!'

Togo stepped out of the ranks and approached the dais.

He bowed again. 'In this war we will not be dealing with simple Chinese bandits. Russian artillery and naval guns are the best in the world. They have infantry regiments with traditions hundreds of years old. We must take every advantage to safeguard the lives of our men and ensure a swift victory. I agree with General Honjo that the czar's message is a declaration of war. Therefore we must strike first without warning to gain maximum surprise. The first action must be at sea. If our navy can contain the Russian fleets at Vladivostok and Port Arthur, their land forces will be left dangling at the end of a six-thousand-mile, single-track supply line. General Honjo's people have promised to cut that line. The Russian army will wither and die.' Togo bowed. 'My vote is for war, and for permission to attack without a formal declaration of hostilities.'

Nogi, Takamora, Sasaki and Honjo each slammed a fist over his heart as a sign of agreement.

Mung stood up, and announced the word he most dreaded. 'War!'

The chiefs of staff and the commanders of the imperial military forces bowed and chorused, 'So it is ordered, so it is done.' They raised their heads and shouted, 'Unto victory or death! Dai Nippon banzai! Long live a great Japan! Dai Nippon banzai!'

It was after dark when Hiroki returned home. Noriko took one look at him and knew something important had happened. She helped him on with his house slippers and led him in to dinner. He ate in silence.

After the meal Hiroki finally spoke. 'We ship out tonight.'

'It is three weeks earlier than your orders,' Noriko said.

'It is war. Grandfather Mung saw no alternative.'

'Can we defeat the Russians?'

'Other than General Stossel at Port Arthur, most

Russians think of Japanese as Oriental adolescents. This is to our advantage. At the latest intelligence briefing, Honjo predicted our success in six months.'

'According to the western press, Russia's army and navy are among the best in the world,' Noriko said.

'Western journalists promote that myth because they have only seen the European military in action. Our men's excellent behaviour in battle was completely disregarded at Peking in 1900 and against the Chinese army in 1894. The West is colour-blind, and Mung is distracting foreign correspondents away from our training bases and naval depots. He invited them on a special train ride to Kobe. They are being wined and dined and will be on a yacht sailing the inland sea when war breaks out. We also have orders to keep war correspondents away from field units, and to stop any mail or telegrams they send.'

'But I assumed Mung would uphold freedom of the press,' Noriko said. 'He always did in the past, no matter how unfair or derogatory they were to him or his ideas.'

'It is not his future at stake, but Japan's. Grandfather knows that every overseas Japanese newspaperman works for military intelligence. Honjo convinced Mung that war correspondent is another term for professional spy. The Russians read newspapers and journals too. Letting foreigners write about our military aids the enemy.'

'May I help you pack?' Noriko asked.

'My orderly has my kit ready.'

'Then wake the children to say goodbye. I will be waiting.'

Noriko heard Hiroki say goodnight to the boys. She stepped to the doorway of their room and let her robe slip off. She had positioned the lamp so it threw a soft ruddy glow on her naked body.

Hiroki walked down the hall deep in thought. He looked up and saw her, a golden statue perfect in form, yet alive. He hurried forward but stopped one step away to gaze at her glossy shoulders, at the beautiful curve and flow of smooth muscles down to shapely legs.

Noriko reached out and undid his tunic. He watched her beautiful breasts rise and fall as she unbuttoned his shirt. She undressed him and he caressed her thighs, kissed her face, neck and lips. They sank together onto the sleeping quilt and made love. In the quiet moments they whispered of their adoration for one another. Time passed and they lay entwined.

'Your mother always worried about you going up in the air,' Noriko said.

Hiroki kissed her eyes closed. 'I will not go up on a kite again. But balloons are safe. They rise so high, we will be out of the enemy's sight and reach.'

'If it were so easy, they would have women doing such work.'

Hiroki laughed. 'One day I shall take you and the children up. It is safer than a rickshaw.'

'I fear height.'

'I did not think you fear anything.' Hiroki buried his face between her breasts and felt her shudder.

'I am afraid of losing you,' Noriko sobbed.

'Please do not cry,' he whispered into the warmth of her body. 'It takes all the strength from me. I promise not to die.'

The telephone rang and Hiroki picked up the receiver. 'Yes. Yes.' He hung up the phone. 'That was my orderly. I asked him to ring before he came to pick me up.' He kissed each of Noriko's breasts, then lowered himself and buried his face in her soft rounded belly. He sucked hard and raised his head, pointing at the purple mark. 'I have left this for you to remember me by.'

'I love you,' Noriko whispered, and held him close. 'I love you. I love you.'

412

Chapter 46

It was late in the evening when Mung entered the imperial reception room. The Emperor was alone.

'Your majesty, I postponed the decision for war until the last moment. Further delay would have jeopardized our agents in Manchuria, our troops in Korea, and invited a naval bombardment of our coastal cities by the Russian navy. I have ordered a surprise attack on Port Arthur in order to trap the Russian fleet.'

'I assume you have determined what the international reaction will be without a declaration of war,' the Emperor said.

'I believe America and England will remain silent. Some European countries, such as Germany and Austria, will condemn the action. But Japan will gain respect from the coloured peoples of the world. We shall be the first Oriental country in modern times to engage a white Christian nation in open warfare. This should stimulate Orientals to demand better conditions from the colonial powers, and enhance the possibilities for Japanese business abroad.'

'You sound like those expansionists I have heard about,' the Emperor said. 'We must ask ourselves what will happen if we lose to Russia.'

'Sire, Russia has pushed us into a position where we must fight. Even if our military had voted against war, I would still have used my power as Tairo to send them into battle.' Mung tapped his head. 'I have memorized every army unit, ship and sabotage cell, their locations and objectives. I know the plans of our army and navy, and the ability of our merchant marine to deliver supplies. Everything is in the proper place at the proper time. My son Shimatzu, with the help of President Roosevelt, has obtained an additional one-hundred-million-dollar loan from Kuhn and Loeb Associates in New York. Sire, I do not consider the possibility of defeat. Honjo's ten years of preparations in Manchuria and my grandson's Special Forces in Korea increase the probability of success. We shall never be more prepared!'

'The warriors of Japan have my blessing. Let no man turn back until his objective is taken or his task complete.'

6 February 1904
While Honjo's agents were delivering weapons to a secret congress of Russian revolutionaries in Stockholm, and St Petersburg nobility celebrated the birth of a son to Czar Nicolas, Admiral Togo and his squadron sailed through the cold, dark night towards the Liaotung peninsula. Togo believed with unswerving certainty that to win the war, Japan had to neutralize the Russian fleet in Port Arthur.

'If the czar's navy is allowed to roam the seas unhindered, they will sink our troopships as we did the *Kowshing*,' Togo said to his aides. 'The Japanese army must have the ability to move unhindered at sea while the Russians are restricted to slower land travel. Once our attack begins on Port Arthur, there will be no turning back until we have destroyed or blockaded the Russian fleet!'

Uraga stepped forward with a package resting on the palms of his outstretched hands. 'Sir, it has been ten years since you led the imperial Japanese navy to its first victory. The signal you used was this Z flag.' Uraga bowed. 'I have saved it for this occasion.' He raised up the flag and declared, 'Unto victory or death!'

Each man in the admiral's stateroom slammed his fist over his heart and repeated the oath. 'Unto victory or death!'

Togo's short-cropped hair and Vandyke beard were streaked with grey. He reviewed his men in silence; his dark eyes burned into them. No one lowered his gaze, and a solemn bond was forged.

Togo reached into his desk and withdrew a short ceremonial sword used for seppuku. He held it forward in his clenched fist and repeated, 'Unto victory or death!' He turned to Uraga. 'Have the Z flag run up and signal made to man battle stations!'

Rumours of the impending battle had reached a fever pitch throughout Togo's squadron. For days seamen and officers had talked and argued about where and when they would strike. Now they lay fully clothed in their bunks, staring silently at the bulkheads. They waited, they listened, and prayed they would not disgrace themselves, their families or their Emperor.

At 9 p.m. the sound of the giant bronze propellers driving the ships through a calm, cold sea took on a higher pitch. The ships of the First Imperial Squadron surged forward. Clanging bells set every man rigid. The loudspeakers blared, 'Now hear this! Now hear this! Admiral Togo has raised the Z flag!' There was a pause and then the metallic voice ordered, 'Man your battle stations! This is not a drill! Man your battle stations!'

Ninety seconds later the captain of each ship took the microphone and spoke to his men. 'It is impossible for Admiral Togo to address each crew personally before the forthcoming action. The admiral has made a voice recording which will be played now.' There were scratching sounds as the needle was placed on the record.

Togo's voice came over the loudspeakers of every ship in the fleet. 'Civilized warriors of Japan, you are about to inscribe glorious deeds in the pages of our history! We will be fighting a European enemy for the first time! There is no need to be intimidated! You represent the best trained navy in the world! You can sail faster, fight better and you have more courage than any group of men on the face of this earth! I do not exaggerate! These are facts! The Emperor has given you the most modern equipment! Your officers have trained you well! The outcome of the battle rests on you! The target is Port Arthur! Honour the Emperor! Honour Japan! Dai Nippon banzai!'

The officers led their men in three roaring cheers. Then everyone bowed to the loudspeaker nearest them.

Togo's communication centre was located in the wheel-house aboard the flagship *Hatsuse*. Uraga heard the clicking of the wireless and stiffened. The message being received was from Akichi Shibata.

'Are you on schedule?'

Uraga repeated the question to the admiral. Togo consulted his charts. He looked at his watch and nodded yes. Uraga signalled the radio operator to reply.

A longer transmission clicked in. 'To Admiral Togo. Russian sailors in Port Arthur on liberty. Officers aboard flagship *Czarevitch* at concert. Positions of battleships, cruisers unchanged. At 21:45 enemy anti-torpedo nets will be dropped. Pilot ships will rendezvous at harbour entrance and lead you through mine-fields. Two floating flares will indicate your safe passage.'

'Send this reply,' Togo said. 'Excellent work. Are enemy searchlights in place?'

Uraga repeated Shibata's response. 'Yes. We will wait last moment before shutting searchlights down. Dai Nippon banzai.'

At 10 p.m., while officers of the Russian fleet aboard the *Czarevitch* were listening to a navy band concert, a line of several small navy ships appeared off Port Arthur. The unexpected arrival was not unusual as the Russian fleet had been building for months. Since neither the czar's army nor navy was equipped with wireless, the officer of the day flashed a request for identification to the incoming ships.

Aboard each of Togo's torpedo-boats, Japanese captains

416

referred to a copy of the official Russian signal book supplied by Shibata, and identified themselves as Russian Torpedo Group Five reporting to Port Arthur as ordered.

'Flash signal, permission to enter granted,' the officer of the day said to his signalman. He cranked the field telephone but the line was dead. 'Runner,' the officer shouted.

An enlisted man came from the duty room buttoning his tunic.

'Report to Admiral Kostov or General Stossel that several unscheduled naval craft have properly identified themselves and are preparing to enter port!'

The runner pointed down the hill. 'The pilot boat is going out to meet the ships. The harbour master must know of their arrival.'

Actually the harbour master and his pilots had been compromised by Shibata's agents into leading the Japanese fleet through the mine-fields.

The officer hesitated, then said, 'There've been many rumours of an attack by the Japanese. You need the exercise! Make the report!'

The runner felt no need to hurry. He ambled down the gravel path, chatting up sentries along the way. Slowly it dawned on him that all communications along the entire defence system, from the lookout point on top of the hill to the port below, were out of order. He ran the remainder of the way to the flagships and reported.

Admiral Kostov and General Stossel hurried to head-quarters. German nobles from the Baltic state of Estonia, whose families boasted generations of professional soldiers, they recognized trouble. It was confirmed by a loud explosion.

'A mine,' Stossel said. 'I know the sound.'

Two more detonations sounded closer.

'Those weren't mines!' Kostov banged the chart table and smiled. 'If the Japanese have got into the port, we're ready!

Every searchlight from every ship is mounted on the slopes of the hills overlooking the harbour. Let the little yellow bastards come! When the lights go on, our artillerymen will wipe them out! It'll be like shooting ducks on a pond!'

Seven Japanese torpedo-boats had followed the Russian pilot boat through the mine-field guarding the approaches to Port Arthur. As they drew parallel to the breakwater, a following sea drove boat number five forward. It would have crashed into the rear of boat four had not the captain veered off course, into a mine. The explosion disintegrated boat five.

The blast's concussion sprang the hull of boat six and it began to sink. Rather than block the channel for the rest of the squadron, the captain of boat six ordered full speed ahead. The vibrations were shaking the craft apart but he held course until he passed the two floating flares marking the end of the mine-field. He swerved to the left with the engine's last burst of power, the bow went underwater and the crew leapt overboard.

Uraga relayed the wireless messages to Admiral Togo. 'The attack has begun! Boats five and six lost in the mine-field! Enemy torpedo nets are down! Two torpedoes struck the *Czarevitch* amidship! The battleship *Retzvison* and heavy cruiser *Pallada* have taken hits!'

'Silence on the quarterdeck,' Togo ordered. 'We are about to pass the channel flares. Prepare for a 90 degree turn to starboard at flank speed!'

Bells rang, orders were shouted and the flagship's captain called, 'Prepare to come about!'

'Gun captains, prepare to fire on my command,' Togo ordered.

'Gun crews ready,' the captain said.

'Execute the starboard turn,' Togo ordered. 'Squadron, form battle line behind flagship!'

As the big ship heeled into the turn, Togo watched the

gun flashes from the Russian ships caught at anchor inside the harbour. Only a few of their heavy weapons were in action and none had yet found the range.

'Gun captains, fire your assigned targets,' Togo ordered, and the big guns aboard the flagship roared. Fiery muzzle blasts silhouetted the ships.

Togo glanced behind at his squadron following him into Kostov's trap. Shibata had better stop those searchlights, he thought. With the mine-field at our backs and the artillery looking down our throats, we will pay dearly if he fails.

At Russian military headquarters, General Stossel received his first battle report. He handed the message to Admiral Kostov. 'The *Czarevitch* and *Retzvison* are both hit and listing badly,' the general said. 'The cruiser *Pallada* has been run aground to stop her from sinking, I suggest my artillery commence firing.'

Kostov looked out the window. 'Wait one more minute. The Japanese ships will be trapped in the harbour or caught in the narrow lane between mine-fields. We'll destroy them!'

Stossel pointed out the window. 'I count fourteen of our ships on fire. Your fleet will be wiped out in another few minutes.'

'But we're in our home port and can make repairs. The Japanese will be stranded and die out there in the freezing waters.' Kostov turned to the duty officer. 'Give the signal!'

A bright red rocket whooshed into the air. As it reached the apex of its arch, hundreds of powerful searchlights around the port were switched on. For a moment everything was frozen in harsh white light.

Hidden on the side of a hill, Akichi Shibata thrilled at the sight of Togo's squadron and the Rising Sun flag with its sixteen rays fluttering in the wind. He placed both hands on the plunger of the electrical detonator and jammed down hard. The squat stone building housing Port Arthur's power station erupted in a massive pyrotechnic display. The searchlights on the hills overlooking Port Arthur faded before the first Russian artillery piece could be ranged on the Japanese fleet.

The destruction of the power station was the signal for fires to be lit by Shibata's agents. Those fires acted as aiming stakes for Togo's gunnery officers. They consulted the detailed charts supplied by Shibata's agents and proceeded to reduce the port's defensive positions to rubble.

At 2 a.m. Togo turned to Uraga. 'Give the order to withdraw! I want everyone out of the harbour by daylight!'

It was 8 a.m. before the dense black smoke over Port Arthur cleared and the damage inflicted was assessed.

'Twenty-one enemy ships sunk or grounded,' Uraga repeated in a loud voice. 'Thirteen more damaged or on fire.'

'I require an evaluation of the Russian harbour fortifications,' Togo said.

Uraga relayed the message to the wireless operator below, and they waited.

'There is another signal from shore coming in,' Uraga said. He slammed his hands over the earphones.

Everyone on the quarterdeck watched Uraga. He scribbled quickly on a scrap of paper and looked up, his face aglow. He bowed to Admiral Togo. 'Sir, General Shibata has relayed a message from his agents in Vladivostok. The Russian Admiral Makarov was killed aboard his flagship in an encounter with our Northern Squadron. The Russian ships have returned to Vladivostok in confusion and are blocked in by our mines and ships. There is a second report from the escorts guarding our troopships on the way to the landing at the Yalu river. They trapped and disabled a Russian troopship and its escort. The enemy ships were beached and abandoned on the Korean coast.'

Togo clasped his hands behind his back. 'The destruction of that troopship and her escort will alert the Russians to our imminent landing at the mouth of the Yalu. But it will not help them. Without sea power, Russia has lost the war!' He surveyed the broken ships in the harbour, the columns of black smoke rising above Port Arthur. He bowed his head, closed his eyes and prayed that his ancestors could see the triumph of the Japanese navy. 'Uraga,' he said, 'send this message to his imperial majesty, Emperor of Japan! Mission accomplished. Notify the chiefs of staff at Hiroshima. Japan rules the eastern seas. Then you are free to order troopships and barges for the land assault on Port Arthur.'

Admiral Kostov's face was ghostly white. He dropped the damage and casualty report onto the chart table and looked to General Stossel. 'This is impossible. My fleets here and at Vladivostok have been destroyed or blockaded.' The admiral shook his head. 'I do not understand,' he whispered.

'We used cheap Oriental labour to build our gun emplacements, lay our mine-fields and place your search-lights,' Stossel said. 'There were obviously Japanese spies and saboteurs among the workers we employed.'

Kostov did not respond. He turned and marched into his office.

A short time later the crack of a revolver reverberated throughout headquarters. A clerk ran to the door of Kostov's office and threw it open. 'The admiral is dead,' he cried.

Stossel watched his colleague's body carried out. Then he returned to the chart table and gathered his staff around. 'The Japanese have defeated our navy, but if they want Port Arthur they must come to us! We have 55,000 well-trained soldiers in this city! The enemy must take it from the land side and we'll be waiting! I want existing gun positions reinforced. Every cannon that can be salvaged from the damaged ships should be brought ashore and put into defensive position! I have enough weapons, ammunition and food to last ten years!' He slammed the table with his fist. 'Gentlemen, we fight!' He pointed to his personnel officer. 'The first order of the day is to expel every slant-eyed son of a bitch from Port Arthur!' He pointed to his engineering officer. 'Dig and refortify all positions! I want our trenches so deep and so well-placed that only direct hits will take out our guns or our men!'

'Sir, it is February,' the engineering officer said. 'The ground is frozen to a depth of five feet.'

'Use dynamite! Scavenge every damaged ship of its coal and defrost the ground! But dig! When the Japanese come I will cover the approaches to this city with their dead!'

Chapter 47

Port Arthur, November 1904

Nine long months had passed. It was winter again and the land war in Manchuria and Port Arthur dragged on.

'Did Noriko write you about my family?' Uraga asked.

Hiroki slapped his brother's shoulder. 'I had hoped to hear about home from you. It has been almost a year since I last saw the family, and two months since mail was delivered to us in Manchuria.'

'There are only three things that enter Port Arthur – ammunition, food and replacements. We have not had mail for nine weeks.' Uraga led his brother into a tent. 'This is my rear-area home. I go forward every other night to observe the enemy positions.'

'When we heard in Manchuria that Togo's surprise attack had been so successful, we thought Port Arthur would fall in a few weeks,' Hiroki said. 'But it has been almost a year.'

A sleepy-eyed major raised his head from under a pile of blankets. 'General Honjo predicted six months to defeat the Russians, but he forgot to tell General Stossel.'

'This is Mini, from army intelligence,' Uraga said to Hiroki. 'We work together.'

'Short for Minobe,' the major said. He wrapped a blanket around his shoulders and sat up. 'I think we will not take General Stossel's position before spring.'

'I thought you outnumber the Russians,' Hiroki said.

'We do, but Stossel is smart, and he has good troops who are well dug in. His artillery is so expertly concealed behind the hills, we cannot knock them out. There is no room for manoeuvre. The largest flat area is only seven hundred yards wide. Every attack has to be a direct frontal assault.'

'The Russians have no lack of ammunition or food,' Uraga said. 'They can blanket all avenues of attack. The troops that make it through the artillery and mortar barrages are cut down by machine guns.'

'Our army has taken 19,000 wounded and 8,500 killed, with nothing to show for it,' Minobe said.

'Possibly my aerial observation unit can help,' Hiroki said. 'We were hardly used in Korea and Manchuria because the battle lines were too fluid for the use of balloons. I was a liaison officer with the Korean Special Forces. After our troops swept the Russians into Manchuria, I was assigned to army field intelligence on the drive to Mukden. We know the Russian battle plans for Mukden, but cannot get there.'

'I thought Honjo's spy network was supposed to have everything tied up like a birthday present for our army,' Minobe said.

'It takes infantry to win a war,' Hiroki said. 'The Russians have extended our lines of supply and communication by fighting a withdrawal in stages to the northern capital. They have some good soldiers and able officers, although we are better.'

'In what way?' Minobe asked.

'Discipline, sanitation and training. The Russian units are inconsistent. Some are well trained. But others are conscripts taken directly from their homes, given a rifle and instructed on the line. They outnumber us, but we outflank them and they withdraw. Their abandoned bivouac areas smell like Chinese pigpens.' Hiroki held his nose. 'We thanked the gods for the Manchurian winter in which human waste freezes. Our soldiers say that if the Russians had the wind behind them, they would win the war for certain.' He smiled. 'At least here in Port Arthur with a siege in progress and stable battle lines, I may get airborne.'

'General Nogi wants us to take you into the trenches tonight and show you what is happening on our side from the ground,' Uraga said. 'There is an assault at 1 a.m. and another at 5 a.m.'

After dark, Hiroki followed Uraga and Minobe – through a valley, up a slope and into a shallow winding trench. The familiar sounds of friendly artillery and mortars over their heads was interspersed with the thin crack of rifle fire ahead and the crump of enemy mortars landing on the reverse slope. The glare of brilliant arching flares, which disappeared behind the crest of the hill, outlined the barbed wire where machine guns hammered a background to the deadly scene.

'Stop here,' Uraga said. 'Listen to that battery of enemy mortars firing.'

Hiroki listened to the gentle thumping sound of the smooth-bore high-angle weapons and realized Uraga was counting. 'Seven, eight, nine, duck!' Several explosions boomed on the slope above them and Uraga held Hiroki's head down in the trench. A deadly sizzle of shrapnel cut the air.

Then Uraga pulled Hiroki up. The three hurried through the trench, which became shallower as they went over the skyline.

Uraga talked as they trotted. 'This area is blanketed by that platoon of enemy mortars. When you hear them fire, you have until the count of ten before the shells hit.'

Hiroki puffed as he worked his arms and legs up the steep hill. He heard enemy mortars, ducked and shouted out, 'Incoming!' But Uraga and Minobe were sprinting ahead. Feeling foolish, Hiroki leapt forward after them, realizing he had forgotten to count. He churned his legs to keep his brother and Minobe in sight. When they dived, he dropped full length onto the frozen earth. These explosions were closer and the ground shook under his belly.

'Keep a tight arse,' Hiroki whispered to himself. 'Do not embarrass yourself on the first night in a trench.'

'Stay down and crawl,' Uraga shouted. They crept forward over open ground that suddenly sloped down, and slid into a trench ten feet deep.

Hiroki's eyes grew accustomed to the eerie light and the shadows cast by overhead flares. Snipers and artillery observers stared out into the night from the firing steps. Inside the trench, fighting bunkers with firing slits had been dug into the dirt walls. Opposite were bunkers where the men slept, cooked and waited.

Minobe had disappeared and Uraga led Hiroki to a bunker. 'It is big enough for two to sleep. Mini will wake us in time to see the 5 a.m. assault. The 1 a.m. attack has no chance of succeeding.'

'Then why do it?'

'A diversion. I do not believe the 5 a.m. mission will succeed either, but this is a war.' Uraga shrugged, and crawled into the bunker.

Hiroki followed, into a dark, damp hole so narrow their shoulders touched when they lay down and their booted feet stuck outside. Within moments he heard his brother snoring. Hiroki ran his hand up the dirt wall at his side and touched the rough bark of the tree trunks supporting the sandbag roof. Shells landed nearby and dirt fell into his eyes. He brushed at his face, then pulled his hat over it. He listened to his own breathing, his brother's snoring and the sounds of war outside.

Hiroki dreamt he was sliding down a long, dark, mouldy tunnel, being dragged through the dirt by his feet. He awoke and tried to sit up but bumped his head on the log roof. Uraga was pulling him out of the bunker by his legs.

Minobe handed Hiroki a tin cup of steaming hot tea. 'Drink it fast. The 5 a.m. assault on Rice Cake Hill begins shortly.'

Again Hiroki followed the two men, this time into trenches leading down the hill towards the enemy lines five hundred yards away. They fell in with the attacking force moving into position, men dressed in long coats with fur collars and polished cartridge belts. From their canvas leggings to their peaked caps and chin straps, they and their new rapid-firing Murato rifles could pass parade inspection, Hiroki thought.

'We stop here,' Minobe said. 'It is the best observation point.'

'Why is Rice Cake Hill so important?' Hiroki asked.

Minobe led them up onto the firing step and they peered over the parapet. He indicated a high mound-like hill rising up ahead of them. 'At 203 metres it is the highest point in this area. On top it is flat and extends back behind the Russian lines. It commands a full view of Port Arthur. When we take it, the Russians will surrender.'

'I still do not understand how you could defeat the Russian navy so quickly and be stymied by the czar's army,' Hiroki said.

'The first answer is that Togo caught their navy by surprise,' Minobe said. 'Secondly, the Russians seem to fight better on defence than on offence. Although they outnumbered our Mukden army, they chose a fighting withdrawal to wear our forces down. They defeated Napoleon by their brilliant defence and forced him to retreat through the Russian winter. Thirdly,' Minobe wagged his finger in the air and shook his head, 'do not believe everything you read in the Japanese newspapers. Your brother is in naval intelligence. He can tell you.'

'Some Russian naval officers are incompetent cowards and others quite brave,' Uraga said. 'I can give you a good example. One of their captains noticed that our ships always took the same route outside Port Arthur's harbour and saw a way to trap our morning patrol. He planned to lay mines across our path during the night,

427

but a senior captain aboard the sister mine-laying ship *Yenisei* wanted the glory. The senior captain pulled rank and took the *Yenisei* out. Then he drank too much, ran up onto his own mines and sank his ship. The cruiser *Bojarin* went out to rescue the *Yenisei*'s crew. It was a brave thing to do since our forces were alerted. Togo signalled the *Bojarin* we would not interfere, but the Russian cruiser hit another mine. That crew abandoned ship. There were not enough lifeboats so a destroyer was called to aid in the rescue. Although the *Bojarin* was burning and listing badly, the ship had not sunk. Her captain ordered the destroyer's captain to sink the *Bojarin*, and the destroyer fired two torpedoes. The first ran true and the cruiser went down like a rock. But the second torpedo jammed in its tube. The fuse burnt down and it exploded, sinking the destroyer. We heard all this from the captains of the cruiser, the destroyer and the mine-layer, all of whom we rescued.' Uraga's face became grim as he continued the story. 'We were so overconfident that twenty-four hours later we took the same route on morning patrol. The Russian captain who originally thought of the mine-laying plan had defied orders, come out just before daylight in a heavy fog, and dropped fifty mines along our usual route. Togo was almost killed aboard the *Hatsuse*. The battleship *Yashima* went to the rescue, hit a mine and sank. Our band played the national anthem and I saw the Emperor's picture carried off the *Hatsuse* before it went down. You will not read about that because the Japanese press is forbidden to print bad news and the foreign press is not allowed near the battle zone.'

'Sounds like we have our own incompetents,' Hiroki said. He heard thumping sounds in the trench below and saw men jumping up and down. 'What is that about?'

'The non-commissioned officers are listening to detect noisy equipment.'

'Fix bayonets!' an officer called.

The hiss of long, thin, steel blades sliding out of scabbards sent a chill through Hiroki. 'What about artillery preparation?'

'We hope to surprise the enemy without it,' Minobe said. 'They will not expect an attack just before dawn. Our troops have no intention of coming back across no-man's-land in broad daylight until they have taken Rice Cake Hill.'

From the trench below, the first regiment of General Nogi's Third Army scrambled up the ladders and over the parapets. One thousand five hundred men formed into fifteen companies. They closed ranks shoulder to shoulder and marched forward, wading through the waist-high millet field into the morning mist. At one hundred yards the flag bearers and officers leading the attack were swallowed up by the ground fog. Hiroki watched the troops walk unflinching into the white mist and disappear.

Uraga kept an eye on his watch. 'At 120 paces a minute the lead unit should reach the Russian barbed wire right . . . now!'

Hiroki jumped at the distant crack of rifle fire.

'We are doing well,' Minobe said. 'Those shots are from Russian scouts. Our men must be within three hundred yards of Rice Cake's main trench line.'

'The sun will be into this valley in a few minutes,' Hiroki said. 'Our men will be exposed.'

'So will theirs,' Uraga said. 'They have their trenches at the base of Rice Cake on flat ground. They stand up and fire over the parapet.'

Black dirt and debris were blasted up into the morning light above the ground fog. 'Our men have reached the Russian mine-fields,' Minobe said. 'That is the closest we have ever reached. Maybe there is a chance.'

'Shhh! Listen,' Uraga said.

There was a rumble of thunder from the direction of Port Arthur. Even with the sun illuminating the sky, there seemed to be lightning flashes behind the hills. The thunder continued and Hiroki saw his brother and Minobe exchange worried glances.

'Russian guns,' Uraga said. 'They have set up a killing ground with an artillery time fire.'

Although the explosions were three hundred yards away, the ground under Hiroki's feet shook. The noise deafened him. He pulled Uraga and Minobe down below the parapet. Shrapnel whipped the air over their heads. Dirt, metal, bits of bone and flesh rained down on them as they huddled on the fighting step.

It was several minutes before they could rise up to look. The fog was gone, the day clear and crisp. Everything had been silenced by the guns. Fires smouldered in the centre of blackened shell holes in no-man's-land. A handful of shellshocked Japanese soldiers wandered aimlessly in the field.

'Where is the First Battalion?' Hiroki asked.

'They reached within a hundred and fifty yards,' Uraga said.

'But where are they?'

As if in response, three groups of Japanese infantry rose from the ground, those lead units who had been ahead of the murderous barrage. Two companies formed up in full view of the enemy. They bunched together as they had been trained in the German infantry tactic of Mass and Momentum, and charged the enemy trenches. But the third company turned and came back towards the Japanese line.

'What are the Russians rolling out of their trenches?' Hiroki shouted.

'Those are twenty-pound balls of gun cotton stuffed with explosives,' Uraga said.

They watched several of the deadly cotton balls explode into sheets of flame among the tightly packed Japanese troops. Uniforms caught fire and soldiers ran blindly into mine-fields or barbed wire. The remainder continued the attack, but enemy machine guns cut down every man. Not one reached within fifty yards of the Russian trenches.

Two Vickers machine guns on either side of Hiroki began firing and he flinched. 'They are shooting at our men coming back to the trenches,' he shouted. 'Stop! You are killing our own men!'

Uraga pushed his brother off the firing step into the trench below.

Hiroki looked up and screamed, 'Are you crazy? Those men are not cowards! Everyone in the First Battalion, dead or alive, deserves a medal!'

'Our battle cry is victory or death! There is no turning back!'

Chapter 48

1 December 1904

In the imperial palace a grim-faced Mung addressed the Privy Council. 'Marquis Inei's financial report shows us that Japan is again close to bankruptcy!' He nodded at Shimatzu. 'My son ceased raising money abroad after hearing of our naval victories in Port Arthur and Vladivostok. He and many of us were confident the war would be won in six months.' Mung leaned forward and fixed Honjo with a cold, hard stare. 'The chief of Japan's National Intelligence Service did make that claim?'

Honjo's face and shaven skull coloured an angry red. 'It is as you say, Tairo.' He hated himself for having boasted, and Shibata more so for not having fulfilled his promise. 'I accept full responsibility and will do my duty.'

'Seppuku is not the answer,' Mung snapped. He needed results and an angry Honjo was the quickest way to achieve that. He purposely addressed the most feared man in the empire as if he was a young lieutenant. 'I want you and your agents to accomplish what you have promised! The Russians were supposed to be left dangling at the end of a six-thousand-mile, single-track rail-line which your men pledged to cut! Latest reports indicate the rail-line continues to function! General Kuropatkin in Mukden will have half a million men by spring, twice our military strength! Unless we can take Port Arthur and transport General Nogi's Third Imperial Army to Manchuria, we have lost the land war! In April the larger Russian army will break out of Mukden and push our troops back to the Yalu! Kuropatkin will then sweep through Korea!' Mung pointed down at Honjo. 'Tell Lieutenant General

Akichi Shibata to leave his warm whorehouse and get to work!'

Honjo trembled with fury and Iga Sasaki attempted to direct attention from him. 'Tairo, we can reduce the pressure on our treasury by seeking international loans from the Europeans.'

The lines on either side of Mung's sharp cheekbones deepened. His jaw muscles danced and he glared at Sasaki. 'Mr Prime Minister, since the stalemate on the battlefields around Mukden and in Port Arthur, neither the Americans nor Europeans are willing to advance us funds! Every request for a loan has been denied! Other nations have spies. They know that if Russia can hold Port Arthur until spring, Japan will lose the war. And by next summer the czar's soldiers would be sitting in Pusan one hundred miles from the Japanese coast. We must win the battles of Port Arthur and Mukden quickly, and make peace. Only then will the Occidental bankers advance us loans!'

'We can defeat Russia!' Sasaki said. 'We can topple the czar!'

Mung's voice was laden with contempt. 'Does the prime minister intend to march our troops all the way across the frozen wastes of Manchuria, Mongolia and Siberia to St Petersburg and Moscow, when we cannot even defeat the Russians at Port Arthur? Mr Sasaki, you are . . . ' He hesitated.

Everyone in the room thought Tairo was about to label the head of state a fool, but Mung finished his sentence with, ' . . . you are mistaken, Mr Prime Minister.' There was an audible sigh of relief from members of the Privy Council.

'My son Shimatzu will institute and promote a new savings plan throughout the empire to raise capital,' Mung said. 'It will be directed at the common people, with bank depositories in every post office, railway station and Japanese ship. The Emperor has agreed to help publicize this campaign. In addition, Marquis Inei will float a special war bond issue. I command the members of this council and your families to see the bonds are bought out within a week! That is an order from Tairo! And we shall float other bonds after that.' Mung turned to Honjo. 'Shake your intelligence chief in Manchuria until his teeth rattle! Russian reinforcements must stop reaching Mukden! I am sending a no-second-thought order to General Nogi. Take Port Arthur before March!'

Port Arthur, 23 December 1904
'You two must come up in the balloon with me,' Hiroki said. 'I need you to complete my plan to take Rice Cake Hill.'

'I joined the navy to fish, not fly with the birds.' Uraga laughed. 'What you propose is against the laws of nature.'

'I am afraid of height,' Minobe said.

'Be serious,' Hiroki said. 'Since Tairo sent the order to take Port Arthur, the approaches to Hill 203 are painted red with Japanese blood.'

'If you think I am joking about fear of height, you are wrong,' Minobe said.

'It is a lot safer up there than marching into the Russian guns. I need your knowledge of infantry tactics and expertise in trench warfare.'

'So he will go,' Uraga said. 'But why do you want a naval officer like me up there?'

'Because the battleships and cruisers are included in my plan to capture that hill.'

'You are mad,' Uraga said.

'No, your brother is brilliant,' Minobe said. 'When the Russians see Togo's fleet sail over the mountain, into the barbed wire and through the mine-fields, they will give up their vodka, throw down their weapons and surrender.'

'Not funny,' Hiroki said. 'You two are joking and

434

men are dying. Help me, and I promise Hill 203 will fall.'

'We have to joke,' Uraga said. 'Otherwise we would be mad. When do we fly?'

At 5 a.m., as cooking fires were being lit in the trenches, Uraga and Minobe warily approached the large, oblong observation balloon.

'It looks like a schooner without a cabin or masts,' Minobe said.

Hiroki came up behind the two and slipped in between them. He hooked his arms in theirs and dragged them towards the hovering craft. 'When they first designed this model it was thought a keel was necessary, as on a sailing ship, to stabilize it in the air,' Hiroki said. 'Newer models are shaped like cigars and have rigid frames. This is a giant silk envelope sixty feet long filled with hydrogen gas.' He opened the door in the large wicker basket and ushered the reluctant pair in. He turned around and shouted, 'Cast off the ground lines and let the tether lines out to fifteen hundred feet!'

The men around the balloon jumped to the command.

'How long before we take off?' Minobe asked.

'We are already on our way up,' Hiroki said.

Minobe looked over the side and groaned. He slipped to the bottom of the gondola.

'I guess he really is afraid of height,' Uraga said. 'How will we get down again?'

Hiroki touched two strings leading up the sides of the balloon. 'I loosen these to open flaps on top of the balloon until there is negative buoyancy. If I change my mind, I drop some of the sandbags tied on the outside of the gondola and we rise again.'

There was a hard bump when the balloon reached the end of its tether ropes. The gondola swung back and forth.

'It is time to pray,' Minobe cried.

'The gondola will stabilize itself in a minute,' Hiroki said. 'Now stand up and look!' He and Uraga grabbed Minobe under the arms and pulled him up until he peeked over the side.

'Are you all right?' Hiroki asked.

Minobe did not respond. He gazed down in wonder for several moments. 'I would never have believed it,' he whispered. 'I can see everything. The barbed wire, the mine-fields. And I can look right down into their trenches.' He shook off Hiroki's hand and used his binoculars. 'I can see everything on top of Hill 203. Why didn't you tell me it is like this!' He began scribbling notes.

'How can you use the navy from up here?' Uraga asked.

Hiroki pointed to the twenty-three Japanese ships patrolling offshore. 'The range of the big guns aboard the battleships and cruisers is six miles. Beyond those hills,' he pointed again, 'they would be within four miles of Rice Cake and out of sight and range of Russian artillery.'

'But how do I tell them where and when to shoot if I cannot see them either?'

Hiroki touched a telephone attached to the side of the gondola. 'The wire is wrapped around one of the tether lines and a wireless radio operator on the ground is waiting to relay your messages to Admiral Togo's flagship. Try it.'

Uraga looked down at the battlefield, then out at Togo's fleet. He gaped at his brother. 'You may have found the key to taking Port Arthur! If I can direct our navy guns, our firepower will be tripled!' He picked up the telephone but heard nothing. 'Does this thing work?'

Hiroki cranked the handle and Uraga heard a voice say, 'Standing by to relay orders to Fire Control aboard the flagship *Asahi*.'

Uraga looked at his brother with respect. He spoke into the mouthpiece. 'Stand by for coordinates and a two-round fire mission for range.' He whipped out a field map, oriented himself with familiar landmarks and barked his orders.

Five minutes later two shells exploded on top of Rice Cake Hill.

Uraga shouted into the telephone, 'Correction,' and gave new coordinates.

Three minutes later two more shells landed.

'I have that Russian artillery battery bracketed,' Uraga cried. 'I can wipe them out!'

'Stop jumping,' Minobe said. 'Calm down. Give me that telephone and let me blow up some machine gun bunkers.'

'Not yet,' Hiroki said. 'I want the naval barrage to be a surprise combined with a massive infantry attack. I have other ideas for both of you to evaluate before I present this plan to the general's staff.'

'General Nogi, sir,' Hiroki said. 'Commander Ishikawa, Major Minobe and I have developed a strategy to take Hill 203.'

'A request by three senior intelligence officers is taken seriously,' Nogi said. 'My staff, as well as Admiral Togo and his staff, await your plan. Do not waste our time.'

Hiroki stepped forward and tapped a large wall map of Port Arthur with a wooden pointer. 'The Russians have built bunkers, trenches, redoubts and man traps. They have skilfully placed mines, barbed wire, artillery and machine guns in defence of the city. Their strong point is Rice Cake Hill. That hill is also a major fault in General Stossel's plan because no second line of defence exists behind it. When it falls, Port Arthur will surrender.'

Hiroki saw impatience on the faces of the senior officers. He had not said anything they did not already know. 'Gentlemen, please look at these images taken from a height of one thousand feet.' He distributed photographs. 'You can see all the emplacements at the base of Hill 203. Four thousand men of the Fifth Siberian Rifles have been in those positions for two weeks. The normal tour of duty is three weeks. This is the strategy we bring you. Begin a six-day-long harassment of the enemy with artillery, mortars and infantry probes. Keep them awake every possible moment until the day before they are to be relieved, which falls on January first. I believe the Russians are too disciplined to be caught at a New Year's Eve celebration, but they will be exhausted.'

'The Fifth Siberian Rifles are a crack unit,' Nogi said. 'They never retreat. They have killed a thousand of my men in the last two weeks.'

'On the day we attack, all our artillery should be combined with the navy's heavy guns to blast them out of their holes,' Hiroki said. He stepped back and handed the pointer to Uraga.

'For several days now I have been ranging our naval guns on Hill 203,' Uraga said. 'From the observation balloon I can zero in three times the firepower previously employed on any target. In addition, the biggest guns of our battle-ships can be utilized to blast paths through the mine-fields protecting the enemy trenches at the base of Rice Cake.' He bowed and handed the pointer to Minobe.

'Please look carefully at the photographs,' Minobe said. 'Notice that the Russian trenches are very narrow. Their stretcher bearers have difficulty managing the twists and turns. Once they start moving wounded back, it is impossible for reserves to move up. A heavy bombardment of the trench line just before our infantry attack will send a stream of wounded to the rear. The narrow trenches will prevent their reserves from reinforcing the forward positions. If they should try to step outside the trenches, they will be cut down by our artillery or our snipers. In addition, the Russian commander who selected his position at the base of Hill 203 has erred. His machine guns cannot depress enough to hit our men if they crawl through the millet field in two areas.'

'No Japanese soldier crawls into battle,' Nogi snapped. 'We march or run to a fight, but never crawl! That would be damaging to morale!'

'Sir,' Hiroki said, 'I respectfully request that we abandon the German attack concept of Mass and Momentum. Crowding soldiers together and charging into modern cannon and machine gun fire is wasteful. I suggest our scouts and snipers should crawl through the millet field to approach the enemy trenches. The main attack force will follow. Instead of marching shoulder to shoulder, they should move forward in ranks ten feet apart, each man two arms' length from the men on either side. Such a strategy would prevent several men from being killed by one bullet, one mine or one artillery shell. Enemy machine gunners and riflemen would have to aim rather than simply point at our massed formations. It would reduce casualties.'

'Crawling is not permissible,' Nogi declared. 'It would dilute a soldier's courage and make his comrades think of shirking their duty! I will allow crouching by scouts and snipers only. This new formation of attacking infantry sounds logical, but must be observed and evaluated in training.'

'My plan calls for a week of heavy bombardment before we attack,' Hiroki said. 'That will give our troops time to train.'

Nogi and Togo looked at each other and nodded, indicating Hiroki should continue. For three hours he, Uraga and Minobe detailed their plans and answered questions. The senior officers added their experience to the new strategy. At the conclusion of the meeting, orders were given to the Third Imperial Army to begin practising the new infantry formation.

From the balloon at nine thousand feet, Hiroki, Uraga and

Minobe directed the imperial artillery and mortars to break down the enemy trenches. The weapons pounded the Fifth Siberian Rifle regiment that defended Rice Cake Hill. Uraga zeroed in the big guns of Togo's battleships and cruisers on the enemy artillery in Port Arthur. While, below, Nogi scoured his army for coal miners and formed a Mole Unit to tunnel under the enemy mine-fields.

1 January 1905, 5.20 a.m.
The first rays of the sun had touched the mountain-top and sliced into the valley below. Uraga, Minobe and Hiroki swayed gently in the gondola fifteen hundred feet above the battlefield.

'It is an awesome sight,' Minobe said. 'Twenty thousand men down there waiting to attack.'

'If we fail this time, Nogi will be forced to withdraw the army because we are low on ammunition,' Uraga said.

'Then put all the guns on target,' Hiroki said. 'Every round must count!'

'I do not have a personal weapon,' Minobe said. 'I worry about what would happen if the Russians counterattacked and pulled us down.'

'There is nothing to fear,' Hiroki said. 'We would cut the ropes and float to wherever the wind takes us.' He looked over the side and cried out, 'The scouts and snipers are moving!'

The men below ran crouched over through the waist-high millet field and took up positions just ahead of the Mole Unit. Three lines of soldiers trotted after the scouts and filed into the tunnels.

A thousand men climbed over the parapets and stood in line abreast, both arms out at right angles, finger tip to finger tip. They fixed bayonets, held their rifles at short guard and walked forward. Another thousand men came out of the trenches, formed up and moved forward. And another and another.

'They are magnificent,' Hiroki cried. 'We cannot fail them! Start the barrage on the enemy trenches!'

Uraga and Minobe cranked their telephones and gave their orders. Seconds later, low rumbling sounds came from the sea and from the army's artillery positions behind the mountains. Below, Hiroki saw the muzzle flash of mortars. The lines of men continued coming out of the trenches.

The sun angled down into the valley as shells fell on the Russian trench line. The Japanese infantry moved forward and men were cut down by mortars bursting in their midst, but the extended formation reduced the number of casualties. The forward pace continued.

A bugle sounded on the battlefield. The imperial infantrymen raised their rifles and trotted forward into the attack, the First Battalion with the honour of leading the charge. Hiroki saw individual soldiers race ahead of their units and dive onto barbed wire. Their comrades ran over them into the mine-fields, following shell holes to avoid mines. Many were caught by trip wires and blown up. Where one fell, three followed.

'Mini,' Hiroki shouted, 'two new machine gun emplacements on the right flank! They are cutting our First Battalion to pieces!'

'They were well hidden until now.' Minobe called the coordinates into the telephone, then picked up his binoculars. 'I have direct hits on both guns but they continue to fire. They must be sheltered in concrete bunkers. Artillery cannot do the job.'

'What are the coordinates?' Uraga asked. 'The battleships have armour-piercing shells.'

Two minutes later the three men watched sixteen-inch naval shells explode around the machine gun bunkers. When the smoke cleared, the guns were silent.

Shells began to slam into the millet field, cutting down the advancing troops. 'Russian artillery,' Hiroki shouted. 'Silence them!'

Uraga and Minobe each worked with a telephone and a list of prearranged coordinates. From the time Hiroki gave the order, only eleven minutes elapsed before all the big Russian guns protecting Rice Cake Hill were silenced.

Hiroki cranked the telephone with a direct line to headquarters. 'General Nogi, sir, it is time for the final assault!'

'They are on their way,' Nogi said.

More men climbed out of the trenches and formed spaced lines. They marched forward with fixed bayonets.

'Uraga, Mini,' Hiroki shouted, 'you have time for two more rounds on the main trench line! Then cease fire!' He untied the ropes to the vent flaps and the balloon descended. He tied the flaps down and dropped four sandbags. The balloon's descent stopped at six hundred feet above the battlefield.

The three men in the gondola watched shells blanket the Russian trenches. They heard the banzai war cry and saw their infantry charge. Sharpshooters of the Fifth Siberian Rifles traded fire with the scouts and snipers of the Third Imperial Army. More Russian machine guns opened fire. Japanese soldiers fell like scythed wheat, piled so high the enemy gunners held their fire until the following soldiers climbed over their dead. Hiroki saw Russian gunners pouring water on overheated, smoking gun barrels.

Then out of the ground came the Japanese Mole Unit and the soldiers hidden in the tunnels. They were the first to break into the Russian trenches, with knives, clubs and bare hands. The main body of Japanese infantry reached the trenches and smothered the defenders.

Minobe tugged at Hiroki's arm. 'General Nogi is on the telephone! He wants to know what the situation is!'

Hiroki took the receiver and spoke in a dead voice. 'General sir, our troops have taken the enemy's main trench line. The Fifth Siberian Rifles fought to the last man. Their supporting units have broken and are running. Rice Cake Hill has fallen. Port Arthur is yours.'

'What do you estimate our casualties?'

'More than 50 per cent.'

'You three will be decorated and promoted in rank,' Nogi said. 'Uraga, you are to report back to Admiral Togo. Hiroki and Colonel Minobe will come with me to Manchuria.'

'Thank you, sir,' Hiroki mumbled. His shaky legs would not hold him and he slipped to the floor of the gondola. He looked up at Uraga and Minobe with tear-filled eyes. 'I planned this to save lives. Did you see the slaughter?'

Chapter 49

The Imperial Palace, 3 January 1905

'Tairo has summoned all members of the Privy Council to hear an important announcement,' Admiral Takamora said.

'Gentlemen, word has reached us from Port Arthur that the city has fallen,' Mung said. 'The fortress is ours. We paid a high price for it.' He rested his shaking arm on his knee in order to read the report he held. 'Twenty thousand dead and 60,000 wounded. The enemy suffered 9,000 dead, 20,000 wounded and 26,000 captured officers and men. We took possession of 500 cannon, 35,000 rifles, 180 machine guns and a million rounds of ammunition. From Port Arthur's harbour we have taken four serviceable battle-ships, two cruisers and fifteen gunboats. The warehouses are stocked with food, clothing and field supplies for our army's use in Manchuria.' He waited for the members of the Privy Council to finish congratulating one another. Then he turned towards Takamora. 'The admiral will soon lead a fleet of troopships carrying the Fifth Imperial Army from Japan to join General Nogi's Third Imperial Army and our forces in Manchuria for the drive on Mukden.'

'Gentlemen,' Takamora said, 'the years have crept up on me unnoticed. I now prepare for my last mission in the service of his imperial majesty. Therefore I especially delight in leading you in this victory celebration. Banzai,' he shouted. 'Dai Nippon banzai! Long live a great Japan!'

As the others cheered, Honjo whispered to Sasaki, 'The strain on Tairo is beginning to show. It is the first time I have seen the Great Elder have to read a report and not have it memorized.'

'As much as I would like to see him go, he is the man most responsible for this victory,' Sasaki said.

A senior White Wolf agent entered the room and slipped Honjo a telegram. The general read it and approached the dais. He bowed and whispered to Mung. 'Tairo, this has come from an agent in St Petersburg. You may not wish to make it public.'

Mung adjusted his spectacles and read the telegram. With a frown, he invited Honjo up on the dais. Everyone in the reception room fell silent.

'I have criticized General Honjo publicly,' Mung said. 'Now I am pleased to praise his efficiency. I would rather the news be more pleasant but I must announce that we are threatened again.' He nodded to Honjo to proceed.

'My agents in St Petersburg have reported that upon hearing of the fall of Port Arthur, Czar Nicolas appointed Admiral Rodjestvensky in command of the Baltic fleet. That fifty-ship armada is ordered to sail from Russia and sink the Japanese navy, our merchant fleet, and bombard our coastal cities until we surrender.'

4 March 1905

Tokyo's postal employees had volunteered to sort and deliver the mail from Manchuria long after normal working hours. The capital's streets were alight. People stood outside their homes with lanterns in the cold rain. Wives and mothers moved down to their front gates to meet the mailmen.

Noriko saw the mailman turn into her street and prayed there would be a letter for her. She had not heard from Hiroki for the two months since Port Arthur fell. She watched the mailman leave the neighbour's house and approach empty-handed. She turned away so he would not see her tears as he passed. Hiroki would have written if he was alive, she thought.

'Marquessa? Marquessa Koin?'

Noriko whirled. Through her tears she saw the mailman holding out a fat envelope. She bowed. The mailman bowed. 'It is the thickest letter I have delivered today,' he said, repeating what he told many of the women.

'Pardon me for weeping,' Noriko said as she took the letter.

'Everyone who receives a letter weeps, and it makes me happy too,' the mailman said. 'When there is no letter, I weep.' He bowed again. 'Today we must all rejoice. Mukden has fallen. The land war is over.'

Noriko bowed again and hurried inside. There was no sound from the boys' room and she was pleased. 'I wish to be alone with my Hiroki,' she murmured, and sat near the hibachi. She touched the envelope to her lips and sniffed for his scent, then carefully opened it.

My dearest Noriko,
I miss you and the boys so much. Please tell Yaka's family I saw him three days ago and he is well. We promised each other to pass on this message because we still do not depend on the mail service. Three of your letters arrived at once. I put them in order and read them over and over. Mini did not receive mail so I read my letters to him. He painted your name in bold black letters on both sides of our balloon to honour you. The troops call us Noriko's Eyes.

In truth, our work is not so important as it was in Port Arthur. By the time we inflate our old gasbag, the enemy has fallen back. These Russian soldiers are not the same quality as those we fought in Port Arthur. Most are unwilling conscripts forced into seven years' service by the czar. Their miserly pay does not meet their families' needs at home. We have heard many in Russia are starving.

We surprised the Russian high command by ferrying the Third and Fifth Imperial Armies into Manchuria during February, and launching an attack on a seventy-mile front in sub-zero weather. Our sabotage units and secret agents did excellent work in the enemy rear. They cut communications and rail-lines, blew up mine-fields, and supplied us with accurate information on gun emplacements and troop deployment. The Russians made their first stand in fortified positions seventy miles south of Mukden.

Although outnumbered, we used new infantry formations and the wireless to coordinate with our big guns in night attacks. We forced the enemy back to the Sha-ho river, some thirty miles closer to Mukden. Again they took up defensive positions and outnumbered us by sixty thousand men. They brought in their renowned Cossack cavalry to raid our flanks. Mini and I were aloft at two thousand feet when we spotted the enemy horse. We had no artillery free at the time, so we reluctantly called in our cavalry. The Russians are better horsemen. We are better soldiers. The Cossacks made sabre charges but our cavalry dismounted and cut them to pieces with rifle-fire. The famed Cossacks fled! Our intelligence reports the Russian cavalry has registered eight hundred index finger casualties, which means they wounded themselves to avoid combat.

Our soldiers compete with each other to be first in battle. General Nogi's only son died leading the charge at the Sha-ho river. A junior officer took over for him, was also killed, and then an enlisted man led the assault until the enemy broke. Sometimes from above we count eight and ten Russians carrying one wounded man off the battlefield. Our men make every effort to continue the attack, even when wounded.

From the balloon I watched one of our regiments capture an enemy railhead. The Russians left twenty flatcars behind, but no steam engine. Our officers and men loaded their big guns, ammunition and supplies onto the flatcars. They harnessed themselves to the cars and pulled them fifteen miles in seven hours to outflank an enemy force five times their size. They offloaded the guns and bombarded the Russian division until it fled in panic towards Mukden. I believe that city will capitulate soon. In addition to disgruntled Russian conscripts in the ranks, there are many communist and socialist revolutionaries who encourage defection and surrender. We have taken fifteen thousand prisoners in the last two days.

My dearest, I regret I will not be here to see the fall of Mukden. Mini and I were directing artillery at an altitude of three thousand feet ten miles from Mukden. As the light faded, we began our descent. At five hundred feet two of our own artillery shells went through the balloon. We were lucky they did not explode, but we went down faster than usual. I broke a leg and Mini suffered a nosebleed. He claims your name on the balloon gave me the luck. By the time you receive this letter, I will be on my way home.

Noriko put the back of her hand to her mouth. 'Children,

children,' she called, sobbing as she hurried to their room. 'Your father is coming home!'

Honjo scanned several reports, then turned to Sasaki. 'We have captured Korea, Port Arthur and most of the mineral-rich areas of Manchuria. Mung is correct. It is time to seek peace with the czar.'

'But unless we receive a large indemnity from Russia, Japan could be bankrupt,' Sasaki said. 'The tremendous cost of this war is based on foreign loans.'

'My agents say that Mung secretly approached Theodore Roosevelt through William Whittefield and received confirmation that the American president is prepared to host a peace conference. Roosevelt has been Japan's most ardent supporter. He publicly praised our surprise attack on Port Arthur's naval base and the courage of our soldiers at Mukden.'

'The Russians are in no mood to negotiate. Admiral Rodjestvensky is leading an armada towards Japan.'

'I have given orders for Shibata to monitor the Baltic fleet and delay it,' Honjo said. 'Communists have already sabotaged their own battleship, the *Orel*, by putting metal filings in the engine's ball-bearings. That ship is out of action. In addition, Mung influenced the British to deny use of the Suez Canal to the Russians. It will take them an additional two months' travel around the Cape of Good Hope. Meanwhile Admiral Togo is training his crews, refitting his ships with the new high-explosive shells from Germany, and the Marconi wireless.'

'All that does not solve Japan's financial problem,' Sasaki said. 'If Togo does defeat the Baltic fleet, and if Roosevelt does hold a peace conference, all the Russians need do is stall and Japan will be mortgaged to the western bankers as Mung predicted.'

'That is why your plan to conquer Russia and depose the czar was thoughtless. Immediate wealth lies south, not north. Japan's fate is inextricably bound up with China's. We are geographically nearer, culturally closer and economically interdependent with China. We must begin to milk the Chinese cow as the Europeans have done for the last century.' Honjo leaned towards Sasaki. 'I recommend you send a secret envoy to Peking requesting amnesty for Field-Marshal Tso-lin, and sanctioning his appointment to the governorship of Fentien province. You might wish to use Akichi Shibata.'

Sasaki knew full well the suggestion was a command. He nodded his compliance.

'We own the warlord Tso-lin and his aides,' Honjo said. 'They are dependent on Shibata for opium.'

'Why should Peking agree to such a request?' Sasaki asked. 'It is obvious if they give in now, we shall demand more later.'

Honjo unfolded a map and pointed at Mukden. 'General Nogi has a quarter of a million battle-tested troops three hundred miles from Peking. If China does not agree to our sphere of influence in Fentien province now, we shall take it!'

'What if Togo is defeated at sea? Then our armies will be cut off in Korea and Manchuria.'

'That is in the hands of Akichi Shibata,' Honjo said. 'He is responsible to delay, demoralize and track the Russian fleet so Togo can spring the trap.'

Chapter 50

Formosa, April 1905

The chief of Japan's National Intelligence Service hid his anger at being manipulated into a chair that faced a sunlit window. His protégé had given a curt nod of the head rather than a respectful bow upon their meeting. *Japan needs Akichi Shibata now*, Honjo thought. *There will come a time when respect will be rendered.*

'You redeemed your good name in the battle for Mukden,' Honjo said. 'Our casualties were reduced because of your accurate information. The enemy surrendered sooner on account of your sabotage units.'

'I am pleased that my humble efforts have finally been recognized in Tokyo,' Shibata said, and poured rice wine for Honjo and himself. 'When this is over, I wish to return home for a vacation.'

'There is the matter of the Baltic fleet,' Honjo said, thinking that Shibata's presence in Tokyo would be a threat to his leadership. He opened his attaché case. 'General Kuropatkin sent the following message to the czar just before surrendering Mukden. *Only a decisive naval victory can bring a certain degree of honour to Russia and give us leverage in any negotiations with Japan.* Upon receiving that telegram, Czar Nicolas ordered Admiral Rodjestvensky to take the Baltic fleet into Japanese waters and destroy our . . . '

'It was then you assigned me the task of monitoring the Russian ships,' Shibata interrupted. 'I have filed at least one report on its progress every twenty-four hours.'

Honjo chose to ignore the rudeness. 'Where is the fleet now?'

'Madagascar. Your system of wireless operators at key points around the globe has kept us informed. The fleet stopped in Barcelona, Tangiers and Capetown. Their voyage is now fifteen thousand instead of seven thousand miles to reach Japan because the British closed the Suez Canal to them. The Hamburg-Amerika line was contracted to refuel the ships. I own at least one man in every fleet of coal-tenders that supplies the Russian armada. Immediately after servicing the warships, those men report to me and I to Admiral Togo's intelligence officer.'

'Is that where you spent the million yen? It was listed in your last report as a one-time payment to an unnamed informer.'

'No, the people aboard coal-tenders come much cheaper,' Shibata said. 'The million was used to purchase the fleet's course and destination.'

'From whom?' Honjo asked.

'From the czar's cousin, Charles. Togo can lie in wait for the Baltic fleet in the strait between Korea and Japan. Rodjestvensky's destination is Vladivostok.'

'If correct, the price was cheap,' Honjo said. 'Show it to me on the map.'

Shibata traced a course with his finger. 'They depart Madagascar in two days and sail across the Indian Ocean to Singapore.'

'Does Rodjestvensky plan to give his men shore leave there?'

'No. Communists and socialists are too active in the fleet. He fears mass desertions. His ships will refuel outside of port, then move into the South China and East China seas, past us here in Formosa and into the strait between Korea and Japan.'

'They have an alternative,' Honjo said. 'They could take the longer Pacific route to Vladivostok. Togo would be left waiting with our navy in the southern strait while they sailed north along our coast unopposed to bombard our cities.'

'No,' Shibata said. 'The last refuelling stop is Shanghai. I have paid the captains of the coaling ships to inform the Russians that the Chinese and British will not allow fuel to be sold to them in China. The Baltic fleet cannot carry enough coal to take the longer route to Vladivostok. Togo is to wait for Rodjestvensky in the strait!'

Honjo studied the map again. 'The strait is a hundred miles across. If Togo's fleet spreads itself from the Japanese coast to the Korean coast, the fifty-ship Russian armada might succeed in breaking through.'

'They have been reduced to forty-five ships,' Shibata said. 'One battleship was sabotaged at the outset. The crew of another got drunk, thought they were under torpedo-boat attack and began firing, sinking one of their own cruisers. Three more ships were damaged when the crews mutinied and Rodjestvensky turned his guns on them.'

'Togo's fleet will still be outnumbered, outweighed and outgunned.'

'Yes, but he has newer equipment and braver men. And he will know in advance if the enemy is taking the Korean side of the strait or the Tsu-shima side. That narrows the area to fifty miles. My spies aboard the Russian flagship will signal my fishing boats stationed along their route. The information will be relayed by wireless to me, and on to Togo. Tell our admiral he can expect the Russian navy sometime after mid-May.'

2 May 1905

'Is our navy prepared to meet the Russian fleet?' the Emperor asked Mung.

'Yes, sire. Admiral Togo and his staff exude extreme confidence.'

'Then why is there such a sombre mood among the people? I read it in the newspapers and feel it from my

452

staff. During the Korean and China campaigns the attitude was buoyant.'

'Your subjects were led to believe this would be a short war,' Mung said. 'The enormous casualties, food shortages and 30 per cent devaluation of the yen have made life difficult.'

'Is it still possible to make peace with Russia before our two navies meet?'

'I do not believe so. The American president calls the czar a foolish little dictator who should be put in his place. I have a message from Theodore Roosevelt via William Whittefield.'

'Is he prepared to initiate a peace conference?' the Emperor asked.

'Unofficially William has already suggested a conference in the president's name. The Russian ambassador's response was that the Japanese will drop to their knees and beg for peace when the Baltic fleet bombards Tokyo.'

'But everyone knows our navy is waiting for the Russians. Correspondents have been tracking and reporting the movements of the Baltic fleet to the world. Are the Russians blind?'

'Colour-blind, sire. I have come to accept Iyeasu Koin's premise that Europeans believe all non-whites are stupid cowards.'

'Then why do you trust Roosevelt?'

'He is an American,' Mung said. 'They are a different breed of Caucasian – a mongrel nation made up of the dregs of all societies, which has produced a hybrid people. Theodore Roosevelt epitomizes America. He is a fierce patriot and a fair man. He forced the state of California and six other western states to reverse their anti-Oriental laws forbidding Chinese and Japanese from attending public schools, owning land or conducting business.'

'How do you explain that Roosevelt compelled our navy to return three Russian ships, and his demand that we allow foreign newsmen into Mukden before the battle was over?'

'Adherence to the law and freedom of the press are fundamental beliefs to all Americans. When our cruisers chased the Russian ships into a neutral Chinese port, that violated international law.'

'If the journalists had not been there, the incident would not have been publicized,' the Emperor said. 'On this I agree with Honjo. Newspeople are public spies. What do Honjo and Nogi think of Roosevelt as mediator?'

'They both approve. Honjo has quoted Roosevelt's recent address to the US Naval War College. No triumph of peace is quite so satisfying as the triumph of war. Nogi quoted the American president's well-known axiom. One cannon and a bucket of gunpowder are worth more than all the treaties and volumes of international law ever written.'

'How can our military be so confident of victory when the western press predicts our defeat at sea, the destruction of our coastal cities and our capitulation to Admiral Rodjestvensky?'

'The Occidentals still underestimate us,' Mung said. 'Again I am drawn closer to Iyeasu Koin's belief that Europeans may be incapable of accepting us as social equals. That is unless we first prove our military superiority.'

The Emperor paused to frame a suitable reply. 'I do not agree with you about Americans. The few I have met appear to be Englishmen with poor manners. If they are pressured, Americans will react to us just as the Europeans have.'

'Possibly a decisive victory at sea will convince the West we are their equals. I have always tried to avoid war, but this time it was not possible. Let us hope it serves a positive purpose for Japan.'

26 May 1905
Noriko entered the sitting room ahead of her two sons.

They walked shoulder to shoulder, with hands behind their backs.

'My boys have a mischievous look,' Hiroki said to Mung.

Mung smiled. 'These boys worry me. They are hiding something behind them. I do not know if they have come to play a trick on you or their great-grandfather. How old are you two?'

'I am seven,' Yuhki said.

'I am eight,' Kunio said.

'Well if you want to be any older, do not play tricks on me.'

The boys giggled and looked to their mother. She bowed to Hiroki. 'Your sons request permission to approach their father and make a presentation.'

Hiroki grunted and pulled a solemn face. 'Decisions of such importance require a consultation with Tairo.'

This was a game the boys had played with Mung and their father since his return from Mukden. They watched the two men confer in serious whispers, and giggled nervously.

'Advance and make known your intentions,' Hiroki growled.

The boys shuffled forward and bowed. They stepped apart, each holding one end of a highly polished cane, and handed it to their father.

'What is this?' Hiroki asked.

The boys recited in unison. 'It is for our honourable father, hero of Port Arthur and Mukden, whom we hope to follow into the Emperor's service when we reach military age.'

'Where did you learn that?'

The boys giggled again. 'In school,' Kunio said. 'We are taught to memorize every battle and many things about our brave soldiers and sailors and their glorious victories.'

'Now tell your father why you chose this beautiful cane,' Noriko said.

'To replace the bamboo cane the army gave you so you can walk with us,' they recited.

Hiroki made a ceremony of examining the walking stick. 'What kind of wood is this?'

The boys looked to their mother. Noriko whispered and they repeated, 'Rosewood.'

'And it has a beautiful silver handle,' Mung said.

'That is called a head, honourable Grandfather,' Yuhki said.

'And so it is,' Mung said. 'I think we should see how your father walks with it before you go to sleep.'

Hiroki stood up and tapped the cane on the tatami mat. He limped around the room, coming to a halt before his sons. 'This is the finest cane I have ever seen. My leg feels better just walking these few steps. I am certain I will be able to accompany you to school tomorrow.' He saw their faces light up.

The two boys bowed to their father. 'Our teacher said you can use the cane to beat us if we are unworthy of the name of our family, disloyal to the Emperor, or if we ever become traitors to the state,' Kunio said.

Hiroki glanced at Mung and Noriko. 'Very practical teachers my children have. Possibly you boys should study in the American school as your mother and I did.'

Hiroki saw fright in their eyes.

'No, Father,' Kunio said. 'The foreign devil teachers would put bad thoughts in our heads.'

Noriko quickly whisked the children from the room.

'I have not heard the foreign devil phrase for many years,' Mung said. 'That is Honjo's influence. Patterning the thoughts of the younger generation.' He pointed at Hiroki. 'You young people will have to guard against this.'

'You are Tairo.'

'And I feel every bit the Great Elder. I am weary

456

and the strain of waiting for the coming naval battle drains me.'

'I wish there was a way to be with Togo and Uraga,' Hiroki said.

'I heard that,' Noriko said from the doorway. 'You are staying home until your bones heal properly!'

'Your wife is quite forceful,' Mung said. 'I would have thought the leg was mended by now.'

'Hiroki does not tell when he is hurting,' Noriko said, with a stern glance at her husband. 'Two weeks ago the German ambassador's personal physician took a photograph of the inside of this hero's leg with a new invention, an x-ray camera. He saw that it had been broken in three places, not two as the field surgeon said. They had to break the bone and reset it. Hiroki has a walking splint on his leg now.'

'Noriko is correct,' Mung cautioned his grandson. 'Your health is no longer only a personal matter, but an affair of state. I am here this evening to confirm your appointment as the youngest member of the Privy Council.' He put his hand on Hiroki's arm. 'You earned the position.' Mung looked at Noriko. 'Your father chose well for his son and son-in-law.'

Noriko smiled. 'My father saw Hiroki's potential. Father knew I would be able to improve your grandson.'

'Continue the good work. He is still a bit rough around the edges. I expect if you both apply yourselves to the task, someday Hiroki will become personal adviser to the Emperor. But,' Mung warned, 'no more battlefields. Our family is well represented in the military. Uraga is aboard Togo's flagship and Yaka is on Chefu island. Yesterday we heard from Yaka that the enemy fleet was three hundred miles from Tsu-shima strait.'

Hiroki did a rapid mental calculation. 'The battle could be going on right this minute.'

'More likely tomorrow,' Mung said. 'Now I am going to sleep. You two do not need an old codger with you to celebrate the appointment to the Privy Council. Tomorrow morning, Hiroki, you will accompany me to the imperial palace.'

It was after midnight when Hiroki entered his grandfather's room. He stood looking down at the sleeping figure of the old man who had tried for so many years to guide Japan away from war. Now he commanded the nation as she prepared for the greatest sea battle in modern history. Hiroki saw Mung move and was suddenly looking into the barrel of a navy Colt .44. 'It is me, Grandfather.'

'I cannot see well without my spectacles. Besides that, since you were a little boy I warned the family not to sneak up on me when I sleep.'

A fleeting fear rushed through Hiroki. His grandfather had forgotten he was raised in Korea. 'The enemy fleet was sighted near the Tsu-shima strait an hour ago,' Hiroki said.

'What time is it?' Mung snapped, his voice alert in the darkened room.

'Twenty minutes after midnight.' Hiroki turned up the lamp and saw that Mung had slept fully clothed.

'Bring the messenger in here,' Mung said.

As soon as the man entered, Mung began speaking. 'Send the following dispatch to our fleet: From Tairo to Admiral Togo and men of the imperial navy. 27 May 1905. Order of the Day. The fate of the empire rests in your hands The fire-storm in Tokyo proved that any Japanese city can be burned to the ground. That is the enemy's intention. Raise the Z flag! The battle cry is Victory or Death! Containment of the enemy is not enough! Destroy them! Dai Nippon banzai!'

Chapter 51

27 May 1905

In the wheelhouse of the newly commissioned flagship *Mikasa*, Uraga spoke into a direct telephone line to the communication centre amidship. He adjusted his earphones and completed the repetition of Mung's Order of the Day.

'Victory or death!' Admiral Togo and his staff repeated, and bowed.

'Your grandfather has a way with words,' Togo said. 'Broadcast his message over the loudspeakers of every ship in the squadron! Add my compliments! Either we will triumph or greet our ancestors!' He pointed to the large silk packet tied to Uraga's duty belt. 'Is that the Z flag?'

Uraga took out the famous battle pennant and Togo stepped forward. 'Gentlemen,' Togo said to the staff officers, 'join your hands with mine on this flag in solemn oath!'

The officers crowded around. Admiral Togo peered through each man's eyes into his soul. His voice came from deep in his chest, rasping over vocal cords callused by years of command. 'Before the beginning of the world, there were numerous gods.' He pointed to the heavens. 'The last of the great ones were Izanagi and Izanami.' His eyes challenged the men who waited to hear the old legend from the great warrior.

'The two gods created Japan and later bequeathed it to the Sun Goddess Amaterasu. Amaterasu bestowed sovereignty over the holy islands on her son Jimmu Tenno, the father of all Japanese, the first in the line of successors to the imperial throne.' Togo's voice caressed the ancient tale.

'We are a people descended from a god, and led by a god! The living god has spoken through Tairo! He has ordered victory!' The fire in Togo's eyes burned into the hearts of his men. 'Is there a Japanese alive who will disobey the word of the Emperor!'

'No!' the men chorused, and pressed their hands down harder on the flag. Their hearts swelled with pride. 'No!'

'Take this solemn oath with me,' Togo whispered. 'If I should fail to do my duty, shirk my responsibility or in any way disgrace the Emperor, may the private parts of my body fall off!'

Mesmerized by the force of their leader's will, the men repeated the oath in a low, hymn-like monotone.

'May my children, my family and my ancestors be turned into piles of disgusting filth and my name obliterated for eternity in this life and the next!' Togo's words were repeated by his men. Then he broke their trance with his shout. 'Unto victory or death!'

'Dai Nippon banzai!' the men roared.

'Man your battle stations,' Togo ordered. 'Bosun, time check!'

'Sir, 01:45, two hours and five minutes since first sighting the enemy.'

Uraga cleared his mind of the soul-stirring trance Togo's words had induced. He cocked his head and listened carefully to the voice coming through the earphones.

'Admiral Togo sir, an important message is being decoded in the communication room,' Uraga said. 'It is a delayed dispatch to our agents on land from a fishing boat trailing the enemy fleet: Top priority. Forty-three enemy ships Tsu-shima strait after midnight. Hospital ship five miles behind fleet, lights on. Dirty hulls reduce battleships' speed two knots. Super-structures. Newer battleships cut away. Older ships ornate woodwork. Use high-explosive shells. Dai Nippon banzai. Akichi Shibata.' Uraga choked on the name but Togo was too absorbed to notice.

The admiral paced the wheelhouse and his staff fell back. He glared out of the window into the dark, as if by force of will the night would fade and the enemy would be revealed. He spun around. 'The Russian hospital ship is complying with international laws of warfare by travelling with lights on behind the enemy fleet! Send twelve of our cruisers forward in a picket line to locate that ship! It will tell us exactly where the enemy fleet is!'

'Sir,' the captain said, 'if we meet the Russians before our cruiser division returns, it could be disastrous! Rodjestvensky has more firepower than us as it is!'

Togo smiled. 'I have a plan to negate much of the enemy's strength. Battleships set the pace of a fleet, and we have been informed theirs run three knots slower than ours. They must have grown algae in the warm waters of the Indian ocean. The message said they have dirty bottoms, which reduces their speed by two more knots.' He slammed his fist into his palm. 'I can meet them, chase them or sail circles around them! They are mine! Send an order to all captains: Refer to ship identification charts and use the new armour-piercing shells on the super-structure of the modern Russian battleships! Use high-explosive shells on the older craft! The woodwork will burn and smoke the enemy crews out of their gun compartments!'

Mung and Hiroki sat side by side at a table on the dais, overlooking a maze of wires, telephones, decoding machines and radios prepared to relay information directly from Togo's fleet. The men of the First Imperial Communication Battalion sat at ornate tables and chairs moved in from the imperial ballroom.

'Has the Emperor been behind the curtain since we arrived?' Hiroki whispered to Mung.

'I do not know, but you must read every dispatch loud enough to be heard back there. How long is it since the sighting of the hospital ship?'

'The *Shinano Maru* reported the lights at 4 a.m., then lost them in heavy fog. It is now 7 a.m. Our twelve cruisers are still paralleling the Russian fleet.'

Hiroki was handed a message, which he read aloud. 'Enemy increasingly nervous. Firing at our cruisers. No return fire. Battleships *Mikasa*, *Kasaga*, *Fuji*, *Mishine* and *Shikishima* making a 180-degree turn. Second division preparing to execute same manoeuvre.' Hiroki studied the map and battle chart of the Tsu-shima strait. 'Grandfather, it appears Togo is making a mistake! The Russians are nowhere near his main body of ships and he is turning away!'

'You do not know the man as I do. Togo fears only disgrace. I gave him an order to destroy the enemy. He must be setting a trap.' Mung took the pointer and tapped the battle chart. 'We have twelve cruisers exposing themselves to an edgy enemy. The Russians probably believe our main force is behind them, when in fact Togo is pulling back to plan some manoeuvre to catch Rodjestvensky by surprise.'

Hiroki heard a sound behind him and started to turn, but Mung stopped him. Mung stepped aside so the map and chart could be seen from behind, then used a pointer to trace Togo's turn. 'The enemy is steaming into the Tsu-shima strait at eight knots in four columns, their battleships leading,' Mung said loudly. 'Twelve of our cruisers are shadowing the enemy. The new manoeuvre by Admiral Togo will delay a major confrontation for several hours.'

The curtain behind them rustled softly again.

'I think you and I should have breakfast and rest,' Mung said. 'We shall need our strength later.'

Aboard the flagship *Mikasa*, Admiral Togo had ordered the 180-degree turn, then reduced the battle watch to 50 per cent. Half of his men stood down to eat, wash, rest, and later relieve the second half. The noon meal was served at battle stations.

'Time check!' Togo said.

'13:55, sir.'

'Sir,' Uraga said, 'we have a sighting from the crow's-nest. The enemy is approaching in a formation of four columns, distance nine thousand yards, speed eight knots, direction two points off our starboard bow.'

All eyes in the wheelhouse looked to the right. Although the sky was clear and the sun bright, a haze on the water obscured the oncoming Russian fleet.

Togo turned to Uraga. 'I want my voice piped into the loudspeaker system of this ship, and my message sent to every ship in the fleet!'

Uraga gave the command, then held the microphone up for the admiral.

'To the officers and men of the imperial fleet,' Togo announced. 'We are about to engage an enemy who vows to burn our cities! They boasted to other nations that our Emperor will crawl on his belly to ask for peace!'

Uraga felt anger welling up in his chest. Veins in his head pounded. The man next to him wept with rage. A senior commander gritted his teeth so hard that blood ran from his gums.

'We are the only force between the enemy and the Emperor!' Togo continued. 'It is not enough to die in battle! We must win, or all Japan is dead! Destroy the enemy! Destroy the enemy here! Destroy him completely and totally! Banzai!' Togo cried. 'Dai Nippon banzai!'

The war cry rang throughout the Japanese fleet. 'Dai Nippon banzai!' Every man bowed, then stood to his battle station.

Togo stalked out to the bridge. He called back over his shoulder, 'Gentlemen, follow me!' and the staff trailed after their admiral. Uraga pulled communication wire with him. Armour-plate shutters banged closed, darkening the small area. Viewing ports were opened and the sun filtered in.

The battle of the Tsu-shima strait would be directed from this enclosure.

The *Mikasa* ploughed through a calm sea. The battleship *Kasaga* sailed on her port side and the remaining twenty-nine ships of the line steamed behind in a column of twos.

Uraga moved behind Togo's right shoulder and adjusted his headset. He listened, then said, 'Sir, enemy range eight thousand yards and closing.'

Togo nodded. Tension on the bridge mounted. The two fleets approached each other almost head on.

Togo spoke softly to Uraga. 'Send the torpedo squadron forward at full speed on our left flank. They are to take up positions behind the twelve cruisers paralleling the enemy.'

Uraga relayed the message into the speaker attached to his headset. His heart swelled with pride at sight of the fifteen small boats racing out of the battle line and passing the *Mikasa* on the port side. There were now only fourteen ships in the two columns moving towards forty-five Russian ships, but the Japanese fleet contained the most modern battleships and heaviest cruisers on the face of the earth. Each was equipped with the latest radios, advanced weaponry and navigational devices in the world.

'Gentlemen, we will cross the Russian T no matter what the cost!' Togo said. 'Completion of this dangerous and complicated manoeuvre depends on each of us doing his duty in a synchronized turn while under enemy gunfire! If successful, all our ships' guns will bear on the first four enemy ships! The Russians will only be able to aim their forward guns at us. I sent the cruisers and torpedo-boats ahead to shorten our battle line. According to Akichi Shibata, the Russian gun turrets on the port and starboard sides cannot traverse more than 45 degrees right or left. Sailing in columns they will only be able to bring their bow guns to . . .'

'There they are,' the *Mikasa*'s captain cried.

Four giant battleships abreast broke through the low-lying mist, followed by four more big battleships, four heavy cruisers and alternating lines of four battleships and four cruisers flowing into the mist.

'Cruiser division and torpedo-boats will attack the enemy flank!' Togo turned to Uraga who, with the others, stared wide-eyed at the oncoming might of the Russian empire. 'Mr Ishikawa, relay my order and we shall get on with winning this war!' Togo shouted at his staff officers, pulling their attention away from the enemy's awesome display of power. 'We will sink those big-bellied Russian blow-fish! But you must be patient. Uraga, send this order: Gunnery officers, hold your fire! Captains of the fleet, prepare to execute an in-succession-turn to starboard at flank speed!'

There was stunned silence on the bridge. The admiral had ordered the most difficult manoeuvre in naval warfare. Performing it under the Russian guns would allow the enemy gunners to range their weapons at the point where the first ship and every other made its turn. The imperial Japanese fleet would be in danger of destruction within minutes.

'Enemy at seven thousand yards and closing,' Uraga reported.

'Execute the in-succession-turn to starboard,' Togo ordered.

'Execute,' Uraga shouted into the speaker. 'Execute!'

The *Mikasa* came to life. She charged forward at full speed, and heeled over as she made the turn.

'Time check!' Togo said.

'14:20,' the captain said. 'The enemy flagship *Suvoroff* is firing for range!'

'Distance 6,500 yards,' Uraga reported.

'Gunnery officers, hold your fire,' Togo ordered. 'The enemy is shooting at us and the *Kasaga* and not ranging their guns on the crucial point of the turn! They thought

465

we were behind them and the surprise has put them off balance!'

'Enemy battleships *Oslyabia*, *Borodino* and *Kamchatka* ranging guns on us,' the captain shouted.

'Enemy shells falling short of our port bow,' Uraga reported. 'The *Kasaga* has taken two hits and three close misses!' He listened, then reported, 'No serious damage!'

'The *Kasaga*, *Fuji* and *Shikishima* will broadside the *Suvoroff* with us,' Togo ordered. 'The next four will fire on the *Oslyabia*! The *Kamchatka* and *Borodino* will be engaged by three cruisers each!'

Uraga repeated the orders into the speaker, then reported, 'We have taken a hit on the port bow above the waterline! Not serious! Crow's-nest reports our cruisers and torpedo-boats are attacking! Dark smoke is rising far back in the enemy formation! Two direct hits on our fantail! Superficial damage!'

'Gunnery officers, you have five minutes before the last ship makes its turn!' Togo said. 'Recheck range and direction!'

A sixteen-inch shell ricocheted off the armour plate of the *Mikasa*'s gun turret in front of the bridge. An angry spray of sparks burst off the top and multicoloured light flashed through the viewing ports. Two more shells exploded forward, tearing up the bow. Togo leaned to look out of the viewing port and another big shell slammed into the same gun turret. Uraga saw the admiral come hurtling towards him. They both landed in a heap on the deck, Togo on top. 'Sir,' Uraga gasped, 'are you hurt?'

'It is a bit like the night we went after the *Kowshing*,' Togo said, helping Uraga to his feet.

'Sir,' the captain said, 'the in-succession-turn is complete! You have crossed the enemy's T! All our guns bear on the front of his column!'

'Fire,' Togo cried. 'Broadsides fire!'

Uraga relayed the command, and the big guns roared.

The giant battleship *Mikasa* jumped two feet sideways in the water from the recoil of the heavy weapons. They fired again and again. The smell of burnt cordite was sharp in Uraga's nostrils. Behind the *Mikasa* the ships of the imperial navy rode in perfect battle line, their guns belching red and yellow tongues of flame through clouds of black gunsmoke.

Uraga held his hands on the earphones to hear, and repeated over Togo's shoulder, 'Torpedo-boats report two enemy destroyers sunk and a frigate damaged! The cruiser division has sunk an unidentified enemy battleship, three cruisers and five destroyers!' He looked at his watch. 'Sir, only thirty-five minutes have passed and the battle is in our favour!'

'Can anyone tell me if we are hitting the leading enemy ships?' Togo asked. 'They are wreathed in smoke.'

'The crow's-nest has a report,' Uraga said. Togo and the others on the bridge saw astonishment cross his face.

'What is it?' the captain demanded.

'The *Oslyabia* is down!'

'What do you mean down?' Togo asked.

'Sunk! She broke in two and sank with all hands!' Uraga clamped his hands over the earpieces again, then said, 'The Russian flagship *Suvoroff* has only one gun firing! Her fantail is awash and she is burning! Her crew is abandoning ship! The *Borodino* is on fire and listing to port! Only three of her guns are still in action! The *Kamchatka* is on fire and appears out of control! She has struck her colours!'

The men on the *Mikasa*'s bridge cheered.

'Quiet!' Uraga called. 'Quiet! I am receiving a report from our cruiser squadron.' He listened, then shouted into the mouthpiece, 'Confirm last message!' Uraga's eyes met Togo's as the words came over the wireless. Then he bowed low to the admiral. 'Sir, the Russian battle formation is broken! They are fleeing all over the ocean!'

'So quickly?' Togo said.

No one spoke.

The admiral of the imperial fleet paced back and forth while Uraga verified the reports from other captains. Then Togo took up Uraga's microphone and shouted into it, 'This is Admiral Togo! All units, attack! Attack! Fulfil Tairo's order of the day! Destroy the enemy! Chase him to the ends of the earth! Destroy the enemy!'

For thirty hours Hiroki and Mung had sat on the dais reading battle reports aloud. For the last two hours Mung had slept slumped forward with his head on the table. There was little news coming in now. The men of the communication battalion slept at their ornate tables.

Hiroki was reading a report giving the names of three more Russian ships sunk. A soft voice spoke from behind him. 'According to my calculations, the entire enemy fleet except for a handful of small ships is either captured or sunk.'

Hiroki, shocked by the voice, asked, 'Are you certain?' Realizing to whom he had spoken, he caught his breath and began to tremble.

'What are our losses?' the gentle voice asked.

Hiroki rustled through the papers on the table and examined them again. 'Three torpedo-boats,' he said in respectful awe. 'We have lost just three small torpedo-boats. Only minor damage is reported on other Japanese ships.'

'Help your grandfather to his bed,' the Emperor said. 'Tairo needs his strength to direct the peace negotiations.'

The curtain rustled and in the distance Hiroki heard Tokyo's ancient war gong tolling the victory of Tsushima strait. He turned to Mung. 'Grandfather.' Hiroki touched the old man's shoulder. 'Grandfather, we have won.'

'Help me.'

Hiroki heard Mung's plea and gaped at the bowed head. 'What should I do?'

'Lift me up,' Mung whispered. 'I am having another stroke.'

'Doctor,' Hiroki cried. 'Someone get a doctor!'

Chapter 52

29 November 1905

Mung had experienced neither the warmth of Tokyo's summer nor the winter's first chill. Now, seated in a straight-backed rocking chair, he had been dreaming again. In his dreams, old friends came to visit – his Okinawan body-guard Rhee, Kang Shu the great Chinese tong chief, Lord Hotta of the Fujiwara, Yaka the valiant one-sword samurai for whom his grandson was named, Denise Dubois the sexually aggressive Frenchwoman. Denise smiled into his eyes and he awoke with a start, hearing Noriko's voice.

Mung straightened in his chair and leaned forward. 'It has been five months of dull, insipid conversations with my sons and grandsons. My brain is addled. Where are Hiroki and Shimatzu?'

'On the day of your stroke his imperial majesty ordered that nothing or no one was to disturb your recovery,' Noriko said. 'Specifically excluded were political discussions, talks about finance or anything to do with the military.' She tucked the blanket under the arms of the rocking chair. 'Hiroki and Shimatzu will soon arrive and give you a complete report of the war with Russia.'

'Did the doctor say I could go out for a walk?'

'He recommends a rickshaw.'

'Thank the gods for that. I am tired of playing Tokaido Road with your sons. They always win. And discussions about summer heat or autumn rains are boring.'

Noriko smiled. 'We shall soon talk of winter snows.'

'Young woman, remember I am Tairo. Sitting here with a partially paralysed arm and leg, I may appear invalid. But when I grow angry, even the lions tremble.'

'There are no lions in Tokyo, I am not so young, and the doctor said you are not to grow angry.'

'Sit by me.' Mung motioned Noriko closer and waited until she was seated on the tatami mat next to him. Then he looked closely at her and said, 'You will always be my child. The wonder-child who nursed me through two strokes. If, as the Christians believe, there is a Heaven and your parents are looking down on us, they are proud of you.' Mung reached out and touched Noriko's head. 'Thank you for bringing me back to life. There were times I wished to die. But I have unfinished business that must be attended to.'

'Shhh.' Noriko sniffled back a tear. 'Save your strength. Hiroki and Shimatzu will arrive any moment.'

'I am strong enough for them. You must help Hiroki. His position on the Privy Council gives him access to power that has corrupted older, more experienced men. He should always remember that the spirit of Japan is embodied in the Emperor, and the Emperor's power resides in the people. Honjo and his faction will try to control the new Emperor by isolating.'

'But the Emperor lives,' Noriko said.

'He is sixty-three, fifteen years younger than me. Only Nogi and Takamora were older.'

'You speak of them in the past tense. How did you know about their deaths?'

Mung ignored the question and went on. 'Hiroki should keep the Emperor informed of current political, military and social events. Men who support the Emperor's policies should be placed in positions of power. To accomplish this, Hiroki should use political pressure, the family's personal wealth and influence. The Emperor will assist with appointments to the Upper House of Parliament. Marquis Inei and Shimatzu will cooperate in finance and industry, which leaves Yaka and Uraga to influence the military. Help your husband to do what your father and I did for twenty years. Seek bright, young, dependable people and groom them for public office.'

'But you will be here to guide him.'

Again Mung did not answer.

Sounds came from the front of the house and Noriko started to rise.

'One second longer,' Mung said. 'My family seems to produce only boy babies. If there ever are girl babies, I would like one named Saiyo, another Ukiko, in honour of my wives. And one should be named Gin-ko. Would you tell this to Yaka and Uraga when they return from Manchuria?'

'You will tell them next month.' Noriko patted Mung's hand. 'I shall return in a moment.'

'How is my father?' Shimatzu asked Noriko as he and Hiroki put on their house slippers.

'He is well, but does not expect to be with us much longer.'

'If you think this meeting is a strain on him, we can postpone the report,' Shimatzu said.

Hiroki laughed. 'Tairo would probably chase both of us down the street and shake the information from us. He is on the mend.'

Noriko led them in to sit with Mung. He rocked back and forth, eyeing his son and grandson. 'All this talk of weather, grain harvest and sheep raising has come to an end. Let us start where I left you five months ago, with my face on the table in the imperial reception hall. I know we won the war. Tell me how, why and something about the Portsmouth Agreement.'

Noriko and Hiroki exchanged glances, wondering how Mung knew of the peace treaty.

'We defeated the Russians because of our superior intelligence service, excellent preparations and the most modern military equipment in the world,' Hiroki said.

'Except for three ships, the entire enemy fleet was either sunk or captured in the Tsu-shima strait. Four thousand eight hundred Russian sailors died. Five thousand nine hundred were taken prisoner. We lost three torpedo-boats and one hundred and ten men. William Whittefield wrote from Washington that ours was the greatest naval victory in modern history, although our people feel differently. Until the Portsmouth Treaty, the public thought Giri had been repaid to the Russians. Now they believe the Americans tricked us.'

'I do not understand how Roosevelt convened a peace conference so quickly,' Mung said.

Again Hiroki realized his grandfather had information he was not supposed to have received.

'I was in the United States and involved with the negotiations,' Shimatzu said. 'Our previous dealings with Roosevelt and his derogatory statements about the czar led us to believe he favoured Japan. He was also acceptable as a mediator to the Russians. I made the mistake of being overly frank with the American president.'

'You actually met Theodore Roosevelt,' Mung said. 'What is he like?'

'He fosters the image of a fire-eating cowboy, then surprises people with his brilliant mind and ability to grasp the essentials of any situation.'

'And what did he grab from you?'

'I told him that although we destroyed the Russian navy and eliminated their army in the Far East, Japan was on the verge of economic collapse. Then, at Portsmouth, Roosevelt used that information to enforce a treaty which does not satisfy our people.'

'Why was Portsmouth chosen as the venue?'

'Roosevelt told the press it was to prevent either the Japanese or Russians from being pressured by foreign powers in Washington DC. He told me he could not stand the summer heat in the capital. The New Hampshire weather is beautiful, but Portsmouth was full of journalists. The Russian negotiators wined and dined the press and immersed them in fanciful stories favourable to Russia. Our representatives distanced themselves from everyone and concentrated on the negotiations. The Hearst newspapers whipped up such anti-Japanese sentiments that all Japanese children were taken out of San Francisco public schools. Other American states reinstituted anti-Japanese laws. The bad press affected our people here in Japan. The wire services to the Far East are controlled by western newspapers. The Japanese press reprinted the unadulterated American news and people here grew angry.'

'What made Roosevelt turn against us when he was so helpful before the war?' Mung asked.

'We won too big and too fast,' Shimatzu said. 'Immediately after the war, Lord Cade renewed the military alliance with us and withdrew much of the British navy from the Far East to India. The French and Germans pulled out their fleets to confront each other in North Africa. The Austrians and Russians have had several crises in the Balkans and reduced their military presence in the Orient. William Whittefield predicts a major war in Europe with France and Russia facing Austria and Germany. The Europeans have pulled out of the Pacific and Japan has the largest navy in the Orient. Roosevelt fears we may try to take the Philippines, Hawaii and all the islands in between. He made certain we did not receive an indemnity, and the Japanese economy remains so fragile that we cannot think of military adventures. The Russo-Japanese war cost Japan one billion five hundred million dollars. And the Americans hold most of our notes.'

'I assured President Roosevelt through William Whittefield that Japan has no territorial interest in the Pacific,' Mung said. 'As Tairo I am able to guarantee that promise.'

'Whittefield presented that argument to Roosevelt,'

Shimatzu said. 'But you were incapacitated and Prime Minister Sasaki had sent Akichi Shibata to Peking.'

Noriko flinched and Hiroki's eyes flashed at the mention of Shibata's name.

Mung wiped dampness from his drooping left eyelid. 'Why did Honjo's man go to the Chinese capital?'

'He tried to force the Dowager Empress into appointing one of his puppet warlords as governor of Fentien province,' Shimatzu said. 'When she refused, he threatened an invasion of China. He reminded the Empress that Japan had three hundred thousand battle-tested troops in Mukden, only ten days' march from Peking. The Empress cabled Roosevelt of the threats and the American president was furious. That is probably what convinced him that he must negotiate the Portsmouth Treaty without an indemnity to us. Although we did receive all the territories we gave up ten years earlier under threats from the three European nations. We now occupy Port Arthur, Korea is a Japanese protectorate, and a third of Manchuria is under our political administration.'

'That should have pacified the people.'

'They expected too much,' Hiroki said. 'They imagined a massive cash settlement, even more than we received from the Chinese in 1894 and 1904. The Japanese press reprinted eastern news stories claiming victory for Russia at the peace conference. There were anti-government demonstrations in Hibiya park. People were angered by reports that Roosevelt sided with white Christians against Japanese heathens. Buddhist monks and Shinto priests fanned the crowd's anger. General Nogi and his wife committed seppuku at their son's grave in protest. When word of their deaths reached Hibiya park, the people marched on the palace with the intention of petitioning the Emperor to reject the treaty. Honjo's police were swept aside. He called out the imperial guard and the First Imperial Army division. Scattered confrontations erupted and spread throughout the city. A major anti-western riot developed. The American embassy was surrounded. In Tokyo alone, thirteen Christian churches were burned, fifty-three Caucasian homes destroyed. More than one thousand of our people were injured and seventeen killed.'

'I still do not understand why the people considered the settlement so bad,' Mung said.

'Japan was cheated out of its rightful share of the Boxer indemnity by westerners, and before that exploited by France, Russia and Germany when they forced us to relinquish the territories we had won from the Chinese. The people feel the territories we received now are not enough. Giri required a Russian indemnity payment to Japan. They say that once again we won the war and lost the peace. The reaction was so fierce, Sasaki had to resign as prime minister. People say Giri is owed and Giri will be paid.'

'To whom?'

Hiroki was absolutely certain Mung already knew much of what was being discussed. Tairo had not asked the name of the new prime minister, or commented on Nogi's suicide. 'The anger of the people is against the Americans,' Hiroki said.

'Why did Sasaki authorize the signing if it was so unpopular?'

'My father-in-law and I advised him to sign,' Shimatzu said. 'Japan is now a debtor nation. At Portsmouth, Roosevelt made it clear that his aim is a state of balanced antagonism in the Far East. For this he was prepared to encourage trade, relax American import duties on Japanese goods and arrange low-interest rehabilitation loans to bolster our economy. We agreed to refrain from military adventures and major weapons production. Neither the Russian nor the Japanese people are happy about the outcome, but next month Theodore Roosevelt will receive the Nobel Peace Prize for his efforts at Portsmouth.'

There were sounds at the front of the house. Before Noriko could rise, an officer of the imperial guard entered the room. 'Stand, place your hands in front of you and face the door!' the guard said. 'His imperial majesty is about to enter!'

Mung pushed his quilt off and struggled to rise.

'Tairo has his majesty's permission to remain seated,' the guard said.

'I will die on my feet rather than insult the Emperor!' Shimatzu and Hiroki helped Mung to stand and he motioned them to either side. 'If I falter when I bow, catch me.'

For the first time in his life, the Emperor of Japan entered a private home.

'As head of the Ishikawa family, it is my honour to greet his most royal majesty,' Mung said, grateful for Shimatzu's and Hiroki's steadying hands.

'I greet you, Tairo,' the Emperor said. 'I have come for my button.'

'Sire? Your button?'

'You have not forgotten the button award I made to you and Mori?'

'Noriko,' Mung said, 'please fetch my purse.'

Shimatzu and Hiroki exchanged questioning glances.

Noriko returned with the purse and Mung motioned towards it with his finger. 'There is a black bone button inside.'

Noriko handed over the button. Mung bowed and presented it to the Emperor.

'Young woman, stand next to Tairo, please.' The Emperor motioned the guard to open a lacquer box. The Emperor withdrew a silver pendant on a green ribbon and put it over Noriko's bowed head. 'This is acknowledgement for extraordinary virtuous service to me, and for your care of Tairo during his illnesses.' He withdrew a second pendant, a gold-encrusted ruby at the end of a heavy golden chain.

'Ten years ago I could not acknowledge Mung's meritorious contributions to our country and our people when he negotiated the settlement with China, then later with France, Russia and Germany. Our people were unjustly angered. Before I distanced myself from Mung, I gave him a button from my tuxedo as a symbol of my gratitude.' He placed the ruby pendant over Mung's head. 'I hereby award you the Supreme Order of the Rising Sun in recognition of your many contributions and sacrifices for the people of Japan.'

Mung bowed. Tears filled his eyes. The Emperor took his arm and led him from the room. 'Old friend,' the Emperor said, 'I have missed you.'

Chapter 53

It appeared to Honjo that the old man in the rocking chair was asleep. Mung opened his eyes and the chief of Japan's intelligence service bowed. Noriko led Honjo to a seat directly in front of Tairo. She moved to tuck in the quilt on his lap.

'That will not be necessary,' Mung said. He smiled at Honjo. 'My blood circulation is poor.'

'I hope it will improve soon. Many people have purchased prayer notes for Tairo, at temples and shrines throughout the country.'

Noriko bowed to Mung. 'If you wish, I will remain here.'

'No. General Honjo and I have some unfinished business to discuss. Then I will prepare myself for the dedication ceremony this evening.'

Noriko bowed again, and left the room. The two men waited until they heard the front door close.

'Your granddaughter-in-law is a special person. I have heard how she nursed you back to health.'

'It is strange you should compliment her,' Mung said. 'Considering how you allowed Akichi Shibata's people free rein to seduce and addict her to opium.'

Honjo's shaven skull shrank between his massive shoulders. He leaned forward and his eyes narrowed to slits that raked the thin old man rocking gently back and forth. Only Mung's eyes were vibrantly alive.

Honjo leaned back, wary but confident he was in control. 'There are many things you and I do not agree on, Tairo. But we have worked together for the good of Japan. I admire your leadership skills. Your negotiations with the

British prior to the war negated the French and German military in the Far East. It made victory over Russia possible.'

'We did work well together,' Mung said. 'In retrospect I admit that your assessment of Japan's military power was more accurate than mine. Your intelligence service performed remarkably well. Although I fault some of your methods. It was a waste of human life to have those fifty-three men caught attempting to land near Vladivostok. You betrayed them to give the Russians the impression we were planning to land there instead of on the Yalu. But it could have been done another way. I do not believe human life is so cheap.'

'Seppuku by that many men convinced the Russians and stimulated our people to volunteer for military service. Those deaths saved thousands of lives.'

'What excuse can you give for Shibata's manipulation of Noriko?'

'I had to divert his anger. He would have killed your grandson for breaking his nose and insulting him in public at Shimatzu's wedding. I needed Hiroki alive to lead the Special Forces in Korea, and Shibata alive to take Manchuria.'

'So Noriko was the only diversion a talented man like you could think of for your protégé?'

'I must admit I have lost control of Shibata. He acts as he wishes.'

'You are a liar!'

Honjo braced himself. He would smother Mung and claim the old man had suffered a terminal stroke. He leaned forward, flexing his hands. 'I have let you live because you were an asset to Japan. Your services are no longer needed! You are useless!'

'But not harmless,' Mung said, withdrawing the Colt .44 from under his quilt. He pointed the revolver at Honjo's chest. 'Sit down or I will kill you!'

'Your family would be disgraced.'

'How could the man who so recently received the Supreme Order of the Rising Sun, from the Emperor's own hand in a private visit to his home, be vilified?' Mung shook his head. 'The incident would be hushed up.'

Honjo slid to the edge of his chair; his body tensed to spring. 'Old man, I am not afraid to die. I was about to kill you, but if I cannot others will! Guards,' Honjo shouted, and looked to the door. 'Guards!'

'Enter,' Mung called.

The door opened and four young men stepped into the room, each holding a pistol in one hand and a club in the other.

Mung raised the Colt revolver in Honjo's face. 'You may have incorporated the Black Dragon Society into the National Intelligence Service, but the men remain loyal to me. Your bodyguards are either dead or unconscious. My Black Dragons have never lost touch with me since my exile or during my illness.'

'What is it that you want?'

'Giri,' Mung declared. 'For myself, and in the name of my dead friend Count Iyeasu Koin, I must avenge the cowardly acts of Akichi Shibata on my family. He is here in Tokyo.' Mung was pleased to see surprise register on Honjo's face. 'Your protégé appeared at this morning's practice in the Imperial Hall of Martial Arts. He carried out a threat made twelve years ago when he attempted to disgrace my grandson in a kendo exercise. This morning General Shibata dismissed the headmaster.'

'I thought he was in China,' Honjo said.

'My Black Dragons inform me your protégé has returned to challenge your leadership.'

Honjo breathed deeply. He steepled his fingers and looked past the revolver to study Mung's face. 'Do you wish me to kill Shibata?'

'Yes!'

'That is not a problem. His presence in Tokyo indicates a total lack of respect for his teacher. It will please me to give him a final lesson.'

'Shibata must disappear today,' Mung said. 'He has sworn to kill my grandson, and Hiroki has vowed to avenge Noriko's suffering. There is another complication. Before he died, Udo made arrangements for ninjas to kill Shibata on his return to Tokyo, and leave his body to be found. Such a death would be linked to Hiroki and could force his resignation from the Privy Council.'

'Akichi Shibata will disappear! I guarantee it!'

'If the slightest scandal touches my family, I have ordered the Black Dragon Society to see you dead,' Mung said.

'Shibata's face will not be seen after tonight! He will suffer for defying me!'

'Cruelty is unnecessary.'

Honjo grinned. 'It is a tool. A device to control people. I will make an example of Shibata. Please tell the chief Yakuza in the flower shop on the Ginza that I have need of one of his artists.' He noted the surprise on Mung's face. 'My agents have followed you and your men for many years. I now have need of the tattooed men's experience.'

Westerners, Orientals, men and women of Tokyo's diplomatic corps bowed and curtsied when Tairo entered the meeting of the American-Japanese Friendship League. He was flanked by Noriko and Hiroki. He limped up the steps to the dais and was seated in the place of honour. Above the platform there was a large sign. WHITTEFIELD MEMORIAL LIBRARY.

Hiroki stood up to unveil a brass wall plaque, and read aloud, 'This library is dedicated in honour of the Whittefield family of Fairhaven, Massachusetts, who saved and adopted a shipwrecked fisherboy, Mangiro, of the village of Nakanohama in 1841. That boy rose to the exalted rank of Tairo in the service of the Emperor. May our two countries maintain the ties and warm relations experienced by the Whittefield and Ishikawa families. Dedicated 22 December 1905 by Marquessa and Marquis Koin.' Hiroki bowed to Mung. 'Venerable Tairo, please honour us with a few words.'

Mung leaned on his cane and stood up. 'It has been a long journey since I left home to go fishing. Most of the people who helped me along the way are not here to share the fulfilment of our dreams. The honours bestowed on me also belong to them. There was Lord Shimatzu Nariakira of Satsuma, called the Silver Fox by his fighting men. History books do not tell you that, or of his raising an American to the rank of Senior Samurai of Satsuma. John Whittefield, my adoptive brother, is inscribed in Japan's ancient book of heraldry. John and I stood with Lord Nariakira against the shogun's army in the Hakusar valley. That victory was the first major step in the modernization of Japan.

'There were many Americans at our side in the intervening years. Commodore Perry and his marines who volunteered to teach us how to aim and fire new guns. Members of the Kobe Club helped organize a relief effort after the great earthquake. Of late, the relations between Japan and America have been strained. This is unfortunate. Our countries hold much in common. We are both relatively new in the modern world, and have moved from agrarian to industrialized societies in the past fifty years. Our peoples are hard-working, ambitious, courageous, and each fiercely proud of his country.

'My life has been dedicated to bringing Japan into the modern world, to Japan's acceptance as an equal in the eyes of the great nations.' Mung looked over the podium at the western ambassadors seated before him. 'In part we achieved acceptance from the Europeans with cancellation of the unequal treaties, and with the more recent international trade and military agreements.' He turned to the American ambassador. 'Recognition of the highest form came from the United States. President Theodore Roosevelt feared our military might. At the Portsmouth Conference he attempted to weaken us by not including a Russian indemnity. When a country needs to be told it is great, it is clearly not. When people act towards us as President Roosevelt did, there is no need to be told.

'In the battles of Tsu-shima, at Mukden and Port Arthur, Japan punctured the myth of western military invincibility. For Asians, Africans, Indians and Pacific Islanders, the world will never be the same. Few had foreseen such a decisive defeat of a Christian nation by Orientals. The first American reaction appeared to most Japanese as less than honest – President Roosevelt's attempt to restrict Japan's growth and maturity.' Mung saw Americans in the audience shift uneasily. He aimed his eyes like a double-barrelled shotgun at the Japanese dignitaries. 'The American president may not have been wrong. He might have studied the ancient Japanese philosopher who said, "Big victories lead to great defeats." Americans express that same axiom another way. The cat who chases the dog thinks he is a tiger. Then he goes out to attack the bull and is surprised when he is trampled.' Mung stood erect and adjusted his eyeglasses. His voice filled the hall. 'We Japanese should be careful not to overestimate our strength in the light of recent victories. We are not animals. The colour of our skin does not represent what is in our hearts. For three generations the Whittefield and Ishikawa families have worked to build bridges of friendship between our peoples. This library we dedicate today is another span to strengthen our ties. I ask all of you, Caucasian and Oriental, Catholic and Buddhist, Protestant and Shinto, to continue the bridge-building efforts begun by Captain William Whittefield when he saved me from death on a lonely wind-swept island more than half a century ago.'

Mung bowed to the standing ovation. Westerners and Japanese crowded in to congratulate him.

One tall Japanese politely waited his turn for Mung's attention. He bowed and said, 'Tairo, I represent three of the largest Kabuki theatre companies in Tokyo. We have combined our efforts to produce a play about your life. It has drawn capacity audiences for two months. I respectfully invite you to attend as our honoured guest.'

Mung's face brightened. 'I remember when Kabuki actors were considered just a step higher than criminals. I would be delighted.'

'It may be too much for you,' Noriko whispered. 'The play is five hours long.'

'So you saw it and did not tell me,' Mung said. 'Naughty girl. I will make you sit through it again. Does the playwright treat me well?'

'You are a hero,' Noriko said.

Mung grinned. 'I must see tomorrow's performance.'

A Black Dragon in the crowd caught Mung's eye and nodded. Mung knew that Akichi Shibata was in Honjo's hands.

Chapter 54

In the duty room of the White Wolf Society building, Honjo greeted Akichi Shibata with a wide smile. 'It was good of you to respond so promptly to my invitation.'

Shibata glanced at the two big guards flanking him. 'Your messengers insisted my compliance was mandatory and immediate. They were less than polite to a general of the imperial army.'

'Well now that you are here, tell me why,' Honjo said.

'I do not understand the question.'

'Why have you returned to Japan without my permission?'

'You sent me on a mission to China and I carried it out. Japan's acquiescence in the Portsmouth Agreement and Roosevelt's interference in Chinese affairs put me in danger.'

'Danger has always been the nature of your profession,' Honjo said.

'In the past fourteen years I have worked on my own and produced positive results. There was nothing more to do in China. I was cut off from my network in Manchuria and decided to return home.'

'To displace me as chief of the National Intelligence Service?'

Shibata stiffened. He motioned to the man on his right and the guard closed the door. Shibata grinned at Honjo. 'Did you really think I would enter this viper's den unless these men were mine, you baldheaded fool! I have looked forward to repaying you for those lessons in the Green House!' Spittle appeared at the corners of Shibata's lips. 'Many times I kept warm in the frozen wastes of Manchuria wrapped in my hatred of you. General Honjo, it is time I repaid Giri! These men are mine, this building is mine and you are mine!' He pulled a pistol and ordered the guards, 'Take him!'

The two men spun around and pulled Shibata's arms up in the air. His pistol fired harmlessly into the ceiling. He was slammed back against the door, gasping. 'Why? Why are you doing this?'

Honjo stepped forward and removed the pistol from Shibata's hand. 'You were my best student ever. The most talented man I have ever known in the fields of espionage, sabotage and subversion. But your faults of vanity and lack of humility overshadowed the rest.'

Sweat poured from Shibata's face, dripping into his eyes. He struggled, but the two guards held him firmly against the door.

'You are afraid,' Honjo said. 'Good. That will make my task easier.'

'How did you find out what I was planning?'

'Your personality demands that you be best at everything. That is why I sent you to Manchuria and then on to China. I knew that if you returned it would be to displace me. I tested you from the first day you reached Manchuria fourteen years ago. Every man you recruited to overthrow me belonged to me and reported to me. I have a suitcase full of files on your plans. The only surprise was your sudden appearance in Tokyo. I learned of it from Mung.'

Shibata wilted in the grip of the two men. 'Kill me quickly,' he pleaded. 'I have earned that much.'

'You have one more service to perform before you die,' Honjo said.

The two guards twisted Shibata's arms behind his back and turned him around to face the door. Honjo opened it. Shibata saw that from the time he had passed through the game-room on his way in, everything had been removed except a billiard table at the far end under a single green shaded light. Two rows of army officers stepped out of the shadows and formed an aisle leading to the table.

Honjo whispered in Shibata's ear as he took the small mirror from Shibata's sleeve. 'Your last contribution to the White Wolf Society will be as an example to my students. They will know respect for their superiors.'

Shibata was shoved into the arms of the first two men – propelled back and forth, punched, kicked, his clothing torn from his body. When he fell they raised him up and sent him stumbling down the gauntlet. Until, bruised, bloodied and stark naked, he was thrown onto the green cloth of the billiard table and spread-eagled face up. He spat out broken teeth and prayed for death.

'Gentlemen,' Honjo said, 'General Shibata was the first to introduce electric shock as a form of torture. He taught me all he knows. I shall demonstrate.'

Faces crowded around the table. Shibata twisted and squirmed but he was held down. Someone applied a damp rag to his hands, then wet his feet. He looked unbelieving at wires being taped to his fingers and toes. 'NOOOOoooooooo! I have sacrificed too much for the Emperor, for my country, for the White Wolves! Kill me, but do not torture me into disgracing myself before witnesses!'

'Shibata, Shibata,' Honjo cooed. 'You never did a thing for anyone but yourself. Everyone in this room knows who you are and what you are.' He motioned to a small man seated at a generator.

The man spun the handles and electricity pulsed into Shibata's body. He screeched, his arms and legs quivered. Then the pain ceased and he heard Honjo discussing with the students the proper use of electric shock during inter-rogation. Shibata practised sucking his tongue back up on the roof of his mouth.

'Are you ready for the next treatment?' Honjo asked.

'Your mother fucked horses and your father was a whore

to white men,' Shibata screamed. He sucked his tongue back as the shock slammed into his arms and legs.

'Enough,' Honjo said. 'Enough,' he shouted.

'I have stopped,' the generator operator said.

Honjo looked down at Shibata – arched from his head to his heels. The bones of his rib cage seemed about to burst through his skin.

'His tongue,' Honjo roared. 'He swallowed it! Open his mouth!'

Two officers forced Shibata's mouth open. Honjo reached into his throat, hooked a forefinger under the inverted tongue and pulled it out.

Air rushed into the starved lungs. Shibata spat. He coughed and wept. 'Let me die,' he pleaded. 'Please let me die.'

Honjo signalled and the electricity struck again. Shibata bucked, his body spasmed. For three long hours, Honjo held class on his finest protégé. Shibata lay limp on the table.

'Electric torture could go on for days,' Honjo said to the students. 'You have seen the different applications to various parts of the body. Keep in mind that the more tender areas require less voltage, that use of electricity causes dehydration. When General Shibata regains consciousness he will be extremely thirsty.' Honjo waved forward a man carrying a pitcher. 'We will give the good general this drugged liquid whenever he wakes. Dispensed correctly it will keep our former colleague asleep for at least thirty hours. That will be more than enough time. Bring the Yakuza in!'

Tairo's entrance into Tokyo's Grand Kabuki Theatre became a triumphal procession applauded by the élite of Japanese society. Leaders of the nation had travelled great distances to pay homage to the man who had led them and their fathers into the twentieth century. Mung,

Noriko and Hiroki were followed by spectators, greeted by actors, led by attendants through the theatre and onto the stage to the place of honour.

The curtain rose on a scene in the fishing village of Nakanohama where Mung's mother was mourning the loss of her two sons at sea. Mung's brother Jakato led the parade of his memories from bygone days on the fishing boat. Mung was caught up in the imaginative scenery, brilliant costumes and inspired acting. Drawn back into his own past.

The Whittefield family, arms linked, came forward smiling, followed by Pistchiani, Deacon and Black Ben. The three seamen gave the ancient whalers' cry, 'Town-hoooo!' and Mung was once again racing behind a harpooned whale over deep blue waters. He watched the mighty flukes of the leviathan rise up and whack the sea a thunderous blow. Events and people came alive for him as his life story unfolded.

Seated at a campfire in the gold fields of California, he heard the chrip-chrip of crickets. The smell of wood smoke changed to the crackle of sizzling fat and the aroma of roasting pig at King Kamehamea's luau in honour of Mung's conversion to Christianity. The Lord of Satsuma strode out and ordered him to build Japan's first modern whaler. Battle cries and the fall of the shogun's banner were followed by secret meetings at sea with Commodore Matthew Perry. Gompachi, the flat-faced fighting priest, smiled and willed Mung his position as Black Dragon. Mung fought back tears as he watched his courtship of Saiyo, his first wife, and her death. He struggled to control his emotions in the scenes of his marriage to Saiyo's sister, Ukiko, and her death caused by the Golden Lizard's henchman. With pride and sadness he watched his firstborn son's fatal duel against the Choshu samurai warriors before the gates of the imperial palace.

On and on marched the memories before Mung's eyes.

Iyeasu waddled out with his brother, the giant Danjuro, Lord of Mito. The Vulcan pirates and hired assassins fell before his Colt revolver. He watched negotiations with the Chinese prince and a crucial battle with tong-men aboard the great scrambling dragons in Canton harbour. General Nogi and Admiral Takamora came forward to pay homage to Tairo. The final curtain descended after the re-enactment of the Emperor's visit to Mung's house and his award of the Supreme Order of the Rising Sun medal.

There was a moment of profound silence in the Grand Kabuki Theatre. Then, one after another, men and women came to their feet and bowed. The entire audience, the actors and attendants began to cheer. 'Dai Nippon banzai! Dai Nippon banzai! Tairo! Tairo! Tairo!'

Noriko and Hiroki helped Mung to his feet and an expectant hush swept the theatre.

'Grandfather, they are waiting for you to speak,' Hiroki said.

Mung leaned on his cane and stepped forward. He bowed to the actors gathered on stage. 'You have made the past come alive for me. The journey was more than an enjoyable nostalgic trip on which I renewed old acquaintances. Your professional expertise has allowed me and the good people in the audience to walk through the recent history of our nation. You have given us a unique perspective on what lies ahead.' He turned to face the audience. 'This play gives us all an insight into the future. The sacrifices made by those I was privileged to know during my lifetime were aimed towards gaining Japan's acceptance as an equal by the great nations of the world. And we have achieved that goal. But the end of one era is the beginning of another. Japan will soon be tested again. The withdrawal of the westerners from the Pacific in preparation for a European war leaves a void in the Far East. A vacuum that will draw the United States and Japan into closer contact. Those who desire Giri because of Theodore Roosevelt's Portsmouth Treaty will demand war with America. I strongly advise against this! We must consider the positive parallels between our two nations. A wave emanating from a Japanese beach moves uninterrupted across the face of the ocean until it breaks on California's shore. Japan's and America's destinies are forever linked by the Pacific ocean. Pacific means peace. I advise every effort to maintain a tranquil relationship between Japan and the United States!'

In the basement of the White Wolf Society headquarters, Akichi Shibata struggled to his feet. His face itched, his limbs were stiff and his vision hazy. He wore the clothes of a street beggar. He held onto the pool table and realized that military men stood in the shadows around the room. A captain held out a cup of water and Shibata grabbed it to slake his thirst. Honjo stepped from the shadows and Shibata cringed.

'Do not be afraid,' Honjo said. 'In a moment you will feel bright and alert. Better than you have in a long time. The drink was a stimulant. Soon everything will be clear and perfectly understandable to you.'

Shibata already felt energy coursing through his veins. He stood on his toes, then rocked back down on his heels and clenched his fists. His eyes darted towards the closed door, then the barred windows.

'You are no longer a prisoner,' Honjo said. 'If you wish to leave, no one will stop you.' He stepped aside and the door swung open.

Shibata went into a half crouch. He turned full circle. He rubbed at his face and took one cautious step towards the door. When no one moved, he took another step. His itching face distracted him and he rubbed it with both hands.

Honjo moved forward and Shibata flinched again. The senior White Wolf smiled. 'I wish to return this.' Honjo held out the small mirror. 'Vanity is weakness.'

Shibata reached out cautiously and plucked the mirror from Honjo's hand. He spun around with teeth bared, in a full crouch. No one moved and he brought the mirror to his face. His eyes widened and he glanced behind him. Honjo's smiling face was next to his. Shibata looked in the mirror again, and again turned. Honjo chuckled. Shibata brought the mirror so close to his own face his breath fogged it. He brought up his left hand to his swollen yellow lips and saw the reflection of his fingers below the black nose and red circles around the eyes. He rubbed furiously at the colour.

'It does not come off,' Honjo said. 'The Yakuza are expert at their art.' He snapped his fingers and bright lights flooded the room.

Four men holding full-length mirrors surrounded Shibata. He turned right, he turned left, but a horrible image was always before him. No matter which way he turned, he saw the grotesque yellow, black and red face above the wretched clothes of a Tokyo beggar. He crumpled to the floor and sobbed.

Honjo grabbed Shibata's hair, jerked his head back and dropped a knife into his lap. 'You may take your own life! Or, if you desire, leave by that door!'

Shibata snatched the blade and stuck the point into his throat. Droplets of blood formed on the shiny steel. His hand quivered. Honjo stood over him, smiling and pointing to the open door. 'If you can live with that face, freedom awaits you.'

Shibata's wild eyes questioned the men standing around him. He dropped the knife and began to crawl. Then he scrambled on all fours towards freedom. He leapt to his feet, bolted through the door, and was impaled on a three-foot-long steel sword.

'Discipline, loyalty and respect are most important to remember,' Honjo said.

The officers bowed to the White Wolf.

'Your grandfather has had a long day at the theatre,' Noriko said to her children. 'Put the Tokaido Road game away and prepare for bed.' She watched the boys leave the room, then handed Mung an envelope. 'This has just arrived by special messenger.'

Mung took the envelope to his desk and opened it.

'The unwelcome guest is gone,' he read. It was signed by General Honjo.

Mung put the message aside. He took up paper and brush and wrote quickly. The heaviness in his chest and thickness in his throat were familiar feelings of discomfort he had suffered before each of his strokes. This time he relaxed and did not fight it. He watched the brush slip from his hand. Although his eyes were open, darkness clouded them. From far off he heard Yuhki say, 'Grandfather, we have come to wish you a good night. Your cane has fallen. Grandpa? Grandpa!'

> To the disciples of Honjo
> And the descendants of Mung,
> Dark wings and bare trees
> Or springtime and song.
> Your choice.
>
> JOHN MUNG